For Frank,

JOHN RICHARDS

The Gods of
Fortune

With best wishes,

John Richards

Pease 5th October 1999

British Library Cataloguing-in-Publication Data.
A catalogue record for this book is available from the British
Library.

ISBN 0.85131.680.8

Published in Great Britain in 1996 by
The Caduceus Press, an imprint of J. A. Allen & Co. Ltd.,
1 Lower Grosvenor Place,
London, SW1W 0EL.

Typeset by Textype Typesetters, Cambridge
Printed by Hillman Printers, Frome

Designed by First Impressions, Bradford.

Disclaimer

While many of the people described in this book did exist and are well documented historically, all of the main characters are fictitious and are not intended to represent any real person living or dead.

Author's note

On 31 August 1914 Nicholas II, Tsar of Russia, decreed that St Petersburg be renamed Petrograd as the German name given to the city by Peter the Great was now thought to be inappropriate.

Acknowledgement

With sincere thanks to Chris Eyre for her unfailing patience when deciphering my hieroglyphics and for her precise typing skills.

John Richards was born in 1943 and educated at Shrewsbury and Oxford. His first book, *Stagecoach*, published in conjunction with the BBC, achieved great success. Since then he has pursued careers in publishing and journalism as well as being a director of a Texas bank.

A dedicated four-in-hand driver, he has represented Great Britain at four World Driving Championships as well as being an active member of The Coaching Club.

He is married to Helena and has a daughter, Camilla.

Dedication

To Helena
with love

St Petersburg, Russia, January 1893

Prince Nicholas Orlofski and Count Ivan Korsakov disliked each other from their first meeting. It was as if their genes had marked them out in some strange way to be rivals. Life expected much of them as serving officers in the Horse Guards but it was fate that now intervened to bring their simmering jealousies to the surface. Territorial disputes between their forefathers had long since soured relationships between their two families, which, over the years, had been carried along on a river of bitterness.

It was therefore predictable that, at dawn on a winter morning, they should seek satisfaction for the sins of their fathers in an affair of honour. This was an exquisite moment of truth as, from the cradle, these two patrician heirs had lived in a world of power and privilege, never giving quarter one to the other. Compromise was not in their lexicon as they headed for a showdown from which they knew in their hearts only one would return alive.

Nicholas, for one, did not relish the occasion as he had a well-loved son, Alexander, now twelve, and his wife Princess Catherine had recently presented him with a new-born daughter, Natalia. 'So much to live for,' he thought as he

7

focused his mind on the ordeal to come. He knew his courage and coolness would be on display to the world and he was determined that, whatever the outcome, he would conduct himself with honour.

Unlike his rival, Ivan had no such feelings of honour and he cared even less for his family. He had once married briefly, the union producing no issue, but he had a son, Igor, from one of his many liaisons. He had seen to it that the boy was adopted and legitimised before passing on to him the yellow bile of his hatred of the Orlofski dynasty, which had overshadowed the Korsakovs for generations.

The scene was now set for the two adversaries to write another chapter in the book of conflict that had accompanied their families over the decades. Society, in the main, regarded their feud over the boundaries of their estates with tolerance, while many referred to it in spiritual terms as a clash between the forces of good and evil. On the one side there were the Orlofskis, with their dashing good looks, perfect manners and impeccable lineage, in stark contrast to the haughty and overbearing Korsakovs.

Both men arrived within minutes of each other at the appointed place at the city limits. Nicholas sat in his sleigh, wrapped in a bearskin pelisse, calmly smoking a cigar, while Ivan stalked fretfully about as their weapons were brought forward, and their seconds trampled a path in the fresh snow. An argument now began over distance, with Ivan asking for eight paces while Nicholas wished the distance to be greater so that his skill as a marksman would tell. After a heated exchange, the matter was eventually settled in Nicholas's favour with the distance being agreed at ten paces.

The seconds produced the pistols, having given their solemn assurance that they had loaded according to accepted conventions, and the small party of supporters from both sides retired to a safe distance where they waited in silent anticipation. After a few moments the combatants took up their pistols and stood perfectly still. Nicholas had

8

removed his pelisse and tried not to shiver in the intense cold. He reasoned that a potential injury would be less serious if a ball entered his flesh cleanly. Ivan, on the other hand, kept his cloak on, hoping it would give him extra protection if he was hit. It was agreed that firing would start on a word of command to be given by one of the seconds. They tossed a coin and Nicholas's second, Colonel Antonov, was directed to give the signal.

Both men were excellent shots but opinion had it that Nicholas had the steadier nerve and quicker eye. As Antonov gave the command, the antagonists walked in unison from their barriers but, before they had covered the agreed number of paces, Ivan turned and fired, wounding Nicholas in the back. He fell heavily, his blood staining the cold ground in an ever-expanding pool of cruel red. Antonov restrained the surgeon who tried to rush forward to help as it was obvious that Nicholas was severely wounded. Now, in the deadly hush that fell like a blanket, the onlookers heard Nicholas, in a thin, frail voice, demand that Ivan return to his post and wait for him to take his shot. Reluctantly Ivan walked back and stood sideways on, covering his torso with his right arm for protection. From his prone position on the ground, Nicholas summoned up all the strength he could muster and, after what seemed an eternity, discharged his pistol. The ball passed cleanly through Ivan's neck and he slumped to the ground with a cry of pain. It was all over for both of them.

News of two such illustrious fatalities ricocheted round St Petersburg like a stray bullet. A week later the Court of Honour was convened to examine the circumstances of the duel and witnesses were called. On hearing the grim facts of the encounter, the officers presiding had no option but solemnly to conclude 'that the death of Prince Nicholas Orlofski was unlawful as his opponent had flagrantly and wantonly breached the Code Duello under whose laws duelling is conducted'. To add fuel to the fire, rumours began to circulate that Ivan's pistols had rifled barrels to give them more accuracy, and were also fitted with hair triggers to give him that all-important edge. The whole affair summed up all too starkly the gulf in morals and ethics that had always existed between the Orlofskis and the Korsakovs. In an unprecedented gesture, Count Vladimir Freedericksz, the Minister of the Court, was despatched by the Tsar to carry his condolences to Nicholas's widow, the distraught Princess Catherine. The Korsakovs, meanwhile, waited in the shadows for the storm of disapproval to abate and for an opportunity for revenge to present itself.

Now, twelve years later, another generation of the two feuding families dined in the officers' mess. Igor Korsakov and Alexander Orlofski harboured a deep and corrosive dislike for each other, a hatred that had survived and grown since the fateful day of their fathers' duel.

The hour was late as Alexander Orlofski sat at the green baize of the card table with his friends. Luck was running with him and he was winning. He was in that pleasant state of mellowness that exists somewhere between sobriety and intoxication. Now, from the corner of his eye, he could see Igor Korsakov as he walked slowly across the room to where he was seated. Igor knew he had picked his moment well when he sensed Alexander's mood of euphoria.

'Enjoying yourself, Orlofski?' he enquired condescendingly as he sat down close by.

'Well enough, Korsakov,' was the reply.

The game, momentarily interrupted, resumed and Alexander smiled as he won yet again.

'Your luck is in tonight,' ventured Igor. 'Let's hope you will be equally successful at the Tsar's review in the morning.'

'Why do you say that?' replied Alexander.

'Well, if you drink any more you won't be able to find your horse, let alone ride it.'

'I shall not let the regiment down,' came the sharp reply.

'Just as long as you're properly turned out.'

'That's rich, coming from you,' replied Alexander. 'Why,

I've heard that dreadful old valet of yours uses urine as a cleaning fluid on your uniform and hunting clothes.'

'What if he does?' snapped Igor, scowling.

'Well, you may look very fine but we all know you smell like a bear when it rains.'

A ripple of laughter rang round the table.

'Why, you swine,' replied Igor between his teeth. The large veins in his neck stood out like rope and his face was suffused with anger. So often incidents of a similar nature had ended in him enforcing his opinion with pistol or sword after he had sprung his trap.

'You're also an unprincipled scoundrel and a cheat,' Alexander continued. 'Why, all St Petersburg knows there's bad blood in your family and don't try and tell me it wasn't you who was seen drinking with Rasputin last night.'

Igor now reached for the large white handkerchief that was stuffed up the sleeve of his jacket and dabbed at his forehead. 'If you were sober I'd have no hesitation in killing you and lopping off your ears. Look at you,' he snarled. 'You'll never be a patch on your father, and that's not saying much.'

'You're becoming a bore, Korsakov,' replied Alexander smiling thinly. 'Now, why don't you just let us get on with the game. Please be good enough to leave us.'

'Not before I receive some satisfaction.'

'What have you in mind?' enquired Alexander as a hush descended on the room.

'These matters can often be satisfactorily resolved by the turn of a single card,' was the measured reply.

'As you like. I'm interested to see if you've got a yellow streak at cards when the stakes mean something.'

'You Orlofskis have the nerve of the devil,' Korsakov spat back, his lips drawn tightly against his irregular, shark-like teeth.

The officers' mess was, by now, almost deserted. The stale remains of cigar smoke hung heavily around the room. Those left were either asleep or drunk. Alexander looked about, seeking the comfort of familiar faces for support. He knew that it was already too late to pull back from the climax of a night of high stakes and mad risk but that, with fortune favouring him, this might be a chance to break Korsakov and remove the threat he represented to the Orlofski family.

'I wager my lands in Estonia against your Moscow estates,' he heard himself saying, his heart beating so fast that he was afraid Igor would sense his anxiety. He sat back and tried to appear calm as he waited for an answer.

'We'll play one round for twelve points. My Moscow estates against all your lands in Estonia,' came the precise reply.

'Done.' This was the moment of truth that gave Alexander the surge of adrenalin he loved. It was like watching a woman undress, he thought, as he looked at the virgin pack of cards Korsakov was beginning to unwrap.

The drama that was now about to unfold suddenly drew its inevitable voyeurs. From leather-bound sofas and deep armchairs stumbled the few who had survived the night's serious drinking. They crowded unsteadily round the table and the number grew as Igor calmly repeated the stakes.

An old French card game called Le Truc had become fashionable in the mess. Essentially a bluff and gambling game, it suited the Russian temperament – the need to confront, to accept a challenge instantly, especially if an insult might be imagined. Now that duelling had become so commonplace among the Russian upper classes, gambling for high stakes had assumed a new importance, enabling the participants to savour the seductive thrill of risking all. The Russians had inherited from the West the love of the grand romantic gesture, and from the East the fatalistic acceptance of destiny. Mixed with the Russian character, Le Truc created an explosive cocktail of danger that was quite irresistable.

They cut to deal and Korsakov's ace was too strong for Orlofski's queen. The first hand was played in silence. Korsakov won and claimed the first point. Alexander's head now began to clear. A strange confidence still enveloped

12

him, even though the first point had gone to Korsakov. Alexander dealt. Igor took one look at his hand and exerted the non-dealer's right of calling for a new deal. Was he bluffing? Alexander hesitated. His own hand included a seven and a six, both ranking higher in Le Truc than the court cards. He refused a new deal. The hand was played and Alexander won. One point each.

By now the table was surrounded by tense, drawn faces. The stakes were whispered, the consequences for the loser instantly recognised. Without the income from his lands the loser's commission in the Imperial Guard and his very place in society could be irretrievably compromised. A sobering concentration settled on the spectators.

Colonel Nikolai Ivanovitch had appointed himself adjudicator. Celebrated for the number of duels he had fought and seconded, his authority on this occasion went unquestioned.

The third deal gave Alexander seven, six, ace, a very strong hand. 'Two if I play?' he asked, thereby doubling the points at stake. To Alexander's surprise Igor nodded, 'Yes.'

The seven was played and immediately Igor Korsakov's cold voice was heard. 'Four if I play?'

A spasm of panic flushed Orlofski's face. Did Korsakov hold two sevens. There was no turning back. 'Yes.'

The first trick was spoilt with sevens. In the second, Alexander's six was also covered by Igor's six. Four points rested on the third card. Igor looked sternly from under his leathery eyelids, his black eyebrows bushy like straggling brambles, before placing his king on the table, quickly covered by Alexander's ace.

'Five points to Orlofski, one to Korsakov,' intoned Nikolai Ivanovitch.

Alexander's head was clearing. He was nearly halfway to the victory that would render powerless a hated enemy who guarded a secret that Alexander dare not challenge. Not only would Igor be unable to threaten any longer; he would have no standing in the brilliant, if unstable, society that jealously guarded its own unwritten rules.

'You're doing well, Orlofski. Let us increase the stakes. Add your castle at Ivanhov to your Estonian lands. My palace, along with my estates that border yours, will balance them.'

The familiar surge of adrenalin ensured Alexander's acceptance. 'I agree. Everything but the family silver and portraits.'

Nikolai Ivanovitch signalled his understanding that the stakes had been increased.

Suddenly the mood changed.

'You can also have a night of love with Tamara if the cards should favour you,' said Igor, grinning. Tamara Tereskova was well known to the assembled company by anecdote as Igor's wanton mistress, infamous for behaviour that was notorious even by the Bohemian standards of Russian society.

The onlookers roared their approval for what they saw as an unselfish sporting gesture. As the commotion raged, Alexander remained sprawled in his chair while his adversary sat bolt upright.

Igor dealt the hand, three cards each, placing them very deliberately on the green baize. With a good hand, Alexander tried to bluff, asking for a new deal. Igor refused it. Alexander's cards revealed the bluff and won him yet another point: six to one. Everything was going his way but, even as he tasted victory, a doubt shivered through his mind. The fates were surely with him – or were they the genies of the wine bottle? He thought of his widowed mother and his twelve-year-old sister Natalia and the carefree times they had spent at Ivanhov. He dared not lose.

He gulped a drink and dealt another hand. Seven, seven, ace. A stronger set was hardly possible. Igor asked for a new deal. Alexander refused and asked for a double. 'Two if I play?' Again, to his surprise, Igor accepted and then placed a seven on Alexander's seven. Alexander doubled a second time. 'Four if I play?'

Igor still looked cool and composed, the only sign of tension appearing in the way he held the cards, just a little too stiffly and very close to himself. The nails of his left hand showed white as he looked across at his adversary, his gaze steady and unflinching, seeking out a tell-tale sign that might flicker across Alexander's face. He had mentally rehearsed this scene a thousand times and he knew he must not fail now. Alexander, on the other hand, had lapsed into a seemingly carefree state, the alcohol in his system temporarily protecting him from the vulnerability of his position. He drank deeply again from the Baccarat crystal glass and, as usual, made no attempt to conceal his hand. It was almost as though he wanted those watching to see that he had been blessed by good fortune. He still felt a strong sense of elation, imagining that fate was sitting beside him. Perhaps, together, they could now destroy the Korsakovs.

'I accept,' said Igor in the same sharp voice, cold like a dueller's pistol. The climax was fast approaching. The onlookers held their breath as Alexander's second seven was matched by another from his enemy. Four points were still at stake. Alexander required two more for the twelve needed. One more double with his ace and he was there. Surely Korsakov could not have a six. 'My remainder,' he heard himself say.

A barely audible collective intake of breath came from the crowd and Nikolai Ivanovitch quickly repeated, 'Remainder.'

The watching officers knew the rules of the game. If Igor accepted, whoever won the next trick won the twelve points. They knew the ultimate risk had been taken. They could see the ace of hearts in Alexander's hand and knew that only a six, any six, could defeat it. Their sympathies were with Orlofski but should he not have been cautious and waited?

Alexander threw his ace on the table and leant back, only his heavy breathing disturbing the silence. Igor now slowly lowered the fateful card, produced as if from nowhere, and, with almost surgical delicacy, placed on top of the ace of hearts the six of clubs.

'Twelve points and match to Korsakov,' declared Ivanovitch and a crushing silence descended as both men momentarily took stock of their changed circumstances.

'I'll give you a week to pack your things, Orlofski,' Igor said coldly, before rising from the table. As he was leaving he turned to the stunned Alexander, still slumped in his chair. 'Think yourself lucky you didn't get Tamara. Come to think of it, you probably don't know she claims to be the lovechild of your revered grandfather.'

The remark failed to register fully as the dreadful enormity of what he had done began to dawn on Alexander's confused senses. Slowly, he forced himself to think back over what had happened earlier that night when the seething snake pit of jealousy and intrigue between the Orlofskis and the Korsakovs had opened up.

Gone, on the turn of a card, was everything his family had painstakingly built up over four hundred years. He shuddered when he thought of what his mother, the Princess Catherine, would say, and how he might explain things to his impressionable twelve-year-old sister Natalia.

Still frozen to his seat, Alexander let his thoughts pursue his tormentor out into the night. He imagined moonlight yellowing the hated florid face and glistening on the jet-black, pomaded hair. With his revolver drawn level with the left temple, he would pause to savour Igor's fear before pulling abruptly on the trigger. Plenty of men had died this way and Alexander had had ample opportunity to witness the incongruous mess that a bullet in the brain created.

'By all that's dear to me, I shall get even,' he said, his voice croaking as it passed over a dry tongue and lips.

He pushed back the hair that fell over his bleary eyes and cursed his luck. Despair was written on his lean and handsome face as he rubbed the small cleft in his chin. He knew instinctively that Igor had cheated and he had a strange feeling that the card that had won Ivanhov and his estates for his adversary would eventually cost both their lives. The Orlofskis had always believed in fate and it now seemed appalling that the dissolute Korsakov should become an agent of divine retribution. Alexander would need to act quickly to exact revenge.

A week later Alexander made the solitary, bitter journey to Ivanhov. He had made an agreement with Igor that the latter would follow the next day and would be collected from the railway halt by Yuri the coachman. Alexander now needed to walk round his property for the last time and to visit the small village of Ivanhov which straddled the long straight highway that seemed to lead nowhere.

Dr Kuropatkin, the sole medical practitioner for many miles, lived in his own substantial house in its own grounds, while the rest of the dwellings, or isbas as they were known, were solidly built wooden houses made of unpainted, rough-hewn logs. Until recently, the whole community had been well regulated, with Nicholas, in his time, insisting that tidiness and order should prevail. Under Alexander's regime, however, standards had dropped and it was only when a fresh fall of snow blanketed the village that a semblance of order returned. It was here, among the uncounted acres stretching beyond the horizon, that the Orlofskis had established the base of their power and influence over the centuries, and here the castle had always been a focal point. From the exterior it was both forbidding and entrancing. The central section, constructed of massive, dressed stone blocks, gave it a stern impregnable look, while, in contrast, the golden onion domes, surmounting the old towers and bastions on the western side, shone in the bright winter light.

Once inside visitors were surprised to find the rooms somewhat smaller than expected, with the exception of the great hall with its huge stone fireplace and massive timbered roof. It was here and in the panelled library that the family portraits hung, while family banners festooned the higher reaches of the stone walls. Instead of the jasper and malachite columns and profuse gilding which was found in

St Petersburg, the castle was a maze of plain vaulted halls with faded frescoes on the walls and ceilings. This was Russia in its purest form – simple and dignified, reflecting the creed of the Orlofskis.

Alexander set about the grim business of removing his family's personal effects. It seemed like an act of desecration akin to robbing a tomb. His mind was still in turmoil, but he knew he must think carefully if he was to execute his plan. Igor would come to Ivanhov alone and would doubtless display the Korsakovs' inherent weakness for blood sport. Alexander now determined to snatch the opportunity to turn this hunter into quarry. He also knew his unwelcome guest to be a heavy drinker, especially fond of Dom Perignon, of which there was an ample supply in the castle cellars. With uncharacteristic thoroughness he planned every moment of Igor's last day down to the finest detail, taking a cold pleasure in the scheme.

The following day dawn was punctuated by snow flurries and, after a traditionally substantial breakfast, Alexander took Igor on a tour of the treasures of Ivanhov.

'The Rubens was bought by my grandfather on a visit to Paris,' he said, pointing proudly to a large canvas in an ornate gilt frame. 'Over here, on the bureau, are the miniatures of my ancestors, together with a collection of snuff-boxes presented by the Tsar. Everything in the castle is yours except, of course, the silver and portraits.'

'That was our agreement,' Igor replied stonily.

Entering room after room, Alexander became almost light-hearted. He was determined to show Igor every last Orlofski treasure, safe in the knowledge that he would not survive the day to enjoy them. His triumph would be short.

When they eventually sat down together in the library, with its rows of dusty volumes, Igor was very ready for a drink. As Alexander's hand went to the bell pull, Igor stared into the fierce flames of the log fire and smiled. 'You're very calm about losing all this,' he said, looking quizzically at Alexander. 'It's almost as though you don't care any more.'

'Oh! I care very much,' came the reply, 'perhaps more than you will ever know.'

At that moment a servant entered bearing a silver tray on which stood two tulip-shaped glasses.

'Champagne,' said Alexander, pointing in the direction of the ice bucket in which two bottles were visible. 'Carry on, Igor, it's all yours now,' he said, a hint of a smile crossing his lips. 'After lunch you must try some of the Napoleon brandy, you may be certain that the cellars of Ivanhov will not disappoint you.'

A large lunch and an excess of drink had made Igor boisterous and foolhardy. He was in a jubilant and reckless mood as he struggled to find the necessary co-ordination to put on his furs and felt boots for the hunt. The sleigh was waiting at the castle door and the grey horses snorted and stamped. Yuri, the coachman, wearing his traditional badge of peacock's feathers on a round hat, checked their impatience before gathering the reins into his enormous hands. His face registered distaste as the interloper seated himself, then, hunching his huge shoulders as much in disgust as against the icy blast, he willed the horses forward. As they sped along, Alexander watched Igor drink yet more brandy from a silver-mounted hip flask.

The weather was closing in but even in the gloom it was never really dark as the carpet of snow reflected any light there was. As they sped along the primitive tracks cut between the legions of birch and fir trees, the passengers covered their faces with traditional bashilisk or camel hair hoods as a protection against frostbite. As they progressed further into the forest, the trees rose up on either side like the pillars of a great natural cathedral. Faster and faster they went and soon the cold began to find its way under the furs, numbing their bodies and slowing Igor's already befuddled brain. Travelling so fast was like being caught up in a mysterious wind that propelled them along. Everything passed by so quickly that they seemed to be flying and

Alexander revelled in the sensation of power and speed.

'Isn't it fantastic, Igor?' Alexander shouted. 'Only a bold and great race like ours could give birth to such a way of travelling.'

There was no reply as Igor sat, frozen and speechless, as though in an alcoholic trance.

The moment Alexander had planned was fast approaching. When Igor picked up his gun to shoot it would be easy to push him out of the sleigh. 'Please God, don't let me fail now,' Alexander said over and over again under his breath.

They were approaching a large birch wood, where, five minutes earlier, Alexander's men had dragged a piglet along by its tail, making it squeal pitifully to attract the starving wolves. And the wolves had come in plenty. Suddenly, Igor sat bolt upright. His eyes glinted when he saw them ahead and he laughed shrilly as he took up his gun.

Intent on steadying himself, he reached out to support himself only to find the butt of Alexander's gun in his ribs. Alexander enjoyed the look of terror he saw in Igor's face. His eyes bulged in fear under his bushy brows and his mouth was drawn back in an expression of anguish as the two men exchanged their last desperate glances. Then, with a sickening thud, Igor was plunged headlong into the pack.

It was a quick and vicious death. The wolves' razor-sharp teeth tore at Igor's throat and face until he was almost unrecognisable. With deft savagery, they attacked the exposed flesh in a frenzy of aggression.

Alexander, now fearful for his own safety, rapidly loaded his smooth-bore gun with buckshot cartridges and aimed. Again and again he reloaded and fired until his ears were ringing and six wolves lay dead on the snow which was rapidly turning crimson. A further two had been wounded and were slinking away trailing a tell-tale ribbon of gore.

Alexander now bent down to pull the lifeless body back into the sleigh. He was surprised to find how damaged Igor was. In the background he could hear Yuri saying, 'Thanks be to God.' The corpse lay crookedly in the bottom of the sleigh in a pool of blood. Igor's eyes still stared and Alexander felt the need to close them. Gingerly, he pulled down the dark and leathery lids before recoiling in disgust.

He flinched again from the bitter cold now fastening on his bones. 'Drive on!' he shouted to Yuri. 'Don't spare the horses.'

The huge bear-like figure of the coachman urged forward the three magnificent greys pulling the sleigh. As the miles passed, the vicious thong of the coachman's knout coiled and danced as the hard-pressed horses laboured to drag each breath from the frozen air. The middle horse, or korienik, wore the traditional, wooden, arched douga with its bells, while the two side horses galloped with their heads turned sharply outwards. The wind was now blowing the snow in drifts and, more alarmingly, a blizzard had started up, blocking out any familiar sign in the vast grey waste.

Alexander's mind was in a turmoil. 'For heaven's sake get a move on, man,' he shouted anxiously, his voice almost lost in the wind. He huddled low in the sleigh, seeking what protection he could from the snow that was driving into their faces, making it difficult to discern the track. Yuri now had to rely on the oldest, experienced horse in the lead of the troika, who knew the paths leading back to the castle even when they were obliterated by snow and ice. Bells rang out to guide the party home, as was the custom when the weather turned foul and dangerous. Alexander rejoiced to hear them, knowing that the first part of his ordeal was nearly over.

At last he could see the line of blazing torches which led like some infernal signpost to the huge façade of the castle, its windows ablaze with light. It was a welcome sight.

'Drive up to the main door,' he ordered curtly, 'and then get someone to help you take Count Korsakov's body inside. When you've done that, go and fetch Dr Kuropatkin from the village. Hurry, man, hurry, and remember to say that the Count was drunk when he fell from the sleigh and there was nothing we could do for him.'

21

Alexander bounded up the stone steps leading to the massive doorway and strode past the two footmen into the huge, flagged hall. Dogs lay in front of a log fire which, although burning brightly, only partially warmed the space. Throwing down his blood-spattered coat, Alexander went immediately to wash his face and hands. He was careful to remove every stain and looked coldly in the mirror before snatching up the fine, white linen towel, his long slim fingers drawing comfort from the familiar embroidered crest. He hardly dared look at his own face for fear that something had changed, that his guilt might stare wildly back at him.

He waited anxiously for the doctor's arrival, taking refuge in the study where he had to search for a drink as the decanters, which were customarily placed on the silver tray close to his large roll-top desk, had been packed away, ready for their removal to St Petersburg. His hand shook as he lit a Turkish cigarette. Inhaling nervously, he released the smoke from his nostrils in brief staccato bursts. Soon there came a knock.

'Come.'

A servant announced Dr Kuropatkin.

'Thank you for coming so quickly, Doctor,' Alexander said, rising to greet the grey-haired man who carried a small, battered leather bag.

'There's been a death, I hear?'

'Yes, I very much regret to tell you that the new owner of Ivanhov, Count Korsakov, fell from the sleigh while we were hunting this afternoon. He was dead before Yuri could turn the horses and I could rout the wolves.'

The old man scratched his head. 'We were all very sorry to hear of your troubles, Your Highness.' He paused. 'Will this mean you won't be leaving after all?'

'I'm afraid it won't change anything,' replied Alexander wearily.

'We heard in the village that this Count so-and-so had asked if a bear hunt could be arranged,' the doctor continued in his peculiar, clipped voice. 'I'm glad you

stopped it. It's no sport for nobility. I told them that in my time the Orlofskis have never made sport of bears. Wolves, on the other hand, are born to be hunted.'

Alexander grunted. He knew that, in his own interest, he should say as little as possible. He just wanted the doctor to see the body and certify death. Turning on his heel he led him out of his study and across the hall, their footfalls echoing eerily. They climbed the wide stone staircase and entered the first floor room where the body had been washed and laid out. Alexander looked on calmly as the old man drew back the sheet revealing the cruelly disfigured cadaver.

'Please leave me now. I have work to do.'

Alexander nodded and withdrew, shutting the heavy oak door behind him with a soft thud. He just hoped with all his heart that the old man would sign the death certificate. He knew, however, that the real test would come when he took the body back to St Petersburg.

Some thirty minutes later Dr Kuropatkin was standing once again in Alexander's study. His green eyes looked earnestly at Alexander who could sense his unease.

'I have often seen injuries similar to those sustained by Count Korsakov. Once the jugular vein is severed, death follows quickly.'

'Was there anything else?' enquired Alexander nervously.

'No, except the dead man must have been very intoxicated at the time of the accident. Was he a heavy drinker?'

'We all drink too much in the Guards,' Alexander answered, smiling. 'It was freezing hard so we had some bottles in the sleigh.'

'All I can do is to write a short report, detailing my findings, as no doubt there will be a full post mortem when you get back to St Petersburg.'

Alexander nodded. 'Thank you, Doctor for coming so quickly.'

The next day a sombre procession left the castle. Alexander had sent a messenger ahead to the railway halt some twenty miles away and they had telegraphed for his personal carriage to be coupled to the St Petersburg train. As the runners of the sleigh hissed and creaked over the frozen waste, he had time to reflect. Inwardly, he hoped that most of his brother officers would surround him with a solid ring of silence, but he recognised that it was this very solidarity that would court suspicion. He knew that he could trust Yuri with his life. His family had served the Orlofskis for generations and many had gone to their graves guarding Orlofski secrets. That Igor had been very drunk at the time of the accident would be remarked on but it would be no surprise to those who had known him.

In St Petersburg most people had their own views on what had really happened but no one was able to piece the facts together. Alexander had a loyal band of supporters who protested his innocence but it was impossible to get away from the fact that the motive for killing Igor was all too obvious. Both factions considered it to be an open and shut case, while the police, for their part, refused to be precipitated into action by rumour. For the time being they were prepared to sit and wait as the case against Alexander grew stronger.

Much speculation now centred on Tamara and her son Michael who Igor had recognised and, finally, legitimised. Wagging tongues speculated wildly on what would happen if they were to inherit part of the fortune now made up of both the Korsakov and Orlofski lands. As Tamara was, by her own admission, the daughter of an Orlofski from an illicit liaison, it was the supreme irony that Orlofski blood should inherit, even if she was not recorded as issue in the Almanac de Gotha, the aristocrat's bible containing details of all noble births.

Alexander had come to hate himself for the misery he had inflicted on his family. He knew it was his fault that the house was suddenly full of whispers and hurried conversations behind closed doors. His hands shook and his once immaculate nails were bitten to the quick. Life was no longer predictable, and that frightened him. He loved Catherine, his mother, but even in her presence he was distant and uncommunicative. It was too difficult for him to reconcile himself to the fact that he had to live under the same roof, knowing that what he had done had devastated her world.

'There's nothing anyone can do, Mother,' he repeated in answer to her questions.

'If only you would talk about it, Alexander,' she pleaded. 'I can't do anything to help you if you won't discuss your problems.'

'I'm beyond help. Just leave me alone.' His voice was almost beseeching in its intensity.

'You mustn't talk like that. Let's fight this as a family.'

'Oh, come on, Mother, be realistic. I've ruined your life and Natalia's, as well as dragging the family name into the gutter.'

'But you don't seem to realise that although our circumstances have changed, we have not. We are still the same people.'

'No,' he replied slowly. 'Ivanhov and the estates were the source of all our power. Now they're gone there's nothing. Father would never have forgiven me.'

'It's not a question of forgiveness, Alexander,' she said, searching for the right words. 'Your father would have understood. What he wouldn't be able to forgive, however, is you sitting about feeling sorry for yourself.'

Mealtimes for Alexander were now purgatory. He longed to be left alone. Looking at his sister Natalia he remembered how in happier times she would sit next to him while he rattled off the latest news from the regiment, her large eyes wide with amazement at his stories of heroism and daring. Some tales she never tired of hearing and she would beg to be told them again and again. Now, in stark contrast, Alexander sat pale and withdrawn, playing with his food and hardly speaking. The looks he shot his mother were desperate and anguished as he drank greedily, his glass replenished to the brim and emptied over and over again.

After one such lunch, Alexander retired to his study. He sat at his desk averting his gaze from the photograph of his father that looked out at him from its oval silver frame. Alexander could almost feel the chill of his disapproval and he suddenly broke down, sobbing, holding his head in his hands, slowly rocking backwards and forwards. His outburst of emotion eventually gave way to a strange, detached, icy calmness as his final tenuous link with reason now snapped. He had known for the last week that death, his own death, was the legitimate answer to his situation. The only problem was how to die like an Orlofski with whatever vestige of pride and honour he had left.

He pulled open the top right-hand drawer of his desk. His careful, enquiring fingers passed over the bulk of his service revolver until he felt the familiar shape of the mother of pearl handle of the hunting knife Natalia had given him for his birthday. Picking it up, he shaved the hairs from the back of his hand with the razor-sharp blade before holding it up to the light. 'Made in Sheffield England' was clearly stamped into the shining steel.

Alexander now crossed to the oak chest in the corner of the study and pulled out the imperial flag. It smelt of mothballs. He had kept it ever since the bitter day of his father's funeral when it had draped the coffin as it was taken by gun carriage to the family mausoleum.

Putting the flag to his face he felt the cloth coarse against his skin. He knew that no flag would fly for him on a winter's pole. His would be a grim funeral with the church congregation looking on disapprovingly from a distance in heavy judgement on a noble suicide. As he stopped momentarily before the mirror he saw his face reflected for the last time. For just a moment he considered the tran-sience of human life and the uncertainty of earthly domain as he looked back into his own staring eyes. It was a strange farewell he bade himself before, with flag and knife in hand, he pushed open the mahogany double doors.

He could see the white marble staircase rising from the hall. Since childhood it had always reminded him of the way a swan's wing lifts with the first effort of flight. He walked with echoing tread until he was in the centre of the floor, exactly beneath the huge crystal chandelier. With studied precision he shook out the flag on the cold marble before he lay down on his back, facing east. He said a short prayer, the words of which seemed to rebound around the rafters in bitter intensity – a cry for help from the world he was about to enter, and a statement of contempt for the world he was leaving. Carefully he took the knife and pulled the blade quickly across his throat from ear to ear.

The pain was sharp, like a red hot incision. Blood from the severed artery pumped into the air, covering the marble floor in a red tide and splattering its ugly way into small pools. Death had come with speed and ferocity to claim its willing victim, and was already knotting the first threads of a story that would take decades to unfold.

1

Natalia was in every way a true Orlofski, as witnessed by her raven hair and dark eyes. To see her standing close by the portraits of her illustrious ancestors, recently brought to St Petersburg from Ivanhov, was to recognise her lineage. Orlofski blood was dominant and it had stamped its issue well.

In the days since Alexander's death her emotions had been in turmoil. She was obsessed with a need to understand the events leading up to the tragedy and had carefully pieced together every scrap of information gleaned from conversations with her mother who had been uncharacteristically evasive when Natalia broached the subject. It seemed to her that she was being unfairly denied information that was hers by right. Alexander was her only brother and, in spite of the difference in age, they had been very close.

She was, therefore, particularly interested when Count Freedericksz came to report on the result of the official inquiry into Alexander's death. He was an old and trusted friend of the family and his position as Minister of the Court allowed him to be party to the Tsar's innermost thoughts.

The Orlofskis had always found him the epitome of discretion and, since her husband's death, Catherine had come to rely on his help and advice.

'I told the Tsar that there are several officers in the regiment who feel your family estates were won by a card placed in Korsakov's sleeve,' Natalia overheard him say. 'We can't prove it, but the rumour won't go away.'

'These things are often exaggerated.'

'Yes, I agree, but His Majesty is powerless to help unless there is clear evidence of deception.'

'Even if we could bring a case against Korsakov's heirs, it won't bring Alexander back,' said Catherine, retaining her composure. 'Who inherits now that Korsakov is dead? I should like to know who will be living at Ivanhov.'

'As Igor was unmarried and had no close relatives, I believe that his mistress, Tamara Tereskova, has been left well provided for. The rest of his estate, including Ivanhov, goes to his elderly uncle who spends most of his time in Paris.'

'It's very hard to bear the thought of that terrible woman living on our money.' After a moment's pause, Catherine continued, 'You know, of course, of Alexander's grandfather's indiscretion?'

'Of course,' he replied, holding her gaze.

'She's nothing but an adventuress of the worst kind.'

Freedericksz looked at Catherine, his kind eyes softening almost to tears as he saw her distress.

'She's got a boy, I'm told,' she began again.

'Yes.'

'What is his name?'

'Michael, I believe.'

'Illegitimate?'

'Yes.'

'Korsakov's child?'

'It's widely rumoured so.'

'How old is he?'

'About Natalia's age, as far as I know.'

He now waited in silence until she sought his face with

her eyes again, as he sensed that there was something more she wanted to know.

'What did the Tsar think of the fact that Alexander took his own life?' she asked, her voice fragile with emotion.

'He was dreadfully upset, Catherine.'

'But he must have said something more,' she pleaded.

He hesitated for a moment. Side-stepping the question, he began, 'He was very concerned for you in the light of recent events. In fact, he has instructed me to let you know that he will help in any way possible.'

'That's kind of His Majesty,' replied Catherine. 'Please tell him that I am very grateful, but we shall manage. We still have this house in St Petersburg.'

'As you wish, but the offer stands should you change your mind.'

'Now, tell me what he really said,' she demanded.

'Very well. He is concerned about two matters. Firstly, he asked me to try and establish if Alexander had killed Igor Korsakov at Ivanhov or whether it was purely an unfortunate accident. Secondly, and less importantly, he was upset that Alexander had taken his life lying on the imperial flag.'

'Oh God,' she sighed as he continued.

'I told him that it was intended as a last symbolic gesture, emphasising his loyalty.'

'Anything else?'

'Only that he hoped it wouldn't be regarded as an unfortunate precedent.'

'An unfortunate precedent!' repeated Catherine in amazement. There was another silence before she began again. 'Have you been entirely honest with me? Everyone tells me what they think I ought to hear, rather than the truth.'

Freedericksz nodded his head. He understood. 'I have told you the truth.'

He had always admired Catherine and, even in adversity, he found her still entrancing, endowed with a forceful and charismatic personality. She was regal without being autocratic and her deep brown eyes were set in an

31

intelligent, delicate face complemented by carefully dressed brown hair. Her vibrancy was expressed by her intense manner of talking and when she smiled it lit up the room as well as immediately taking twenty years from her face.

It was now his turn to ask the questions. 'I hear you were seen at Fabergé's shop in Morskaya Street yesterday?'

'Yes, that is so,' she replied defensively.

'Was it the emeralds or the diamonds?'

'The emeralds, Vladimir,' she replied matter of factly.

'It must have been a terrible wrench?'

'Yes. The necklace has been worn by generations of Orlofskis. It was given to us by Peter the Great.'

'I know. I just hope he gave you a good price. It's unique.'

'Fabergé has always treated us fairly, and I have no reason to doubt his integrity.'

'Quite so,' replied Freedericksz gravely. 'Have you told Natalia?'

'Yes, I took her with me.'

'Was that wise?' he asked raising his eyebrows imperceptibly.

'Probably not, but I know she feels upset when I try to protect her from the truth. After all, the emeralds would eventually have been hers.'

Realising that she now risked discovery if she remained by the door, Natalia crossed the marble hall and hurried up the staircase to her room. Once there she felt safe. She lay quietly on her own familiar bed with its blue silk hangings, watching the thin sunlight struggling to pass through the window panes and the frost creating delicate and intricate patterns on the glass. She now had time to think carefully about the humiliation her mother had suffered when they had visited Fabergé's shop the day before.

Natalia shivered as she remembered how she had to watch impassively as her mother entered the shop where Fabergé, dressed formally in a tail coat, had greeted them. As Court Jeweller to the Tsar of Russia and countless noble families, he knew to be circumspect. Highly priced gifts inscribed with the most intimate messages were frequently purchased and given by men to their mistresses. Similarly, exquisite pieces were brought to him by people of rank and position to pay gaming debts. Natalia had hated to see her mother forced by circumstances to place before him several presentation boxes, all beautifully embossed with the Orlofski crest. They were the most precious things she possessed. Natalia felt quite claustrophobic until they had left the dark-panelled office, and she remembered hearing Fabergé tell her mother that she could 'rely on his utmost discretion'.

With the emerald necklace left resting on a plump, red velvet cushion inside the shop, she had hardly dared look at her mother. She knew the loss to the family could never be measured in money, and it seemed to her that the Orlofski dynasty was crumbling to noble dust before her eyes. She could just come to terms with Alexander losing his inheritance in a game where luck was paramount, but to lose to a cheat was something entirely different.

From her earliest childhood Natalia had heard the name of Korsakov spoken of darkly and now, for the first time, she knew what strange relief could be temporarily enjoyed by focusing all her confused emotions on one well-defined object of hate. She was glad Igor Korsakov was dead. In spite of her youth and innocence, she understood the simple equation of one life taken to balance another's death. Alexander's motives in luring Igor Korsakov to Ivanhov were now as clear as day. The scales had to weigh evenly and, until the moment of his death, there had been a singular imbalance in the divine mechanism. Deep inside she knew that the moment for revenge would reveal itself one day, perhaps when she least expected it.

The bizarre set of recent circumstances now made her suspicious of things she had hitherto regarded as the bedrock of family life. Only her love for her mother remained untarnished. Natalia knew how much Alexander's death had affected her and it was clear that she would now have to be the strong one if they were to survive as a family.

It was a difficult path that she trod. Noble by birth, impoverished by circumstance, she now concluded that the Korsakovs must be made to pay a ransom for past sorrows.

Six years later, at eighteen, Natalia was beautiful and intelligent. Her Slavic, high cheekbones and delicate chiselled nose were perfectly complemented by a mass of shiny, raven-coloured hair that danced about her shoulders. Her brown eyes were wide set and large, with long lashes, and her mouth was full and generous. Her elegance was accentuated by her long, swan-like neck and flawless pale skin. Hers was no static beauty, and every emotion was mirrored in her face. She was now a woman at the pinnacle of her considerable powers but with the bloom of youth on her skin she confused her admirers with a mixture of innocence and sensuality. Her aloofness was often commented on but it also served, in some strange way, to attract eligible men who jostled each other in their eagerness to be seen at her side. Unlike other young women in her position, she shunned facile liaisons and was careful and discerning in her choice of friends. Those close to her knew they could count on her endearing quality of total loyalty to those whom she liked and admired. Deep down she felt that she was the last remaining standard-bearer of the family and, although their flag was tattered and torn, she was determined it would fly proudly with the best in Russia yet again. Despite the gentle and loving side to her nature, she had yet to come to terms with her anger.

Now in her late fifties, Catherine had watched Natalia conform to the gentle road that led to womanhood and had guided her as best she could. It was, however, now well known to all who knew her that she was suffering from a cancer which was quite advanced. It had not dimmed her spirit, but it ravaged her looks as her weight fell and the skin on her face wrinkled. There were few people whom she would see, let alone dine with, but she had accepted an invitation to dine at the British Embassy with her old friends

Sir Edward and Lady Milner. Edward Milner had been Ambassador for some ten years and she knew that he and his wife, Lavinia, were the two people in St Petersburg whom she could trust to look after Natalia after her death which she sensed would not be long in coming. There was now much pain to cope with, as well as other physical symptoms of her illness, which she accepted with her usual dignity.

She had a particular affection for the British Embassy with its beautiful snow-white ballroom whose windows fronted the Neva. As a young woman she had sat there with Nicholas on long summer nights when they were first married, gazing at the gilded spire of the Fortress Church. Now all of that seemed so long ago as she arrived with Natalia, the snow scudding through the city streets and the wind whipping round the corners of the old building.

Leaving their furs, they were ushered by a liveried servant into a warm and beautifully furnished room where Lady Milner greeted them and took them to the fire which burned brightly. The conversation quickly turned to the Milners' impending retirement and they enthused about the prospect of taking up permanent residence at Larkhill Park, their Georgian mansion near Henley-on-Thames.

'We've never had time to enjoy it to the full, Catherine,' began Sir Edward.

'Oh, I envy you so much,' she replied, smiling. 'I fell in love with England that time when you invited us to stay when Natalia was still only a girl.'

'It was one of the happiest summers of my life,' said Natalia. 'I remember it so clearly, particularly that wonderful wall-eyed pony called Coco that you let me ride.'

'Do you really remember him?' asked Lavinia Milner. 'He's getting on for twenty-five now and in retirement, but he's still very much part of the family.'

'I'm interested to know what you feel the future holds for you, Natalia,' said Sir Edward, suddenly fixing her with bright, intelligent eyes from beneath bushy eyebrows.

For a moment Natalia was taken aback by his directness.

'I shall eventually go to England, Sir Edward. I like the English. Our class in Russia is in terminal decline, perverted and feckless.'

'Go on,' he said, his eyes dancing.

'Why I might even marry a rich landowner or someone "in trade" as I believe you call it. It could be quite exciting, although possibly not what my family might have wanted.'

'Well, since you mention it, I could introduce you to my godson, Peter Duff. His father owns newspapers. But let's not rush our fences.'

Natalia now looked across to where her mother was sitting. For the first time she noticed the strange, transparent look of her skin, and the greyness of her complexion.

'You must do what you think best, my dear,' Catherine began. 'Life is short, so make the most of it. I just want to die knowing you're safe,' she continued wearily. 'I have so little to leave you.'

A silence descended on the room. No one queried Catherine's statement. It was clear to them all that to question her presumption would be futile. Lavinia Milner eventually broke the spell by turning to Natalia.

'We would love you to be with us at Larkhill. The house needs someone young to prevent it feeling like a mausoleum.'

'I'd like that very much,' said Natalia. 'When the time is right, I'd love to go to England with you.'

She got up and spontaneously kissed them both before going to sit beside her mother who was squeezing Lavinia's hand, her eyes moist with emotion.

'It's an answer to my prayers,' Catherine said softly.

'Well, I'm glad that's settled,' said Sir Edward to Natalia. 'Who knows, you may even establish a new Orlofski dynasty in England. Why, there's Peter Duff, my godson, and so many families with eligible sons who need an infusion of new blood,' he continued enthusiastically. 'You may, however, have to kiss a lot of frogs before you find your prince.'

'Edward, that's not very appropriate,' said Lavinia, at the

same time scolding him with her glance, uncertain of Natalia's reaction.

'You seem to have it worked out, Edward,' said Catherine. 'Just one word of warning, however. What I have to say is difficult for me, but it's important you all know the truth. It will prove crucial in the future, mark my words.'

'What is it, Mama?' asked Natalia, sensing her mother's discomfort.

'I think you know, or have guessed,' Catherine began slowly, 'that Tamara Tereskova has an illegimate son, Michael. Keep away from him. He will bring nothing but trouble.'

Worried about her mother's increasing breathlessness, Natalia tried to stop her.

'Let me finish,' Catherine said. 'Tamara was the lovechild of your grandfather, Boris Orlofski. It was a dreadful indiscretion.'

This was something Natalia had long suspected and it came almost as a relief to know the truth, unpalatable as it was.

'What you are saying, Mama,' she said carefully, 'is that Michael Korsakov and I share the same grandfather?'

'Exactly.'

A month later Catherine Orlofski died. It was a swift and simple end. She let go of life without a struggle, her breath carried off like a feather on a current of warm air.

Her mortal remains were brought to the Church of the Fortress of St Peter and St Paul. The Tsar allowed the body to lie in state and it was guarded by soldiers of the Imperial Guard. Litanies were sung at regular intervals, and many filed past to pay their respects. After a short service, conducted by the Archimandrite, Catherine's body was interred in the Orlofski vault to the tolling of the great bells of the Fortress Church.

Natalia was now a child of circumstance, freed from her family but still bound by the shackles of the past.

2

Michael Korsakov was born by caesarean section one wintry morning in his mother's house in St Petersburg. He was in the truest sense 'from his mother's womb untimely ripped' and he deeply resented his premature and undignified arrival in the world. He had a good head of black hair and, even as a newborn infant, he kicked and struggled with his mother who soon tired of his antics and was pleased to pass him to a wet nurse to whom he bonded well.

His eyes were dark and slightly sunken but strangely bright with an almost hypnotic stare. It was clear that this was no ordinary child. 'A child from God,' whispered Lena, his wet nurse, as she cradled him in her arms. 'More like spawn of the devil himself,' was the often-repeated reply from the household staff who had taken against him from the moment of his birth.

'You wait and see. With my milk and God's hand to guide him, he will walk with princes and have a charmed life.'

Tamara at first dismissed this as 'peasants' talk' but soon she, too, began to see the developing power of Michael's still-fragile personality and somehow they formed an uneasy bond of affection. It was not the love of a mother and child in the accepted sense but perhaps the next best thing as it was ever-present and the one constant point in both their lives. Such was the lot of the child who now waited to act out his role. Born in shame to a despised mother and a high-born father, his genes seemed at odds with themselves as nobility and baseness fought for supremacy.

From his earliest childhood Michael had heard tell of the death of his grandfather in the duel with Prince Nicholas Orlofski, and he was used to hearing his father and Tamara speak of the Orlofskis with a bitter rage. His formative vocabulary therefore became full of the language of hate, which he acquired by osmosis. He resented the fact that when his father visited them, he would invariably leave early the following morning without a word or glance in his direction.

'But why does Papa not live with us?' he would ask Tamara.

'He is a soldier with many responsibilities,' she would answer evasively.

It was a reply born of desperation, for although Igor still visited her for his own pleasure and kept her and Michael in style, they were seen by him as chattels rather than loved and valued members of his unconventional family. In this atmosphere Michael soon realised that fate had robbed him of a childhood where he could have a full-time father like everyone else, and he reacted by being disruptive and quarrelsome. A tutor was appointed who quickly learned the magnitude of his task and, in the space of a week, despaired of keeping discipline. Although he was quick to recognise Michael's undoubted talents, he was unable to make him concentrate on anything for more than a few minutes. When he reprimanded the boy, he was met with a volley of punches and kicks and if this tactic did not work, Michael would then lie down and scream, defying every attempt to calm him. His violent and aggressive behaviour, coupled with his controversial background, isolated him from other children whose mothers saw him as a dangerous influence on their own offspring who were being so carefully raised.

Michael was twelve years old when his mother heard of the death of Igor Korsakov at Ivanhov. She knew there was bad news immediately she saw the tense face of the man wearing a black armband who stood before her.

'Count Igor Korsakov died in a hunting accident yesterday afternoon,' was all the frightened messenger could say.

'Tell me more, man,' Tamara yelled at him blindly.

'I know nothing more, madam.'

'But you are certain?'

'I have it on the authority of my commanding officer. He sends his condolences and will keep you informed officially when the facts come to be known.'

'It's those Orlofskis,' she moaned. 'It's always them.'

The soldier left hastily as Tamara raged hysterically about the house until her grief and anger were exhausted.

She could see no future for herself and Michael without her protector. She had money put by, a considerable amount in fact, as Igor had been generous, but it was the loss of position that she mourned. She loved the life she lived among the raffish end of St Petersburg's high society where she held a position of importance as Igor's favoured bedfellow.

In the months following Igor's death Michael turned all his hatred on the Orlofskis who, he firmly believed, had brought him the misery he was now enduring. Even the news of Alexander Orlofski's suicide had done nothing to alleviate his animosity. He and Tamara had no sympathy for the Orlofskis and regarded the death as just punishment for opposing the Korsakovs. They now lived on the uncomfortable cusp of society, with most doors slammed in their faces.

Furthermore, Michael hated his mother's new lifestyle and despised the strange men who came in and out of her life with monotonous regularity. Equally, Tamara knew that she and Michael were destined to be stepping-stones for the disreputable and the parvenus seeking to place a first, faltering step on society's ladder. However, even that existence was not to last and Michael found his mother, tears coursing down her cheeks, carefully placing the jewels that represented the prizes of her youth, in a cavernous velvet bag with a silk drawstring. She was equally careful when she placed a pile of elaborately printed bonds in a battered crocodile-skin attaché case. He looked at the portrait of his father, mounted on his favourite charger, which brooded over the mountain of luggage piled in the hall.

It was clear to Tamara that life in St Petersburg held nothing but unhappiness for both of them. Together, they had become a peepshow, providing the city's café society with salacious gossip. They left Russia like a breeze on the water – hardly creating a ripple.

Their arrival in New York, some two weeks later, was therefore all the more remarkable. At first the city had been a shock to Michael who, for the first time in his life, had been overawed by the brash arrogance of his surroundings. He looked disapprovingly at the gentility of their Fifth Avenue apartment, missing the gilded chandeliers and marble columns he had always known so well.

He sensed, by his mother's obvious discomfort, that their presence in the city had caused quite a stir. What he didn't know was that the New York *Chronicle* had plastered news of their arrival all over the front page. The article was less than flattering. Not only did it refer to Tamara's more colourful past, but it also brought up the spectre of the Orlofski-Korsakov feud.

The following day, with Michael as support, Tamara entered the *Chronicle's* impressive building in Franklin Square like an avenging angel. Michael looked on impassively as his mother demanded to see the proprietor.

'Who are we seeing, Mother?' he asked sulkily.

'The man who runs this place. He's Irish.'

They waited with mounting impatience, Tamara tapping her fingers on the table while Michael sprawled on a leather sofa. When they were finally ushered into Joe O'Donnell's office, a large, genial, balding man with short stubby fingers got up to greet them.

Tamara swept past the secretary, her long wheaten hair escaping from under her fur hat and her sable coat swinging loosely from her slim shoulders. The flush of anger she felt brought her a look of well-used, careworn beauty. Every faint line on her pale face was a testament to trouble and desperation.

Joe O'Donnell was momentarily stunned as he studied Tamara and the sullen young man at her side.

'I'll come straight to the point, Mr O'Donnell,' she began in the broken English that had become her second language since her liaison with Igor. 'You're a rotten bastard. This is, how do you say ...?' she said, holding up the offending page and struggling to finish the sentence.

Joe O'Donnell was quick off the mark. 'They usually say "a gross libel",' he volunteered, 'but I don't think so in your case.' He smiled. 'We always do our homework.'

'You must be crazy to print this. I am no bad woman.'

'You're clearly one hell of a woman, Miss Tereskova,' he replied.

'You can't have any idea what pain this has caused me and my son Michael,' she continued, changing her approach.

'We have a job to do. The public had a right to know.'

'Even at the expense of my private life?'

'Yes, I'm afraid so.'

Tamara had never met a man like this before in such a position of authority. In Russia, he would have been the younger son of an aristocrat or an academic in a grey suit, toeing the official line. His power attracted her. It was the greatest aphrodisiac to a woman of her background.

Joe, likewise, found her exciting and unnerving. He had never married, waiting, as he put it, 'for the right woman to come along'. From the first he had recognised that she was the 'right woman' but with the wrong background. He was gripped by a reckless desire to own and possess Tamara and, over the course of the next year, he became obsessed by her. She was all that mattered and he focused all his energies on winning her at any cost, financial or emotional.

Tamara, for her part, was well used to being flattered and pursued, but even in her extravagant repertoire of romantic or erotic experiences, she could find nothing to rival Joe's raw enthusiasm and passion. The following June they were married and New York held its breath. It was like a social thunderclap in the city and the resultant lightning flashed for some time.

Michael very much resented his stepfather. He found himself unable to relate to this extraordinary man and his unconventional ways. Everything about him was strange, from his loud check suits to his white spats and rattlesnake-skin shoes. He failed to understand why his mother felt a fascination for such a man, and he hated to see her happy while he languished in this new and unprecedented misery. Joe, in return, sensed Michael's dislike and failed in his first clumsy attempts to win the boy's approval.

School became another problem, with Michael seeming increasingly withdrawn.

'They call me a Russian bastard,' he said simply when questioned by Joe.

'Can't you do something to stop them, Joe?' asked Tamara angrily.

'There's not a lot I can do – they're not saying anything that's untrue.'

'You unfeeling swine.'

'Don't give me that, Tamara. You've got to realise that in this country things work differently. Michael's got to learn to hold his tongue and gain respect.'

'He should have respect by right,' she spat back.

'No, Tamara,' he said solemnly. 'Here we have to earn it.'

Deep down she knew he was right. She remembered clearly how she had fought against putting the words 'father unknown' on Michael's birth certificate. She recalled the sullen face of the registrar in St Petersburg and the money she had to give him to see that Igor Korsakov's full title was inscribed on the appropriate line. It was her method of brazening out society's disapproving gaze with as much of a flourish as she could muster. She was, besides, very proud of Michael's origins. In Russia, the aristocracy often committed minor indiscretions, while New York's Irish Catholic society, in which Joe had his roots, was far more straight-laced. In New York her condition was considered sinful, but less grievous because Michael's father was at least a foreign aristocrat.

Everyone knew about the O'Donnells and their social aspirations for Michael but it was one particular incident that brought things into stark focus. In the short time he had been at his exclusive private school, Michael had already acquired a reputation among the other boys for boorish behaviour. Among the sons of 'old money' his pedigree was flawed, while 'new money' found him conceited and arrogant. His origins, and those of his mother, were of the greatest interest to most of the school, and they hung like a millstone round his neck. He became the butt of jokes and an object of ridicule. His instinct was to fight and, when roused, most times he gave better than he received.

One day, after just such an encounter, he was dragged struggling to the locker room which, in normal school hours, was strictly out of bounds. His pants were pulled down and he was held down, face forward, on the slatted wooden bench by the showers. A sudden shudder excited the boys as one of them produced a battered tin box. Removing the lid with a gloved hand, he produced a live, fully grown scorpion. In the now deadly hush it was shown to Michael before being scooped up by his tormentor and placed on his naked backside.

Michael was rigid with terror. He felt the creature begin its slow journey across his skin, expecting at any moment that it would use its deadly sting. He had read about such insects in books and he was all too aware of the consequences of their venom. For what seemed an eternity he stopped struggling, he even stopped breathing as he tensed the muscles on his buttocks, waiting in horrified silence as the insect sustained its intimate contact with him. Suddenly, when he felt his head would burst with fear, he heard a voice saying coldly, 'You can get up now, you Russian bastard. It's quite harmless. It's had its sting removed. Tell that whore of a mother of yours about this if you must. We don't want you here.'

Michael did, indeed, tell his mother and Joe about the incident with ice-cool clarity. At a safe distance he felt rather proud of his ordeal which he even embellished as Tamara listened horrified. Her mind was now made up to withdraw Michael from the school and have him educated at home. She would hire the best tutor there was in New York.

Joe O'Donnell strongly disapproved of her decision and told her so in no uncertain way.

'These things happen all the time in boys' schools. You can't wrap him up in cotton wool. He's got to mix with other boys and have the rough corners knocked off.'

'He's had all his corners knocked off before his time,' Michael's mother replied angrily. 'I'm keeping him here and that's final.'

'For God's sake, he's got to be part of the real world,' Joe said, pointing to the bustling avenue six storeys below. 'Look, that's where it's all happening, Tamara. I can tell you it's not here behind closed doors. Don't pander to him. Let him off the leash and I promise you he will grow into a fine man. Hide him away and he'll either become maladjusted and arrogant or a shy, diffident nobody.'

'It's my decision, Joe,' she said, fixing him with her steely gaze.

Michael was impassive when Tamara showed him her advertisement in the *Chronicle*; not so the well-qualified tutors of New York who applied in droves. Her choice eventually settled on Dr Hal Morrow, a Harvard graduate in his early thirties. Tamara particularly liked the fact that he was unmarried. She didn't enjoy the thought of a wife and children intruding into Michael's life. Total dedication, nothing less, was what she required. Wit, humour and urbanity were Hal's undoubted coinage and he used them freely. Prematurely grey and ramrod straight in his bearing, he gave the impression of breeding and substance even though his background was crammed full of middle class virtues.

It was abundantly clear to Joe that Tamara's decision was a good one, but made for the wrong reasons. He could see that she had thought Morrow's outwardly benevolent approach and twinkling eye would ensure an easy time for her son, but Hal had other ideas. He saw potential in Michael, and the challenge was to bring it to the fore. He welcomed the opportunity to groom the boy for greatness.

At first, it was difficult for him to break the tough outer shell that Michael had grown to protect himself from the world. As he slowly chipped away, however, he was able to get an insight into what lay beneath the defences. Initially, Hal concluded that Michael was schizophrenic but he soon modified this view to one of 'temporary lack of balance' as he described it to Tamara. There were certainly elements of Michael's personality that would have been more at home in a state penitentiary but, just occasionally, a glimpse of his soft, inner centre exposed itself, only to retreat quickly before it had time to register fully. It was on this dimly flickering flame that Hal concentrated as they picked their way through the wide ranging curriculum that he had set. He winced as he saw Michael struggle through adolescence with all the ease of a snake shedding its skin on a warm stone, powerless to help in his real struggle with himself.

Two years later, just as things were starting to improve, a shock wave of anxiety momentarily rocked Tamara. Joe was piloting a single-engined bi-plane when it crashed in a strong crosswind when landing on a grass airstrip in the Midwest. The plane brushed a wing and spun around, burying its propeller in the mud. By a remarkable stroke of good fortune, Joe escaped with only a collection of formidable bruises to show for his ordeal. Tamara wept with joy as she heard the news of his escape and Joe sent her a telegram full of bravado.

The following day he arrived home to a hero's welcome and that evening they went out to celebrate at his favourite Irish restaurant, surrounded by his cronies. He told them the story of his escape in minute detail.

'I fought with the controls, but the devil was whipping up such a wind it blew me clean off the airstrip,' he explained to the wide-eyed diners as they sank glass after glass of stout. 'Lucky we ended up in a bog – so it was just like being back in Tipperary!' he joked.

Arriving back at the apartment, Tamara knew exactly what Joe was expecting because he had expressed his intentions in the most basic language and could hardly keep his hands off her. She was anxious to please him but she hoped that he would not expect too much of himself as, after all, he was in his mid-sixties and out of condition. She knew from experience that she could not count on the clinical finesse in lovemaking that she had been used to with the Korsakovs, but then Joe was different in every way. He was a carthorse where Igor had been a Thoroughbred and, like Tamara, a specialist in the art and craft of sex. Joe's technique left much to be desired but she accepted his clumsy advances.

Fired by unbridled passion, Joe began to crush her fragile frame with his sweating body and she could feel his breath coming in heavy, laboured gasps. Suddenly, he convulsed and she knew instinctively that what was happening was a heart attack. Tamara recognised the symptoms as the very same thing had happened to her, many years ago, while entertaining an over-enthusiastic elderly lover in St Petersburg. She lay helpless, crushed by the weight of his body as the life drained from him and his breathing stopped.

Joe's body lay in the drawing room of their apartment with the lid of his coffin open, much to Michael's fascination. It was about the only custom of death that the Russians and Irish agreed upon.

Tamara was now the sole heiress to Joe's fortune which, when added to her own personal wealth, made her a powerful force. She immediately threw her energy into running the O'Donnell Group, finding she had a natural aptitude for business. Her dashing style captivated the city business community and, surprisingly, she soon achieved a cautious level of acceptance by the establishment. Forthright and eccentric she might be, but her good looks, sensuous charm and endless capacity for hard work won her and the *Chronicle* many admirers.

3

Time had not mellowed Michael's outlook on life. The years, if anything, had made him even more arrogant and unfeeling. He knew there was such a thing as love but he had never experienced it and he looked on enviously while it passed him by. Central to his whole personality were his dark staring eyes set openly in a face that was alive with changing emotions which were patently visible for all to see and which he took no trouble to conceal. Young women, when first meeting him, felt like prey trapped in the glare of a hunter's light. They found him at one and the same time strangely attractive and frightening, his presence being overwhelmingly physical. He looked mature beyond his years, and this was accentuated by the hint of dark stubble on his chin and by the sleekness of his black brilliantined hair, which he wore in the manner of Rudolf Valentino. 'A nasty piece of work' was how mothers would sum him up to their excited and restless daughters.

Michael enjoyed knowing that women could sense that everything about him was made for unrestrained pleasure. In short, he was like a dominant dog who clearly marked his territory as a warning to all-comers.

Unknown to his mother and Hal, he had been seeing girls, the like of whom had brought many a pimply-faced youth face to face with beckoning manhood and roughly cast them aside after a lesson. Michael, however, took what he wanted, and then it was he who decided the next move. He was intent on hacking his own path through life and it seemed that he knew no barriers when seeking fulfilment of knowledge or sensation. This was the dark side to a golden future which held a place at Harvard and a seat at the boardroom table of O'Donnell's.

Since childhood it had worried Michael that his mother had never fully explained the circumstances of his father's death in Russia, preferring to say that he had died in an accident while serving the Tsar. He soon realised that even Hal had not been taken into Tamara's confidence on this most delicate of subjects.

'If you really want to know', Hal said, 'then you must ask your mother, but tread with caution.'

Michael picked his moment carefully. Late at night was always the time when Tamara relaxed with a drink and he knew from past experience that delicate subjects could be introduced at such an opportunity. He was acutely aware that anything connected with their past in Russia needed handling with kid gloves or the subject would be closed immediately.

'I see that Rasputin is in the headlines again,' he began cautiously.

'Yes. He's certainly come a long way from when your father first met him in St Petersburg.'

'Did you meet him?'

'Yes, frequently. He was always posing as a humble penitent, but we all knew better.'

'It would seem he knew how to have a good time,' Michael said.

'He was more careful in those days about his behaviour because he was attached to Father John of Kronstadt who had been confessor to Tsar Alexander III.'

'What did Father think of him?' asked Michael.

'They got on well together. Your father liked outrageous stories and Rasputin would tell us about the days he spent at the Monastery of Verthoturye.'

'I've heard the name,' Michael interrupted.

'He used to tell us that sinning was the first step to holiness and it cheered your father up to hear that. There were tales of orgies and all manner of goings on.'

'Wasn't Rasputin a member of the sect they called the White Doves?'

'How did you know about them?' Tamara asked suddenly.

'Well, the boys at school used to say they often castrated their followers in mystical rights.'

'That is so,' she replied. 'Your father had far too much to do with mysticism. I will always believe that it was Rasputin's influence that made him bait the trap for Alexander Orlofski.'

'What do you mean?'

'Your father was wild and reckless when I first met him. He was determined to bring down the Orlofskis and Rasputin helped him to dream up his plan.'

'Did father really win the estate on the turn of a card?'

'Yes. If only he had been contented with what he had,' she added wistfully. 'To gamble for such stakes was madness. Even though he won, he lost.'

'What do you mean?' Michael asked.

'After your father's murder, Orlofski, as you know, committed suicide and we were made outcasts by those in society who claimed that your father cheated in the card game.'

'Was there any proof of that?'

'No one could ever prove it but the Orlofskis' version of the story was backed up by Count Freedericksz. The Tsar believed them. He always liked Catherine Orlofski.'

'Didn't she die when we were in St Petersburg?'

'Oh no, she died some years after.'

'Who's left in the family?'

'Only her daughter, Natalia, who, from what little I hear, has the Orlofskis' good looks but is very hard up. She must be about your age. But let's not dwell on the past, Michael, for my sake,' she said looking up at him. 'I'm only glad that we both have a future. When you graduate you will be joining the company and, eventually, it will be yours. Thank God the past is dead and gone.'

Michael frowned. 'The past is right here in front of me, Mother,' he replied firmly. 'It's not going to go away as easily as you hope it will. There's so much I need to come to terms with.'

Two weeks later Michael took his leave of his mother at the office before preparing to depart on the Pullman to Boston.

'Thanks for the chat the other evening, Mother,' he said. 'It helped me to understand how you felt about Father and the pressures upon you.'

'I loved your father very much. We came from different backgrounds but we were good for each other. Please remember that.'

'I shall,' he replied.

'Now good luck, and give my regards to Hal.'

Michael kissed his mother stiffly and was gone.

Ten minutes later he met Hal at the apartment where he was seated in the study.

'We haven't long before the train,' Hal began tentatively. 'I know you'll take this opportunity with both hands.'

Michael grunted. Finishing his cigarette, he bent over the table and stubbed the cigarette butt out firmly in the cut-glass ashtray. Before Hal could continue, Michael put his hand inside his jacket and pulled out a large, folded sheet of paper which he threw carelessly across the table to Hal. 'Read that,' he said.

Hal picked up the paper and opened it carefully. It was a chart drawn up in Michael's clear hand, meticulously detailing the blueprint of his life for the next thirty years. Looking closer, Hal saw that it was divided into decades, with each major goal set out in chronological order and underlined in red. He sat for some time studying it as Michael watched intently for the first sign of a reaction. When Hal looked up, his face was creased in a broad smile. 'I'll say one thing, Michael, you're not lacking in ambition.'

'There's nothing I've planned that, with application and a slice of luck, I can't achieve.'

'You're starting from a firm foundation,' said Hal. 'Brains and family money are always a good beginning but the further you progress down the road, the harder the going becomes. There are, however, several things', he continued, 'that you must beware of.'

'What are you referring to?' said Michael, visibly stiffening.

'Well, your intention to marry an aristocrat who must be able to add to your fortune could be flawed thinking for a start. As you know, I have never married, so perhaps am not qualified to judge, but I would suggest to you that marriage should be for love. If, by good fortune, money and position come as well, then count your blessings. You can also put out of your mind any thought of a political career as you must know you aren't cut out for it. I know that you have all the right connections and the money to succeed but you don't have the right make-up to be a politician. As for standing for President, your high-born wife of ample means might just be an impediment before you even stand for the Senate. You're too damn wild and if they dug into your past, as they're bound to do, you would never survive unscathed.'

'What you're saying, Hal,' replied Michael coldly, 'is that there's no room for bastards at the White House.'

'I'm merely saying that everything is possible in this great country but it's not a good idea to start on a path with the odds already stacked against you.'

'And what about my other goals?' Michael asked mockingly.

'You have every chance of building O'Donnell's into a large and powerful corporation as the foundations are

53

sound. There's no reason why you shouldn't, in due course, rival Randolph Hearst and his empire. Tenaciousness is your greatest asset and you've got a ruthless streak that will enable you to step over the prone bodies of your adversaries. Your other ambitions simply seem to need great physical endurance and I'm not certain you will be able to sustain your strike rate into the projected third decade.'

They both laughed, breaking the tension.

'I'd better jettison any hope of political ambitions,' said Michael, turning to Hal. 'Hey, give me that piece of paper.' With a bold flourish he put a line through the offending lines. 'You're right, Hal, I'm not cut out to be a politician,' he smiled. 'Maybe, in due course, a grateful President will offer me the post of United States Ambassador to Imperial Russia.'

Suddenly, Michael's mood changed. Hal was used to his mercurial temperament and took little notice as he began, 'I wish Mother was more forthcoming about what really happened in Russia. She has told me a fair bit but I'm absolutely certain there's more.'

'For God's sake, Michael, why do you have to keep trying to open up old wounds?' asked Hal.

'It's just something that I heard when I was at a dinner party last week with the Browns who live two blocks away. Bud Brown has just graduated from Harvard and he was telling me that he saw a picture of the Orlofski girl in a magazine. She's evidently quite a beauty.'

Hal sensed trouble. 'For Pete's sake, just concentrate on the job in hand.'

Michael hardly heard his words. All he could see was a mental picture of Natalia Orlofski.

4

Edward and Lavinia Milner had been kept well informed of the fortunes of Tamara and Michael by the embassy staff. It was only now, however, as they returned from St Petersburg to England with Natalia, that their thoughts turned to John and Elizabeth Duff and their children, Peter and Emma. As Sir Edward's favourite godson, Peter had been placed at the top of the list of eligible young men for Natalia to meet. He might not have the bluest blood, nor the largest fortune in England, but he had the one cardinal virtue that Edward Milner admired – constancy.

Throughout their marriage Lavinia had been fond of reminiscing about her childhood in a village in the Welsh marches close to where Elizabeth lived. She remembered how strikingly blonde Elizabeth had been as a girl, and how fearless when riding to hounds. At that time she had also had a more than passing admiration for young John Duff, very much the Byronic hero, dashing, chivalrous and loving. She freely admitted to shedding a tear when Elizabeth and John had married. Money from a family trust, and the timely intervention of Sir Hugo Ballard, chairman of the Cheshire Bank, had helped the Duffs to purchase the

Liverpool *Daily Record*, a newspaper in terminal decline.

After many battles, they had pulled the paper up by the scruff of its untidy neck, paid off their borrowings, and had, at last, begun to consider themselves comfortable and secure, 'a dangerous feeling' as John had frequently warned.

They were, by anyone's standards, rich, influential and powerful. Liverpool now had a paper that was its dominant voice, fighting the city's battles and rejoicing in its many successes.

The Albany Group, as the business was known, now published periodicals and magazines alongside its newspaper interests with the *Record* being considered as a serious contender to the London daily press. To safeguard the family's control, a sizeable block of Albany shares had been put in trust for Peter and Emma when they reached the age of twenty-five.

Pre-eminent among the directors and staff was George Gerrard, the editor-in-chief of the *Record*. He had helped to make crucial decisions at times of crisis and had established a unique editorial policy for the paper. His shrewdness and sound judgement were, therefore, much respected, and it was with him that Elizabeth was currently talking through her plans for expansion into America to form a truly international publishing empire. Currently, John had no great desire to encourage her, relying on the strength of Albany in its well-researched and familiar markets at home. While being open-minded, he was anxious that nothing drastic should put at risk the foundations of the family's prosperity, now rooted firmly in the Lancashire soil. To most onlookers the Duffs led a charmed life of privilege, blessed as they were with more than their fair share of nature's gifts.

It was with just such a sense of God-given security that Elizabeth approached every day and today was no exception as she faced the full force of a gale. There were few out that morning with the hunt to see her mounted, as usual, on her bay gelding with a fine, intelligent head and kind eye.

Riding side-saddle, she looked elegant even in the atrocious conditions as she waited with the rest of the field. Suddenly the hounds started running. The fences were big and the ditches blind. To go fast over this country required a cool nerve and a sure-footed horse. Mistakes almost always led to disaster in such conditions. Elizabeth was alongside Randle Baguley, a dashing young man with a reputation for boldness. He rode with panache and daring on a fine chestnut Thoroughbred with an extravagant jump, and Elizabeth kept close to him almost as though seeking shelter from the gale. Together they galloped, half-blinded by the lashing rain, over the yielding grasslands. Elizabeth felt herself on the ragged borderline of control as they approached a wide, open ditch. They were going too fast. She struggled with the slipping reins to regain control before the horse took a mighty leap. It was like being catapulted madly through the air. For an age they seemed to stay in flight before landing heavily on the slippery mud. The horse's legs slid from under him and Elizabeth fell headlong in the path of Randle's horse. Randle saw the horror of his situation with terrible clarity, powerless to stop the animal from trampling her prone body.

John Duff waited in turmoil for the funeral. When the day finally came it was a cold, dull, December morning, one of England's starkest. The churchyard trees creaked and strained in the wind, while beneath their massive boughs there waited a dramatic personae of stone angels and biblical saints. The wind blew cruelly, shaking and tugging at the purple plumes on the black horses as they came in sight of the church. The hearse they pulled contained the mortal remains of Elizabeth and as the cortège came slowly to a halt outside the church, a small knot of onlookers craned forward to gain a better view. The sombre bearers carefully removed the oak casket from the hearse, under the watchful eye of the undertaker. To a whispered command they lifted it to their shoulders before walking in practised unison to the church door, preceded by the intoning vicar, his vestments whipped by the wind as John, Peter and Emma followed, their heads bowed in silent grief.

Watching them as they walked slowly to their seats were the ruddy and broken-veined faces from the hunting field where Elizabeth was killed, and the paler ones of the City establishment. Peter and Emma sat rigidly between their father and Lavinia Milner whose face concealed any hint of emotion. In his eulogy the vicar started by reminding the congregation of much they had treasured about Elizabeth.

'We have not only lost a woman at the height of her powers,' he continued in his clear, thin voice, 'but a wife and mother.'

On leaving the church, the sombre procession wended its way to the graveside, the wind striking bitterly at the bare-headed mourners. They stood in silent prayer and watched in stunned disbelief as the casket was slowly lowered into the ground. The vicar's words were tossed and buffeted by the gale as John stepped forward to cast the first handful of earth. It seemed such a futile thing to do when such a weight of clay would soon be unceremoniously shovelled into the grave.

A few close friends shook John solemnly by the hand, muttering kind words which meant little. To each one he mechanically repeated, 'Thank you, thank you.'

He shivered with the cold. It was not just the raw creeping cold of the day, but a deeper numbness that seemed to chill him right to the soul. Without Elizabeth he would have to be all things to all men, but he couldn't help wondering if the task was beyond him. It wasn't the *Record* that bothered him unduly. He knew its future was secure with an experienced and dedicated staff. Peter and Emma were his main concern. How would they manage without their mother? Who would help to guide them? The questions came thick and fast, and no answers presented themselves.

Night after night John sat alone at Charnley Lodge, his elegant mansion in a leafy part of the city known as Sefton

Park. Through the haze of his cigar smoke he looked quizzically at Elizabeth's portrait which hung in a heavy gilt frame over the fireplace. It was a spectacularly good likeness which captured her ambition, so riveting in its intensity. Subconsciously he listened to the memory of her voice as she spoke of the hopes she held for Peter and Emma, and her ambition that they would, one day, inherit a newspaper empire that spanned the Atlantic. If her dream was to be realised, he knew that central to any plans must be two key figures, his banker, Sir Hugo Ballard, and his old friend George Gerrard. These two men were his trusted advisors and he set much store by their wise counsel. He knew that the decision to expand Albany interests to America could not be taken lightly.

5

Peter had inherited his father's charm and easy manners, but it was Elizabeth's legacy of piercing blue eyes, blond hair and startling good looks that set him apart. Now eighteen, he was Head of the School at Shrewsbury and one of the finest scholar-athletes of his generation. He had won a scholarship to Christ Church, Oxford, from a sixth form that lived and breathed the classics, and a brilliant future seemed assured. Most important, he had now almost come to terms with his mother's death, finally exorcising the demon of despair that had come so uncomfortably close.

Peter knew that much was expected of him as he sat in the school chapel for matins on this, his last Sunday. At the back of the nave sat the masters, their wives and families in the carved stalls, while five hundred and fifty fresh-faced young men were assembled to accept the compulsory placebo of religion. He sat through the long sermon, paying scant attention except when the chaplain addressed his closing remarks to the boys who were leaving. They were trite and totally predictable, and Peter groaned inwardly at his painful lack of imagination. After twenty minutes, a familiar creaking of the pews showed the chaplain that his course was run and he knew that the span of attention allotted to him by the boys had expired. Prayers and hymns then intermingled and, by force of habit, Peter stood, knelt and sat in all the right places. He ran his fingers through his hair and pulled at his tight, starched collar, the front stud of which pushed at his Adam's apple when he swallowed hard. The noise seemed so loud that he glanced at his friend, James Ponsonby, who was sitting next to him, and was relieved to see that he had not drawn attention to himself. He looked up at the altar, remembering how hard he had prayed when his mother died, before repeating the Lord's Prayer with a stern conformity, curbing his inclination to anticipate the familiar sentences.

Soon the red-cassocked trebles of the choir were following the crucifer down the aisle. The older boys of the choir followed and the procession was completed by the chaplain and headmaster to the accompaniment of the swelling organ. After a short interval, Peter got up and led the school in regimented order out of the gloom of the chapel to blink in the summer sunshine.

He now walked alone to the chapel garden and sat on a cedarwood bench, deep in contemplation. Here, he was at the pinnacle of his youthful success and yet he realised how little of the world he understood. He had never earned money, fathered children or felt hunger like the masses who left school at twelve in the slum quarters of Liverpool, and who, at his age, were well worn with a knowledge of life. True, he had felt his share of pain after his mother's death, but he knew instinctively that his path was fixed and that fate controlled his destiny.

With these thoughts still fresh in his mind, he left the school that had formed and moulded his character over the most impressionable years of his life, having passed the first real milestone of youth.

As Peter crossed the Kingsland Bridge, on his way to the station, he took a wistful look at the River Severn flowing some forty feet beneath, licking against the pontoons of the boathouse. Walking beside him was James Ponsonby, a cheerful young man with a mass of unruly ginger hair and an ever-present smile. They had been friends from the very start of their schooldays and he was pleased that James had secured a place at Oriel College, Oxford, to read history.

'It'll be good to see you next term at Oxford, even if you are not at one of the grander colleges,' said Peter jokingly as they walked past the hideous red brick edifice of the Ear, Nose and Throat Hospital.

'It's a good solid college. Most of my family have been there,' James replied smiling good naturedly. 'Let's just hope you can keep up with that high-spending lot at yours.'

'Father will just have to stump up,' said Peter defensively.

They now walked through the familiar streets of Shrewsbury, past the Raven Hotel to the mock-Jacobean façade of the railway station. It was from here that they were leaving for London to catch the boat train from Victoria en route for Leichtenstein. James's father was Court Physician and Surgeon to the Grand-Duke, and they were to spend part of their summer vacation with him and his wife Caroline.

The early morning sunlight pierced the window of the sleeping car as the steward announced their imminent arrival in Vaduz, the principal town of Leichtenstein.

Peter and James washed, shaved and took a light breakfast of coffee and croissants before preparing to alight.

As they walked through the ticket barrier a cheerful, if slightly down at heel, servant met them. He took their luggage from the porter and carried it to the waiting horse-drawn omnibus. Once aboard, they sat back on the deep-buttoned leather seats as they progressed slowly through the ancient streets and avenues until the shadow of the great castle lay across them.

James's mother, a tall, elegant woman dressed in a green loden suit, greeted them warmly.

'Your father, James, is in his rooms attending to some elderly patients, most of whom seem to be suffering from gout or lumbago.' Without pausing, she continued, 'I'm sure you'll want to attend the reception at the castle tonight. You're both invited. The Grand Duchess tells me that Princess Natalia Orlofski is staying with her. She's living in England with her guardian, Sir Edward Milner, and she's anxious to meet you both.'

'That's a coincidence,' said Peter. 'Sir Edward is my godfather and he's often spoken of the Orlofskis and Natalia in particular. He tells me she's one of the most beautiful and eligible ladies in Europe,' he said flushing slightly.

'If I'm given any choice I would prefer an heiress from America,' laughed James. 'Let's hope Father gets the post of Surgeon General next!'

'Little hope of that,' replied his mother. 'Leichtenstein is the zenith of his aspirations, and it'll probably be retirement in Sussex next stop.'

At seven o'clock precisely, the party left the house. Peter felt from the outset that it was an evening of rare promise, and he determined to savour every moment to the full. As they approached the castle it was bathed in amber light. From the open carriage he could see the mountains that ringed the principality and smell the sweet scent of blossom that was carried on the breeze from the lower pastures. Leaving the carriage, they joined the line of guests waiting to be received. Moving forward slowly, they were soon before the Prince and Princess. When his turn came, Peter took the white-gloved hands offered to him and bowed from the neck as he had been taught.

As they walked through the ornate rooms, servants in knee breeches and livery coats sewn with gold thread offered champagne to the guests, many of whom were wearing a bewildering assortment of court and military uniforms. The ladies were decked out in a dazzling array of silks and satins set off by an abundance of jewels, while their escorts displayed a rash of medals and sashes.

Wherever they looked they saw the shimmer of crystal and gilt, the effect heightened by reflection from countless mirrors. The richly decorated walls and ceilings displayed the shields of arms of noble families, many of whom were watching carefully as their sons and daughters danced to the music of the orchestra.

James pointed out the more illustrious guests to Peter, including a Portuguese nobleman well known in court circles and a patient of his father's. 'Doesn't he look unpleasant,' he whispered to Peter, 'but, surprisingly, despite his looks he's a huge success with the ladies. I believe that in his youth he was an intimate of the Prince of Wales. Apparently, they attended many racy parties organised by the Garde du Corps.'

In the shimmering light of five thousand candles, Peter's imagination ran riot. This was a new and strangely enticing world in which he became more aware of the passionate undertone of feelings.

'My God, James,' Peter said, drinking in the scene. 'It's like something you dream about.'

'You'll soon find that life here is not too far removed from romantic fiction.'

'All we need now is to meet the beautiful Natalia Orlofski,' said Peter smiling.

Hardly had he finished speaking when he saw Caroline Ponsonby making her way through the throng of guests while chatting earnestly to a tall, stunningly elegant young woman who moved with the lithe walk of a gazelle. She was introduced first to James. Peter waited for his turn, his mouth suddenly going dry.

'I should like you to meet Princess Natalia Orlofski.'

He looked into the large brown eyes that returned his gaze. There was something about her that quite literally took his breath away and, for a moment, he remained speechless.

'How do you do, Princess?' he said, at last recovering some of his composure.

There was an uneasy silence for a moment before James suggested they should all sit at one of the gilt tables on the terrace.

'I believe you're staying as a guest of the Royal Family,' Peter began as they were seated.

'Uncle Max, the Grand Duke and cousin to the Prince, is an old friend of my family,' Natalia replied softly. 'I've been staying with him, but I leave for England tomorrow.'

'Are you going to Larkhill?'

'Yes. How do you know that?' she asked in surprise.

'Sir Edward is my godfather.'

'Oh! so you're the famous Peter Duff. He's talked about you so much.'

'You too,' he replied smiling.

'It seems then that we shall meet again as I believe you are going up to Oxford next term.'

'I very much hope so,' was all he could manage. He could hardly bear to look at Natalia. It was her eyes that transfixed him. In some strange way she was telling him to tread carefully if he wanted to see more of her. The promise was there but he knew instinctively that the path would not be so easy.

6

The clear blue days of summer were about to give way to the mists of autumn as Peter prepared to leave Charnley Lodge for his first term at Oxford. He had been unable to think of anything else but Natalia since returning from Vaduz and he longed for the beginning of term which would bring him closer to her. His mind was in turmoil and he lived in that heightened state of awareness that is often mistaken for love.

'It can't be love because I've only met her once,' he reasoned. 'Yet, by the same token, it can't be infatuation.' The more he thought about it, the less he needed a rational explanation. He knew that his father would strongly disapprove if he were even to whisper his intention of marriage. The finger of logic pointed quite clearly to a youthful fantasy born out of one romantic evening spent in Leichtenstein.

'The boy is obviously rushing headlong into something he will regret' were words he knew would be banded around. 'Marry in haste, repent at leisure' was another well-worn phrase he expected to hear trotted out, for he clearly understood that his father's ambitions for him rested on the important years he was to spend at Oxford. Nothing was to upset the 'grand plan'. In another set of circumstances things might have been different. He knew that his parents themselves had married young, and that his father's views, in the main, were liberal and often flexible. The best plan, he reasoned, was to keep his powder dry and to wait for events to unfold.

Christ Church, or 'The House', as it was known to all in Oxford, welcomed Peter warmly. He knew, however, that rank, breeding and a long distinguished family lineage had, over the centuries, been more important attributes for the college than sheer academic brilliance alone. Peter typified the new breed of gifted, prosperous, middle-class boy from public schools other than Eton, upon whom the future of the college would partly rest.

As he walked through Wolsey's Gateway he was acutely conscious of the vast scale of the place as he surveyed the huge bustling college quadrangle. Strangely, he was very much aware that he was living out his father's unfulfilled ambitions as well as his own. He thought of him as he heard the great bell of Tom Tower chime out the hour. 'It tolls longer and louder than any other in Oxford,' he could hear his father say. He pondered momentarily on the significance of this as the porter took him to his rooms which he was to share with Charles Finch, a pimply, arrogant young man who had come up straight from Eton. Finch's father and grandfather had been up before him and eaten dinner in Hall and prayed in the College Chapel. It was, therefore, home ground to him, even though he had arrived barely an hour before Peter. Both were reading Greats, but it was soon apparent that they had very differing ideas about how their time should be spent. Their first argument began on the second day of term.

'Come on, Finch, don't start worrying about work, there's so much else to do,' Peter chided.

Finch eyed him coldly. 'If you have simply come here to enjoy yourself, then count me out.'

'But you've got to have an interest outside your studies.

This place is supposed to bring out the complete man. That's the whole object of coming here.'

'It's a bit late for character development now, old boy,' sneered Finch looking down his long, pointed nose at Peter as he sprawled languidly on the faded chintz-covered sofa. 'It's always the same with you fellows from the provinces – you're too pushy.'

'Now hang on,' interrupted Peter angrily.

'Too much to prove,' Finch continued airily. 'Your father might have made some money and given you the advantage of an education, but my family have enjoyed four hundred years of wealth and privilege, so we instinctively know how to handle ourselves.'

'Well, if that's so, all I can say is that you're not much of an advertisement for the system,' replied Peter. 'For God's sake, get off your high horse. I hope you can see that it will be better for both of us if we could rub along.'

'A sort of armed truce?' asked Finch smiling frostily.

'I suppose so,' said Peter. 'But all work and no play makes . . .' He didn't bother to finish the sentence as it was obvious that he was talking to himself. 'This isn't going to be much fun,' he thought as he gathered up his books and, with a long, pained glance in Finch's direction, walked slowly to his bedroom where he threw himself down on the freshly made bed after kicking off his shoes. 'What a bore to be stuck with a toad like Finch,' he thought, cursing his luck.

From his prone position on the bed he was unable to see out of the lead-paned opened window, but he could hear the earnest chatter that came from the quad below. A sense of calm seemed to envelop him as he took stock of things. It was a bit early to make any rational judgement but he knew that his world would soon be full of new challenges. A smile creased his face as he thought of the prospect of seeing Natalia.

He reached over to the bedside table and re-read the letter he had received from Lady Milner in the morning's post. It was written in her bold, fluent style and as he read he paused when to came to the all-important line: 'We greatly look forward to seeing you and James next weekend at Larkhill'.

The following Saturday, Sir Edward sent his chauffeur, Grainger, in the Daimler to Henley Station to collect Peter and James from the Oxford train. After a drive of some twenty minutes, which they spent in animated conversation, they passed between the impressive stone lodges that guarded the entrance to Larkhill Park. Eventually the huge façade of the house loomed in the distance at the end of a seemingly endless tree-lined gravel drive, flanked on either side by carefully tended box hedges. Peter had seen pictures of the house and immediately recognised its Palladian elegance executed in white Chilmark stone.

As the car pulled up at the colonnaded front, Lovatt the butler was waiting at the door to take their coats before announcing their arrival.

Sir Edward greeted them warmly in the library where a large fire was burning. Natalia was seated on a sofa by Lavinia and the two young men first greeted their hostess before turning to her.

'I'm delighted to see you again,' Peter started awkwardly.

Natalia inclined her face towards him with just a hint of a smile appearing in her eyes. 'Thank you, Peter,' she replied softly.

The colour raced uncontrollably to his face as he looked at her. He had thought of her countless times since that evening in Vaduz but he couldn't remember her being so beautiful. He could now see what James meant when he said she had the looks favoured by the Pre-Raphaelite school of painters, with her fine features and swan-like neck accentuated by the upward sweep of her hair.

At first he felt tongue-tied but soon he began to relax. Seeing Natalia in the unlikely setting of a great English country house, he remembered clearly their conversation in Vaduz. Was this the future she wanted? Great as his expectations might be, they could never match the accumulated wealth of centuries controlled by just a few families. The thought worried him as they talked until Lovatt discreetly announced, 'Lunch is served, your Ladyship.'

Lavinia Milner, small in stature and swathed in pearls, led the way across the elegant hallway with its fluted columns and marble statuary set in regimented order. In the dining room the polished walnut table reflected the glitter of silver and crystal and Peter now found himself seated next to his hostess. He liked Lavinia's relaxed manner which he assumed owed much to the hundreds of embassy parties she had either thrown or attended in her twenty-five years of marriage to Sir Edward.

'Your father has certainly made a success of the *Record*. I remember when your parents bought it. It seemed such a risk at the time.'

'But you helped them.'

'Yes, but they had commitment,' she replied.

'Father still works too hard. Publishing is a very demanding industry.'

'Are you going to join him, or perhaps I should say "when?"'

'That's the general idea. Recently my sister Emma and I have heard about nothing but his great plan for expansion into America. I rather think he's waiting for me to join him before he makes a move.'

'It was always your mother's dream,' Lavinia said, eyeing Peter. 'It's a rare challenge, but I'm certain you will be up to it.'

'I hope so,' he replied carefully. 'Father feels he's got to do it for Mother.' Then, as if to change the emphasis of the conversation, he continued, 'My parents always loved this beautiful estate. I'd be interested to know more about it, Lady Milner. It must be a joy to live here.'

'Yes, we love the place dearly. Unfortunately, at this time of year the gardens are past their best. They're my particular love. You probably know they were designed by Repton.'

Peter nodded, aware of the lasting fame of the great landscaper.

'Unlike Capability Brown', she continued, 'who wanted to reorganise everything in a big way, Repton was content to bring the best out of what already existed. We still keep his original Red Book which has views drawn before and after the proposed works so we even know how the landscape used to look.'

'I'd love to see the gardens sometime,' he began hoping that after lunch was finished she would invite Natalia to accompany them if his request was granted.

Lavinia did not need to be clairvoyant to read his thoughts. They were written all over his face and she was prepared to give him more than a fair chance with Natalia. She and Sir Edward had always regarded Peter as a young man of high principle and talent. Anyway, she was also enjoying the role of matchmaker.

'They tell me, Peter,' she began again tantalisingly, 'that you're a fine oarsman. You are welcome to stay here at Larkhill whenever you're rowing at Henley.'

'Thank you,' he replied with genuine delight. 'I shall look forward to it.'

'As you know, Edward rowed in the Oxford Eight and got his blue,' she continued. 'It will be fun for him to hear some towpath gossip.'

After lunch Lavinia cornered Peter. 'You were asking about the gardens. Time for a conducted tour.' There was just a gentle hint of command in her voice, but, anyway, Peter was delighted to comply.

They had hardly started before she began, 'I know you have more than a passing interest in Natalia. I think, therefore, I should tell you more about her background.' Her directness took Peter by surprise. 'My husband and I have known the Orlofskis since we first went to St Petersburg. They are an old and noble family who have served Russia well. You probably know Natalia's father died in tragic circumstances when she was young and she was brought up by her mother. Her brother, Alexander, was quite a lot older. He inherited the family estates which he dissipated by neglect and imprudent speculation. As a serving officer in the Horse Guards he seemed only interested in military matters. It was widely rumoured that one fateful evening, after drinking heavily, he became involved in a card game with a brother officer, Count Igor Korsakov. He had had too much to drink', she continued, 'and lost everything on the turn of a card. A week or so later Korsakov was killed in a hunting accident at Ivanhov when he went to claim the estate. Alexander committed suicide and what was left of the Orlofski estates was seized to pay his debts. It was a terrible blow for the family but their friends rallied round.'

'I didn't know,' said Peter. 'I'm glad you've told me.'

'Well, that's not quite all,' she said, weighing his reaction carefully. 'I'm sorry to say her mother never recovered from the scandal and died a short time ago in St Petersburg. She had been surviving almost entirely by selling the family's fabulous collection of jewels. Unfortunately, there was very little left for Natalia by the time of her death.'

'It all seems unbelievable,' Peter said as Lavinia continued.

'Your father knows the whole story well – it was covered at great length in the *Record*. I remember him saying it was very good for circulation. The English middle class love to cling to romantic notions about Russia, you know, and Natalia's family have a head start in that direction.'

Peter nodded gravely.

'More importantly,' she continued, 'Natalia has never been able to accept what Alexander did, as it all but destroyed the family. She is, in reality, the last of the line but, thank Heaven, is made of much sterner stuff.'

'And what about the Korsakovs?' asked Peter.

'Well, they seem set to make mischief. Igor's mistress, Tamara, was pretty well hounded out of St Petersburg when we were there. She left with her illegitimate son, Michael, and moved to New York where she seems to have fallen on her feet. However, mark my words, we haven't heard the last of them.'

'What do you mean?' asked Peter fascinated by these revelations.

'Let's just say that rumour has it that Michael Korsakov is a bad lot. If he runs true to form he could cause trouble for Natalia before too long.'

Peter flushed at the thought but before he could say anything, Lavinia continued, 'Perhaps you can now understand why Natalia's mother's last wish was that Edward should become her guardian. As we have no children of our own we were only too happy to agree and she has already brought us much happiness and love. James Ponsonby knows fragments of the story from his parents, but I must ask you never to discuss what I have told you with Natalia.'

'I can't believe that she won't tell me herself,' he said, his voice showing just a trace of irritation. 'After all, I'm no stranger to misfortune. I know, all too well, how it can hurt.'

'Give her time, Peter. Don't go treading on ground that might just turn out to be mined.'

'Mined?' he repeated, furrowing his brow.

'Yes, you must learn to respect the fact that some people have deeply hidden feelings of insecurity and resentment. A psychiatrist would put a name to it.'

'In the short time I've known her, I would have considered that Natalia was the best adjusted person I've ever met,' he said with amazement.

'Who can tell?' she said, smiling softly.

7

'Keep your smelly feet off that chair,' said Michael, brushing past his Harvard room-mate, Chuck Murray, with lordly disdain.

'For Pete's sake, Michael, what's biting you? You're like a bear with a sore head.'

Michael chose not to reply. He was looking at the torn and faded magazine photograph of Natalia Orlofski. She was certainly as beautiful as he had been led to believe, perhaps even more so.

'What's that you're looking at?' asked Chuck.

'Just a photograph of a girl I'd like to know better.'

'Let me have a look!'

Michael grudgingly handed him the torn page. 'Be careful, you damned fool,' he growled, 'can't you see it's ripped already.'

Chuck studied the picture carefully for a moment, holding it up to the light. 'She looks a bit of all right,' he said casually.

'That girl has haunted me,' Michael replied, his tone altogether softer. 'Her family and mine knew each other in Russia. It all ended in disaster.'

'Keep away then, Michael. Why go chasing ghosts?' Chuck asked, a hint of exasperation creeping into his voice. 'Sometimes I can't help but feel you have the craziest notions.'

'There's more than a bit of madness in all of us,' replied Michael coldly. 'The secret is to identify it.'

'God help this place with guys like you on the loose,' said Chuck warily, handing back the paper.

In the weeks that followed, Natalia was never far from Michael's thoughts as he focused all his wild imaginings into a strange, compulsive, all-pervading veneration, while at the same time the darker recesses of his soul sought vengeance for the past and the sins of their fathers. Because she was the last remaining true Orlofski, it was important for him to see Natalia further humiliated and humbled before he could hold out a hand of appeasement. He didn't fully understand his reasoning but it drove him ferociously forward down a slippery path.

It was an advertisement that appeared in the *Chronicle* that suddenly grabbed Michael's attention. The famous New York jeweller, Tiffany, was announcing that it 'could now proudly offer the Orlofski emerald necklace for sale'. Michael blinked and read the advertisement again carefully. 'Half a million bucks,' he said under his breath as he let out a loud whistle. 'It must be the very same necklace that mother told me had been sold by Natalia's mother to Fabergé in St Petersburg.'

Ambition was never slow to grow in Michael and after a morning's thought he determined that any price must be paid to get his hands on such an important part of the Orlofski history.

His initial approach to the jewellers was motivated more by bravado than realism.

'I'll offer you three hundred and fifty thousand dollars,' he had stated abruptly over the telephone.

'I am very sorry, sir, but that price would be unacceptable. We have had many enquiries. You must, of course, come and look at the necklace, it's of beautiful quality and ...'

'Just give me a little time,' Michael interrupted. 'My name's Korsakov. Michael Korsakov.' With that he replaced the receiver.

He now broached the subject by letter with Tamara and, eventually, persuaded her to go to Tiffany for a private viewing.

'You've got to buy it, Mother,' he had written earnestly. 'It's the one object that epitomised the power of the Orlofskis. It was their talisman, the one Orlofski heirloom that you always ought to have had by right,' he continued. 'Don't miss it as it might never come up for sale again in your lifetime.'

Tamara arrived at Tiffany determined not to be tempted but as she looked at the flawless stones, finally revealed before her in the mirrored brightness of the jewel room, she had fallen under their spell. Breathtakingly beautiful in its simplicity, the necklace was the most stunning thing she had ever seen. She didn't need the formally dressed manager to sell it to her. She had to have it and that was the end of the matter. Finding such a large amount of money would not be easy but, after all, she had reasoned, O'Donnell Publishing was a well that replenished itself swiftly even when drawn from freely.

'Tell your client that I shall have the banker's draft here in the morning,' she told the bemused man as she swept out.

Michael was overjoyed when his mother's letter reached him. 'Hey, listen to this, Chuck,' he yelled excitedly.

'What now?'

'Mother's just bought that emerald necklace I told you about.'

'Good luck to her,' Chuck replied flippantly.

'Is that all you've got to say? It cost half a million bucks.'

'Out of my league, Michael,' was Chuck's cold reply.

Michael failed totally to understand Chuck's patent lack of interest.

Like so many things, life at Harvard had been a rude shock to Michael's system. He was used to being the centre of attention and, with Hal, he had always worked on a one-to-one basis. He now found the presence of other undergraduates at lectures and tutorials irritating, especially if they held views contrary to his own. He had chosen to read history and already he had impressed his tutors with his tight, perceptive essays. His only fault was that he peppered them with colourful, and sometimes offensive, adjectives. Socially, he had made a formidable reputation for himself with the racier set as a high-stakes gambler but there were many who already found his arrogance too much to stomach. He drank too much, swore with the seasoned accomplishment of a docker and bragged with all the subtlety of a circus ringmaster.

His only real release from the tension he built up around him was the punishing time he spent in the gymnasium. Over the years, Hal had turned him into a strong and competent boxer. His technique was now almost flawless and, when coupled with his ruthless, aggressive streak, it made him a feared opponent. He trained most days with a huge, black, raw-boned, professional fighter called Boo. They sparred until their bodies glistened with sweat and blood. However, training with a professional, and worse, a negro, soon had him banned from the sport by the university authorities for improper conduct unbecoming to a gentleman.

'Fools! They don't seem to realise I'm not a gentleman. I'm an aristocrat. The rules are different for us.'

The university disagreed.

Michael made much of this reverse and thoroughly enjoyed the limelight, revelling in his new-found mantle of folk hero. His story had become a *cause célèbre* with the press and his rooms were besieged daily by the press corps, to the horror of Chuck and the authorities.

Meanwhile, Michael seemed oblivious to the hurt he was causing his mother by allowing the whole Korsakov legend to be raked over by the scandal sheets and sensation seekers. Much was now made of Tamara's purchase of the emeralds in what was popularly seen as the last act in the ritual humiliation of the Orlofskis by the Korsakovs. It was strong meat and too rich for many of their so-called friends. Rarely were the press barons able to smear one of their own with such vitriolic attacks. Even those publications which prided themselves on their impeccable standards of professional journalism couldn't resist a dig at Tamara, and the mud stuck. Only when he received an angry letter from Hal did Michael make some attempt to moderate his behaviour, but the Korsakov bandwagon was now well and truly rolling, gathering speed all the time.

Chuck had looked on in amazement. His own outlook on life stemmed from a conventional upbringing in a small town in the Midwest. His father was a lawyer and Chuck was destined to step into his shoes in due time. He was, therefore, totally unprepared for Michael's eccentric and outrageous behaviour. It was he who, in an act of self-preservation, suggested that Michael might find a sporting future on the river.

'Yeah, Chuck, that's not a bad idea,' said Michael when the proposal was put to him.

'Anything to keep you from driving me nuts, Michael,' Chuck said, smiling good naturedly. 'Just try not to upset too many people and remember you've got a lot to learn.'

'Yeah, yeah,' said Michael sullenly.

In spite of Michael's bravado, Chuck had noticed that parts of his personality were frail, even vulnerable. Although his early life had been picked over by the press, he shied away from questions about his life in Russia and detailed questions about his father. Spiders of all sorts held a terror for him that Chuck found inexplicable in one who seemed so brash and confident. In an unguarded moment, Michael had once begun to tell him about his experience with the scorpion at school, but had clammed up when he realised the revelation might make him look foolish or lose face. More worryingly, Chuck had noticed the fascination that the occult held for Michael. This had come to light when he stumbled across a pamphlet that lay between Michael's books. It contained a detailed account of the notorious White Doves in Russia, whose rights included indiscriminate sexual intercourse and even allowed for the mutilation of their followers, allegedly to purge them of wickedness.

It was, however, the sickening discovery of a crucified frog pinned to a wooden cross that most appalled Chuck. This was the most bizarre and chilling insight into Michael's mind that he could imagine and it filled him full of alarm. He had carefully, almost reverently, unpinned the small creature and buried it with infinite care, praying that Michael might be forgiven for this act of cruelty and blasphemy, before pointedly leaving the empty cross for him to find.

The end of term could not come too soon for Chuck. He had grown to hate Michael and everything he stood for. Never in his life had he encountered such a destructive force laced with so much talent and ability. It was this potent cocktail that made Michael so dangerous.

Michael, for his part, cared little for what Chuck thought as he prepared to catch the Pullman for the bright lights of New York.

Tamara greeted him as a prodigal son, the emeralds gleaming against the pale skin of her neck.

'Hello, Mother,' he said coldly. His eyes were held by the necklace. He was almost annoyed that she had actually worn it. In spite of his feelings for the Orlofskis, he recognised, grudgingly, that the only person he really wanted to see wearing the necklace was Natalia. He and he alone must be the one to give it to her to symbolise his power. Only then would he show magnanimity. 'You look marvellous,' he added, matter-of-factly.

'Beauty at my age has to be bought,' she smiled, 'but with

half-a-million bucks hanging round my neck, what man wouldn't want to look at me?'

'Sure, Mother, sure,' he replied gently. 'More importantly, you've got the thing the Orlofskis prized most. Don't you see, at long last we can dictate events. We must make certain Natalia knows it's ours.'

'Just forget her, Michael,' Tamara snapped. 'Don't seek out the lightning – it may just strike twice.'

8

'I hope you're getting by on your allowance,' said John Duff pointedly. 'After all, you're not at Oxford to play the fool.'

The colour rose in Peter's face. 'Well, Father, it's been a bit tight recently,' he explained awkwardly. 'The House is an expensive place, and I have to keep my end up.'

'I warned you from the outset that you would be mixing with young men, some of whom have never had to worry about money.'

'I know, Father, but that's the way of things, I'm afraid. They're used to living in London or the Shires and they have large private means.'

'I take your point, Peter, but do try and be a bit more careful,' John continued, conscious of Peter's discomfort. 'What do you owe the bank?'

'A few hundred, Father.'

'Will five hundred sort your problem out?'

'That's most generous,' Peter replied. He just hoped that his father would have the restraint not to ask him where the money had gone.

His financial problems resolved for the time being, Peter presented himself early at the House at the start of the new year with the river rather than the lecture hall his priority. To his dismay, he found Finch in college already, deeply engrossed in his books. It took only a few days for the old animosity to surface.

'Why do you waste your talents in such a wanton way, Peter?' he asked peevishly.

'It's all about commitment and sportsmanship – something you would know very little about.'

'I suppose it's just to impress that foreign woman of yours?' Finch continued. 'I know her sort: sable coats, French perfume and no knickers.'

Finch was ready for the wild lunge that Peter aimed at his receding jaw. With unexpected agility, he ducked beneath the white knuckles and grappled Peter to the ground while he was off balance. Peter's head struck the floor with an audible thud. As he lay half stunned on the Persian rug which had helped to accelerate his fall by skidding over the polished parquet, he saw Finch grinning at him and felt his forearm pressed against his windpipe. What was more, he felt Finch's left hand viciously pinching the flesh on his right thigh.

From the earliest years of his childhood at prep school, Peter had always despised boys who resorted to pinching. They had usually been sneaks, cheats and classroom worms who lacked any vestige of courage. They were the sort who missed games practice to do their Latin construe and blubbed under the sheets at night.

They lay like this for a full thirty seconds as though locked in some slow, ritual, animalistic dance. Peter quickly regained his senses aided by the pain that Finch was inflicting on him with his long fingernails, and he could feel the warm sticky trickle of fresh blood on his trousers. Suddenly, with the strength and commitment of a Cumberland wrestler, he threw Finch off and, scrambling to his feet, dragged him from the floor to pin him against the oak door. He could feel the rapid beating of Finch's heart and smell stale tobacco on his breath which was escaping in pained gasps.

'Let this be a warning, Finch,' he hissed through gritted teeth, before grabbing the dandruff-caked velvet collar of his smoking jacket and sending him crashing onto the bookcase which spilled its contents over the prone body.

Next morning, bruised but with his honour satisfied, Peter received a letter requiring him to report to the Dean's rooms at five-thirty that evening.

He spent the afternoon with James in his rooms at Oriel, rehearsing the defence he would put forward.

'Just make your apologies, Peter, and take your medicine. Whatever you do, don't get involved in an argument you can never win,' said James.

It seemed sensible advice and Peter made up his mind to resist the temptation to fight his corner.

The Dean's rooms were daunting in size and portraits of generations of academics looked down on Peter as he waited. On the chimes of Great Tom, the Dean entered and sat down at his desk leaving Peter standing.

'Mr Duff,' the Dean began, fixing Peter with his steady gaze, 'you have a good brain and a well-developed intellect but your results show a complete lack of application. You may indeed be in the running for a place in the Eight for this year's Boat Race, but you must remember that you have duties other than the river. Furthermore, I may assure you that your deplorable conduct yesterday has not gone unnoticed. Under no circumstances will I allow a gentleman of this college to assume the manners of a bar-room brawler. If you are to remain with us you will have to give me your solemn assurance that you will spend more time at your studies and that you will behave in a civilised manner.'

Peter winced inwardly and almost let his guard slip. His best line of defence was complete agreement. Sir James impatiently intoned, 'Well?'

Peter looked up. 'Dean,' he said quietly, 'I shall make every effort this term to work towards the standards you set. It will be easier after the race as the river does take up much of my time. There will be no recurrence of the incident with Finch.'

'And what about the Princess Orlofski?' demanded the Dean. The question was thrown at him with all the venom one would expect of Zeus hurling a thunderbolt. Before Peter could answer, the tirade continued. 'I hear she has been instrumental in keeping you from your books, and that you have been seen at Larkhill in whatever free time your activities on the river permit. Need I remind you that you have a responsibility to this college and to your family to behave in a circumspect way.'

'Sir, I must make it quite clear to you that my relationship with Princess Orlofski is an entirely proper one and I am greatly upset that you might think otherwise.'

'Do not bandy words with me, Mr Duff,' the Dean replied curtly. 'You may go now, but be assured we shall meet again in these rooms if you let me down.'

Peter left the room biting his lip, the blood singing in his ears.

The following weekend Peter related his encounter with the Dean to Sir Edward who listened impassively until he was finished.

'Those damned academics, they can't see the wood for the trees,' he began. 'It was the same in my day. When you look back at your time at Oxford you'll always be proud that you had the opportunity to row in the Boat Race. It's a rare honour to win your blue.'

'That's how I see it,' replied Peter, 'but I also realise that I can't get away with cutting lectures. It's just that it takes up so much time.'

'Yes, I can imagine,' said Sir Edward. 'When I was young, Peter,' he continued, 'we didn't go through all the rigorous preparation you chaps go in for now. We just got in the boat and worked together for some months before the race. Ours was the true amateur spirit.'

'Perhaps there is something in what you say, Sir Edward,' Peter replied respectfully, 'but you must admit the standard of equipment and training has come a long way since your day.'

Sir Edward seemed not to hear him as he continued, 'We had Meredith Brown stroking the boat in sixty-five. He gave us a victory over Cambridge by rowing them down at Chiswick when they had a clear length at Crabtree. Bridges, who later became Poet Laureate, was a damn fine stroke. He had a talent for catching the beginning of a stroke and then infusing the devil into it. Let's hope you chaps can do the same.'

Gilbert Bourne, the Oxford Head Coach, had assured Peter of his place in the boat as the Oxford crew continued training on their home water, suffering through the bitter onslaught of a cold winter. As usual, Peter struggled to find sufficient time for his studies but it always seemed to be a losing battle.

As the new term wore on, he saw as much of Natalia as possible. Their meetings were all too fleeting but he knew that she understood that things would soon be different.

Eventually the crew moved to London and the Tideway. *The Times* had Cambridge as slight favourites for the race, but there was little to choose between the crews. The light blues had the advantage of weight but Oxford's blade-work and general cohesion were good and it was reckoned that it would be a tight-run thing. This year Cambridge had the heaviest crew in the history of the Boat Race, averaging twelve stone nine pounds, and this was thought to augur well for them in the difficult conditions that were predicted. It was an uneasy time for both crews as the rowing press unmercifully exposed even the slightest weakness in style or technique.

The day before the race the mood in the Oxford camp was quarrelsome and depressed. Things hadn't been going well and morale was at a low ebb. To add to their troubles, an argument now erupted between Peter and George Wilson, an experienced American rowing at number five. Their dislike was mutual and complete. Wilson had secured his place in the boat only recently, after an impressive display of guts and technique, displacing Egerton-Green who was one of

Peter's close friends. Dr Bourne knew that the engine room of the boat must operate efficiently and that if they were to have a chance of winning against Cambridge the American's role, and that of Peter rowing behind him, would be crucial.

From the outset Wilson had been aggressive and moody. The towpath gossips had it that his father had ruthlessly exploited immigrant families in the ghettos of New York where he was a notorious slum landlord. Peter and Wilson maintained a running battle of words which spilled over even when they were rowing. Peter used the anger that Wilson generated in him to fuel his aggression and channelled it into the slim and graceful blade that cut swathes of water with every stroke. It was, however, Wilson's constant tirades against the English that annoyed the whole crew in general, and Peter in particular. One favourite topic was the colonies. 'Your government exploits downtrodden people with a cynical disregard for their rights,' he would begin.

Peter would respond by supporting 'British paternalism' as he called it, accusing Wilson of hypocrisy when his family were responsible, as he chose to believe, for so much misery and degradation. 'You seem to think that the English are responsible for all the ills that beset mankind.'

'I'm just interested to see what makes you Limeys tick,' was Wilson's stock answer, to which he added darkly, 'particularly you, Duff.'

'You seem very interested in me,' Peter snapped. 'What the hell is this all about?'

'Well, it may interest you to know I have a friend back home called Korsakov – Michael Korsakov. It seems you're taking out a girl he's very interested in.' He smiled, sensing that Peter's blood was up.

'Mind your own bloody business, Wilson.'

'My friend says that Natalia Orlofski, although he's never met her, might just be the girl he's always wanted. So don't handle the goods. Understand?'

With a great effort of will Peter turned away, ignoring the provocation.

That evening Peter could hardly wait to telephone Natalia.

'That damn fellow Wilson is trying to cause trouble,' he began. 'He keeps on linking your name with Michael Korsakov. It seems Korsakov might even be coming over to visit Henley this year as part of the Harvard crew.'

For a moment he misunderstood Natalia's silence. 'For God's sake, what's going on?' he demanded angrily. 'I just hope you're not treating me as some pawn in a greater scheme you've got worked out.'

'Don't question me like this, Peter,' she said defensively. 'You have no right to interrogate me. I think you ought to be able to trust me by now.'

'Of course I do,' he replied, his mood softening. 'Just tell me why everyone seems so nervous of Michael Korsakov.'

'I'm certain that Lady Milner, with her usual diplomacy, will have told you something about my family's problems with the Korsakovs,' Natalia began. 'Michael Korsakov, as you probably know, is the illegitimate son of the man who robbed us of our estates and caused my brother's death.'

'And you tell me this with such ice-cold detachment!'

'Yes, I've long since learned to control my feelings in matters relating to the Korsakovs. My time to redress the balance will come. In time I'll tell you the full story.'

'Do you have to sit next to me, Wilson?' asked Peter, scowling, as the Oxford crew gathered for breakfast at the Star & Garter Hotel, Richmond.

'Have it your own way, Duff,' Wilson replied, getting up and pointedly moving to the other end of the table.

'Quiet, you two,' rapped Dr Bourne. 'I won't put up with any foolishness now.' He was reading the morning papers as the crew tucked into a huge meal of kedgeree, bacon and eggs, toast and fruit, washed down by pints of Jersey milk.

Outside it turned blustery and cold as the morning progressed and the sinking of both crews in rough weather some two years before was very much on the minds of the university presidents as they tossed the coin for choice of station.

Fortune favoured the light blues and they elected to take the Surrey station. Both crews now went through those agonising moments which united nervousness with apprehension and hope. As they placed the boat carefully in the water before returning with their oars to take their places in the seemingly fragile racing eight. Peter wondered if the long months of winter training and the sacrifices they had all made would be worth it. At one o'clock, to the clipped commands of the cox, they pushed off from the pontoons and paddled lightly under Putney Bridge, already packed with spectators, before the umpire in his launch called them to the stake boats. Once this delicate manoeuvre had been completed, the crews took off their sweaters and passed them from man to man back along the boats. Peter felt the cold whip of the wind as he sat waiting for the flag to drop. The next twenty minutes would confirm if they could succeed against the odds. Initially, Oxford went off at forty-three to Cambridge's forty-two. They knew that they had to show clear water between them and their adversaries if they were going to take advantage of the long bend in the river starting at Harrod's Repository and continuing for almost a mile beyond Chiswick Steps.

From the start the awesome power of the Cambridge crew was apparent and by the mile post they had established a half-length lead. As they shot Hammersmith Bridge with its cheering crowds, Peter instinctively knew they were in serious trouble.

He could feel the boat was not running and they had now to contend with a strong headwind dashing the water over the splash-boards. By contrast, Cambridge had made light work of the difficult conditions and had a commanding lead by the time they reached the calmer waters approaching three miles. Oxford now set up one last, desperate attack, raising the rate of striking to thirty-six. They knew that this was their last real chance to keep in the race. Suddenly, as the two crews passed Dukes Meadows, Wilson caught a crab. His oar hit him with ferocious power in the stomach. He groaned and slumped over, his blade dragging in the water. Peter gasped as the crew came almost to a dead stop.

'You damn fool,' he shouted, adding to Wilson's pain by ensuring that the long handle of his own oar crushed into his spine.

To the frenzied commands of the cox, they attempted to regain their rhythm. Wilson was now almost a passenger, barely able to go through the motions. With what breath he had left, Peter swore incessantly at him. Defeat seemed inevitable as the familiar sight of Mortlake Brewery came into view and Cambridge now put on a final spurt to underline their superiority, crossing the finishing line seven lengths ahead of their demoralised rivals. For Peter it was a disaster of epic proportions and he felt sick to the bottom of his stomach.

9

'I'm very pleased for you,' said Chuck.

'Yeah – it's been a good day,' Michael replied with a faint smile. After two terms of intensive preparation, he now rowed with a polished authority born of the fusion of great physical strength and perfect co-ordination. So good had he become that he had secured his place in the Harvard crew entered for the Grand Challenge Cup, the premier race of England's most famous regatta at Henley. Against all the odds, he had edged out his rivals for a coveted place in the boat. His inclusion, however, had undergone close scrutiny by the university authorities, anxious to preserve Harvard's good name abroad. Her representatives, it was argued, must be beyond reproach and he hardly fitted that category.

Michael placed great store by representing his university and his adopted country. To have had such a prize ripped away when it was almost in his grasp would have been unthinkable. It was the prospect of going to Henley and securing a famous victory for Harvard that had fuelled his desire. In his imagination he could see Natalia Orlofski, cool and elegant in a stunning wide-brimmed hat and silk dress, watching from the stewards' enclosure while he won the plaudits of the crowd as Harvard beat Leander by a canvas in a thrilling finish. It was a moment he had savoured many times as he looked into the red embers of countless winter fires.

The following day Michael rose early. A stiff breeze was driving rain against the window pane. The night's rest had transformed his mood. Gone was the flushed perspiring face of the previous evening, to be replaced by a look of purposeful endeavour.

'Just a week before we leave for England, Chuck.'

'I know.'

'At last I shall meet Natalia Orlofski.'

'I really don't know why you're so obsessed with her. Just suppose she won't see you?'

'Oh come on, Chuck, what do you take me for?'

Chuck now got up from the table where he was writing and took off his glasses. With an air of pained resignation he walked across the room and sat down opposite Michael.

'I've never met anyone like you,' he began, his blue eyes blinking in his round, plump face as he pushed back a strand of ginger hair. 'Just tell me what drives you?'

Michael waited for a long moment before replying. 'I approach life from a different angle to you, Chuck,' he said. 'You're all for church on Sunday and observing the Ten Commandments in your blue suit and clean shirt, while I enjoy everything that you would tell me is considered base or unworthy in your creed.'

'That's what puzzles me,' Chuck interrupted. 'You want the world to see you as a rebel. However, just once or twice, very briefly, I've seen a spark of goodness in you.'

'Perhaps,' replied Michael, 'but I'm not going to let your pious sentiments deflect me. Now, if you don't mind I've got a lot to do before we leave for England.'

On arrival in Liverpool the Harvard crew found themselves the subject of much attention from the press. Michael recognised the irony of this as the principal newspaper in the city was the *Daily Record*, owned by Peter Duff's family. He had little time to dwell on it, however, before they were swiftly conveyed from the Cunard landing stage to Lime Street Station. He had, none the less, made it his business to find out that Peter had been invited to row in the élite Leander crew who would be one of their foremost rivals for the Grand Challenge Cup.

When they arrived at Henley, the town sat shimmering in the summer heat while great activity centred on the river where workmen were fixing wooden booms in place along the course to keep the spectators' boats from interfering with the racing. The marquees and stands seemed to stretch further along the bank every day. As well as the Americans and the Swiss, several other countries had sent entries, ensuring a truly international flavour.

It was only a few days after his arrival that Michael decided to make his move. One warm Friday afternoon he arrived at Larkhill in a rickety old Renault taxi which had seen better days and which had boiled furiously before reaching the house. Instructing the driver to wait, he walked purposefully to the massive front door and, grabbing the handle that hung beneath the leonine mask of the knocker, rapped out two firm blows, before carelessly tossing away his half-smoked cigarette.

He waited a short time before Lovatt opened the door; visitors were not expected and he had cursed beneath his breath as he struggled to find his tail coat.

'Yes, sir?' he asked.

'I wish to see Princess Natalia Orlofski.'

'Are you expected, sir?'

'She's been expecting me for the last few years,' Michael replied, 'but not specifically this afternoon.'

'Your name, sir?'

'Korsakov, Count Michael Korsakov,' he said presenting his card.

'You'd better come in, Count. I will see if Princess Orlofski will see you.'

Michael declined the offer of a seat. He paced slowly up and down, grudgingly admiring the formal grandeur of Larkhill. The steel tips on the heels of his leather shoes rang out as he walked on the marble floor. By the door was a small table, covered by a green baize cloth. On it was a battered Panama hat, a clothes brush and a silver-topped walking cane. Michael picked up the hat. The label inside read Lock & Co, and he noticed the initials E. M. Going over to the fireplace he was about to examine the picture that hung over it as Lovatt reappeared.

'Princess Orlofski will see you now, Count. Please follow me.'

Michael could hardly believe his luck as he followed Lovatt's measured tread into the blue drawing room where Natalia was standing looking out of the window over the manicured lawn. He had not expected the house to be so grand and he wished he had worn something different from his old pullover and faded blue trousers.

'Count Michael Korsakov,' announced Lovatt and then shut the double doors behind him.

Natalia turned from the window and, for a moment, they stood looking at each other.

'I didn't expect you to see me,' he began. Seeing Natalia's composure, he felt, for once, that he had lost the initiative. Maybe, he thought, it had been a tactical error for him to precipitate a meeting on her home ground. 'You're as beautiful as I expected.'

She felt strangely violated by his directness.

'Why have you come?'

'Curiosity, I suppose.'

'Is that all?'

'No, not quite.'

'Well, what is it then?'

'I just wanted you to know that I haven't forgotten the outrage your brother Alexander committed.'

'You talk of outrage,' said Natalia, her voice taking on the ring of cold steel. 'It was your father who was a cheat. He

93

deserved the fate he suffered.'

'I hope one day we will talk about what happened in Russia,' Michael said. 'Revenge has always appealed to me. It's a word that tantalises, especially when spoken in the same breath as your name.'

Michael noted the flush of anger that had come to Natalia's cheeks and he knew that he only had a short time before their meeting would be at an end. 'You heard that Mother bought the Orlofski emeralds?'

'Yes.'

'It was poetic justice that they should be returned to someone with Orlofski blood.'

Natalia caught her breath and swallowed hard.

'It must be difficult for you to come to terms with the fact that we share the same grandfather, albeit from different sides of the blanket, as the English say,' Michael continued.

'Life has many unpleasant truths, as I'm sure you also have found out to your cost, Count Korsakov. Now, if you have nothing further to say ...'

'Only a warning,' he interrupted. 'My mother's family come from the gypsies and they, like Rasputin, have the power of prophecy. I tell you this – marry Peter Duff and death will hang around his neck like a silken cord ready to be pulled tight.'

'Enough!' ordered Natalia, reaching for the bell to summon Lovatt. 'How dare you,' she added, suddenly aware of the ugly upturn of his lip and the whiteness of his knuckles as he clenched and unclenched his fists. 'Never, ever return, do you hear,' she said as Lovatt entered the room. 'Count Korsakov is just leaving, Lovatt. Please show him out.'

Without a further word, Michael turned sharply on his heel and strode across the hallway before pulling the great door closed behind him with a thud that seemed to shake the very fabric of the house.

'The stupid broad,' he snarled as he jumped into the waiting taxi. 'Drive on, man, damn it, drive on,' he ordered, looking back vengefully at the house as the wheels crunched on the gravel.

Once the anger had drained from him, he derived considerable pleasure from reviewing the havoc and hurt that he had surely caused at Larkhill. In his mind's eye he could see the anguish that his visit would cause to all who loved Natalia. He knew from his own life that seeds of impending disaster had every opportunity to flourish if they were planted deeply enough and watered with venom. A gypsy's curse, he knew, could play havoc with the mind in the small hours of the night. He imagined Natalia in bed between the crisp linen sheets, her mass of dark hair billowing out on the embroidered pillow. He hoped that she, too, would perspire with fear as his mother had done so long ago in Russia when society had rejected her. 'After all,' he thought, 'I alone have the antidote. I alone can remove the fear that I have planted today.'

It was only now, however, that Michael realised the risk he had taken by visiting Larkhill unannounced. He knew it was only by good fortune that he had found Natalia at home alone. Had Sir Edward Milner been in residence it would have been a very different story.

Not everything was destined to fall so easily into Michael's grasp. Against the odds, a week later the Leander crew, stroked by Peter Duff, rowed down Harvard in the final of the Grand Challenge Cup to win a famous victory in what the pundits called the race of the decade. It was a cruel blow to Michael and he took it very badly. Those who knew him best, however, realised that it was in the despair of defeat that he was at his most dangerous.

At Larkhill Leander's victory had been celebrated with style and verve. Now, a week later, all was quiet. The crews had left the green meadows of Henley and the river was returning to normal.

Natalia and Peter were dining with Sir Edward and Lady Milner.

'Thank Heaven that dreadful Michael Korsakov has

95

finally departed,' said Sir Edward wearily as Lovatt entered the dining room with an envelope on a small silver tray. He hated meals being interrupted except for important news.

He opened the envelope carefully. 'Always knew those damn fool Hapsburgs were trouble. It could just be the spark that ignites the world's powder keg in the Balkans,' he said gravely as he announced the news that the Archduke Francis Ferdinand, the heir to the Hapsburg throne, had been assassinated by a madman at Sarajevo while on a tour of Bosnia.

Natalia had been listening. She had a sharp mind and a good grasp of European affairs.

'The Archduke will be no loss to his people, Sir Edward,' she began, 'but the act is symbolic. It will, no doubt, be taken as an excuse for all manner of foolhardy actions.'

'I absolutely agree,' he replied. 'There's no knowing where this may lead.'

'How do you think the Cabinet should react?' Natalia asked.

'Diplomacy, patience and low cunning, in reverse order, are the three ways I would approach the situation,' he replied, wiping his grey moustache with a defiant flourish.

'The Crown Prince only went on this tour because he was upset that the Serbs had stopped buying armaments from the Skoda factory where he was a major shareholder,' Natalia added defensively.

'Well, perhaps it was a wise move for them to decide to favour Schneider-Creusot in France with their business rather than purchase them from a potential enemy,' Sir Edward replied thoughtfully.

'Yes, I see that,' replied Natalia, 'but I'm sure you remember that they retaliated by stopping all Serbian pigs from coming into Austria. That really is diplomacy for you!'

'I know, I know,' said Sir Edward, 'but you have to consider that these princes are playing at politics. They're not men of stature in the international arena.'

'No wonder Europe is in such a mess,' retorted Natalia sitting bolt upright on her chair.

'Come on, don't let's get too excited by all this,' Peter interrupted.

'That's easy for you to say, Peter. You seem to think you're isolated from all the world's problems by your navy and the English Channel, when all you're really good at is sending a gunboat to frighten some poor natives in the colonies into submission.'

After dinner, Natalia and Peter made their excuses. They took their favourite walk down the woodland path leading to the water meadow. The evening sun cast its fading light over the tall trees while the birds fluttered and fussed knowing that dusk was approaching. The long, silver line of the river was just visible from where they stood and, for a moment, Natalia seemed lost in thought.

'I often dream of my childhood haunts in Russia. We used to spend evenings like this playing among the pines until late. Like you, Peter, I've been a prisoner of the past for so long. I suppose I've only just been able to come to terms with the present and the assassination of the Archduke has brought all the old bad memories flooding back.'

Peter caught her gently by the arm and she turned to face him. She hoped that he would not see how truly vulnerable she was.

She pulled him down to sit beside her on the soft grass. Her deep brown eyes transfixed him as he ran his fingers through the raven hair that hung down her back. They lay in each other's arms, enjoying their closeness. Peter felt Natalia's long slim fingers locked between his and as he looked down at her he could see her long elegant neck as she bent her head backwards for him to kiss her. He felt her body pressed close to his as their lips met and she trembled momentarily. He could feel the fullness of her breasts through her blouse as he began to focus on the inevitable result of their togetherness.

Peter's senses were taut and receptive to a degree he had never experienced before as he breathed in the lingering sweet scent of her skin, soft and lustrous with the smooth sheen of youth. He was carried along on the swift flowing river of his instinct until the heat of love came to him, overpowering him with its force.

Natalia lay still for a moment before opening her eyes and smiling a wisp of a smile. She propped herself on one hand before pulling him down to her once again, kissing him gently.

'I felt that I was dying with love for you,' he said slowly. 'You're so beautiful.' Then, holding her in his arms again, he added, 'I'm so glad the first time was with you.'

She smiled back at him but he sensed that this was not the time to expect Natalia to return his confidences.

'I love you, dear Peter,' she said slowly. 'I'm just glad that I found you. There's so much I want to tell you.'

For one wild and liberating moment Natalia felt the bitterness and disappointment of the past flowing away. 'I love you, Peter,' she said again, looking up at him as he held out his hand to draw her to her feet.

The sun had almost disappeared and they watched its lazy descent, lingering until the red glow had finally faded, before starting to climb the hill to Larkhill.

In the gathering darkness Natalia sensed that Peter had something on his mind. His conversation became stilted and nervous.

'God help the English,' she thought. 'If I live to be ninety, I'll never fully understand them.' She was, therefore, surprised when he stopped beneath the great yew hedge that dominated the perimeter of the formal gardens. For a moment she waited almost anxiously. Suddenly he seemed to find the courage he had been seeking and Natalia was momentarily taken aback by his directness.

'I love you, Natalia,' she heard him say with an ease that surprised them both, 'and I hope you will marry me.'

She looked up at him. 'Oh, Peter, I love you too, but marriage is so final, so complete in its commitment. I'm not sure I'm ready.'

'You've spent too much of your life among the ghosts of the past,' he interrupted. 'For God's sake, can't you see I'm real, and I care for you very much?'

'Let's say I'll think it over seriously,' she smiled.

Natalia sat alone on the chintz-covered chair in her bedroom, looking out over Larkhill Park, the large trees clearly visible in the moonlight. She was surprised by the orderliness of her thoughts as she reviewed Peter's proposal. It was predictable, yet she was still surprised. It was not what she had come to expect of the English upper-middle class with their reserve born of a single-sex, privileged educational system.

She loved Peter, which was reason enough to marry him, but she could not deny that she also saw him as the first stepping stone to rebuilding the Orlofski pride. Added to this it had been hinted that, the Milners having no family, Larkhill would one day be hers. At long last the river of fate seemed to be running in her direction, and the Korsakov gypsy curse was no more than a bad dream which, for the time being, was pushed to the back of her mind.

10

Emma Duff had tried to fill the void her mother's death had left. She was naturally optimistic, cheerful and positive. Her ready smile and sharp wit had helped the family through their grief. She knew only too well the loneliness her father had endured, and she was therefore delighted when he married Lucinda Cameron, a regular contributor to the *Record* on Scottish affairs.

As the only daughter of an Edinburgh physician, Lucinda had never married until now, much to the chagrin of her many suitors. Tall and dark, she had a lively mind but was well aware that she must tread carefully with Peter and his sister, Emma. On the subject of Natalia, however, she had proved a staunch ally for Peter. It was she who had softened any resistance that John might have when it came to talk of an engagement.

Since Lucinda's arrival at Charnley Lodge, Peter had appreciated the wind of change that had blown through the house, sweeping away the dust of old, unhappy memories. He just wondered how she had remained unmarried for thirty-five years as he watched her, poised, elegant and beautiful, at his father's side.

Emma also liked and admired Lucinda. She enjoyed the fact that family life had suddenly grown and blossomed. It was what she had missed since her mother's death, and she regarded Lucinda as the one who had caused the miracle to happen.

'Papa seems so happy now,' she began excitedly as they sat at breakfast. 'He used to talk only of business, but now you're here everything's changed for the better.'

'I'm so glad, my dear,' Lucinda began. 'I know he's delighted you've started work at the *Record*. He's counting on Peter joining him when he comes down from Oxford, and we all keep on hearing about this plan to expand into America.'

'Yes, I know,' Emma laughed. 'It was Mama's idea so many years ago. He's always talking about it.'

'Listen to him then, Emma. The one thing he's really good at is running newspapers. He'll know when he's ready to make a move. His timing is always impeccable.'

For a while, Emma had stayed in Peter's shadow, content for him to take centre stage, convinced at first that only he had inherited their father's considerable intellect and talents. Now, slowly, a new self-confidence was emerging, and even Peter was forced to notice that his sister had grown into a well-balanced, graceful young woman. Since leaving school at Ascot she had started work on the *Record* and was now a junior sub-editor. At her own request she ate with the staff in the canteen rather than with her father in the boardroom. Today, however, John had sent a message asking if she would join him as there was something he wanted to discuss.

Looking at her, John couldn't help noticing the resemblance to her mother in her fair hair and oval face.

'What's this exciting news you want to tell me, Papa?' she said, her eyes shining as she drew up a chair opposite him at the polished mahogany boardroom table.

'Be patient,' he said gently. 'Let's ask for lunch to be served so we can talk without being disturbed.' He got up and pressed the brass bell push set into the panelling. Almost immediately a light lunch, beautifully served on the finest china, was placed before them.

Emma took up her crisp, white linen napkin.

'The smoked salmon looks marvellous. The food here is almost better than at home.'

'Don't tell Lucinda that,' John said, laughing at her infectious enthusiasm.

'But do come on, Papa, I'm dying to hear your news,' she pleaded.

John looked at her over his glasses.

'Peter is going to be married,' he began. 'Now, what do you think of that?'

'Natalia?' she asked, her eyes wide.

'As as matter of fact, yes.'

'I gather you approve?'

'If it's what Peter wants then I'm happy for him.'

'I'm so eager to meet her. What's she really like? Is she as beautiful as everyone says?' Emma asked, putting her head on one side and fixing him with a direct gaze.

'Wait and see,' he replied warily. 'I've asked Peter to invite her to stay shortly. I don't think you'll be disappointed.'

'I'm worried that I'm going to look very dreary in comparison. You'll have to buy me a new wardrobe so that I can keep my end up.'

John frowned momentarily as Emma's reaction put him on his guard. It suddenly dawned on him that Natalia's presence in the family might just fuel the fires of jealousy and envy, emotions that he counted among the most destructive. With practised deftness he changed the subject but Emma had immediately read his mind and regretted the remark which he had taken too much at face value. She knew it was no good explaining.

'Before you go, I need one favour, Emma,' he said. 'Go and root out the Orlofski file.' A personal request from his office would draw unnecessary attention to his interest in Natalia. 'The truth, the whole truth,' he murmured to himself.

Half an hour later, Emma brought the file he had requested and laid it on the desk.

'Well, what do you think?' said John, looking at her quizzically. 'I assume you've seen the contents?'

'Yes, I've had a quick look,' she replied directly. 'You'll have to read it in detail but it certainly seems the death of Igor Korsakov at Ivanhov caused much speculation. There was insufficient evidence at the official enquiry to point the finger at Alexander Orlofski for his death but there were many malicious rumours. The only witness was the coachman who gave evidence that it was simply an unfortunate accident. The cuttings certainly show that society shed few tears for the Korsakovs. The rest of the story is very sad. Natalia and her mother must have had a dreadful time,' added Emma, looking carefully for any reaction from her father.

John sat back in his chair. He filled his pipe from the silver-banded alabaster jar that held his favourite brand of tobacco. Emma watched as he pulled at it until the blue smoke rose.

'It speaks volumes that the Grand-Duke and Duchess of Leichtenstein, and the people with all the right connections, like the Milners, should stand so unflinchingly behind Natalia and her mother,' he began. 'It's always as well to know the facts. It saves worrying thoughts later when you can't do much about it.'

'I understand, Papa,' she said solemnly.

'Don't let Peter know that I've been checking up on Natalia.'

'It's our secret,' said Emma, smiling.

A week later, Peter brought Natalia for her first visit to Charnley Lodge. Lucinda greeted her with a friendly hug.

'We're so pleased you've come to stay with us,' she said warmly. 'I just hope you will regard this as your second home.'

'Thank you,' said Natalia. 'We're already very much in

your debt, according to Peter. It was good of you to smooth our path with Peter's father,' she said. 'I'm very glad that we're going to be friends.'

'I'll second that,' said Peter interrupting as he helped the servants to wrestle with one of Natalia's hat boxes.

'You're in the Blue Room. Pearson will show you the way and have your luggage taken upstairs.'

That evening John returned from the office strangely preoccupied. He welcomed Natalia warmly but it was noticeable that he was not his usual self at dinner.

By contrast, Emma was irrepressible as she questioned Natalia at length about Russia, the latest fashions on the continent and about Leichtenstein.

'For heaven's sake, Emma, don't ask so many fatuous questions,' said Peter, beginning to be mildly irritated by his sister's domination of the conversation. Natalia shot him a look of silent rebuke as Emma continued unabated.

'What's the news from the office, Papa? Is it something serious?'

'Well, I don't want to spoil the evening,' he said gravely, 'but I gather that it looks as though war is now almost inevitable.'

'You mean that Austria-Hungary really are going to take on the Serbs?' asked Peter, glancing at his father.

'The situation is volatile,' John replied, 'and it's impossible to predict with accuracy which way it's going to go. If the worst happens, Britain will be dragged in whether we like it or not.'

There was a brief silence.

'What does Sir Edward make of the situation?' John asked, looking at Natalia.

'He's convinced that if there are hostilities and they are not over quickly, things could deteriorate badly. His opinion is that it could end in a war fought on an unprecedented scale.'

'I'm afraid I tend to agree,' said John.

A damper came over all those sitting at the dining table as

104

the possibility of both war and peace was discussed. It was only towards the end of the meal, when they paused for reflection, that John, intent on ending the evening on a more positive note, turned to Natalia.

'Why don't you and Peter come to the office tomorrow? I think we might have some brighter news to report.'

'I'd like to very much,' Natalia said, smiling.

'Good, I'll send the car to collect you both at eleven. I've got an early morning meeting with George Gerrard, the *Record's* editor, and then I'm free until after lunch.'

The next morning, the Rolls-Royce, immaculate in dark blue livery picked out with gold coach lines, drew up outside the Queen Anne-style doorway of Albany House. The doorman stepped forward to open the door and Peter jumped out first to help Natalia from the car. Once inside the building, they crossed the impressive foyer, its elaborate plaster ceiling accentuated by crystal chandeliers hanging like wreaths of ice, bathing the walls in a thousand dramatic fragments of light. Peter led the way as they walked up the green marble stairs, stopping to show Natalia the elegantly framed photographs of his maternal grandfather who had founded the business, and of his mother. On entering his father's impressive office suite, he shook Miss Jones warmly by the hand. She had been John's secretary for twenty years and was now one of his most trusted employees. There was nothing she didn't know about the business or the family, and her loyalty was beyond question.

'Your father's expecting you,' she beamed, after Peter had introduced Natalia.

'She's saved my bacon with Father on more than a couple of occasions,' Peter said, grinning at Natalia.

As they entered the panelled office, John was already on his feet and he greeted them both warmly before motioning them to sit down. He could now see clearly exactly why Peter had fallen in love with Natalia. She radiated an extraordinary beauty which was highlighted by her perfect complexion. Natalia immediately sensed that he was looking at her closely and smiled back softly. If there had ever been a doubt in John's mind as to the wisdom of Peter's choice, it was now erased completely and utterly.

As though to ease the moment, he took out a large cigar. 'Do you mind if I smoke?'

'Please do, Mr Duff. I love the smell.'

As he removed the band and took up the cigar cutter which rested on the desk, he asked earnestly, 'Do you want me to put a formal announcement in the *Record* about the engagement? Here's a draft I prepared this morning. If it suits you we can also send it to *The Times* and *Telegraph*.'

'Steady on, Father,' laughed Peter.

The conversation was abruptly cut short by the telephone ringing. John picked up the receiver and listened attentively. It was the newsdesk to say that they had had a flash from Reuters that Germany had declared war on Russia.

Peter looked at Natalia. He half-expected to see her crushed by the news. Instead, she was sitting erect, looking directly at him. He could sense the strength of her feelings as she searched for words. After a moment she began, 'My people have a great capacity to survive. We always win through in the end but there will have to be great sacrifices.'

'The rumours are that Germany is now intent on invading neutral Belgium,' said John. 'If that happens I'm afraid, for all our sakes, that Asquith, with the consent of Parliament, will have to go to war. I can't see Germany giving way.'

As John predicted, Germany refused to comply with the British ultimatum to withdraw from Belgium and war was declared.

'Act with circumspection and care,' was John's advice to his editorial staff. 'We have a great responsibility to our readers now that we are at war. They are going to rely on us for accurate reports of the fighting.'

As Peter prepared to return to Oxford, he felt strangely divorced from reality. With Europe involved in a titanic struggle, academic life seeeemed almost irrelevant and he knew that it would be only a matter of time before he would be at the heart of the conflict, enduring all the risks that came with such an epic upheaval.

11

'That bloody Korsakov still haunts me even though he's over three thousand miles away,' said Peter turning to Natalia. 'I only have to close my eyes to see him menacingly close to you.'

'For Heaven's sake, Peter, stop fretting.'

'I can't help it. There's something really sinister about him.'

'I know what you mean,' she replied, 'but there are more important things to worry about.'

Although Natalia put on a brave face, she still shuddered inwardly when she remembered the grim prophecy that Michael had made about Peter when he visited Larkhill. She had tried to put the memory of that unwelcome encounter to the back of her mind, but there was something about the look in his eyes that still haunted her. It seemed all the more real now that the country was at war and like so much about the Korsakovs it assumed a malevolent and chilling importance in her life.

For a brief two weeks Peter returned to Oxford. The university seemed to be full of ghosts with so many of her sons already buried under the stinking mud of Flanders. The remorseless roll-call of the dead mounted daily, with some of her brightest lights destined to be remembered merely as chiselled names on a marble college memorial tablet. Everywhere there was a semblance of normality, but scratch the surface and it was clear that the city and the university as he remembered them had changed forever. Peter was truly sorry to break with Oxford on such terms but he knew that there was always the possibility of returning after the war to make peace with the place. One thing he knew for certain was that if he did eventually go back it would be a different person who walked under Tom Tower. Gone would be the carefree spirit of youth, replaced by maturity forced upon him by circumstance.

Peter was desperate in his frustration, torn between Natalia and the knowledge that he could not honourably escape his duty to king and country. It would be the last straw, he thought, if Finch, of all people, told him he had enlisted first.

Towards the end of the second week of term, Peter sat in his rooms with James. The flickering coal fire was inadequate in combating the chill that struck to the bone. Untidy heaps of books and paper littered the floor. In the corner were some empty Bollinger bottles from which Finch had freely imbibed the previous night before retiring, in stupefied incoherence, in the early hours. He had arisen at lunchtime in a foul mood, treated his hangover with a mixture of beaten eggs and garlic, and retired to the library to read Tacitus. Peter and James, thankful for his absence, sat looking into the bleak college garden.

'You're a deceptively fast worker, Peter,' said James, pouring out a cup of tepid Earl Grey tea which had been left to stew in the pot. 'I really never thought you had it in you to carry off such a peach as Natalia.'

'Appearances can be deceptive,' replied Peter with a flash of his old good nature. 'But, joking apart, it worries me what Natalia's going to say when I enlist. I can't really gauge how she's going to react.'

'That apart, you should also be thinking of drafting a letter to the college authorities,' said James. 'It's important to leave on good terms in case you want to return when the war is over to finish your degree.'

'If I ever come back alive,' said Peter, his morose mood returning. 'Judging by how things are at the moment, I have less than a sporting chance.'

'You've always had the luck of the devil,' said James, his voice lacking conviction as he declined to meet Peter's eyes. 'I'll be joining you over there soon,' he confided. 'It's just taking me a little more time to reorganise my life. I've decided to apply for a post in intelligence.'

'Cloak and dagger stuff at headquarters?'

'Yes, more or less,' replied James defensively as he read Peter's tone.

'For as long as I've known you, you've always found a way of never totally committing yourself. One day you may just have to.'

The decision to leave Oxford made Peter sleep fitfully. The following day he telephoned Natalia early to tell her he was coming to Larkhill. He asked her to arrange for Grainger to meet the mid-morning train with the Daimler at Henley Station.

'What's so urgent?' she asked anxiously. 'I had arranged to go into Henley with Lavinia but I'm sure she will understand.'

'Thanks. I'll tell you everything when I see you,' was all that he could say before the telephone clicked off.

When the train arrived Natalia hurried to meet him. At once she found him different. He spoke in a rapid, controlled voice that she hadn't heard before.

'I'm going to join up in January. I simply can't stay at Oxford when most of my friends are in the front line. I want us to be married as soon as possible so that I have the best incentive of all to return in one piece.'

Natalia looked at him with the piercing gaze he knew so well.

'Oh, Peter, I do understand your feelings,' she replied, 'but don't you think we should wait? We could still be married after Christmas and then you could become a war correspondent for the *Record*.'

'Can't be done,' he replied quickly. 'Kitchener has just issued a directive banning all correspondents from the Front.'

Natalia sat in silence for a minute. She could see that Peter was determined and she knew from past experience that at times like these it was better to say as little as possible.

'You must do what you want,' she said thoughtfully. 'I should be disappointed if I saw any lack of courage or any weakness in you.'

Peter was slightly taken aback by this utterance. He had expected tears but instead he had found the true measure of Natalia. He knew that she was strong but he had no idea how she really ticked. Such practised detachment made him feel better and, in some strange way, helped the difficult moment to pass.

'How about December for the wedding?' he said casually.

'Why not?' she smiled, slipping her arms around him.

Sir Edward listened gravely to what Peter had to say. He knew better than to argue the point with him as he remembered how he would have felt as a young man in the same position.

'Would it be all right if Peter was to come and spend some time at Larkhill as usual?' asked Natalia. 'At least we'll be together for a little time before the wedding.'

'Of course, my dear,' he said. 'If you're to be married in early December, I had better get a move on. It takes a while, you know, to read the banns and get things organised,' he added, busily writing notes. 'What date had you in mind?'

'The first Wednesday in December would be ideal,' said Peter. 'It need only be a simple affair with just the immediate families. I'll make sure that Father and the family are told right away.'

That weekend, Peter and Natalia took the train to

Liverpool to spend some days at Charnley Lodge. It was a bittersweet occasion with everyone seemingly sailing serenely along but paddling hard beneath the water.

'Please tell us about the plans for the wedding,' asked Emma.

'Well, most important of all', replied Natalia with a smile, 'is that I'd very much like you to be chief bridesmaid. That probably means the only bridesmaid,' she laughed.

'Oh! I'd love to be,' Emma cried. 'I haven't been a bridesmaid since I was ten.'

'I know Peter has asked James to be his best man and the Milners have organised the parish church at Henley. Sir Edward has agreed to give me away,' continued Natalia.

'But don't you want to be married in a Russian Orthodox church and have those lovely crowns held over your heads?' butted in Emma excitedly.

'My home is here now and my faith is Peter's,' Natalia answered simply. 'I've got to put down roots. I've had lots of time to chat with Canon Saunders. He's full of practical commonsense and I feel very happy he's to take the service. He's been so kind to both of us. Peter also frequently reminds me that he umpired the Boat Race in nineteen hundred.'

'What's that got to do with being married?' asked Emma.

'Nothing,' replied Natalia laughing, 'but if it makes Peter happy, that is half the battle.'

In the weeks that followed, Natalia busied herself in preparing for the wedding. Peter, on the other hand, seemed to be living in a strange world of fantasy. It was almost as if he was waiting to recreate the stories Nanny Baxter had read to him as a boy. He had often told Natalia of the book he used to keep by his bedside as a child. It extolled the exploits of fresh-faced British officers gallantly leading charges against the Boers while hopelessly outnumbered, and of countless deeds of valour guaranteed to stir young blood. The characters were always oblivious of danger and often died gloriously in the service of their country, which was the supreme mitigation. It was this boyish enthusiasm, near to

112

recklessness, that had first attracted Natalia to Peter, but she knew a much deeper strength of character lay beneath the thin veneer. She felt it had something to do with schooling. Phrases such as 'it's not cricket' and the 'code of the amateur' confused her. Russian men never bothered with such strange things, she mused. Englishmen, she thought, too often took their pleasures and worldly affairs in an unabashed, full-frontal attack.

'Perhaps that's why I love him,' she thought.

Returning to Charnley Lodge by train, Peter now set about putting his life in order. He set great store by visiting his mother's grave. His memories of her were still vivid and he recalled with anguish the days after her death and the awful final realisation that she was not coming back. He stood bare-headed, deep in thought by the simple headstone. It crossed his mind that he might soon join her in this seemingly desolate spot. Worse still, he thought, if he were to die in some foreign field and be buried amid a mass of regimental graves. It even occurred to him with horror that he might be left to rot, a stinking corpse in the barbed wire jungle of No Man's Land. Such thoughts preyed heavily upon his mind as he retraced his steps until he stood under the shadow of the church. The thought of death, his own death, had never really worried him until now. Suddenly it became an unwanted companion who walked beside him, prodding him if he dared forget its presence.

All, however, was not shaded by sombre thoughts. He was keyed up and excited as the wedding drew close. Natalia had suggested that it should be a simple but dignified service with just the two families and their close friends present. Peter agreed wholeheartedly that it was far more suitable kept that way, especially as so many of their friends would be missing.

The flint and chequerwork church seemed to shine in the winter sun as John and Lucinda stepped out of the Rolls-Royce to join the small party of family guests already seated in the pews. As they looked round they could see the elegant and varied monuments to wealthy benefactors of the town.

'Elizabeth would have been proud of Peter,' John thought and wondered how life might have been if circumstances had been different.

Five minutes later Peter and James came in and sat down in the pew in front of them. As the clock struck the hour a hush fell on the congregation who waited expectantly for the arrival of Natalia on the arm of Sir Edward. As they walked serenely up the aisle, Natalia remembered a Russian proverb taught to her as a child by her mother. In her mind's eye she could see her in the nursery, saying, 'Great is Holy Russia, but the sun shines elsewhere too.'

'Well,' she thought, 'the sun has at last come into my life,' and she turned and smiled at Peter who had taken up his position with James before the chancel steps. James stared at her just a little too long and, realising his mistake, flushed.

Natalia was wearing a white silk dress trimmed with lace and her train was embroidered with the letter 'O' surmounted by a tiny coronet. Her shining dark hair was piled high on her head, accentuating her graceful neck and contrasting with her paleness. Over her face she wore a lace veil held in place by a small circlet of pearls and she carried a posy of pink flowers. Canon Saunders, who had been standing at the top of the chancel steps, waited for stillness to settle on the congregation before starting the service in ringing tones with the passage on the meaning and purpose of Christian marriage.

Natalia couldn't help but smile at the turn of events that had brought her to marry in an English country town, far away from the swinging censer and gold crowns of the Russian Orthodox church of her childhood.

The ceremony progressed in ordained fashion until it was the time for the giving of rings. To Natalia this was the moment that she became Peter's. She therefore let out a small gasp when Peter dropped the ring as he was about to place it on her finger. She shivered as James moved quickly

114

forward to retrieve it from the stone floor. Momentarily he was caught in her gaze and she thanked him silently with her eyes. Was it, she thought, the first portent of the Korsakov curse?

12

Hal raced to St Patrick's Hospital when he received the news that Tamara had been taken there, seriously ill. He waited in the depressing, antiseptic corridor of the old building before being allowed to see her. Sitting by the bed he took her hand and pressed it. There was no discernible reaction. She stared at the white ceiling as though in a trance. He stayed with her for a while, sitting quietly and talking gently. It mattered little to him if he received a response, he just wanted her to know she was not alone.

'Dr Morrow,' began the sister in her starchy voice, 'you wanted to see me?'

'Yes.'

'We can talk in my office.'

They left the private room and walked a short distance down the corridor, their footsteps muffled by the oilcloth. Once in the claustrophobic closeness of the office, the woman began, 'I'm afraid Mrs O'Donnell has had a severe stroke.'

'Are you sure? She's only fifty-one. There must be a mistake.'

'There's no mistake. Most of our tests have now been

completed. Although she has lost the use of her right side, with consequent impairment of speech and sight, her condition is stable.'

'Will she recover?'

'That depends on her. If she fights back then it's surprising what can happen.'

'She's an O'Donnell. She'll fight.'

'Good, then see how things are in a month or so.'

As the days and weeks passed, Hal waited anxiously as Tamara explored the limits of her damaged body. Knowing her as he did, he could see that her clarity of thought was unimpaired, but the co-ordination between her brain and tongue was obviously missing. He waited patiently as she battled to escape from the wheelchair which constrained her more fiercely than iron bars. Looking at her he just wished he could take the terror from her eyes and let her resume her place in the world she loved so much, free from any disability. He roundly cursed Michael for his all too obvious absence and he wondered if the years he had spent with him had been in vain.

When Michael eventually did come to visit his mother, Hal could sense her agitation. He noticed how, in some strange way, a chasm had opened up between them. Michael's eyes now seemed to bore unblinkingly into her soul, probing and searching the hidden ground. Unbridled ambition and the scent of real power and influence seemed to have overridden any filial loyalty that he had once felt. Hal knew him too well, however, for Michael to disguise his feelings. Michael's worst instincts, which he had previously managed to suppress, were now bursting out like boils. Hal suddenly remembered what Tamara had said about his father in an unguarded moment. 'Yes,' he thought, 'she's quite right. He's inherited bad blood.'

Michael didn't stay long. He had seen as much of his mother's physical condition as he needed to reinforce his claim as the heir apparent to O'Donnell's, and Hal knew he would move with all speed to seize power from Tamara. In a

117

last desperate effort to upset his manoeuvrings, Hal consulted Tamara's doctor and the following day he was able to arrange for her discharge from hospital. 'We're going home, Tamara,' he said simply. The tears, never far from the surface, were now staining her pale cheeks. Taking her lace handkerchief he wiped them away with undisguised tenderness.

'Is Michael coming to see me today?' she said, struggling with the barely formed words and inclining her gaze away from Hal.

'Be patient. He'll come when he's ready.'

He knew, however, that Michael would already have laid plans to take his place at the helm of O'Donnell's and his first move would be to challenge Dean Jones who, since Joe O'Donnell's death, had run the company. Tamara and Dean had a warm and cordial relationship and during her stay in hospital he had been a faithful and regular visitor.

'He's more like the brother I never had,' she said when describing their relationship to close friends. Hal knew that Dean found Michael's presence in the company irksome but, for Tamara's sake, he had put on a brave face. She had always listened to him, even if she disagreed with his point of view, and he had been counsellor, guide and friend. Michael, Hal knew, would transform this relationship to one of master and servant.

As Hal predicted, it was only a matter of days before the board of O'Donnell's were forced to accept Michael as president in place of his mother. Hal knew that Michael's new position would fail to impress the city establishment or his rivals. It was clear that they regarded him as wet behind the ears. Most laughed openly at his posturing pride in styling himself Count Michael Korsakov and they regarded it as only a matter of time before he would be humbled and they would be able to pick up the pieces of O'Donnell's for a knockdown sum. It was obvious to Hal that Michael was drinking too much, but what alarmed him more than anything else was the company he kept. It seemed that most of the low life of the city passed through Michael's apartment. Gone were many of his Ivy League friends, to be replaced by shadowy figures with dubious backgrounds. In short, he was seen in the best places in town in the worst company.

Hal knew that since his fleeting encounter with Natalia Orlofski, Michael had been fascinated and captivated by her, even though she had so fiercely rebuffed him. He had even ordered an English press-cutting service to forward every detail published about her, and he noted with particular interest the news of her marriage to Peter Duff. He had ringed the date on his calendar and then gone out and got liberally drunk. Hal did not have to be a mind reader to see that the momentous happenings that linked the Orlofskis and the Korsakovs in a sinister embrace seemed to exert a strange hold over him. Like so many other rich young men before him, it had come as a shock when he found that money could not buy the object he desired. He was used to taking his pleasures ready-packaged and available from the shelf. To find Natalia not only unavailable but also hostile was more than his ego could bear.

Along with their propensity for evil, Michael had inherited the brash, wayward charm of the Korsakovs. Tamara had told Hal the sketchy details of Igor Korsakov's death, but he had never delved too deeply, leaving it to her to tell him just as much as she wanted.

'I don't want a word breathing to Dean,' she would say when she thought she had gone too far. 'It's important to me that Michael must believe his father was a good man. Things might have been very different if I had been just a few years older,' was her constant lament. She had always known that, somewhere in Michael's make-up, lurked the dark side of the Korsakovs which time and circumstance were now unleashing, and which she was powerless to stop. He had come on the back of a hurricane, she reasoned, and she had always felt that it was through him that the family's destiny would be worked out.

119

13

The honeymoon over, Peter and Natalia returned briefly to Larkhill before travelling north to spend Christmas in Liverpool. They found Charnley Lodge, set as it was in the fashionable part of the city, a far cry from the rolling meadows of Larkhill. Natalia at first found it difficult to understand the native Liverpudlian who spoke with a distinctive catarrhal intonation. She was amazed to see people of all races and creeds living cheek by jowl close to the waterfront and mixing easily with the Irish Catholics who made up the principal workforce at the docks. They laboured tirelessly, and for the most part with good humour, loading and unloading a bewildering variety of cargoes from ships sailing under a diversity of flags.

The Mersey was the great artery which served the city and its hinterland, bringing trade and prosperity to the port. From here the thriving industries of the North West exported goods to the Empire and beyond. The grim reality of a protracted conflict now seemed inevitable as steam lorries and teams of magnificent heavy horses on the Dock Road conveyed a seemingly endless stream of goods and supplies for the troops abroad.

Natalia tried to maintain an outward veneer of calm but she knew that the death rate among the inexperienced young subalterns at the Front was frighteningly high. Each night she prayed fervently, her hands pressed together as she knelt by the bed, that Peter would be spared. Sometimes she prayed in Russian to her Orthodox God, and at other times in English to the God of the Empire and the Dominions across the Sea. All she could do was to support Peter in every way possible now that he had made his decision. On the surface he remained calm and unruffled but deep down he knew he might not live to see another Christmas. It was at night, in bed, that she really knew how much Peter meant to her and she clung to him obsessively. There was little she could do but to make the most of their last days together and look forward to his first leave.

When the day for Peter to leave came, Natalia saw him off from Lime Street Station. John and Lucinda had elected to stay behind, unwilling to intrude into their private moment. It would have been too painful to see them struggling with their emotions. Upon her return home, Natalia joined them in the drawing room.

'How was he?' asked John gently.

'Fine,' she replied.

'He never gives much away.'

'No. He's learned to hide his feelings very well,' she smiled. 'He simply knows that he's honour bound to fight.'

'All you Duffs are obsessed with duty and honour,' interrupted Lucinda. 'It's very plausible until someone gets hurt.'

John gave her a cautionary glance.

'No, I won't be silent,' she said. 'I know he's doing the right thing, but it all seems unnecessary.'

'That's what I think, Lucinda,' said Natalia. 'All this because one man is assassinated in the Balkans,' she added, looking at John.

He refused to meet her gaze, the tears pricking the back of his eyes as he thought of his son.

Picking up the paper Natalia began to read the headlines.

'Terrible, isn't it?' said Lucinda softly. 'I can't believe that by Christmas nearly a million of your countrymen had died.'

'I just can't bear to think of my childhood friends who will be in the thick of it,' replied Natalia. 'The Russian cavalry with horses and sabres are no match for the Prussians and the Austrian hussars with their modern weapons. It's mass butchery.'

'Please, that's enough,' said John stiffly. 'The day's painful enough without reading any more about the war.'

The following week Natalia received a letter addressed in Peter's hand and with an Aldershot post mark.

'He says his fellow subalterns in the Coldstream Guards are a good bunch,' she read aloud to John and Lucinda over the breakfast table. 'They're all terribly conscious of how little they know of real warfare. Read it if you like,' she said with a wry smile.

Peter had obviously chosen his words carefully knowing the letter would be seen by all the family. He told how they were taught the lessons learned in past colonial wars. 'We officers have to lead by example,' he wrote. 'It means exposing us to more risk but at least it shows the men we aren't shirking our duty.' He explained how they were expected to use this dubious tactic against well-equipped and carefully trained German troops who would be a very different adversary from the enemy in previous conflicts in Africa. He was full of praise for the NCOs, adding that they all realised they were going to need their help and experience to cover up the initial mistakes they were bound to make.

Natalia, for her part, wrote to Peter every day. She cautioned him to look after his health and pleaded with him to be careful. She kept her letters strictly matter of fact and concentrated on news from home. 'Your father's having trouble with the Press Bureau in London,' she wrote. 'He's having to submit copy sent to the *Record* from the Front and, more often than not, it's savagely cut. He's really annoyed.

You know better than anyone else, Peter,' she continued, 'that rumours and intrigue are rife. Your father has refused to run that story of the supposed sighting of Russian troops who are said to have landed in Aberdeen last September with "snow on their boots" on their way to reinforce the Western Front. He said that many of the less responsible papers blew the whole thing out of proportion and he was outraged that even *The Times* hinted at the story. Apparently they bolstered it with accounts of trains travelling with their blinds down, station slot machines jammed with roubles and men kept busy sweeping snow from carriages.'

Peter smiled as he finished reading the letter. 'God help Britain', he thought, 'if those in high places think that's going to fool the enemy.'

14

'Come on, Dean. Get off your butt and start things moving!'
Michael was enjoying 'cracking the whip' as he called it at
the office. His attitude was aggressive and abrasive. He
disliked fat men and he found Dean's large stomach
particularly irritating. Dean was, in fact, the epitome of all
Michael despised in men already into late middle age.

'Why don't you go back to Harvard, Michael, and leave
things to us?' suggested Dean lamely. 'You can be certain
that we'll look after your mother's best interests.'

'Get lost,' Michael replied acidly. 'For a start, I don't trust
either you or Sam Goldman, that wily old attorney of
mother's. You'll both stitch me up.'

'I'll ignore that remark, Michael,' Dean said stiffly. 'Now
don't go criticising Sam. He's a good man and devoted to
your mother.'

'That's as may be. Just draw up the itinerary for my trip to
the West Coast. You've always been too cautious, Dean,' he
chided. 'We've got to expand our interests before the
competition gets a head start on us.'

'Your mother, with the support of the board, always found
it best to consolidate as we went along. Financing this new

building has been onerous. We're only just beginning to see daylight. If we split our resources we'll have real problems before too long. I strongly advise against it, Michael.'

'Well, we'll see,' was the non-committal reply.

Dean hoped that Michael's absence might give him some breathing space as he was convinced that it was not the time to have an all-out confrontation.

The following week Michael was packed and ready to leave.

'Try not to get us into trouble, Michael,' said Dean eyeing him peevishly.

'Just look after the store while I'm away,' Michael replied coldly as he picked up his raincoat and hat. With that he was gone, striding across the lobby to the elevator and then to the front of the building.

'Thank God for small mercies,' Dean thought before putting a call through to Goldman and Co. Sam Goldman, and his father before him, had always been close to Joe O'Donnell and they had dutifully seen Tamara through the minefield of legal problems after his death. Sam was a small, lantern-jawed man with the deep-set eyes of an owl. He had a shrewd business sense, coupled with complete loyalty and a straightforward approach to the thorniest of problems. He had always been secretly in love with Tamara but he also had the good sense not to press his suit with her. Even after her stroke, he had been content to admire her from afar and to continue diligently to look after her interests. Dean knew that he could count on him as a staunch ally against Michael whom they both disliked and mistrusted.

As the limousine left the O'Donnell building, Michael instructed the driver not to take him to the station as planned but to drive back to his apartment and unload his luggage.

'You may assure anyone who asks you that I caught the train with fifteen minutes to spare,' he said, slipping a twenty-dollar note into the driver's hand. 'I'm relying on your discretion. If you breathe a word of my change of plans to anyone then you will never work for me again.'

'Yes, sir, you can rely on me.'

As soon as he was in the apartment, Michael picked up the telephone. 'Has everything gone according to plan?'

'Yes,' he was assured. 'A man resembling you has boarded the train. We have made certain that everyone who needs to know believes you are en route for Chicago.'

'Just as long as there isn't a slip-up.'

With that, he replaced the receiver and poured himself a whisky from the cut-glass decanter on the sideboard. He sat down, dialled the number of Frinksteins, O'Donnell's merchant bank, and asked to be put through to the chairman. After a short delay he heard the familiar voice of Stewart Armstrong.

'What can I do for you, Michael?' he asked.

'Just tell me where I stand, Stewart.'

'I can only tell you what all New York knows already. Dean Jones and your mother's attorney, Sam Goldman, are hoping to have you removed from the board of the *Chronicle*. As you are aware, O'Donnell's publish for the establishment, and many readers disapprove of your lifestyle. I must warn you', he added, 'that your behaviour of late has given grounds for concern. You have been seen with the wrong company and many people are talking. Your rivals are making capital out of it.'

'Don't lecture me, Stewart, just tell me what I should do,' Michael interrupted.

'Keep a low profile for a while. Don't give them any more ammunition,' was the grumpy reply. 'I would also suggest you try to be more understanding with your mother. Don't, for God's sake, do anything rash. I'll let you know if I have any more information. Don't, however, be surprised if someone makes a bid for the *Chronicle*. It's a delicate time.'

'Yes, I understand. If you have any further information I shall be at my apartment and not in the office. Dean thinks I'm on a train bound for Chicago. I don't want him alerted that I'm still in town.' He put the telephone down and considered his situation. 'Interfering old fool,' he thought indignantly as he decided on his next move.

The following morning Michael arrived at the office and, brushing aside the surprised commissionaire, took the elevator to Dean's office on the tenth floor. He entered without knocking and stood staring at Dean and Sam who were deep in conversation.

'Surprised to see me, you cunning bastards? I just couldn't trust you not to double-cross me while I was away. You're both fired. You've done enough damage and I want you out!' Turning to Sam he pointed to the door saying, 'I won't bother to see you out, Goldman. Tell your henchmen that it will take a stick of dynamite to remove me from the *Chronicle*.'

'There are simpler and much more congenial ways within the law, Michael,' Sam answered, picking up his briefcase. 'You may have gone too far this time. If I were you I would consider your position very carefully.'

'I think we both knew from the start that working together would be purgatory,' said Dean, scooping up a handful of papers and stuffing them into his case. 'What I didn't know was that you have no sense of morality in either your business or private life. You're a bad lot, Michael. Mark my words, you'll pay for this.'

'You'd better be out in an hour or I'll have you thrown out. I've already instructed security to change the locks on the filing cabinets. See you take away nothing of importance.'

'Go to hell!' said Dean as he looked into those cold blue eyes.

15

Peter's first days at the front line shattered any illusions he might have harboured about the glamorous side of combat. As he marched his sweating and cursing men up to the front line he couldn't help wondering how he would feel when, alone and vulnerable, he had to lead them over the top from the relative safety of the trenches. He knew fear distorted and shrivelled men, and he just hoped that if it placed its clammy hand on him he would still do his duty unflinchingly. Honour, duty, sacrifice were all words he had heard since childhood. They had become part of his subconscious lexicon, but they had never been put to the ultimate test in a bizarre lottery of life and death.

He was forcibly jerked out of his own imaginings by the approach of a convoy of horse-drawn wagons moving supplies to the trenches. He ordered his men to stand by the side of the dusty road to let them pass. He could see the weariness in the men's eyes and sensed the desperation of the horses as they searched for a secure foothold, the carts creaking under their heavy loads of shells, munitions destined for the large howitzers positioned a mile or so behind the trenches. These big guns were capable of striking some ten miles into enemy territory to do terrible damage.

It was not, however, until he reached the front line that the full horror of the war assailed his senses. The area twenty yards in front of the trenches was covered with a contorted and chaotic jumble of barbed wire, with tin cans filled with pebbles fixed to the wire to give some warning of an enemy attack.

It was a landscape of total desolation, vandalised by man in his crude efforts to win his own particular crusade in the name of justice or freedom. The whole barren scene horrified Peter as he surveyed it in all its stark disarray, and he wrinkled his nostrils at the putrid, all-prevailing smell of death. Sniper fire made it impossible to move the rotting corpses, and rats and flies abounded, bringing disease and discomfort to the suffering men.

Sergeant Boon soon proved a great help in showing Peter the ropes. He was a leathery little man with the alert look of a whippet. 'You just get your bleedin' bearings to start with, sir,' was his sound advice.

He'd seen two of Peter's predecessors killed in as many months and he looked at him with a mixture of pity and genuine anxiety, knowing how ill prepared he was.

'Don't teach a lot about trench warfare at Aldershot, sir?' he ventured.

'Not a lot,' replied Peter. 'I shall need all the help I can get, Sergeant.'

'You can count on me, sir,'

Looking at a map, he asked Boon to explain the set-up. Peter knew that the trenches were carefully planned networks with the front line or fire trench heavily fortified and well guarded. With a blackened fingernail, Boon then pointed to the area on the map showing the support trench with dug-outs.

'This is where the command posts are, together with medical 'elp and stores. It's a sort of staging post for supporting the lads in the front line. It gets to yer, waiting there not knowing when you'll be wanted. The reserve trenches are behind, and there are communication trenches enabling the lads to move all lines under cover.'

Peter could see the trenches had been dug in a dog-tooth shape which, he remembered from his training, was to stop enemy fire from raking along the lines and to minimise shell blast.

As Peter craned his neck for a better view, Boon pulled him unceremoniously back.

'For Gawd's sake,' he yelled. 'That will get you killed in short bleedin' order, sir. You'll have to move around more careful than most as you're so tall. It's all right for short-arsed people like me as we've got less to shoot at,' he cackled.

Peter could see that it was a constant fight to keep the trench walls repaired and that timber and wire netting were used to restore some order after shelling and heavy rain.

'Never bleedin' well stops raining 'ere,' complained Boon. 'The duckboards used to keep the mud at bay when we first came but they're no bloody good now. You'll have no chance to have a bath for some ten days, sir. A lot of men have lice but there's not a damn thing we can do about it. All that seems to keep 'em going is the thought they might get some leave, but I doubt it, the way things are going. We never seem to get a real bloody break. Just as the lads try and relax we have to stand 'em to again in case of attack. We seem to spend most of our time wet, cold and waiting for a ruddy shell with someone's name on it.'

Pointing across to the shell holes he continued, 'Just be bleedin' careful you don't slip into one of those, sir. You'll never get out and it's an 'orrible death to be drowned in filthy, bleedin' mud. Most of the lads know what they're doing so just concentrate on keeping yourself in one piece. I'll be keeping things together so don't try and be a bloody 'ero, sir.'

Peter smiled. 'Thanks, Sergeant.'

They grinned at each other and Boon offered Peter a cup of tea which had just been brewed in an old petrol tin.

130

Disgusting as it was, it helped to keep the cold at bay.

The one small privilege Peter and his fellow subalterns enjoyed was sleeping and doing paperwork in cramped dug-outs built near the trench walls.

There was never an air of permanence about these arrangements as the sad fact was that their occupants only lasted a few short weeks before the suicidal policy of leading by example ensured they were picked off in terrifyingly large numbers. Peter shut such thoughts out of his mind, an old trick he had perfected in the nursery after his mother's death, and set about writing to Natalia.

'Waiting must be the worst punishment of all,' he thought as he looked at her photograph which he carried in his wallet.

Peter soon resigned himself to the barbaric ritual of trench warfare. He grew in confidence, thanks to Boon, until he almost started to believe that he had some control over the situation. He was rudely jerked out of his complacency when the Germans started shelling the area behind the trenches where they thought the reserves might be concentrated. The noise and devastation were horrendous, with shells falling in quick succession at the rate of about a hundred an hour. The support and communication trenches soon became impassable and it was necessary to run at the double across one hundred and fifty yards of open ground to the firing trench.

'Follow me and get the men across when the enemy machine gunners are blinded by the smoke and debris, Sergeant,' ordered Peter.

In the swirling smoke they ran across the open space, stumbling, cursing and falling in shell holes. No sooner had they finally reached the firing trench than several six-inch shells burst, burying Privates Skinner and Jones alive. When rescuers finally got to them and dug them out, they were horribly mutilated but had obviously died quickly, if not from their wounds then from asphyxia. The attack continued throughout the day and, as soon as dusk fell, reserves were pushed up into the front line. Enemy fire still raked the area as Peter waited with his cold and exhausted men. Soon the worst part began, with shrapnel shells falling every five seconds or so, covering them with mud and dirt from the trench parapet.

'Keep a good look out for an infantry attack, Sergeant!'

Peter knew from his short experience that it would not be long in coming. Then, chancing a look for himself, he put his head above the parapet. In that split second a shell burst in front of him, hurling him back on to the stinking floor of the trench where he lay stunned. As his head cleared he knew that he was in trouble. Boon got to him as soon as he could.

'Stupid bastard,' he said under his breath. 'You'd have thought he'd 'ad more sense than to do such a bloody stupid trick. Don't move, sir,' he said, raising his voice. 'I'll staunch the bleeding.'

Using his pocket knife he cut a tourniquet from Peter's uniform. Eventually he was able to control the flow of blood from what was left of Peter's arm which had been severed by shrapnel below the elbow. Shells continued to rain down all around them and Boon knew from experience that the pain would begin soon. By a stroke of good fortune the regimental doctor, who kept a watching brief in the trenches, was close at hand.

'Over 'ere Major Kingsley,' Boon called out as he held Peter who was now lapsing into unconsciousness.

'Well done, Sergeant, you've probably saved his life,' said Kingsley. 'I'll do my best to make him comfortable.'

With the help of an assistant from the Royal Army Medical Corps, he cleaned the jagged wound as best he could and applied an antiseptic dressing. When he had given Peter a shot of morphine he instructed a wide-eyed private to stay with him before moving on to do what he could for the other wounded and dying.

Peter knew that his worst enemies would be the cold and mud. He gritted his teeth and looked down at his shattered arm. As the pain washed over him he lapsed in and out of consciousness. At such times the memory plays strange tricks and he imagined himself in the Saville Row shop of Huntsman, the tailors, on a strange wooden horse on which he sat in some embarrassment while his buckskin breeches were fitted. He remembered the hundred pounds that he had won at cards from Rupert Carlyle and had never been able to collect. 'It'll buy me a new hunting coat and breeches,' he said to the startled private before slumping into unconsciousness again.

The shelling continued for what seemed hours until, just before five in the morning, there was a lull. Peter now seemed oblivious to the pain as they carried him behind the lines to a Red Cross ambulance already containing two other weakened and broken men, and pulled by a weary horse. Peter hardly cared whether he lived or died.

'Better move him to Boulogne as soon as possible,' he heard the doctor say after he had been examined at the improvised clearing station. 'He needs urgent specialist care.'

Something about the smell of his festering arm told Peter that all was not well. 'Gangrene,' he heard them mutter.

'Oh God,' he sighed, already seeing the spectre of his own death.

The long journey from the Front to Boulogne without proper medical help took its toll on Peter. It was becoming increasingly obvious that his chances of survival were precarious. When the fever had abated, the surgeons were forced to amputate the upper part of his arm in an effort to halt the spread of gangrene. By now he had assumed a deathly pallor and was hardly recognisable as the handsome, dashing young man who had enlisted a few short months ago.

It was decided that, the following morning, he would be taken back to England on one of the hospital ships moored by the quay. He was slung in a shallow, precarious cot and, once on board, was taken to a special ward for infectious diseases. The other wounded men were housed either in what had once been the dining saloon or in wards running the length of the ship below decks. Each ward had double rows of cots slung to minimalise the movement of the ship but giving ample room for the motion encountered in rough weather. Peter felt groggy and found it difficult to comprehend that he was on the way home as the throbbing of the ship's engines indicated they were leaving the harbour. In the airless ward he could smell the angry nature of the gangrene that had taken hold of his wound. The fever was now returning and he was soon covered in sweat. Mesmerised, he watched the other cots swinging with the swell of the sea. The overworked nurses tried to make him as comfortable as they could, helping him to wedge himself in his cot. He hadn't realised how awkward it was to have only one arm, and movements that before he would make naturally now had to be thought out carefully. After what seemed an eternity he lapsed into a confused state where he became almost detached from the pain. He now experienced a strange feeling of coming out of his body and rising up to the deckhead where he found that he could look down on himself. It was an eerie sensation and, although delirious, he knew he was in that strange twilight zone that lies between life and death. As he fought against the desire slowly and painlessly to give up the struggle, it was the thought of Natalia that dragged him back to the living.

'Tell her she must keep away from that Russian,' he repeated over and over again as he swung ceaselessly while the sea carried the ship towards England.

16

The rain fell steadily, running in long rivers down the windows as John sat drinking tea in the drawing room of Charnley Lodge with Lucinda and Natalia. It was a bleak and depressing afternoon and the wind rattled the panes erratically as it tugged at the ivy-covered walls of the house. Life, once so full of promise for the family, had lost the bloom it had bestowed on them. Peter was on everyone's minds.

In a vain attempt at conversation, Lucinda, who had all but given up reading about the war in the newspapers, decided to broach the subject of the Russian Front with Natalia who she knew was following the fortunes of her fellow Russians with an obsessive interest in every detail of their plight.

'It's just too terrible to contemplate,' Natalia replied, her voice monotone. 'Being posted to the Front is like a death sentence. At least the Empress cares about the troops. I only hope that now she's turned part of the Catherine Palace into a military hospital she'll see with her own eyes the direct result of the army's strategy. The generals are using the ordinary soldiers as cannon fodder.'

'God knows it must be difficult for her', said John thoughtfully, 'with her brother the Grand Duke of Hess fighting in the German Army. You could say it's the classic case of divided loyalties.'

'Oh no! She's fervently Russian,' Natalia replied firmly. 'I know it must be agonising for her, but she would never betray her adopted country. It's in some ways the same for me. I feel Russian, but I'm committed to Peter and England.'

After a moment's pause, Lucinda asked, 'Have you heard any more about your application to join the Red Cross as an auxiliary nurse?'

'My offer was politely refused. It seems only the best nurses are required.' After a moment's pause, she began again, uncertain of Lucinda's reaction to what she had to say. 'I've joined the Liverpool Voluntary Aid Department instead. I'm starting work at the hospital next week. It's only washing and bed making but at least I'll be doing something useful instead of sitting around all day.'

'Good for you,' said John, puffing at his cigar. 'No good waiting around here for news of Peter. It's better to be busy. Time goes faster that way.'

She smiled at him. His very presence was comforting. There was something about his large figure that inspired confidence and, at this time, she needed all the support she could find. She had always known that it was the agony of waiting that was to be her worst enemy. How many times had she been told that no news was good news? 'The English are so stupid,' she thought angrily.

'Why don't you phone Colonel Hawksley at the War Office this evening, John?' asked Lucinda, suddenly seeing the tension in Natalia's white, clasped hands which she held tightly in her lap. 'He might be able to tell us something.'

'I doubt it, but I suppose it's worth a try,' said John frowning. 'I know it's a dreadful thing to say but, subconsciously, I often find myself hoping that Peter might get wounded. Nothing too serious, God forbid, but just enough to ensure he would have a desk job for the rest of the war. At least we would know he was safe.'

'I know exactly what you mean,' said Natalia, 'but he's always keen to do his duty to the full. You taught him that lesson as a boy, and Shrewsbury helped to reinforce it.'

'I know,' said John, 'and I don't regret it for one moment.'

Natalia smiled weakly at him. He could see the pain that was so close to the surface.

Pearson knocked and entered the room as Lucinda was pouring tea from the large silver teapot with the infuriating spout that always dribbled. He caught John's eye and inclined his head to the telegram sitting on the silver tray he carried. John rose to his feet, the colour draining from his face as he walked hesitantly across the Turkish carpet to where Pearson was standing. The others sat frozen in their chintz-covered chairs and it seemed to Lucinda that they were seeing the scene unfold in nightmarish slow-motion. John picked up the telegram and, seeing that it was addressed to Natalia, he handed it to her. Summoning up her courage, she tore open the official brown envelope and read the short crushing message it contained:

'DEEPLY REGRET TO INFORM YOU THAT SECOND LIEUTENANT PETER DUFF ...'

She read no further but simply looked at John and Lucinda like a stricken animal that had just been kicked in the stomach.

'Who brought the telegram?' she asked Pearson in a hollow voice.

'The boy is in the hall, Mrs Duff,' he replied.

'Give him sixpence and send him on his way,' John ordered. It seemed strangely important, for Peter's sake, to do the right thing by the innocent messenger. The boy, who by this time had left a small pool of water on the mosaic floor of the hallway, accepted the money somewhat diffidently before turning and hurrying off into the rain. John felt despair, pain and outrage but he was a helpless prisoner of his emotions.

Natalia's brain at first felt numb. Slowly, as the terrible

truth sank in, it seemed to flash back disconnected images of Peter, jumbled and meaningless. 'Just tell me he died without pain,' she said, looking beseechingly at Lucinda who was powerless to console her. 'I can't bear to think of him suffering and alone.'

She didn't cry, however; it was John who wept like a child. He sat, his head in his hands on the bottom rung of the ladder of despair, little knowing that time and ill fortune would now place a heavy responsibility on Emma. He knew she must be told about Peter but he dreaded being the bearer of such news.

17

Michael blamed his mother. He blamed her both for the circumstances of his birth and for the predicament in which he now found himself. Predictably, his vindictive dismissal of Dean Jones and Sam Goldman misfired and he was outraged when the board sided with his mother.

'Remain a vice president with a seat on the board, Michael,' said Sam coldly, 'but you have no option but to resign as president.'

'And if I refuse?'

'Then we shall have to prove that you are unfit to hold office. It will be a dirty business but, believe me, we have more than enough on you to force your hand.'

'Where does Mother stand in all this?' Michael asked icily.

'Naturally, she is anxious to resume her place as president of O'Donnell's now that she is on the road to recovery,' Dean replied defensively. 'We feel she has made sufficient progress to make a substantial contribution to our meetings.'

'As your puppet?' demanded Michael, his eyes narrowing as he looked around the boardroom.

'We just need a period of stability, Michael. You must realise that it would be impossible for you to continue in office. There's too much gossip and innuendo about your lifestyle and our readers are very conservative in their views.'

'Don't give me that. You're just using my mother so that you and Sam can manipulate the company.'

'I don't have to take that from you or anybody else,' said Dean angrily, only to see the back of Michael who, ungracious as ever, got up from the table and kicked over his leather-seated chair before leaving the boardroom, his face white with anger.

The hastily taken vote was unanimous in restoring Tamara as president. Sam ensured that the minutes of the meeting read: 'After a lively discussion, the Board unanimously ratified the appointment of Mrs Tamara O'Donnell as President and thanked Mr Michael Korsakov for standing in for her during her indisposition.'

Michael knew he was out-manoeuvred. All he could do now was notch up another wrong on his mental scoreboard, to be righted at some time in the future. He knew he must get away. The pressures he had inflicted upon himself were becoming unbearable and had been added to by the fact that he had just read Peter Duff's obituary which had appeared in the *Record*. There and then he determined to leave for England and he read with considerable interest the morning edition of the *Chronicle* which carried the following advertisement:

Travellers intending to embark on an Atlantic voyage are reminded that a state of war exists between Germany and her Allies, and Great Britain and her Allies; that the zone of war includes the water adjacent to the British Isles; that, in accordance with the formal notice given by the Imperial German Government, vessels sailing in the war zone in ships of Great Britain and her Allies do so at their own risk.

Imperial German Embassy, Washington, 22 April 1915

He threw the paper at Hal who had come to his apartment at Tamara's request.

'I don't want my epitaph to read "he died peacefully after a long illness bravely borne". I'd prefer a watery grave if I had to choose,' he said.

Hal eyed him coldly but refrained from replying.

'I'm going to England to find Natalia and to see if I can buy that newspaper the Duffs own in Liverpool,' Michael added grimly.

'For God's sake, Michael,' said Hal, exasperated, 'just let go of the past. Remember that sheet of paper you showed me before going up to Harvard? Do you want to fall at the first hurdle?'

'Come on, Hal. I'm allowed some latitude.'

'Don't be a damn fool, you've already had your nine lives.'

Michael ignored Hal's admonition.

'Just help me to see what this is all about,' he said, pointing to the advertisement.

'It's possibly a bluff. The German Embassy has been making hostile noises about what they call "ships of the enemy mercantile marine" since the fifth of February when they issued their proclamation to neutral countries. They couldn't possibly endanger the *Lusitania*. World opinion would be outraged. It's unthinkable,' Hal added, 'but to be on the safe side I'll ring the British Embassy and speak to Lord Campden if you really want to travel.'

'Do it right away,' said Michael. 'I'll try to contact the German Ambassador, Count Bernstorff, myself.' He picked up the telephone and asked to be put through to the Ambassador's office. After a moment's delay, the operator answered. 'Imperial German Embassy. May I help you?'

'This is Count Michael Korsakov of O'Donnell Publishing speaking and I would like to be put through to the Ambassador.'

'Please wait a minute, Count. I'll see if his Excellency can take your call.'

After what seemed an eternity, the operator informed Michael that the Ambassador was not available and asked him if he would like to speak to a senior attaché.

'Very well, I will speak to the Naval Attaché.'

There was another lengthy pause before Captain Boy-Ed, the German Naval Attaché in Washington, picked up the telephone.

'May I help you, Count?'

'I will come straight to the point, Captain,' said Michael. 'I'm travelling to England on the *Lusitania* and I have read the statement put out by your embassy. I would be grateful if you could expand and clarify it for me.'

'Count, I can neither add to nor subtract from the statement issued from our Press Office. I would have thought that the meaning was quite clear.'

'Captain, I'm sure you're aware of the American note to Germany dated twelfth February. The United States Government warned your people that it would hold the Imperial Government to strict accountability for any loss of American lives on the high seas.'

'We have studied your government's note, Count, and we have talked to Mr James Watson-Gerard, your ambassador in Berlin. I now beg you to excuse me as I have a pressing engagement.'

With that the telephone clicked off leaving Michael stranded.

'Arrogant swine,' he said to himself, angrily thumping the desk with his fist.

A few minutes later, Hal walked into the room. 'I've spoken to the British. While they can give no firm assurance for the safety of shipping, they feel that, on the face of it, there's little risk. They seem to think it's all a bluff.'

'Sounds sensible to me. What you are, in essence, saying is that the British have no real idea of what the Germans are going to do.'

'I'm saying', replied Hal, 'that no one in their right mind would attack the *Lusitania*. Just think of the repercussions and the wrath it would bring down on Germany. It's out of the question, Michael.'

'I agree. I don't know what all the fuss is about.'

'Quite,' said Hal. 'Now I've got a lot on my plate and I could do without worrying about you and piracy on the high seas.'

Michael knew the die was cast and he felt strangely relaxed as he contemplated the future. Then, with sudden venom, he threw his shoes at the framed photograph of Tamara in its silver frame. It shattered, sending fragments of glass flying to the floor. 'I'll show you,' he said, staring at the broken remains on the carpet.

All Michael could think about was returning to England and seeking out Natalia. She dominated his thoughts with an obsession fuelled by a compelling mixture of emotions. Jealousy, lust and hate all had their part in the poisonous cocktail. Half-told stories from his boyhood heightened the sense of mystery and intrigue which had always surrounded the Orlofski family, with Natalia the main focus of his lingering vendetta. It worried and confused him that one so beautiful and desirable could be the object of his hate. He felt he was living his life in front of a mirror which insisted on reflecting the passions and desperate needs of a past generation. Still deep in thought, he left the city centre and was soon approaching Pier 54 where the *Lusitania* was berthed.

Once alongside the embarkation hall, the cab stopped suddenly, throwing Michael forward in his seat. He cursed the driver and jumped out angrily ignoring the outstretched hand waiting for a tip. Once he had completed the boarding formalities, he pushed his way through the crowd to the first-class gangway. He paused momentarily as he recognised a group of reporters huddled together in their long raincoats and Derby hats, then he pulled up the collar of his coat and joined a group of chattering passengers as he made his way aboard. Hoping that he had not been recognised, his immediate concern was to find his state room and get his steward to unpack his luggage.

'What the devil is all this fuss about, Simms?' he asked the perspiring steward who, at first, seemed reluctant to answer. 'I suppose a few idiots are getting the wind up about the war threat to the ship.'

'Well, since you mention it, sir, not all the passengers want their luggage unpacked because of the scare. Captain Turner has told us that there is nothing to worry about.'

Abandoning conversation, Michael lounged about the cabin as Simms unpacked. When the task had been performed to his satisfaction, he dismissed Simms who left the cabin cursing under his breath at his ill luck in having such a demanding master. Sitting on his bed, Michael set about studying the passenger list which was set out in alphabetical order. As he came to the short section of names beginning with the letter 'V' he put a red line underneath that of Alfred Gwynne Vanderbilt.

The vibration of the ship eventually told Michael that they were putting to sea. He went on deck as the ship nosed her way down the North River with the city skyline silhouetted against a clear sky. A confusion of thoughts came to him as he watched the Statue of Liberty glide into the distance as they made for the Narrows and the grey ocean. Only a few short years ago he and his mother had passed this way together but he was now determined to make his own mark on the waiting world.

Dismissing such thoughts, he returned to his mahogany-panelled state room to change for dinner, where he found his clothes laid out neatly on the bed. He looked anxiously for the invitation which he hoped would be forthcoming, asking him to sit at the captain's table, and heaved a sigh of relief when he saw an envelope sitting on his desk. He ripped it open quickly and removed the gilt-edged invitation. He scanned the card: 'The First Officer invites Count Michael Korsakov ...'

'Damn, damn!' he shouted thumping his fist on the desk. Throwing the invitation to one side he started to change, dropping his clothes haphazardly around the cabin and brooding on the imagined slight Captain Turner had dealt him. He tied and untied his bow-tie with increasing anger as it refused to adopt the immaculate formation he desired. Eventually he finished dressing and made his way to the huge, ornate dining saloon, decorated in white and gold, where the chief steward pointed out the first officer's table. As Michael crossed the room he noticed the magnificent sideboard and then looked up at the domed ceiling with painted panels after Boucher. Dutifully, he greeted those already seated at the table and took his place next to a middle-aged Jewish matron and the elderly wife of a New Jersey industrialist. His heart sank as he surveyed the rest of the fat faces at the round table with the gleaming silver cutlery and shining glasses. Eating his consommé, he cursed his luck and glanced across to the Captain's table where he saw Alfred Vanderbilt in animated conversation, surrounded by the rich and famous.

'Damn,' he thought again as he broke open his bread roll, realising that, yet again, he had been left out of the golden circle in which he wanted to be included.

Michael slept fitfully until Simms woke him at 8.30 a.m. with coffee and fruit juice. He was still smarting from the imagined slight of the previous night and he felt hungover, with a mouth like dry sandpaper and a ringing in his ears.

'Draw me a salt bath, Simms,' he commanded, 'and put my clothes out.'

'Very good, sir,' Simms replied in a tired voice.

When he had bathed, Michael set about shaving. He didn't like what he saw in the mirror. The bags under his eyes were blue and heavy, and his skin held a hint of yellow which conspired to age him. After he had dried his face, he applied an astringent lotion from a gold-topped bottle.

Breakfast in the dining room made him feel better. He ate frugally and then went out on deck to blast his lungs with clean, fresh air. As he walked around the promenade deck he stopped and looked down at the water racing past in white billows as the ship's hull cut through the grey ocean. Deep down inside he knew that he had made a fatal mistake in not staying in New York to fight Dean and Sam and he promised himself that he would use his time wisely once he arrived in England. Thoughts of Natalia dominated his planning. How would she react to him once they came face to face again? Could he win her over to be his ally in his proposed takeover of the Albany Group by O'Donnell's? He knew that bereavement left people feeling weak and vulnerable and he hoped to play this card for all its worth.

18

Emma threw a despairing look at the bland white face of the clock. Throwing on her coat she hurried out of the office, down the stairs to the foyer and into Dale Street where she hailed a cab. Ten minutes later she was at Aigburth Hospital where she had arranged to meet Natalia who was on duty. The *Record* was highlighting the plight of men gravely disabled at the Front. Emma was convinced it was a story that needed to be brought to the public's attention.

'Sorry I'm late,' she said breathlessly.

'Don't worry,' replied Natalia, smiling. 'I know what a treadmill you live on. Come on, Matron says I can show you around.'

As they walked through the scrupulously clean wards between neat rows of beds, they were watched in silence by the dull staring eyes of the wounded.

'It's what you don't see that's the greatest enemy,' Natalia said. 'Some of these men have been made to endure terrible things and in some cases it's temporarily deranged them. There's a young man I want you to meet,' she continued. 'He's in one of the private rooms over here that we keep for officers who need specialised treatment.'

'How bad is he?' asked Emma with some trepidation.

'Nothing to upset you. He's just very breathless.'

'Gas?'

Natalia nodded as she opened the door. The young man was lying on the bed, propped up on three pillows. He was dark and conspicuously handsome but his pallor and the blueness of his lips told his story clearly. He looked up and smiled at them in a disarming, though distant, way. Emma could see that even the slightest movement made him struggle for breath and she worried that her presence would upset him.

'I'm going to leave you now,' said Natalia. 'The only thing that Matron has asked me to ensure is that you don't ask the identity of this officer.'

'I understand,' replied Emma. 'I gave her that undertaking before I came in.'

Natalia smiled as she shut the door behind her.

'I hear you're making a good recovery,' Emma started, producing her notebook and pencil. 'Perhaps you could try to tell me your story ... from the beginning?' she continued, drawing up a chair by the bed.

'It's difficult to know where to start,' the young man replied, speaking in a hoarse whisper. 'I was one of the first to volunteer. At the Front we were shelled incessantly and we got very little sleep. It was a constant bombardment of high explosive. I suppose it was made worse because many of us were totally unprepared for what we had to go through.' At that point he stopped, holding himself up on his arms while he struggled for breath.

'Shall I call for a nurse?' Emma enquired anxiously.

'No,' he said, turning to look at her, his dark brown eyes almost masked by tired eyelids. 'They can't do anything.' For a few minutes he lapsed into a fit of coughing and it was some time before he was ready to continue.

'I found that a useful way to survive', he began, 'was to accept that I was going to be killed. That way every day I was spared was a bonus. It was the gas attacks that put me here.

148

They were horrible and cause the most atrocious suffering. I was caught in one of the first series of attacks by chlorine gas at the beginning of May, near Ypres. It was all so sudden. A cloud of yellow-green gas came towards us on the breeze. It hugged the ground, never reaching more than ten feet in height as it rolled slowly forward at no more than walking pace. We didn't panic because we had never seen gas before. It was only when choking men came rushing back from the forward positions that we took out our flannel belts, soaked them quickly in water and put them over our faces. The affected men were choking and gasping as the gas slowly filled up the trenches. It was too late for some who lay writhing on the trench floor. Others trampled straight over them without a second thought in their bid to escape. It was terrifying to watch so much suffering. We were lucky in so far as we didn't take the heaviest losses because the wind changed direction and blew the gas away.' The young man now lapsed again into convulsive coughing.

Visibly shaken, Emma did what she could to ease him before he slumped back exhausted on to the pillows, his ashen face streaked with sweat.

'Sorry,' he whispered. 'Sorry.'

Natalia now returned and motioned to Emma: 'You'd better go now and let him rest.'

Rising from her chair with tears rolling down her cheeks, Emma thanked the young man before leaving the room.

'Dear God,' she said under her breath, 'how can we let these things happen?'

The next morning the whole of page four of the *Record* was devoted to the horror of gas attacks, coupled with a condemnation of the use of chemical weapons by the Germans.

Reaction to Emma's article was swift. It was soon clear to George Gerrard that she had pinpointed something which, when spelt out in all its terrible starkness, shocked and enraged the *Record's* readers.

'Go and see that young officer again as soon as you can

and get more of his story,' he said to Emma. 'Better still, find out about his background and make him a bit of a hero.'

'I don't make heroes. They tend to make themselves,' she said simply.

That night at dinner, Emma sat picking peevishly at her food.

'George has gone too far this time, Papa,' she said moodily. 'He wants me to go back and see that poor chap at the hospital, the one who was gassed.'

'You did a good job telling the public about the consequence of chemical warfare,' said John. 'You should be proud of what you've done.'

'I don't quite see it that way,' she replied. 'Why should I have to go and dig into the poor man's identity. It's a gross invasion of privacy and I gave my word to the matron.'

'It would make a wonderful local interest story, my dear,' he replied. 'You're too sensitive, Emma,' he continued. 'We're here to influence and guide public opinion. Gas is an evil and we're showing the misery and suffering it brings.'

After a moment's pause, Emma began, 'I know you aren't supposed to tell us,' she said looking earnestly at Natalia, 'but it would help to know who that chap is.'

'Why?'

'There was just something about him I couldn't quite put my finger on. It was like a deep sadness which was very transparent in such an obviously gentle person.'

'I know what you mean,' Natalia replied. 'It's against all the rules but I can't see any reason why you shouldn't know who he is. I know you won't breathe a word. His name is Captain Baguley, Randle Baguley.'

The following morning, Emma was still feeling dazed as she arrived at the office. The unexpected revelation of the previous night had stunned her. She had never dreamt that, so soon after the devastating news of Peter's death, she would come face to face with her mother's unwitting assassin. However, she could feel no hate for him. It had all been so long ago and she knew instinctively that he had died himself hundreds of times reliving the horror of that moment. She could now feel only compassion for him, lying breathless in hospital and, subsequently, she felt that it would be important for both of them to meet again so that the past, while never forgotten, could be put behind them.

She worried about Natalia. She was not to know who had been involved in her mother's fatal accident. It was never talked about as it had been a taboo subject.

'Coincidence and fate are so closely linked,' she thought as George Gerrard shouted to her across the office.

'Come on, Emma. Your taxi's waiting. You'll miss the train if you don't get a move on.'

Emma caught the express from Lime Street with only minutes to spare. Her mind was still racing but she knew that she must keep calm. It was an important day. She had been granted an interview with the celebrated Lord Lonsdale at his Cumberland seat, Lowther Castle, and she was determined to make the most of it. She knew he had controversial ideas on how to support the war effort and she was anxious to do her homework thoroughly as she headed for the restaurant car.

As the Edinburgh-bound express shuddered to a halt at Penrith Station, Emma stepped down from her first-class carriage and made for the ticket barrier, avoiding the puddles left by a heavy spring shower. Pulling her cape close around her as a protection against the light rain, she easily recognised Lord Lonsdale's distinctive yellow omnibus which was waiting for her outside the red stone station. Once she was seated, the horses set off at a brisk trot and Emma collected her thoughts. She sat alone in the carriage, watching the rolling hills through the window until, at last, they passed between two large stone lodges and started up the long drive to the castle which commanded an elevated position above Askham village. It was a truly spectacular setting, with the pink stones of the castle shining in the watery light. Emma was met at the grand entrance by Coombs the butler.

Once inside they crossed the entrance hall and Emma

looked in vain for the bust of the German Emperor which, in happier times, had had pride of place. Coombs knocked on the door of the library and, entering, announced Emma's arrival to Lord Lonsdale.

'Good afternoon, Miss Duff,' the resplendently dapper Lonsdale enunciated crisply. 'Please be seated. I'm sure you'd like some tea?'

Before giving Emma time to reply, he dismissed Coombs with an instruction to return promptly with refreshment for his guest.

'You're an enterprising young woman,' he said, his blue eyes made all the more dazzling by his red face. 'I congratulate you on your article in the *Record* exposing the horrors of chemical warfare.'

'Thank you,' Emma replied. 'I'm glad you approve of our policy of exposing the enemy's tactics.'

'About time someone did,' he replied, lighting a large cigar.

Emma used the pause to extract her notebook and pencil from her large bag.

Lord Lonsdale now turned his gaze directly on her. 'What exactly do you want to know?'

'You're the most powerful and influential landowner in the area and a maker of public opinion. Don't you think you have treated recruitment in a rather cavalier way?' she began.

'What do you mean by that, young lady? You've got to present things in a colourful way up here. You're dealing with countrymen and a sporting public.'

'But I hear that the Mayor of Whitehaven was so annoyed with your references to rotters and cowards that he drove here to complain about what he regards as a slur on the men of the region.'

'Fiddlesticks!' replied Lord Lonsdale. 'Damn fool fellow couldn't understand what we were trying to achieve. The campaign was a great success. It appealed to people's sense of duty and service to their country.'

'Do you really not think that the first line of your poster, with the legend, "Are you a man or a mouse?" is a bit too blunt?' Emma asked.

'No, of course not. Wrote it myself, you know, in this very room. You must understand that there's a skill in presenting the cause you want men to fight for.'

Emma bit her lip and didn't reply.

'Besides,' he continued, oblivious of her amazement, 'I personalised the appeal by printing it in my racing colours.'

'I hear that you were strongly advised against devising your own grey uniforms for the battalion of local men known as the Lonsdales?'

'You don't seem to understand that people from this part of the country have their own, very strong identity. Their own uniform would have united them as a complete fighting force. So much claptrap has been talked about a national identity when we've got Derby's Docker Battalion and even Lord Nunburnholm's Bantam Battalion for short men. Makes sense don't you think?' Emma had no time to reply. 'Why, even the formidable Mrs Cunliffe-Owen is raising a Sportsman's Battalion of the Royal Fusiliers.'

Coombs now entered bearing tea on a silver tray and set it down on the table before Emma. As there was only one cup she looked enquiringly at her host.

'Never drink the damn stuff,' he said. 'Go on, help yourself.'

Emma picked up the Georgian silver teapot and poured tea into the thin china cup. While she did so Lonsdale watched her as though weighing up this young lady. 'Not at all bad looking,' he thought. 'Plenty of spirit, too.'

Glancing up, Emma now phrased her next question carefully. She was aware that she was treading a fine line and her questions might be considered by some to be ill-mannered.

'Lord Lonsdale, what is your contribution to the war effort you expect other men to support? After all, you have just taken over the National Stud and are also keeping the Cottesmore Hunt at full strength. May I respectfully point out that these activities could be misconstrued?'

'The Stud is a great national asset and we've got to protect it at all costs. Anyway, I'm making drastic cuts by disbanding my private orchestra.'

Emma smiled at this unexpected reply.

'Enough of this tomfoolery,' Lord Lonsdale continued, 'Why don't you let me show you around?'

'Thank you.'

'One condition,' he said smiling. 'There's to be no more questions, only serious talk of horses.'

She nodded her agreement, returning his smile.

'Why don't we go and look at the garden? The rain has stopped and the sun's quite warm now.'

'I'd love to see your sunken garden,' said Emma enthusiastically. 'Wasn't it reproduced at the International Horse Show at Olympia?'

'Yes,' he said cheerily. 'Cost me some ten thousand pounds. We used fifty thousand potted plants to create a riot of colour. I did it to add some style to the proceedings. Anyway, we had to put on a good show for our visiting American friends such as Vanderbilt and 'Judge' Moore who were there with their horses.'

Emma nodded. 'Yes, I saw Mr Vanderbilt at Olympia with my father when I was still at school. Together with another American, Walter Winans. He had some of the finest Hackneys, Orloff and Austrian trotters and American Sadddlebreds money could buy.'

'You've got a good memory,' said Lord Lonsdale, smiling. 'I hear Alfred Vanderbilt is bound for Liverpool in a week or so. I just hope those Germans stick by the law of the high seas and respect the integrity of merchant vessels in international waters.'

'There are rumours that the *Lusitania's* carrying munitions', said Emma, 'which would make her a legitimate target.'

'That's silly nonsense,' he replied angrily. 'The Germans know there are important and influential American citizens on board and, anyhow, a ship with her turn of speed would be a difficult target.'

19

Captain Turner was about to go down to dinner with the passengers when he received a message from the wireless room. It was simple and to the point: 'Submarines active off the south coast of Ireland'. Turner was not overly worried. He had already taken action after acknowledging an earlier order from the Admiralty warning of the danger of submarines off Fastnet. The *Lusitania* was now steaming at reduced speed so that she might round Fastnet in the dark, hoping not to jeopardise her rendezvous with the cruiser HMS *Juno* which was to escort her to Liverpool.

At dinner Turner did his best to appear calm and relaxed and to answer questions from those passengers sitting at his table. Later, standing before the towering carved fireplace flanked by twin pilasters, he told those present that everything was being done to ensure their safety.

'It is a fact, however,' he said calmly, 'that there has been a submarine warning.'

'But why, Captain, have all the lifeboats been swung out and our portholes blanked out by our stewards?' asked one woman, her voice shrill with apprehension.

'Just routine precautions, madam,' he answered. 'It's my

responsibility to do everything possible to ensure the safety of this ship and her passengers.'

As the questions continued, Michael sat at the far end of the room looking up at the huge skylight which vibrated with the pulse from the ship's engines. 'It's a good job they don't realise how much danger we're in,' he said softly to the immediate circle of passengers sitting around him.

'What do you mean?' asked a red-faced elderly gentleman sitting bolt upright and eyeing him warily.

'Well, you must have heard the story that's going around that we're carrying a large consignment of arms for the Allies?' said Michael. 'It's bound to make us a prime target for the U-boats.'

'They would never dare! Any more talk like that and I'll see the Captain puts you in custody until we arrive in Liverpool.'

Michael smiled thinly and lit his cigar, watching the small cloud of smoke drift upwards.

The next morning saw the great ship steaming at fifteen knots in fog which reduced visibility to thirty yards, with no sign of the *Juno*. When he heard that the German submarine 'U-20', commanded by Captain Schweiger, had been sighted on four separate occasions since dawn, Captain Turner posted extra look-outs. At 9.20 a.m. news came through of the sinking of the steamer *Centurion* the previous day, and then further information was received of the sinking of her sister ship, the *Candidate*. This was followed by a signal that enemy submarines were active in the southern part of the Irish Channel, twenty miles south of Coningbeg Light. The *Lusitania* acknowledged the warning at 11.52 a.m.

The fog was now clearing and Captain Turner soon ordered speed to be increased from fifteen to eighteen knots. The problem he now faced was how to deal with the threat of hostile submarines twenty miles south of Coningbeg, exactly in the centre of the entrance to St George's Channel. Patiently, Turner awaited the arrival of HMS *Juno* which, he concluded, he had missed in the fog. At 12.15 p.m. he finished decoding instructions from the Admiralty and abruptly gave instructions to change course to port so that he could fix his precise position from the coast of Ireland. There were no second chances in these dangerous waters and he was anxious not to get caught with the fog closing in again and such a dangerous coast on the port side. When he saw the lighthouse standing high above the coast on a rocky projection, he breathed a sigh of relief. 'The Old Head of Kinsale,' he muttered beneath his breath as he ordered a change of course to starboard to take him to Queenstown which was now only some twenty-five miles away.

Aboard the submarine 'U-20', Captain Schweiger could not believe his luck when he saw the bulk of a great liner surmounted by four funnels some fourteen miles ahead. He submerged immediately and set a course that would bring him in close contact with the prey and give him the chance of a flank shot. As the U-boat closed, he knew that the ship was either the *Lusitania* or the *Mauretania*. He quickly deduced that it was the former as the *Mauretania* was currently docked at Avonmouth embarking troops for the Dardenelles.

'U-2' was poised to strike and Schweiger and his crew worked feverishly to ensure that the attack proceeded with all speed. With more hope than conviction, Schweiger gave the order for a torpedo to be fired at the target and waited anxiously for the result. As he watched through the periscope he carefully dictated an account of the scene to the pilot standing beside him.

Aboard the *Lusitania*, Captain Turner was standing on the bridge when the look-outs reported a torpedo heading towards them on the starboard side. It was too late to take evasive action. It hit them just forward of the bridge, sending up a great plume of water.

Michael Korsakov left his cabin and ran round the deck to the starboard side. Even as he did so, and only seconds after the explosion, a further explosion rumbled deep down inside the hull and Michael could have sworn that he heard, quite distinctly, the reports of thousands of exploding cartridges. 'My God,' he thought, 'I wonder if the rumours are true and we really have been carrying munitions.'

Before he could put his thoughts in order, the ship took a fifteen degree list and the bow dipped into the water, forcing him to hang on to the ship's rail to save himself from being flung along the deck, The lifeboats on the port side had swung in over the rails while those on the starboard side swung wildly outwards. It was clear that the forward lie of the ship, coupled with the crazy angle they had adopted, made them almost impossible to launch. Water was pouring in through open portholes on D and E decks and soon the *Lusitania's* stern was out of the water, exposing her huge propellers. Suddenly her bow hit the bottom which held her in that position as she started to settle.

Confusion and panic set in among the passengers as they realised that the ship was foundering so quickly and the whole ship then took on a terrifying aspect when number three boiler exploded, blowing off a funnel and sending a cloud of steam over the decks. Michael had pushed his way through the press of frightened passengers to the huge entrance hall just as Junior Officer Albert Bestic called for their attention. 'Get into your lifejackets. We have only three minutes before the ship sinks,' he said urgently. 'Prepare to do all you can to save yourselves.'

Despair and terror were written on the faces of those present as they fought to get into the boats. Realising the hopelessness of the position, Michael chose to remain behind. He recognised the figures of Alfred Vanderbilt and Carl Frohman and offered to join them in making lifejackets for the children who had been sleeping in the ship's nursery after lunch.

'We need all the help we can get,' replied Vanderbilt.

'You certainly do,' replied Frohman acidly. 'I can't understand why you never learned to swim.'

Suddenly Bestic appeared, shouting, 'For heaven's sake gentlemen, don't you realise what's happening?'

Looking at him with his usual deliberate gaze, Vanderbilt shrugged his shoulders and replied softly, 'All we can do is to make certain the children have something to float in until help arrives.'

Michael was amazed to hear Frohman respond, 'Why fear death. It is the most beautiful adventure of life.'

'For you, maybe,' Michael thought, as a great rush of water swept over them, knocking him down and leaving him unconscious as he hit his head a terrible blow on one of the many doors.

20

News of the *Lusitania* soon reverberated around the world. The stock markets went into a nosedive and rumour and counter-rumour were rife. New York received the news of this disaster with surprising calmness as first reports indicated that the ship was beached off the Irish coast and that all the passengers were safe. In Liverpool, the Cunard Company waited before releasing an official statement but George Gerrard had already gleaned most of the facts from sources he knew and trusted.

He met John Duff on the staircase of the *Record's* offices in Liverpool. 'I was just coming to see you,' he said breathlessly. 'Our sources close to Cunard tell me that the *Lusitania* has sunk with considerable loss of life. It seems she's been the subject of a submarine attack off Ireland.'

'Yes, I've heard as much,' said John. 'What else do you know?'

'The unconfirmed news is that she altered course to avoid enemy submarines and was unable to make contact with her escorting cruiser in the fog.'

'Apparently there's wild speculation in America that she was carrying munitions. I heard that six million rounds of ammunition were loaded before they left New York,' replied John.

'It's all rumour and speculation. I don't think anyone outside official channels knows exactly what's going on. The censor is bound to delete any hard news,' said George. 'Well, at least let's be prepared and get the human interest angle. With your permission I'm sending Emma right away to cover the story for us.'

John thought for only a moment. 'By all means send her if you think she's the right person.'

'Thanks,' said George. 'She is. I'll get her moving right away. She'll have to take the train to Fishguard and then the Irish ferry. She may be too late but, if the worst happens, we can use a local correspondent before Emma arrives.'

Almost as they spoke, on the stroke of five, the *Record* was already receiving the first official reports of the attack and sinking.

When Emma arrived in Southern Ireland, tired and dishevelled, Queenstown, where the relief effort centred, was buzzing with rumour and counter-rumour. The local fishermen and beachcombers were already recovering hundreds of bodies, which earned them one pound for an 'ordinary' body and two pounds for an American. One thousand pounds was the sum offered for the remains of Alfred Vanderbilt and the story was being followed by every paper.

After a while it became clear that there were many survivors, all vying with each other to make a name for themselves. They saw the chance of instant fame and invented dramatic stories of the last moments of the *Lusitania*. Notable among them was Ernest Cowper who was now making himself a worldwide celebrity. His wild exaggerations were snapped up almost without a quibble by the waiting newsmen and relayed with relish to all parts of the globe. George had warned Emma to be very selective about her sources but even she showed interest when

Cowper told of the use of poison gas against the passengers. The censor, naturally, was pleased to let these sensational allegations against the Germans go out unedited. Emma could see that they were manna from heaven for the authorities as they distracted attention from any potentially damaging stories about munitions.

Putting behind her the temptation of sending George the sensational but misleading copy which was easily available, she decided to dig deeper. Wesley Frost, the American Consul in Queenstown, seemed worth a try as he was bound to be at the centre of events. Frost was, at first, unhelpful. He was already besieged with enquires from frantic relatives of those travelling and was anxious to get news of their loved ones to them as soon as was reasonably possible. In spite of her inexperience, however, Emma stood her ground when asked to 'leave us to more important matters', until, in exasperation, he pointed to a young man sitting in the corner of his bustling office. 'Talk to him, if you must,' he said shortly. 'His name's Korsakov, Count Michael Korsakov. No doubt he's got a story.'

Emma started in surprise but, before she could move, a throng of reporters, who had overheard the conversation, suddenly headed in Michael's direction.

'Hey, Count, let's have your story!' shouted a fat man clutching a camera while the others crowded around, pushing Emma out of the way.

'Not much to tell,' started Michael nonchalantly. 'I was knocked unconscious as the ship went down and was saved by my lifejacket which kept me afloat until I was picked up by a fishing boat.'

'What about the gas?' shouted one reporter. 'You must know something about that?'

Michael ignored the question with disdain before continuing, 'Thank God the sea was relatively calm. I can't remember anything about what happened while I was in the water.'

'Come on, Count. Tell us what it was like when the

torpedo hit. What's the story about the munitions she's supposed to have been carrying?'

'I don't know anything about all that.'

'Hey, aren't you Tamara O'Donnell's boy?' shouted one of their number suddenly. 'Does your mother know you're safe?'

With that, a dozen shutters clicked, ensuring that Michael would be front-page news in twenty countries around the world as they rushed to send off their copy, spiced with fictitious quotes.

Emma, meanwhile, hardly had time to consider her position. It was a cruel coincidence that Michael Korsakov, of all people, should have been on the *Lusitania* and was now sitting near her in this cramped and noisy room. She remembered the file marked 'Orlofski/Korsakov' that she had brought to her father some months ago in the *Record's* office, and its riveting contents which she knew by heart. Here he was in the flesh – brutal, charming, physical and uninhibited. Like her mother, she was attracted to danger and she felt her blood racing as she turned to Michael.

'Is it true? Are you really Count Michael Korsakov?'

'Yes,' he replied, returning her gaze. 'I'm here trying to get a bit of peace and quiet to file my own story for the *Chronicle*. It hasn't helped to have that stupid official drawing attention to me.'

'It's not his fault,' said Emma. 'Everyone here just wants a story that's different.'

'I understand,' he replied. 'Then why don't we go and have a drink somewhere more agreeable?'

'Very well,' replied Emma carefully.

'What's your name?' he added as they left.

'Emma Duff. I work for the Liverpool *Daily Record*.'

Michael stared at her in disbelief.

When Emma filed her copy it put George Gerrard in a quandary. It was just the human story he needed but he immediately groaned as he read the name 'Korsakov'. He telephoned John at Charnley Lodge for guidance. 'Can we use any of this copy?' he asked with exasperation.

'Give me ten minutes and I'll have an answer for you.' With that John put down the receiver and rejoined Lucinda and Natalia at the dinner table.

'I still don't know what on earth possessed you to agree to George sending Emma to Ireland to cover the *Lusitania* story,' said Lucinda.

'I knew I was taking a risk,' John replied solemnly, 'but if she is to continue to work on the paper I can't keep her in cotton wool just because she's my daughter.'

'Don't be pig-headed,' Lucinda retorted sharply. 'You know exactly what I mean. You mustn't put Emma in danger.'

'Just hold on a minute. We can talk about the quality of my decisions later, but there's something important that needs discussing now. I know what I have to say may cause distress to you, Natalia,' he said scratching his moustache thoughtfully, 'but sometimes fate works in strange ways.'

'For Heaven's sake, John, What are you trying to tell us?' asked Lucinda.

'What is it?' asked Natalia softly, certain that something unpleasant was about to be revealed.

'George has just been on the telephone to say that Emma has filed a story from Queenstown of an American survivor of the *Lusitania*.'

'But that's what she's there for,' said Natalia. 'What's the problem?'

'Simply that his name is Michael Korsakov.'

Lucinda looked despairingly at John as Natalia flushed.

'How could she do this?' she asked, looking angrily at John. 'Why, oh why, did she have to choose him. If only he'd drowned.'

'It's not Emma's fault,' said Natalia composing herself. 'It's just an unfortunate coincidence.'

'I'll tell George to find a different angle and we'll go with something more conventional,' said John.

'It would be dreadful for Emma if you did that,' said Natalia. 'I appreciate your desire to protect me, but I've got to face up to the past especially now Peter is dead. Tell George to go ahead with my blessing.'

John looked across at Lucinda and their eyes met as she nodded her tacit agreement. 'Just make certain that George treats the story with his usual tact,' she said, her icy tone reinforcing the point.

The story, as it appeared in the *Record*, was a model of good objective reporting. The main narrative of events surrounding the sinking of the *Lusitania* was clearly chronicled and based on eye witness reports that Emma had gleaned from reliable sources, backed up by official statements from Cunard. The piece about Michael Korsakov occupied half a page and described his lucky escape. Little was made of his background and Natalia was much relieved. It was only later when she saw what the bulk of the popular press had splashed across their inside pages that she recoiled in shock. The city editors had not been slow to do their homework and Michael Korsakov's photograph grinned back at her as she read with disbelief Fleet Street's version of the Orlofski/Korsakov feud. Something that, for years, had merely simmered on the back burner of history was now brought to the fore and picked over by every sensation-seeking journalist anxious for a story that contained all the classic ingredients of a blood feud. It was a story that she knew would run and run and, in desperation, Natalia fled to the safe haven of Larkhill and the Milners.

22

'I know it wasn't Emma's choice to go to Ireland and that it can be argued that she was just doing her job, but she should have known better,' said Natalia as she sat in the library at Larkhill with Sir Edward.

'I agree, but you can't place all the blame on her,' he replied softly. 'She couldn't have foreseen things turning out as they did. I suppose it might be argued that she was using considerable initiative.'

'I suppose so,' replied Natalia, 'and yet, deep down, I still feel a sense of betrayal and outrage. How dare the papers print all those dreadful things about my family and the Korsakovs.'

'Well, at least John Duff and the *Record* showed their usual restraint.'

'Yes, but the circumstances were rather exceptional. I was, after all, married to Peter.'

Sir Edward nodded gravely as Natalia looked at him with a hint of defiance, before continuing, 'Emma shouldn't have been sent on such a big story. She's too young and inexperienced, and she should have had more sense than to agree to talk to Michael Korsakov alone.'

'Perhaps, in all innocence, she didn't know the full story of the difficulties between your two families?'

'She knew exactly what had transpired. I'm told that she even read the file at the *Record*, which I'm certain leaves nothing to the imagination.'

'Do you really think so?'

'Oh, it's true. Emma has really overstepped the mark this time, especially as it's no secret that Michael Korsakov's plan is to launch a bid for the *Record*.'

'But I thought that it was John Duff's plan to expand Albany interests into America?'

'Yes it was until Peter was killed. Now it's not being given the same priority.'

'The whole business is very unfortunate,' Sir Edward said after a pause. 'Do you know where Michael Korsakov is now?'

'Yes, it appears he intends to take the boat to Liverpool.'

'What bad luck,' he said tapping his silver-topped cane on the parquet floor. 'Have you decided what you are going to do now?'

'Yes, I'm going back to Russia. I'll see Count Freedericksz first. Then I'm going back to Ivanhov.'

'Do you really think that's wise, my dear?'

'I've made up my mind. It's like finishing a difficult jigsaw that's been left on the nursery table,' she added.

'Isn't the castle a military hospital?'

'Yes. As you know it's passed through several hands since our time and now it's been taken over by the army.'

'I won't try to stop you going,' he said solemnly. 'I know how important it is to you. Just promise me that you won't do anything to endanger yourself.'

'I promise,' she said smiling. 'Somehow I need to get back to my roots more than ever, even though I swore after Peter's death that my future lay here in England. It's funny how things can change.'

'You don't have to explain,' replied Sir Edward reassuringly. 'There's one bit of good news I have for you,' he

167

continued. 'As you know James Ponsonby joined the Diplomatic Service after Oxford and he has just surfaced in the embassy in St Petersburg, or Petrograd as we now have to call it.'

'Yes, I heard as much,' she replied. 'He wrote me a long letter after Peter's death. It will be very comforting to know he's near at hand.'

Sir Edward paused. 'I'll drop a line to George Buchanan the British Ambassador and tell him you're coming, just in case you need anything.'

'That would be kind,' replied Natalia. 'I've already written to Count Freedericksz to ask if I can stay with him and to see if the embassy can arrange for me to go to Ivanhov as a nursing auxiliary.'

In the days that followed, Natalia's thoughts were confused. Even in the peace of Larkhill the spectre of Michael Korsakov was never far away. She tried desperately to erase the memory of his visit and the look in those strange eyes when he had placed the gypsy curse on Peter. No doubt, she thought, it was the same look Michael had seen in Rasputin's eyes when the monk had visited Tamara in St Petersburg. It was the same mocking, goading side of the Korsakovs that her brother Alexander had been subjected to that fateful night when Ivanhov was lost.

Later that afternoon Natalia sat, pen in hand, drafting a further letter to Count Freedericksz. There was so much she had to say and she sought desperately for a way of expressing herself that he would understand and act upon. She was now certain that Michael was too dangerous to be left on the loose any longer. She had come to the conclusion that he had to be taken out of society permanently and that he must be taught a painful lesson so that the scales of natural justice could balance. A plan was forming in her head and she knew that only Count Freedericksz had the power to help her by instructing the Ochrana, the Russian Secret Police, to ask one of its cells working under cover in Britain to turn its attention to Michael and to deal with him.

Finally satisfied with her last draft, she wrote:

I fear that by the time I arrive in Russia it may be too late. Only you can help me by using your influence to remove Michael Korsakov, and I shall shed no tears for him. First it was Alexander, then Mother. His father killed them as certainly as if he had held a gun to their heads, and he is heir to that wickedness and perpetuates it. You, of all people, know what my family has suffered at the hands of the Korsakovs, and I beg for your help. I can only hope that when we next meet you will tell me that my wish has been granted.

You are my only hope as the English cannot fully understand our code of honour. They tend to be too squeamish in righting wrongs. Their legal processes are too cumbersome and cases like this are not understood. As long as Michael Korsakov is allowed to remain free he will be a threat, and I can only wish with all my heart that fate had allowed him to drown.

If you think I sound callous, you are right. I long sometimes to ask for the forgiveness that only the Orthodox Church can grant me. The memory of a thousand candles illuminating the holy icons in church still haunts me, and I can almost smell the incense coming in clouds from the censer.

With all my love, Natalia.

As Natalia finished the letter she felt drained of emotion. She couldn't exactly gauge how Count Freedericksz would respond, but she knew she could leave retribution in his hands.

23

Once Tamara had recovered from the euphoria produced by hearing of Michael's lucky escape, she grew increasingly incensed with him for taking such a high profile with the world's press who had latched on to him eagerly. After his initial reticence, they found him a most colourful character and drew copiously on his chequered past. His despatches from Ireland annoyed Dean who already had Jim Roberts, one of his senior reporters, covering the disaster. Roberts cabled angrily, asking Dean to clarify exactly who was the *Chronicle's* accredited reporter and received the firm reply that he alone was responsible for the story and that Michael was to watch what he said and make no further comments.

Tamara had even cabled Wesley Frost, pleading with him to restrain Michael from taking so much of the limelight. She knew, however, that he was used to being the centre of gossip and conjecture and that he was not likely to give up at such an important stage. To her despair, Michael now talked freely to the press, destroying every last shred of family dignity that she and Hal had worked so hard to preserve. The full dramatic story of their past was laid bare for the world to gaze at as every angle was exposed and picked over by the vultures.

'He's become a bizarre celebrity,' Tamara said coldly to Dean at their daily meeting at her apartment, 'but the price we all must pay is yet to be reckoned.'

'Natalia Orlofski is not going to like this either,' Dean replied carefully. 'I just hope that all this doesn't fan the flames of revenge for another generation.'

'I know what you mean,' said Tamara. 'She's a proud and determined woman and the Orlofskis have always been fond of grand gestures. There's little, however, that we can do. Once he gets to England he'll make straight for Liverpool and we can expect another firecracker to explode.'

'I just hope that, for once, he'll act with discretion,' sighed Dean. 'I don't think he'll get a very sympathetic hearing if he's foolish enough to try and see John Duff.'

'Who's he?' asked Tamara irritably. 'I sometimes have the greatest difficulty in following you, Dean.'

'He's Natalia Orlofski's father-in-law,' Dean replied. 'Don't you remember Michael talking about him and the Albany Group?'

'Now you mention it, I do. Wasn't he anxious that we should consider taking a look at them with a view to purchase?'

'Yes, he had an idea that it would be a useful acquisition, and, for once, he might have been right, but for the wrong reasons. Albany are the correct size and structure for us and would complement our operations. It makes very good sense to have a British connection but the timing would have to be right.'

'It wasn't Albany that Michael wanted. It was a way of getting to the Orlofski woman,' replied Tamara tartly.

'Well, I suspect they would not sell at any price anyway, especially as I believe Natalia Orlofski holds a substantial shareholding,' Dean replied.

'Don't believe anything Michael tells you.'

'I don't. Now, can we please get on with the business in hand?' asked Dean, annoyed that what little time he had with Tamara was always taken up with talk of Michael. 'I just need you to sign these documents before you leave for your vacation. You are still going, aren't you?' he continued, seeing a strange look on her face.

'Yes, of course, Dean. I'm looking forward to it. I'm off to take a cure at the Homestead in Warm Springs Valley, Virginia, so, as usual, you're in total command in my absence.'

'I'll telephone you if anything important crops up, especially if there is any news of Michael.'

At exactly the same time that his mother was leaving New York, Michael was arriving in England on a boat from Ireland. He had made a reservation at the Adelphi Hotel in Liverpool.

'Your suite is on the third floor, Count,' said the manager as he led Michael to the elevator. 'I sincerely hope you'll enjoy your stay with us.'

Michael ignored him for a moment. 'Just make certain there's plenty of bourbon in the room and see to it that there's enough ice.'

'Very good, Count,' he replied. 'Your luggage has been taken care of.'

Michael had heard his mother talk of the Adelphi. First impressions backed up all she had said. The hotel had obviously been built to cater for a discerning clientele, many of whom used the Cunard service to New York or took passage to farflung corners of the Empire. It was solid and dignified and his accommodation was sumptuous without being ostentatious.

As soon as he had taken stock of his surroundings, Michael went down to the lobby in search of that day's copy of the *Record* which he purchased from a smiling girl at the bookstall. Then, on impulse, he went to the front of the hotel and asked the doorman to hail him a cab, with the single intention of visiting Charnley Lodge.

When they reached the leafy carriage drive encircling

Sefton Park, the cabbie pointed out the Duff residence with its imposing tower. It was much as he had expected, solid, with impeccably maintained lawns and shrubs in the formal gardens which lay behind the wrought-iron gates. He thought of Natalia and Peter making love in the house and wondered which of the upstairs windows had been their bedroom. It was a trivial thing but, to Michael, it assumed huge importance. For a moment he felt like bursting in and making an unpleasant scene but, with a supreme effort of will, he held himself in check.

Taking a deep breath, he turned and walked slowly back along the tree-lined road before stopping to sit on a green wooden bench from which he could see the full sweep of the carriage drive. Elegant motor cars and beautifully turned-out carriages lazily conveyed their occupants to and fro and the scene brought back memories of Central Park. Puffing on a cigarette, Michael was pleased to be so much in command of himself as he knew he must act with patience if he was to succeed in manoeuvring the Duffs into selling their controlling interest in the Albany Group. He congratulated himself on his foresight in ordering copies of the *Record* to be sent to his office in New York. Over the past months he had read the paper religiously and had come to admire the professionalism of John Duff and his editorial staff. As he compared O'Donnell's to Albany he saw two very similar animals. Of course O'Donnell's was bigger, with more heavyweight titles in its magazine group but, somehow, Albany had style.

'They're about where we were some ten years ago', he thought, 'and the market is bound to be hungry for new titles when the war is over.'

It seemed strangely unreal that he was here in Britain and in a position to influence the destinies of so many people he had lived vicariously close to in his imagination. It was, however, galling to know that Natalia was not even in Liverpool. He had been irritated to learn that she had left the city and he immediately assumed she was with the Milners

173

at Henley. He thought that it was just another example of the wilful streak he knew she possessed, and which he secretly admired. Natalia's stubbornness, born of adversity, was what he found so attractive. He was unaccustomed to being shunned by women and, for some perverse reason, it served only to increase his interest.

Returning to his hotel, Michael was sitting, mulling over the events of the day, when there was a knock at the door. He got up slowly from the sofa, walked across the thick carpet to where his jacket had been flung over the arm of a chair and casually removed a cigarette from the case in its pocket.

'I'll be with you in a moment,' he called out as he pushed his hair back from his eyes. 'Who's there?' he added as he took out his lighter.

'Telegram for Count Michael Korsakov,' came the answer.

Michael opened the door and looked at the nervous messenger holding a silver tray on which rested a telegram. Taking the envelope, he dismissed the boy curtly and ripped open the envelope to read the terse message.

'SINCERELY REGRET TO INFORM YOU YOUR MOTHER DIED OF A STROKE YESTERDAY STOP DEAN'

Michael stood still staring ahead vacantly, stunned by the news. The ash fell from the cigarette he held between trembling fingers and he pulled at his collar which seemed to be strangling him. Eventually, he did something he had rarely done since a child and dropped to his knees. The prayer he said was simple, taking him back to the troubled days in Russia with his mother. In form and content it wasn't much of an offering but it seemed to calm him. Although Tamara had been ill he had somehow never really considered the possibility of her death. Death was for others. He had always felt that he and his family were strangely protected, almost immortal. He cursed the fact that he was so far away and an angry scowl crept across his face.

Quickly regaining his composure, Michael lost no time in wiring Dean. With a limited service now operating to the United States he knew he wouldn't be able to set off for at least a couple of weeks and, with the usual delays and other factors that governed transatlantic travel in wartime, it might be a month or more before he could get to New York. He therefore wired Dean to proceed with the arrangements and advised him that he was remaining in England. Tongues would wag maliciously but Michael cared little what anyone thought and at least, begrudgingly, he knew that with Dean in charge everything would be in good hands.

Suddenly he picked up a vase and hurled it at his reflection in the long mirror behind the door. It broke into a thousand jagged pieces.

Composing himself, he sauntered down to the cocktail bar and set about drowning the pain of the day. It didn't take him long, however, to realise that drinking in the very proper confines of the Adelphi was not for him and he left to join the coarser crowd at the Red Lion across the road.

For their part they were pleased to talk to a prosperous-looking American who was obviously intent on getting through the thick wad of notes in his hip pocket, which he unwisely brought out with a flourish.

After about an hour Michael left the pub with a young blonde woman on his arm. Watching him intently was Tom Smith who had been told by John Duff to keep a precautionary watching brief on this unwelcome visitor. Tom was average by anyone's standards: average height, average build, mouse-brown hair and definitely no distinguishing marks – a useful man to have working on a newspaper, as John had often remarked.

Tom followed the couple to a rundown house in a row that, fifty years previously, would have been considered quite good style. He noted the time as they entered. A light went on in an upstairs room and the curtains were carefully closed.

Tom waited in the warm evening air for some forty minutes before the door opened again. To his horror, he then saw Michael stagger out on to the dimly lit street only to fall face downwards and lie gasping in a pool of his own blood.

Rushing to him, Tom saw the whiteness of Michael's face and felt the weakness of his pulse and knew that he needed urgent and skilled attention if he was to live. He carefully considered his options. He could either leave Michael in the street and rush to find help, by which time Michael might have bled to death, or he could try to carry him bodily the four hundred yards back to the Adelphi. He soon realised he had little choice. Without further ado, he sat Michael upright and, with an almighty struggle, lifted him on to his shoulders. He staggered along feeling Michael's warm blood seep down his shirt. His lungs and heart seemed to be bursting with the effort as he crossed the road and stumbled up the flight of steps leading to the hotel.

Leaving Michael propped up against the wall, Tom entered the lobby covered in blood and began to plead with the hall porter to get a doctor without delay.

'The Count! The Count!' was all he could say, pointing to the swing doors through which Michael had now managed to drag himself before collapsing once more. A woman screamed as she saw the bloodstained figure lying on the marble floor, like elegantly dressed meat on a butcher's slab. As well as a deep stomach wound, Tom could now see that Michael had considerable bruising and lacerations to his face and throat.

'My God,' he thought, 'he's going to die.'

For two days Michael lay in the twilight no-man's-land between life and death, and the news of another Korsakov incident fed the frenzy of the press. It was a story that they could not have dreamed of – Michael lying at death's door in hospital while his mother, embalmed and cold, awaited burial in New York.

John Duff's urgent cable to Dean Jones describing Michael's plight received an immediate but laconic reply. John knew that Michael and Dean had an uneasy relationship which might well prove to be the Achilles' heel they were looking

176

for. Somehow he felt that he had learned more from the brevity of the telegraphic exchange with Dean than could have been gleaned in a telephone conversation, had that been possible.

Sitting back in his chair, he saw clearly for the first time how vulnerable O'Donnell's had become with Tamara dead and Michael, her only son and heir, clinging to life by a precarious thread.

After a week Michael had improved sufficiently to be moved to the First Western Hospital where it was thought their experience of treating bayonet wounds from the battlefield would give him a better chance of recovery.

One further strange and disturbing fact shocked and mystified both the doctors and the police who had come to the conclusion that Michael's injuries were consistent with some form of bizarre ritual punishment. It had been pointed out to them that similar injuries were sustained by the followers of the White Doves of Russia.

The police had little else to go on as Michael's blonde companion had vanished and, in short, no one but Tom Smith had seen anything and he was left wondering if he could believe the evidence of his own eyes. As the key witness, he had made a long and detailed statement to the police, describing Michael's movements on that day. Even with his keen eye and investigative journalist's training, Tom was at a loss as to what to make of the story. He was sure that the woman had followed Michael into the Red Lion. He even thought she might have been at the Adelphi but he could not be certain. One thing he did know was that the incident bore all the hallmarks of a well-trained and professional gang, possibly hired by Michael's enemies in either Russia or America.

Sir Edward passed *The Times* to Lavinia, indicating the headlines about Michael. 'Korsakov's certainly become a celebrity since the *Lusitania*,' he commented dryly.

He rose from the breakfast table, brushing crumbs from his

tweed suit as he did so, and then walked the short distance to his study. Once inside, with the door firmly closed, he settled in his armchair, drew the telephone closer to him and put a call through to his contact in Whitehall.

'I was most interested to read this morning's paper, Philip,' he said. 'I knew your people could help us sort out the trouble in Liverpool. I am very interested to read about the unorthodox methods our Russian friends used. As you know, Natalia is staying with us at the moment and she told me about the letter she had written to Count Freedericksz asking for his help. It seems they have responded very quickly.'

24

One week after Tamara had been laid to rest in the family vault at St Patrick's Cathedral, Dean received a telephone call from Stewart Armstrong of Frinksteins Bank.

'Now that things have settled down a bit I would welcome an opportunity to talk over your corporate borrowing requirements for the future. After all, it's not beyond the bounds of possibility that Michael, if he survives, may wish to take O'Donnell's business elsewhere.'

Dean laughed at this unexpected remark. 'Come on, Stewart, you know damn well we wouldn't change banks after such a long and happy relationship.'

'Michael may have other ideas,' Stewart replied crisply.

'Well, Michael is in no condition to do anything right now. Even if he wishes to make major changes, he would have me to contend with. Tamara has left me fifty per cent of the voting shares in O'Donnell's as a means of tempering his wilder schemes.'

'I'm delighted for you, Dean,' said Stewart with genuine pleasure. 'She certainly was shrewd: she could read him like a book.'

They both laughed.

'How is Michael?' asked Stewart.

'It's too early to say yet. There's more than an even chance he will make a full recovery, but it will be a long time before he's fully fit. As you know, he's always had this thing about us expanding into England. It would appear he was sizing up Albany Publishing when he got himself into trouble.'

'What happened, and what about the part the Russian White Doves are supposed to have played?' asked Stewart.

'We don't know any more than has been reported in the press. I presume you've read the various reports?'

'Yes, yes I have. Revenge seems the likeliest motive, but even I wouldn't have wished him to have been so cruelly dealt with. It seems his chances of perpetuating the O'Donnell dynasty may have taken quite a knock.'

After a momentary pause, Stewart continued suddenly, 'By the way, Dean, I need to talk to you about a disturbing matter that has just come to light. Could you come round and see me at the bank tomorrow when I hope I will be in a position to give you chapter and verse. Would eleven o'clock suit? I need you to be well briefed before our board meeting as it is important that we act decisively.'

Two days later Sam Goldman acquainted the board of O'Donnell's with the salient points of Tamara's will. He suggested that Dean be voted president with the widest-ranging executive powers. This was unanimously agreed, with the proviso that the situation would be reviewed in a year's time.

'Thank you, gentlemen for your vote of confidence,' said Dean looking at the four ageing faces staring at him anxiously from around the table. He had long thought that new blood was needed to see O'Donnell's safely into the next decade, and today reinforced this opinion. Marvin Jeffries was the oldest of them and was now eighty. He had been a loyal supporter of Joe O'Donnell in the early days and had seen all the great changes in the company over a span of nearly fifty years. Dean had no intention of removing him as he considered him part of the furniture and he valued his unswerving loyalty even though he contributed little these days.

Josh Wilson, Tom Davis and Howard Eisner were, however, another matter altogether he thought, looking at their podgy grey faces. Tom was sweating, he noticed, and one eye twitched nervously as Dean looked at him. All three, he knew, had toadied up to Michael and had shamelessly drifted in the direction of the faction they thought would hold sway. They were weak and ineffectual and he knew that what he was about to say would test them to the limit. It had been Tamara's idea to promote them from within the ranks of the company as she hadn't wanted trouble from cliques that were not of a like mind to her own. Dean had always looked on them as harmless clay which could be moulded to whatever stance the company and its owner wanted, and he knew they were all too well aware and resentful of the role they had played.

'Gentlemen,' Dean said quietly, 'you all know why Sam Goldman is here and we extend our thanks to you, Sam, for setting out in simple terms Tamara's wishes. I have, however, asked Stewart Armstrong from Frinksteins Bank to attend and he is waiting in the anteroom. With your permission, I shall ask him to join us as he has an important statement to make.'

Josh Wilson fingered his collar nervously at this unexpected turn of events. As financial director, he had not foreseen Dean's move and protested that this was not the time nor the place to invite the company's banker without giving him warning. His protestations were in vain as Dean's steely gaze settled on those who might have considered opposing him. Josh looked around anxiously as Stewart Armstrong was duly invited to sit with them at the long mahogany table.

Sam couldn't help but enjoy Dean's sense of theatre as he sat watching the proceedings. He could see his friend was now the complete master of the game and was pressing home his advantage with every word and gesture. Marvin was placidly sucking at his unlit pipe while the others wriggled and squirmed in painful disarray like schoolboys waiting for the cane.

'I shall come straight to the point,' said Stewart. 'Information has been passed to me which leads me to believe that one or more of our senior executives at O'Donnell's has been defrauding the company of considerable sums over the last twelve months.'

'What on earth are you driving at?' asked Tom Davis angrily. 'Everyone who works in my department is beyond reproach.'

'If you will let me finish, Tom, I will explain,' Stewart said sharply. 'We have, for some time, had our suspicions about a company called Eisco which opened an account with us last year. After making enquiries it turned out that they were a phoney supplier of newsprint, and regular sums were being transferred by O'Donnell's to their account. At first, care was taken to ensure that the sums were not excessively large, but for the last two months extremely large amounts have been paid to their account. When we investigated Eisco, we unravelled a carefully constructed façade. As we dug deeper we found that the directors were merely front men and the real owner of the company was Thomas R. Davis of New York.'

'I've heard enough of this nonsense,' said Tom, rising from the table, his face flushed and blotchy.

'I would advise you to sit down, Tom,' said Sam Goldman quietly. 'I am sure we would all like to hear the full story.'

With that, Tom sank back into his chair, wiping his forehead with a large white handkerchief. 'Go on then,' he said hesitantly, allowing Stewart to resume his narrative.

'Eisco has been under investigation by the government for some time. The company was known to be a front for an active service unit of German sympathisers intent on lobbying to keep America out of the war. The trail led eventually to the German Press Bureau and the formidable Dr Dernberg who is now safely back in Germany. They were, of course, hoping to undermine the finances of the *Chronicle* after Tamara refused to sell to them. They hoped to weaken O'Donnell's by fraudulent payments from company funds into various cleverly constructed "shell" companies so that, eventually, we would have no choice but to sell. It was all part of a wider German plot to weaken American industry and get their hands on the news media so that they could control the anti-German hostility after the sinking of the *Lusitania*. A friendly press, presenting the German point of view, has been a prime objective of the German Embassy. Howard Eisner was, of course, the link man but, surprisingly, the real brains were those of Tom Davis.'

'I never thought you had such initiative,' said Dean smiling sarcastically at Tom who was by this time sitting as though transfixed.

'You stupid bastard, Tom!' shouted Howard. 'I should have had better sense than to trust your judgement.'

'Hear, hear,' said Marvin quietly and he began to light his pipe and send plumes of blue smoke into the air, while Stewart pressed a button to summon the FBI agents who were waiting outside. White-faced, Josh Wilson took his leave.

'Quite a story,' said Sam quietly after Tom and Howard had been taken out. 'There must be more of it. Come on, tell us everything now those traitors have gone.'

'Well, we first got wind of things in August when, you will remember, there was a series of articles in the *New York World* about German undercover activities,' said Stewart. 'They published a series of secret German Government papers which had been lost on the New York elevated railway. The documents indicated that the German Ambassador in Washington, Count Bernstorff, had a budget of four hundred thousand dollars a week to influence public opinion and sow the seeds of agitation in American factories with the connivance of the unions. Furthermore, the documents showed that the German Foreign Office regarded it as a priority that pro-German propaganda be fed to our newspapers. Biased and distorted reports were sent from Germany, Austria-Hungary, Turkey and the Balkan States.'

'Don't forget also', interrupted Dean, 'that the German Press Bureau recruited Davis and others like him. The *Chronicle* was targeted by them as we have a large readership and a substantial turnover. They didn't like our support of the Allies and they would have done anything to silence us. Further proof of the intrigue', he continued, 'was provided when Dr Dumba, the Austro-Hungarian Ambassador in Washington, was convicted last month of conspiring with Captain von Papen, the German Military Attaché, to undermine American factories supplying munitions to the Allies. If you recall, they preyed on the guilt feelings of Austro-Hungarian workers with some success.'

'Thank Heaven the President took a firm line and sent him packing,' said Sam.

'Just one question,' enquired Dean. 'What part, if any, did Michael play in all this?'

'None at all. He's had nothing at all to do with it.'

'Yes, I guess that makes sense, but I had to ask.'

'Now we've located and destroyed the vipers' nest,' continued Dean, 'we've only Michael to worry about.'

'I think that's wishful thinking,' said Stewart wearily. 'I'm afraid that I have to remind you that the fraudulent outflow of cash over the last year has seriously weakened O'Donnell's position with the bank. Have you seen how your borrowings have soared recently?'

'Yes,' said Dean warily, 'but it's nothing we can't handle.'

'I think if you look at things in the cold light of day, Dean, you will find that you are very close to being over-borrowed and that you may have to arrange to reschedule repayments on this building.'

'I know we shall weather the storm, Stewart,' Dean said with as much conviction as he could muster. 'Can we try to recover the money that was stolen?'

'My advice is to be very careful,' said Stewart. 'You could lose a lot of face.'

'Don't worry,' Dean replied. 'I shall be discreet. I know the whole subject will be a bit of a hot potato. Incidentally, on reflection, I would bet my life that Michael would have torn Davis and Eisner limb from limb if he'd known what they were up to.'

'I'm sure you're right,' agreed Stewart. 'He was always fiercely proud of his Russian blood and was horrified at the losses his countrymen were sustaining at the hands of the Germans.'

'I think we ought to have him back here in New York as soon as possible in view of the circumstances,' replied Dean. 'Sam has written to him at length. He's put him in the picture from the legal standpoint about the missing funds but it's important that he knows the current problem and its implication. After all, it could be difficult having one of the major stockholders on the other side of the Atlantic and not easily accessible.'

'I think it's the first time I've heard you advocating his presence,' said Marvin, smiling.

'God knows I don't relish having him here,' Dean replied, 'but need's must. After all, he is due out of the hospital soon and should be well enough to travel.'

'What address did Sam use when he wrote to Michael? I hope to Heaven it will find him!'

'Don't worry,' replied Dean. 'He sent the original letter to the Adelphi Hotel and a copy to the hospital just to be certain. And before you ask, they were both marked "Strictly Confidential".'

'Good,' said Stewart. 'Now, let's get Jake Toomey in here. As senior accountant he can bring us up to date with the projected figures.'

After some time the four concluded that, with buoyant sales of the *Chronicle* and an above-average return from the magazine group, they might just scrape by without selling any assets.

'It's going to be close, Stewart,' said Jake, smiling for the first time, 'but by God we're going to do it. Tamara would

185

never have agreed to sell anything unless it was absolutely
necessary.'

25

'Welcome home,' said James Ponsonby with a smile as he greeted Natalia at the British Embassy in Petrograd.

'Thank you, James,' she replied, 'but it's not really home any more. Too much has happened to me since I left.'

He looked a little crestfallen at her reply. 'I just hope that this time you will be able to put the past behind you.'

'I don't think so,' she replied with a hint of a smile. 'Memories, good or bad, last a lifetime.'

Natalia was tired after her long and dangerous journey to Petrograd. She had travelled despite the gentle opposition of Sir Edward who wished her to remain at Larkhill for the foreseeable future. He had finally arranged for her to go straight to the embassy where James had a car waiting to take her the fifteen miles to Tsarkoe Selo, and he made no secret of the fact that he was relishing the thought of being alone with her on the short journey.

Aware that she had been a little distant, Natalia chatted animatedly until the Rolls-Royce passed into the Imperial Park guarded by bearded Cossacks. It was suddenly brought home to her that she was entering a world that only a privileged few had an automatic right to visit. She remembered the hidden domain of the Tsar's family from the distant past. It was here that the mysteries of monarchy were perpetuated and legends were born.

'Funny to think that all this came into being at the whim of Catherine the First who sought to escape while her husband, Peter the Great, was building St Petersburg,' said James, unaware of her thoughts. 'I've never quite understood why two great palaces should have been built only five hundred yards apart.'

'I agree,' said Natalia, smiling. 'It might have been more sensible not to have used the space so economically. After all, the great St Petersburg plain does stretch rather a long way and it's not exactly overcrowded.'

They both laughed, enjoying the pleasure of each other's company. James felt the fleeting touch of Natalia's gloved hand on his arm and he glanced at her. He longed to kiss her but he knew that this was not the time nor the place to see if the boundaries of their friendship could be extended. The day was difficult enough for her without any pressures he might create.

Soon the car made its near-silent way down a wide street lined with trees to the elegant mansion in which Natalia was to occupy a suite of rooms before leaving for Ivanhov. As the car passed through the gilded gates and up the gravel drive of the house, Natalia caught her breath as a whirlwind of childhood memories met her. Before she knew it, they were at the white stone steps leading to the huge entrance door surmounted by a cartouche. A liveried servant ushered them into the spacious hall with its highly polished pine floor, oriental carpets and crystal chandelier. The day was damp and cold but large, decorated pottery stoves kept the house pleasantly warm as well as filling the rooms with the soft, sweet aroma of burning wood and the smell of incense. On the hall table was a large envelope addressed to Natalia. The reverse of the envelope carried the imperial arms. She opened it carefully and stared at the folded sheet of writing paper.

'Can I help?' asked James, as he watched her struggle to decipher the spidery writing.

'Thanks, no,' she said quietly handing him the letter. 'We don't have much time, I'm afraid. On the Empress's instructions Count Freedericksz has invited us to join him for tea at the Alexander Palace at four o'clock.'

'I shall be most interested to meet him,' said James. 'There's been a lot of talk about him at the embassy. Now that he's eighty he's been getting very absent-minded, but I believe he knows more about the intimate secrets of the Imperial Family than anyone else alive.'

'Yes,' said Natalia coolly, 'that's true. I shall always be grateful to him as he was a great support to my mother in her troubles. He has always been a dear, faithful friend and ally of the Orlofskis. We both share a loathing for the Korsakovs. It's a strong bond.'

'I think we had better go and change,' said James softly. 'There's barely an hour before we meet the Count.'

Their eyes met momentarily but then, turning aside, Natalia laid her furs on the table and called a maid to show her to her suite.

As James and Natalia entered the Alexander Palace, Freedericksz met them before the state apartments. Despite his age, he still cut a dash in his elegant, tailored uniform. He kissed Natalia on both cheeks in the accustomed fashion and his genuine affection for her was plain to see as they hugged before he shook James warmly by the hand as though greeting an old friend. 'I'm delighted to meet you, Mr Ponsonby,' he said in a deep, husky voice.

As they moved through the sumptuous rooms, the Count chatted ceaselessly to Natalia while James kept a respectful distance behind them. It was clear that they were going in the direction of the private apartments where four tall black guards kept watch. James noted that they were dressed as Ethiopians and wore full state livery of coats embroidered with gold thread and scarlet trousers, while on their heads they wore white turbans. As they passed, James wondered which of the four was the famous black American Jim Hercules whom he had heard about and who had held a high position in the State Guard since the days of Alexander III.

Eventually the Count led them into a small anteroom where a log fire burned. He motioned Natalia to sit next to him on the sofa, while James chose a buttoned leather armchair.

'When the Empress heard you were coming to see me, she at once insisted we should meet as soon as possible.'

Just then one of the Ethiopians caught the Count's eye and he now beckoned them to follow him into the presence of the Empress Alexandra in her private drawing room. The Empress had changed from her nurse's uniform and was dressed in a long, white, flowing dress trimmed with yards of lace and offset with two rich ropes of pearls. Her hair, red-gold in the fading light, was piled high, lending her face a delicacy and clarity that James could only compare to the very finest porcelain. Natalia curtsied low and deep as the Count announced her. The Empress smiled and reached out to embrace her before saying, 'Natalia, dear, we are so pleased to have you among us again after so long. I do hope your apartment is to your liking?'

'Thank you, Your Majesty, it is very comfortable,' Natalia replied, 'but I am anxious to see your hospital before I have to leave for Ivanhov.'

'I didn't know that you had some nursing experience, my dear, until Count Freedericksz told me,' the Empress said, 'but don't be too impatient. You will find conditions hard enough when you do get to Ivanhov.'

Turning to James, the Empress thanked him for bringing Natalia safely from Petrograd. Giving a hastily rehearsed bow from the neck, he replied, 'It is a privilege to be of service to you, Your Majesty.'

The Empress then rang the silver bell in front of her and a maid entered with one pot of China tea and one of Earl Grey. She placed them before the Empress on a small table covered with a white, embroidered cloth.

'You will probably be amazed', the Empress said, turning to Natalia, 'that I still haven't managed to persuade the dear Count to allow gâteaux and other frivolities to be served at teatime at court. I am therefore risking his displeasure', she continued, her eyes twinkling, 'by adding a chocolate cake to the usual frugal fare that has been served for so long in this country.'

The Count stroked his moustache as he smiled indulgently, then said disarmingly, 'Your Majesty, there are extenuating circumstances today, we have a visitor from England.'

The whole of the ritual of a traditional Russian teatime gripped Natalia. One part of her remembered her childhood days while the other, now more dominant side, looked at the whole scene through the eyes of her adopted country. She knew she was in the presence of the Empress of All the Russias and everything that meant to the oppressed masses, however, she couldn't help but wonder if the old sense of awe and reverence remained intact. Controlling her thoughts, she chatted in her usual engaging way before the Empress indicated that the audience was at an end as it was time for her to make her inspection of the hospital, leaving them both in the trusted care of Count Freedericksz.

As though he had read her thoughts, after a pause, the old man began, 'What news of Michael Korsakov?'

'He will recover, eventually,' Natalia replied.

She smiled thinly at him, her eyes intense and focused. 'I very much appreciated the prompt and appropriate action you took in response to my letter.'

'That is the advantage of living in what you call a backward country, Natalia. Our people in Britain can be relied upon to use their initiative in cases like that. They still have a surprise or two up their sleeves.'

She smiled at him before looking at James.

'Don't tell me anything more,' he protested. 'I know that we are officially turning a blind eye to the Ochrana cell operating in Liverpool, but we can't be seen to condone it.'

'Of course, of course,' replied the Count. 'It might offend your English sense of fair play.' Turning to Natalia he began again, 'I saw Felix Yussoupov last night. He'd been at The Bear, dining with Rasputin. He asked if he could see you.'

Natalia's reaction was immediate. 'I'll see Felix, but I'll never agree to meet Rasputin.'

'I understand completely,' the Count replied.

'I've not seen Felix since he was up at Oxford,' she continued. 'He came to dine with the Milners at Larkhill. How could he mix with that terrible man Rasputin?'

The question went unanswered.

James kept silent while this exchange took place. He knew all about Prince Felix and his fabled wealth and Bohemian lifestyle. The Moika Palace was the setting for many a racy party since Felix had returned to Russia to claim his inheritance following the recent, sad death of his elder brother Nicholas, killed in a duel. He was married to Princess Irina, a niece of the Tsar. It worried James that Natalia might be drawn into their circle, with disastrous results, and it was not lost on him that Rasputin had been a key figure at the inquest convened to determine the cause of death of Natalia's brother, Alexander. Even more worrying was the rumour, known only to a few trusted friends, that Felix Yussoupov was planning to dispose of Rasputin and that his friendship with the mad monk was one of deliberate convenience. Would Natalia, he conjectured, be the bait he needed to help spring the trap?

26

'He's an arrogant so and so but you have to credit him with guts, Matron.'

'I'm reluctantly forced to agree,' she replied severely, before adding, 'However I've rarely seen anyone with such a compelling will to heal themselves.'

Looking directly at Mr Fanshawe, the surgeon in charge of Michael's case, she continued, 'There's something unwholesome about Count Korsakov. I can't quite put my finger on it but I shall be glad when he's well enough to leave.'

'I know what you mean, Matron,' he answered thoughtfully. 'God knows what really happened to him. We'll probably never know the true story but I'm certain the papers will continue to have a field day with fanciful speculation.'

'What chance is there of him making a complete recovery?' she asked.

'Pretty good, but time alone will tell if he will ever be able to become a father. Anyway, it's little short of a miracle he's walking so well, even if it is with the help of a stick.'

Since sustaining his injuries, Michael had spent a lot of

time with the police. He had tried again and again to piece together the events of that fateful night but could remember little that was of real value. There was, however, just one small thread in the tapestry that he was able to highlight. He wasn't sure if his memory was playing tricks or if it was just the effects of inebriation, but he thought he had smelled the pungent aroma of incense in the house of his assailants, the same smell there had always been on the clothes of his mother's pious friends long ago in Russia when they returned from Mass.

'You've given us very little to work with, Count,' said the police inspector, 'but we are doing all in our power to find those who are responsible and bring them to justice.'

'Pompous fool,' thought Michael, fixing his interrogator with a piercing gaze.

'It's a shame, Count, that a man of your standing should find it necessary to keep such company,' the inspector continued before being stopped dead in his tracks by Michael.

'I do not require a lesson in morals, Inspector. What I do need is for you to find those who laid what was obviously a well-rehearsed trap for me. It doesn't take genius to see that they were well acquainted with my habits and knew a great deal about me and my connections.'

'We are fully aware of the circumstances, Count,' came the measured reply, 'but there is one question that we come back to repeatedly.'

'What's that?'

'Why do you think an attempt was made to injure you in other ways besides stabbing? After all, it does seem slightly bizarre. We get to see most things in this city,' he continued reflectively, 'but I must confess I've rarely seen ritual disfigurement attempted. We have a full statement from Mr Duff's employee who had been following you for some days and he mentions nothing about women apart from the blonde at the hotel.'

'There were no other women besides her,' said Michael coldly.

194

'I'm sorry to ask these questions, Count, but we've got so little to go on that every scrap of information helps,' said the inspector, picking up his hat and setting it on his pomaded hair.

Michael watched him as he left the room and then plodded down the white-tiled passage like some dreary automaton whose mainspring has been weakened through continual overwinding. He felt lonely and depressed, relying on his irritability to goad him into action like a sharp pebble in his shoe. He knew that much discussion would be taking place in the boardroom of O'Donnell's and that his predicament would be seized on as yet another sign of his unsuitability for high office within the company. It now took Michael only a moment to make up his mind to discharge himself from the hospital. An hour later he hobbled into the lobby of the Adelphi Hotel, leaning heavily on his stick.

'Any mail?' he asked the surprised concierge.

'Just one letter. It came this morning, Count.'

He could see it was from Sam. As he read, the contents seemed to jump out at him, burning themselves into his mind. He reeled at words like 'fraud', 'deceit', 'conspiracy' and there and then he determined to revenge himself on those who had set about bleeding O'Donnell's of cash. It didn't escape him that his own actions had diverted Dean's attention and provided a cover for this elaborate fraud. As he took the elevator to his suite, all manner of emotions welled up within him. Anger, hate, self-pity, even fear, brought him out in a cold clammy sweat as he struggled unsteadily with the key to the door.

The day passed slowly. Drink numbed his senses as he lay sprawled on the sofa, his clothes reeking of spilled bourbon, and a large stain had developed and spread on the pale carpet where the contents of the overturned bottle had dripped. It was not until a chambermaid came at seven o'clock to turn down the bed that the manager was called and, seeing Michael's state, arranged for the hospital to send a private nurse to sit with him during the night.

195

It was approximately two days later when Michael finally determined what course of action to take. He knew he had to capture the initiative and, true to form, decided on a desperate gamble. For the first time in weeks he knew precisely what he had to do. He sat down at the writing desk and replied to Sam's letter. It was a detailed narrative in which he vested his O'Donnell shares in Sam for the term of one year, or until he returned to America, whichever came sooner. He also instructed Sam to use the voting rights that had been given to him in the company's best interests. Furthermore, he asked that his salary and dividends as a director of O'Donnell's be paid into an account he had opened with the Midland Bank in Castle Street, Liverpool. After repeating his assurance to Sam that he was quite recovered, he went on to warn him against attempting further contact. 'If no word has been received from me in twelve months, then I have left my will and other instructions in the vault at the bank.' For further security he sent a carefully written copy of this letter to James Sloan, the frock-coated manager of the bank, by special messenger.

He was tempted to seek out Emma but, with a great effort of will, he decided against it. Instead, he looked at the new leather case he had bought in Ireland and smiled wryly as he surveyed the tangle of garments which he had packed so haphazardly. Summoning all his strength, he sat on the case and secured the strong brass fasteners. For a moment his resolve failed him but, after a few minutes' rest, he rang the front desk for someone to collect his things. Paying his account with a flourish of new banknotes, he airily dismissed the farewells of the manager and staff and was soon in a taxi on his way to the ship that was to take him to Russia.

The docks were alive with activity at that time of the day. Heavy horses hauled laden wagons while, off in the sidings, hissing shunting-engines clanked about their business. Passing through the dock gates, Michael paid off the cab and approached a rusty tramp steamer tied up under the looming hulls of larger ships. Looking round for help, he saw two men who were lounging idly by the gangplank. Calling them over to where he was standing in the shadow of a great brick warehouse, he asked if they would help him to find the captain.

'You're not going anywhere, Korsakov,' said the larger of the two, landing a blow that took all the wind out of Michael's body, doubling him up on the ground. 'Don't worry,' he sneered, 'I know exactly where I put my knife in you and I won't open it up again, just yet.'

After regaining some of his breath and composure, Michael looked at the man defiantly. 'Who the hell are you?' he demanded through clenched teeth.

Another blow, this time to the head, gave him the only answer he would receive. With no delay the two men picked him and his case up from the cobbles, dumped them unceremoniously in the back of a van loaded with tea chests and made for the dock gates where, after the briefest of checks, they emerged from beneath the overhead railway into the city traffic.

After some minutes Michael regained consciousness and cautiously shifted his cramped position. He was bound hand and foot and already the ropes had made his hands too numb to attempt untying himself. To add further to his misery, he was almost suffocated by a roughly applied gag. He could just make out the voices of his captors speaking softly and he strained, in vain, to hear what they said over the harsh note of the engine. The stone setts of the road buffeted his bruised body as they drove on through the city for some twenty minutes or more. Eventually they turned off into the drive of a large suburban house set back from the road and screened by a thick laurel hedge. The van scrunched up the gravel drive and continued round the back of the house before parking in a small walled courtyard where Michael was roughly bundled into the house.

'Just one word of advice,' said the big man as he untied Michael, 'I shall have the greatest pleasure in shooting you if you try anything foolish.'

The door to a large, sparsely furnished room opened and in walked an attractive woman in her late twenties, her blonde hair tied up in a bun. She looked at the two men and then at Michael who immediately recognised her as the woman who had picked him up at the bar.

'So we meet again, Count,' she said, smiling at him. 'Last time we met you were very fortunate to escape with your life. This time it's possible that you won't be quite so lucky.' Before he had time to reply, she continued coldly, 'Now, down to business. As you probably know, the British Government are going to a lot of trouble to ensure you are not called to the *Lusitania* enquiry to be conducted by Lord Mersey. It's most unfortunate that you put two and two together and found out about the fifty tons of shrapnel shells in the ship's manifest.'

'Now just wait a minute!' Michael said angrily.

'Quiet!' shouted the big man, catching him across the face with his huge hand.

'You also found out', she continued calmly, 'that there were one hundred and seventy-three tons of ammunition from the Remington Small Arms Company destined for the Royal Arsenal at Woolwich, plus other consignments that would have been very useful to the Allies. Hot stuff, I think you'll agree, if the Germans could get proof of the ship's cargo. The official enquiry will, of course, quash reporters' stories that there was ammunition on board which caused the second explosion and the matter will then be discreetly placed *sub-judice*. So you see, when you took up with Miss Duff of the *Record*, something had to be done to make certain you kept quiet.'

Michael stared in disbelief. 'You're all crazy!' he said. 'Surely ... surely you don't think that ... that I, of all people, was party to this plan? After all I'm Russian and bleed for my people's cause.'

'Somebody in Whitehall pointed a finger at you,' came the reply. 'Besides, we all know that there's an old score to settle going back many years.'

'They asked that the assault on you be done in the most painful way possible, in the manner of the White Doves,' said the big man grinning, while his smaller companion bit his lip nervously.

Michael could feel the blood draining from his temples and his head swam as he was manhandled up the stairs and into a small bedroom before the door was shut and locked. He sank back on to the bed, drawing himself up into the foetal position.

Michael lay staring at the bare wall of his room. He was cold, hungry and in pain. When dawn came it was a welcome relief from the dirty blackness of the night. His head and body still hurt horribly whenever he moved and he knew that his wounds had opened up. He could feel dampness where his shirt stuck to him and the growing light showed the crimson colour of fresh blood. He felt weak and desperate, perhaps for the first time in his life, but this was soon overtaken by a more positive emotion – burning anger directed towards his captors.

He heard a noise and, turning towards the door, saw the thin man entering the room carrying a wicker tray which he placed on the bedside table.

'You'd better eat,' he said, gesturing towards an unappetising meal. Then, seeing how deathly white Michael was he continued, 'What the hell have you been doing to yourself?'

Michael eyed him without relish, then attempted to slip off his tweed jacket. He was so weak that his efforts were in vain but they were enough to expose the extent of the blood stain that, by now, had blossomed across his shirt. 'I think your friend got it a bit wrong,' he said in a hoarse whisper. 'If you don't get me a doctor quickly you'll have a corpse on your hands.'

'Nobody would have to know,' came the surly reply. 'You could just have gone missing without trace.'

'Don't forget the whole of the American press corps will be looking for me if I don't show up,' Michael countered weakly.

199

After a moment's indecision, the man screwed up his weasel face. 'I'll see what can be done. I'm not promising anything, mind,' he said before locking the door again behind him.

Michael heard him clatter downstairs and caught quick bursts of conversation but couldn't make sense of what was being said. After some minutes he heard the heavy, deliberate tread of the big man as he climbed the stairs and he braced himself as the door opened.

'Let's have a look at you, then,' he said gruffly. Michael winced as he was turned towards the light now streaming in through the uncurtained window. There was the slight but instantly recognisable smell of an infected wound and he bent over and unbuttoned Michael's jacket for a closer examination.

'Lie on the bed and don't move,' the man said. 'I'll have to fetch a doctor. There's one we use for safe-house visits. So you needn't start thinking you'll be able to raise the alarm.'

Michael had ceased keeping track of the hours by the time the door opened again. The doctor was a tall, gangling type with the inevitable black Gladstone bag which he opened, taking out a number of dressings. 'Get some hot water quickly,' he said to the big man who promptly passed on the order to his colleague. 'It's always the same with you fellows,' continued the doctor, as he carefully opened Michael's shirt. 'You don't seem to know your own strength. You just never learn.'

'Don't lecture, just fix him up,' came the reply.

'Impossible,' said the doctor when he had examined the extent of the wounds. 'If you don't get him to hospital within the day he will most certainly die.'

At that moment the blonde woman entered the room.

'Doc says he's got a problem and we've got to get him looked at,' the big man said, anxiety showing clearly in his face.

'You idiot!' she railed. 'Everything you get involved in goes wrong! Why can't you both handle a simple job without acting like gorillas?'

They all now turned their gaze on Michael.

'Get him to the special ward in the Lunatic Asylum,' she directed. 'Make sure, Doctor, that he's admitted to the secure section. Tell them he's dangerous and that you've had to sedate him because he was trying to injure himself again. We've prepared false papers for him and make sure your partner countersigns the certification documents tomorrow. You'd better get moving as soon as you've patched him up.'

'I don't like this one bit,' said the doctor, looking at the woman. 'One day you'll go too far.'

'Just remember I can get you struck off tomorrow,' she answered coldly. 'All it needs is for me to use the signed testimonies of those two poor girls. You'll be finished, Doctor, finished.'

Sensing his hesitation, she reinforced her point by opening the cardboard box she was carrying. She held it out towards him. Inside, on a bed of straw, was a black, hairy-backed spider the size of man's fist. 'It's a Guatemalan bird eater, it can kill a dog with its venom or paralyse a man for ten hours. It's not very pleasant. Now, let's get on with it,' she said, pointing to the hypodermic needle on the bedside table.

Bending over him, the doctor emptied the contents of the syringe into a vein in Michael's arm. Its effect was almost instantaneous and he slumped on to the soiled pillow.

'Pick him up gently and put him on the back seat of the car.' The doctor established that Michael was completely unconscious. 'Careful mind, I don't want you doing any more damage,' he added crisply to the big man who carried Michael out of the house as though he was a sack of potatoes before placing him on the car seat with as much finesse as he could manage.

'There must be no mistakes,' said the blonde woman addressing the doctor through the window of the car.

He turned to look at her and, as he slowly wound down the window, he said abruptly, 'There's too much at stake for me to let anything misfire. After all, you have made your intentions quite clear as to what you would do if things went wrong.'

'Just as long as we both know where we stand,' she said smiling thinly.

The car set off slowly down the drive before halting briefly at the junction with the road. Michael looked as though he was sleeping off a hangover as he lay stretched out on the leather seat, covered by a tartan rug. The doctor cursed as he turned to look at Michael's sprawled body. He had telephoned ahead to the City Asylum and orderlies were waiting when they arrived at the forbidding brick building more akin to a jail than a hospital for the disturbed. Leaving Michael to be taken to a ward on a stretcher, the doctor went into the office to complete the paperwork for his admission.

'He'll need to be with you for the foreseeable future,' he said. 'He's made a pretty nasty mess of himself and I've had to sedate him heavily to avoid him doing any more damage. He's lost a lot of blood and I'm certain that the wound is infected.'

'What's his background?' asked the superintendent.

'I don't know a lot about him but he's got Irish papers and I'm told his name is Michael Brady. His sister tells me he's spent some time in America. He had a bad accident when he fell during a storm on the ship coming over from Ireland, which seemed to result in a major personality disorder.'

'Who's paying?' was the direct enquiry.

'No problem there,' replied the doctor. 'Just send the bills to me and I'll make certain they're attended to promptly. In view of his confused and violent state, the family just want him put away with as little fuss as possible. To me it looks as though he won't see the outside of here for a very long time.'

With that the doctor put on his hat and walked out of the austere building, more than ashamed of what he had been forced to do.

'One day I'll get the bastards on my terms,' he said under his breath, 'and I shall particularly enjoy my revenge on that blonde tart. Now, back to the real world,' he thought, simmering down. 'Let's see if I can do something to help someone for a change.'

27

'Good Heavens, what on earth's worrying you?' asked George as he walked into Emma's office to see her at her desk, her head in her hands.

'I just seem to have made a dreadful mess of everything lately, George,' she sighed. 'I feel so guilty because of all the trouble I've caused over Michael Korsakov. It's a heavy cross to bear. I just hope that I haven't completely lost Natalia's trust.'

'Well, I did warn you to tread carefully,' was his measured reply.

They sat in silence for a moment, George surveying Emma's troubled features.

'It's funny, really,' she said. 'He's a complex personality with so much charm. It's just a pity that he's got such a brooding and vicious side to him which seems to take over at times of stress.'

'I understand how you feel,' he replied. 'That's why your father and I decided to take you off the Korsakov story. The series you started on the war-wounded is becoming quite important to us.'

'Thank you, George,' she replied. 'You're very under-standing.'

'The moral of the story must be never to make the same mistake twice with the Korsakovs,' he said with a twinkle. He got up slowly and, as he walked to the door, he stopped and turned round to face Emma. Looking at her directly, he said carefully, 'I think it's important that you put things right with Lucinda as soon as possible. She's very protective of Natalia.'

'I know, George,' she replied. 'It's weighing very heavily on me and I'm not certain how to make her understand that there was no malice in what I did.'

'If I were you,' he replied, 'I'd simply tell her the truth and say you're sorry. Simple explanations always carry more weight.' With that he was gone, leaving Emma to her thoughts.

For a moment she sat motionless at her desk. She then picked up the pencil that lay before her and rolled it between her fingers. Her pulse quickened and a burning sensation came to her cheeks as she thought in anger and frustration of the mistakes she had made. Suddenly, she grasped the slender shaft and snapped it into two pieces. 'It's no good,' she thought, 'I've got to do something now otherwise it will drive me mad.' Five minutes later she was in a taxi on her way to see Lucinda at Charnley Lodge.

Pearson hurried to find his jacket as the front door bell rang in the servants' quarters. He was surprised to see Emma who rarely, if ever, came home on a weekday afternoon.

'Good afternoon, Miss Emma,' he said. 'I'm sorry to keep you waiting, but you weren't expected.'

'That's all right, Pearson,' she said, taking off her coat and handing it to him, then, 'Where's Mrs Duff?' she asked quickly.

'In the drawing room,' was the reply.

Emma walked deliberately across the hall before gingerly opening the mahogany doors. Lucinda was seated at the writing desk and their eyes met as she looked up.

'I'm sorry to break your concentration,' Emma said softly. 'I do so much want to talk to you if you could spare me a few minutes.'

'Come in and sit down,' said Lucinda giving her a thin smile.

Looking at her stepmother intently, Emma started to explain. 'I know that you think I have been the source of unnecessary worry for Natalia,' she said. 'I can fully appreciate that you have every right to feel that I have let both her and the family down by acting irresponsibly. I hope that you will find it in your heart to forgive me. I still don't quite know what happened. Events just seemed to take control of me.' Her voice trailed off as Lucinda laid down her pen on the blotting paper in front of her.

'I don't think you realise what a dangerous man Michael Korsakov is,' she said looking at Emma. 'He is capable of causing great unhappiness. What I cannot understand is that you must have known how much pain it would cause Natalia.'

'Unfortunately, I can't put the clock back,' said Emma wearily.

'Just promise me you'll never, ever attempt to see that man again.'

'I promise,' said Emma simply. 'I never thought before I acted – it was such a good story.'

'Your father says Michael Korsakov is over here to gather as much information as possible on the *Record* so that when he gets home he can mount a bid for the Albany Group.'

'That could well be so,' Emma replied. 'If he's correct it would affect us all. I think, however, that it's more likely that he's come over to see Natalia again. From what he said he's only interested in her because he feels there's a score to be settled.'

'We'll never fully understand the Russian nobility,' Lucinda said. 'They have deeply ingrained instincts which we regard as rather feudal. They live in a world of fantasy where everything assumes a larger-than-life importance.'

'I know what you mean,' Emma replied.

'It would be dreadful if he did try to take over the Albany Group. Your father would be devastated.'

206

Emma hesitated for a moment. 'There's something else that's bothering me, Lucinda. I could do with a little advice.'

Pleased to be taken into Emma's confidence at last, Lucinda said, 'I'm a good listener. Tell me what's on your mind.'

'Well you know that I have been seeing Randle Baguley. It's not a distant relationship and we do seem to have grown fond of each other.'

Lucinda nodded. 'Go on.'

'It's a bit difficult to say but I thought you and Papa might have realised that I've become very attracted to Randle. This business with Michael Korsakov has only helped me to see things more clearly.'

'And you wonder', Lucinda interrupted, 'how your father will feel about it if you continue seeing each other in the future?'

'Yes, that's right,' Emma replied softly.

'I think I can reassure you that it won't distress him. We've talked about Randle often and he realises that what happened in the past was the kind of accident that could happen to anyone.'

'But it was Mother who died,' protested Emma.

'You, yourself, have made up your mind not to blame anyone, and so has your father. Accept what happened the best way you can. Would your mother want your future happiness spoilt? I think not.'

Lucinda had rarely probed beyond the point that was the line in the sand which separated her and Emma and their past lives before she had married John Duff. There was so much they still had to learn about each other and she hoped that they could now become closer. She had known for some time that Randle Baguley was waiting in the wings to take centre stage in Emma's life and she only hoped that past unhappiness would not reappear to haunt them both.

Furthermore, she understood that Emma's friendship with Randle would not be without problems. Somewhere in the intervening years must still lie guilt over what had happened to Elizabeth Duff that fateful day, and Lucinda knew that Randle would never really know how John viewed him in spite of his forgiving words.

'For pity's sake, Crabtree,' said Randle. 'Don't fuss. It's just something I'm going to have to live with,' he continued, looking away from the elderly manservant as he began another bout of coughing.

'Very good, sir,' came the reply. 'Is there anything further I can get for you?'

'No thank you,' said Randle. 'Just let me know when Miss Duff arrives.'

He was sitting in the comfortable drawing room at Wethersfield Hall, his favourite black labrador, Jimmy, sprawled at his feet. Out of the long Georgian windows he could just see the Welsh hills across the wide expanse of the Cheshire Plain. He turned to look deep into the crackling wood fire that burned strongly in the basket-grate before getting up and walking to the fireplace which was flanked by two bookcases, each crammed with rich leather bindings. On the chimney breast hung a finely carved gilt mirror beneath which several invitations were trapped by a large, alabaster paperweight.

Randle was in low spirits as he had seen nothing of Emma for the last week and it was only at times like this that he realised how much he depended on her. He also brooded on the fact that he had been spared death at the Front, whereas Peter Duff and so many of his contemporaries from school and the county had never returned. The hunting season had just begun and he found it difficult to reconcile himself to the fact that because he had been so badly gassed he would never again enjoy the thrill of a day out with the hunt. Wethersfield was, however, a great consolation to him with its three thousand fertile acres and the elegant Georgian mansion which he had inherited five years ago on the death of his uncle, Sir Edwin Baguley. Since being invalided out of the army he had begun to take quite an interest in the church which was half-hidden from the house by a dense copse. As well as being lord of the manor, he also claimed the right of patronage to St John's, whereby the choice of a new incumbent to the rectory was his alone. He remembered his Uncle Edwin telling him that he might consult the Bishop if he found difficulty in choosing the parson, but not to take too much notice of the old fool.

'Put an advertisement in *Horse & Hound* for a good sporting parson and you'll be sure to get the right man. Tell him the sermon is to be ten minutes and cough loudly and blow your nose if he exceeds the allotted span.'

Randle was smiling to himself as he remembered that conversation just as Emma's car came into sight on the gravelled drive that swept elegantly up to the house.

'Leave the door to me, Crabtree,' he ordered.

'Thank God you're all right. I was worried about you,' he said as he greeted Emma.

'No need,' she said, laughing. 'I just got a bit delayed. You know me.'

He looked at her and then, smiling, he led her by the hand across the hall into the drawing room. Pouring two glasses of Madeira he said, 'I've really been looking forward to seeing you, but first things first. Crabtree insists that dinner is burning to a cinder and cook is having a blue fit.'

Emma laughed.

It had been a struggle but Randle had by now managed to put aside the feelings of guilt that had dogged his relationship with Emma.

'What does your father make of this strange story I've been reading about Michael going missing?' asked Randle as they ate.

'He's not really sure,' replied Emma. 'Michael is such an unpredictable fellow, anything could have happened. He may even have decided to take a few weeks' convalescence and forgotten to tell anyone. It's on the cards that he's upped and gone to London for a while.'

'Seems a bit surprising to me,' said Randle.

'Well, the last I heard', Emma replied, 'was that his colleagues at the *Chronicle* were very concerned about him; they even asked Father and George to help to find him.'

'As far as I'm concerned', Randle said vehemently, 'he can go to hell! I wouldn't lift a finger to help him.'

Natalia always said that the mere mention of his name was enough to spoil any occasion,' Emma said quietly, 'and she was right.'

'I am sorry, Emma,' Randle said reaching for her hand. He realised how insensitive he had been in pursuing the subject. 'I suppose you've heard nothing from Natalia?' he said, trying a lighter tack.

'Well, as a matter of fact Lucinda received a long letter only yesterday. I think she's finding it a bit of an ordeal meeting so many old friends from her childhood. She particularly mentions the Yussoupovs, and a chap called James Ponsonby who is now third secretary at the embassy.'

'Ponsonby's a good fellow; straight as a die,' said Randle.

'Yes, you know Peter and he were best friends at school, and Oxford. It was through him that Peter met Natalia in the first place.'

'I know, you chump. I was at school at the same time but older and in another house, if you remember,' he replied.

They both laughed. Emma paused while she looked at Randle, her eyes brighter.

'I've been to see Lucinda this afternoon,' she said. 'That's why I'm so late.'

'Ah,' said Randle, 'and is everything all right?'

'Yes,' she said, 'it's fine now.' Then she added, 'I talked to her about us.'

'What did she say?' he asked, anxiety showing in his voice.

'Well, it was quite revealing, actually. I had to set the record straight about Michael and an apology was a bit overdue. She accepted it with good grace. So I asked her how Papa felt about you and me.'

'You were treading on dangerous ground, Emma,' he said gravely.

210

'No, not really. Both she and Papa are quite happy about us seeing each other. They feel that the past should not be a millstone round our necks.'

'If only I could be as certain as you are,' he said.

28

'My God, Wigram, what's the matter with you?' boomed Sir Hugo Ballard as he bounced up the long flight of green marble steps to John Duff's office. He had eschewed the elevator, choosing to prove his fitness to his panting, young assistant, Paul Wigram, who had been with the Cheshire Bank for only four years but who had already proved that he had the flair and sound judgement so needed in his profession.

They were greeted by a secretary who informed Duff of their arrival before formally ushering them into his large, panelled office.

The two older men were good friends and had shared a mutual respect and trust over more than thirty years.

'Hope you don't mind, John, but I've brought Wigram along,' said Sir Hugo. 'He's now directly responsible to me for the Albany account.'

John shot a glance at the young man before welcoming him to the meeting and putting him at his ease. 'Glad to have you here, Wigram,' he said cordially. 'Now, Hugo,' he continued impatiently, 'what conclusion have you come to about lending us the money we need to strengthen our position in the marketplace? We still have to resolve the matter of expansion into America. However, most importantly, we have to ward off the unwelcome attention of O'Donnell's and, in particular, Michael Korsakov.'

'How is he, by the way?' interrupted Sir Hugo.

'He's out of hospital but seems to have gone missing for the time being,' said John peevishly, before quickly returning to the matter in hand. 'Now you realise, I'm sure, that we have to grow considerably if we are to protect ourselves from predators like him who seem to have the mistaken idea that we might be on the market.'

'Some take the view, John, that as you no longer have a male heir you will sell the company in the next few years,' replied Sir Hugo.

'Rubbish!' said John. 'Emma is certainly capable of carrying on and already owns twenty-five per cent of the shares, as does Natalia.'

'But they're both women!' Sir Hugo protested. 'And the establishment would give them a very rough time, especially as one just happens to be in Russia.'

'I know what you are driving at,' said John, 'but it's not beyond the bounds of possibility that they will marry soon and then our problem will be solved.'

'You mean the power behind the throne?' asked Sir Hugo, smiling.

'Yes, if you want to put it like that,' said John, showing he was not amused by the direction the conversation was taking. 'Now, down to brass tacks, Hugo. You said at our last meeting that you were putting our case before your fellow directors and that you hoped for a favourable reaction.'

Looking over the top of his horn-rimmed glasses, Sir Hugo began, 'We had our meeting yesterday and I am pleased to be able to tell you that we are prepared to lend you the money, on two conditions.'

John was now listening intently.

'We shall need our loan to be secured either by shares in Albany or by your personal guarantee to the bank.'

'Of course,' said John. 'That's no problem.'

'The other condition of the loan is that Wigram is to sit on your board. It's our opinion that, besides the family members who are there by right, you only have George Gerrard to help you steer what will become a very large ship.'

'I have no objection to that', said John, 'as I am sure that he will have much to contribute. We shall need ideas and energy to help us in the months and years ahead. But what if you decide to enlist?' he added, suddenly eyeing the young man.

Wigram was caught off guard for a moment and flushed before answering, 'I'm afraid, sir, that the army won't have me. I've tried twice to join up but on both occasions I've failed the Medical Board. Apparently recruits are not allowed to have flat feet and asthma. One or the other perhaps, but not both.' For a moment there was an uneasy silence as John collected himself. It was the small things that reminded him of Peter and the hurt was still only just concealed below the surface.

'I understand,' he said softly, looking at the young man kindly. 'Better ask George to come in and meet Wigram,' he added, ringing the bell. 'There isn't any time to lose.'

As they talked further, John had time to study the young man with whom he would be working to expand his empire. 'The classic mould of a city banker,' he thought. 'Probably Eton and Oxbridge with the family estate going to his elder brother.' He knew that the upper classes were rather keen on primogeniture with the second and subsequent sons destined for the City, the Church or the colonies, depending on their aptitude. Quite a strong face, he thought, but a pity about the receding jawline. His cursory examination now completed and well satisfied with his first impression, he looked in the direction of Ballard.

'While we're waiting for George,' he said, 'how are you getting along with my own personal affairs. I don't want Lucinda to face swingeing death duties when I die you know.'

214

Ballard smiled with easy confidence born of years of knowledge that the bank worked with clinical efficiency on the affairs of its leading clients. 'Over to you, Paul,' he said. 'You've been working hard to see to it that the Chancellor gets as little as possible when the time comes.'

Without recourse to his papers, Wigram spelt out the measures he recommended and within a few minutes his carefully reasoned case had impressed his two companions.

'Good planning, Wigram,' said John smiling. 'I think you and I will get along well enough.'

At this point there was a knock on the door which opened to reveal George Gerrard who politely acknowledged Sir Hugo's greeting before being introduced to Wigram. John motioned George to sit down and told him of the bank's decision to finance their new acquisition.

'I'm delighted that we've got the go ahead,' George said. 'It means a lot to all of us, but there's something I think you will all be interested to hear.'

'Go on,' said John impatiently. 'What is it, George?'

'Tom Smith has just given us the latest news on Michael Korsakov. He could well have been abducted by the same Russian group who were thought to have attacked him!'

Two days later John Duff and Paul Wigram were sitting together after dinner at the Savoy. They were deep in conversation after a day spent with Sir Melville Crichton-Buchanan at the Fleet Street offices of the London *Globe*, and all now seemed set for the orderly takeover of that once great paper, now floundering for lack of strong management.

'Give Melville a contract for one year only,' said John to his young colleague. 'He's weak and ineffectual, and I'm only agreeing to put up with him for a short time to help save his face.'

'I agree,' said Paul. 'It's amazing to think that such a nincompoop could have been in sole command since the death of his father last year. I suggest we keep a pretty close eye on him until we can move him somewhere he can't do any more damage. There's something about him I don't trust.'

'His father was a good man,' replied John. 'It was his mother who was a no-good scheming baggage. They say she was very pretty but she led him a dance.' With that John sat back, eyeing Paul. 'What would you do next?' he said after a moment's pause.

'I'd send for George Gerrard immediately,' Paul replied. 'We've got a great opportunity here and George is just the man we can rely on.'

John nodded as Paul continued, 'We need his expertise to help rationalise the new group and get to grips with solving the problems we're bound to encounter in the first month or so.'

'I think you're right. Emma's willing to hold the fort in Liverpool so that the three of us can concentrate on clearing up the mess Melville has made. Anyway, it will be good experience for her,' John said reflectively.

'I agree,' replied Paul. 'She knows the ropes and, after all, she only needs to pick up the telephone if she needs help.'

'You know, Paul, I so much want to see Emma settled,' said John, suddenly adopting a milder tone, 'especially as she's our only child since Peter was killed.'

'From the bank's point of view, it would be very satisfactory,' smiled Paul. 'You remember Sir Hugo's views which he expressed so forcibly at our first meeting in your office. He'll be even better pleased when Natalia marries a suitable Englishman as I know he's worried about her living in Russia.'

John remained silent for a moment before beginning, 'There's a lot to look forward to and a great deal to be done if we're going to be ready for the takeover deadline of the first week in February. Now, Paul, I want you to give me a report as soon as possible on what our rivals in Fleet Street are planning to do to steal our thunder. They're not pleased that a provincial paper is muscling in on what they regard as their personal domain.'

'I'll let you have my thoughts very quickly,' Paul replied.

John liked Paul and enjoyed working with him. He was precise, reliable and courteous, all the attributes John looked for at the boardroom table. At that moment, above all, he needed men like that around him and he was grateful to Hugo for suggesting that Paul should join Albany's board. He knew that Emma and Natalia, both major shareholders in Albany, were at critical points in their lives and that much would depend on them and who they married. He now saw that Hugo Ballard's over-view of the family situation had been entirely correct and, after dinner, he excused himself. 'Just going to my room to make a telephone call,' he said. 'Get yourself another brandy, Paul.'

John's room at the Savoy overlooked the river. It was spacious and comfortable and he knew why Lucinda enjoyed staying there with him. He missed her now and placed a call to her through the operator. 'Sefton Park two three two, please,' he said. After a moment's pause there was a click and the ringing tones began.

Lucinda answered. 'Oh! John, I'm so pleased you rang,' she started. 'I was going to telephone you but I thought you'd be out for dinner.'

'What is it, Cinny?' he asked, calling her by the name he used when the two of them were alone.

'Well, I just hope you'll be pleased,' she said. 'Randle has asked Emma to marry him. He wants to come and ask your permission.'

There was a long silence.

'Are you still there, John?' she asked.

'Yes, yes. I was just thinking,' he replied. 'Although I've been expecting the news, it's still come as a bit of a shock. Strangely enough I can still see the expression on the poor boy's face that terrible day when Elizabeth died. He looked like a ghost.'

'Marriage is difficult enough without memories like that,' Lucinda replied softly.

'I just hope he knows that I don't hold him responsible.'

'Don't worry, I told Emma your views when she asked me.

They must have talked about it more often than I like to think of.'

'I'm genuinely sorry it's been such a burden for them,' said John, 'but you have to agree it's a very strange set of circumstances. All I do know is that he's not after Emma for her money. His Uncle Edwin left him a very rich young man.'

'Money's not everything.'

'I know, Cinny, but Emma holds a large block of Albany shares and it's quite important for all of us to trust the man she marries, especially as Natalia's future is so uncertain.'

'I hope that Michael Korsakov doesn't try to make trouble, especially as you've just bought the *Globe* which he will see as a move to block his ambitions,' she remarked.

'It's possible but just let him try,' said John angrily. 'I don't think there is any worry on that score as he seems to have gone misssing. I've really had quite enough of that unpleasant young man, particularly as his activities have temporarily thwarted our plans to expand into America. Now don't forget to give Emma my love.'

29

'Maybe next week we'll have the gold caps off his teeth,' said the nurse as Michael lay weak and delirious.

'I'll bet they're worth a pretty penny,' his companion said grinning.

The ward in which Michael found himself was sparse and cold with a lofty ceiling and long, barred windows. All around him he could hear the grunts, groans and moans of the insane. It seemed like some dreadful dream and, for a moment, he wondered if he was dead and in the land of lost souls. As the long days dragged by he was conscious of little except the drugged world in which he was imprisoned. Fever racked his body and he tossed and turned, fighting violently against the restraints that confined him to his bed. The sweet stench of urine was everywhere and many of the patients were left in their soiled bedclothes for hours to punish them for their miserable lapses. It was a hell which Michael had only experienced before in his worst nightmares, but this time it was ten times more horrible because it was a dream with no easy awakening. He could now just focus on the white-coated doctor, accompanied by a male nurse, who was preparing him for another injection.

'This one's got a bit of a past,' said the doctor. 'Even his family have disowned him.'

'Pity we didn't get him put in prison,' replied the nurse. 'He'd be better off in a gang breaking stones on Dartmoor.'

'He's too violent for that. From what we can gather he tried to kill a man.'

Michael bit hard on the rough sheet as he waited nervously for the hypodermic needle to pierce his flesh and for the fluid he feared so much to gain control of his mind and body. He knew that in seconds he would be reduced to a vegetable again with no free will. Hard as he tried to resist, a wave of nothingness washed over him and he retreated into himself.

'That should make certain he doesn't give us any trouble,' said the doctor turning to the nurse. 'Anyhow, he's better off sedated until those wounds heal properly and he's fit to join the others. Let me know if he gives any more trouble.'

'You can move him now, nurse.'

The words brought Michael some small ray of hope. He had pieced together the events leading up to him being brought to the City Asylum but he knew he had little or no chance of escape. 'I don't want to die here,' he thought to himself as he was taken, with scant respect, to the secure wing in which he was now to be imprisoned. He soon realised it contained the criminally insane and habitually violent who were restrained by all manner of formidable contraptions when not sedated. The treatment was designed to stop the most violent from hurting themselves or those who looked after them, and in such conditions it was almost impossible to prevent the orderlies from becoming brutalised themselves by continual assaults.

'My name is not Michael Brady,' he would say over and over again to anyone who would listen. 'I'm Count Michael Korsakov and I demand to see the superintendent.'

'And I'm the Queen of bloody Sheba,' was the reply he most often received although usually he was simply ignored.

Michael had by now stopped arguing about his identity. For the most part he kept a sullen silence until his pent-up rage and frustration boiled over. However, the moment he started to cause trouble, the staff had no hesitation in confining him a straightjacket until he calmed down.

The punishment was even worse than he expected and it took four strong men to subdue him sufficiently to get the jacket in place. This was achieved by spreading his arms which were then placed in the sleeves of the jacket before they were folded across his body and strapped up from behind into a tight bundle. While this was going on everything within him fought against the humiliation he was enduring, and he abandoned himself to formidable bouts of rage.

'You'll pay for this,' he would yell. 'I'll have every one of you brought before the courts. You don't know what you're doing.'

At other times he would be placed, screaming obscenities, in a padded cell where he would be kept for a day or more. He hated this punishment more than anything. The eerie sound-proofed chamber, often smeared with excrement, was frequently used by those with schizophrenia, mania or terminal syphilis.

'Dear God', he said between his tears, 'have mercy on me.' It was something he had frequently heard Tamara say and he now repeated it over and over again.

For the first time in his life he pondered on the meaning of life and the existence of God, and he came face to face with the possibility of death. At moments like these he seemed to lose contact with reality as wave after wave of blinding rage swept over him. Eventually, when he was unable to struggle further, he subsided into limp exhaustion with rivulets of sweat running down his forehead and into his eyes, stinging them.

Unwisely, he now began provoking the orderlies with crude insults. As a consequence, certain of them singled him out for special punishments which included having to stand under a cold shower for long periods until he felt he could take it no more. On these desperate occasions his mind went back to his childhood days in Russia with Tamara and he cursed her for bringing him into such a world. Human nature, he decided, was equally unpleasant if you were five or twenty-five.

It was only at night that he could begin to gather his thoughts. When he looked back he could hardly believe it was only a few short years ago that he had defiantly drawn up his blueprint for life and shown it to Hal.

'I've hardly cleared the first hurdle before I've fallen flat on my face,' he thought, cursing his arrogance.

The situation he now found himself in was so unexpected and alien that, for the first time in his life, he was genuinely frightened and hardly dared think what the future held. He knew one thing for certain and that was that he would rather die than spend the rest of his life locked away in this terrible place. It therefore came as a relief when he was prescribed mild sedatives which held him in a semi-soporific state. He knew he needed something to dull his senses otherwise he might very well have surrendered his reason and joined the tormented souls whose company he was forced to share. Their screams and low moans now hardly crossed the threshold of his consciousness and all he saw was a shadowy world of figures.

Occasionally he let his mind drift back to the happier days of his boyhood with Tamara and Hal in New York and Long Island. However, most times darker dreams would disturb him. One of them came to him over and over again, with monotonous regularity. He dreamed he was floating and could see the bulk of a great liner slipping beneath the waves. He was desperately trying to swim to a lifeboat but, when he got near, the occupants beat him off with their oars. He could clearly see Natalia in the boat imploring them to row away and leave him to drown. He would invariably wake up, wet with sweat, his heart throbbing.

In this state of utter confusion the days merged one into

another and he almost gave up hope of ever seeing the outside world again. It seemed so unfair that help was just a few miles away while he existed in such stinking surroundings with life's criminally insane flotsam and jetsam.

'Why in Heaven's name doesn't someone get me out of here,' he thought bitterly. 'What the hell are Dean and Hal doing? They owe everything to Mother and me.'

Then the realisation of his fate finally came over him like a dark cloud. 'If only I hadn't covered my tracks so carefully,' he thought.

The reality that in under a year he would be presumed dead, on his own instructions, if he didn't make contact with someone from the outside, left him cold with fear. He buried his head in the pillow in frustration at the hopelessness of his situation.

30

'Gentlemen, we have important matters to discuss this morning,' said Stewart Armstrong as he called to order the monthly board meeting of Frinksteins Bank. 'I know there has been much speculation recently about the problems faced by O'Donnell's and the disappearance of Michael Korsakov in particular. That is why I have placed it at the top of our agenda. Some of the speculation about Count Korsakov has got out of hand. As you probably know there are wild rumours circulating that he has either been the victim of the Mafia or that he has killed a man in Britain and is on the run. It's just the sort of thing that can be very damaging for O'Donnell's now they are under siege after the revelations of fraud perpetrated by their former vice-president, which leaked out like gas from a sewer.'

Stewart now took his colleagues through the background of the case and read out a statement from Sam Goldman setting out the intricacies of the action being pursued by the State against Davis and Eisner. He went on to indicate that the Midland Bank in Liverpool had advised him that they were holding Michael's will and various other instructions to be opened in the event of his death.

'Luckily, gentlemen,' said Stewart clearing his throat, 'Michael Korsakov had the good sense to vest his voting rights in O'Donnell's in Sam Goldman. In essence, Sam and Dean control the company now, and with them in charge we stand a good chance of retrieving the situation. To pull the rug out now would be unnecessary and foolish.'

'It's a hard world out there,' boomed Charles Lassiter from behind a blue haze of cigar smoke. 'You've seen that the Chronicle's rivals, sensing that they have difficulties, have shaved their prices, hoping to put them to the sword.'

'Yes I know that there's a war raging now among the mass circulation papers but Dean and Sam have called in a few favours from influential friends and the increase in advertising revenue is keeping them afloat temporarily.'

'Come on, Stewart,' said Charles hoarsely. 'It's all right in the short term but it can't keep them alive indefinitely.'

This point was greeted by a ripple of agreement among the other members sitting around the polished table and Stewart knew that he must make a concession to keep the hounds at bay.

'I propose to write to Dean explaining that we are very concerned about the present situation and that, as a condition of renewing O'Donnell's overdraft at the present limit of one million dollars, we are insisting that the speculative land holdings acquired for the company some thirty years ago by Joe O'Donnell be sold. That should raise at least seven hundred and fifty thousand dollars at current market prices and take the pressure off everyone.'

'Supposing he doesn't agree?' said Charles. 'I know that Sam Goldman would be dead against selling those fine tracts of land in Texas at the moment as they are increasing in value almost by the day. I also know that they're waiting for a geological survey to ascertain if there's oil in the ground they own near Houston in Brazoria County, west of the Brazos River. Let's not be too hasty, gentlemen, there is a certain public sympathy for the Chronicle which will, I dare say, increase as the facts come out in the court case.'

'We do, however, have a duty to our shareholders, need I remind you,' said Stewart. 'But, having said that, I have to declare a sympathy with Dean who, you all know, is a great friend of mine as well as controlling a fine company which has grown with the bank over the years.'

'I know you, as Chairman, have to be seen to be looking after the best interests of the bank,' said Charles, eyeing Stewart, 'but none of us want to take advantage of old friends so let's see how they envisage increasing their collateral. Give them seven days' grace to come up with an alternative suggestion and, if we are not satisfied, then we shall have to act immediately to protect our position.'

'Thank you, gentlemen,' said Stewart. 'I will pass on your views to the board of O'Donnell's. Now, if we can move on to the next item on the agenda . . .'

After the meeting was concluded, Stewart telephoned Dean.

'I'd like to come over and see you immediately, if possible,' he said. 'There's a lot to discuss.'

'Give me an hour, Stewart, and I'll try to have Sam Goldman here as well,' Dean replied, sensing that there was trouble afoot.

There were few smiles when Dean led the assembled party from his office to the boardroom at O'Donnell's. As he entered the room, he immediately felt that the piercing eyes of Joe O'Donnell were looking at him from the gilt-framed portrait which hung over the mantelpiece. He was glad that Sam was there as they sat down and waited for Stewart to say his piece.

The ensuing discussion was tough and uncompromising and was only concluded when it was agreed that Dean and Sam would attempt to come up with a plan that would satisfy Frinksteins without selling the Texas tract.

'That land has enormous potential', said Sam, 'and we must do everything to hold on to it.'

'I understand your position, Sam,' replied Stewart gravely, 'but you have to understand that I am under considerable pressure from my board. Believe me, we want you to succeed.'

'Thank you, Stewart,' said Dean. 'We also know you have to be seen to do your duty.'

After a moment's pause, Dean began, 'It might serve some useful purpose if we now asked Hal to join us just in case he might have any thoughts about Michael's whereabouts.'

'Good idea,' replied Stewart. 'If anyone knows how Michael's mind works then Hal's our man. I'll ask him to come up right away.'

Within a few minutes the sprightly figure of Hal entered and sat opposite them. His new position as senior feature writer was obviously suiting him and he beamed as he asked, 'What can I do for you, gentlemen?'

'As you know, Michael's gone missing after discharging himself from hospital,' said Dean sternly. 'We wondered if you could help us to think where he might have gone?'

'I'll do all I can but it's a bit of a mystery. Before that terrible stabbing I received a letter from him telling me about his meeting with Emma Duff. It seems that he had become very interested in her and then, for some reason, things turned sour,' replied Hal thoughtfully. 'That might have something to do with it. Women have always been his downfall. I remember when he was sixteen . . .'

'Yes, yes, Hal,' snapped Dean impatiently. 'We know all about that. What we want to know is if you have any clues about where he might be heading?'

'In a word, no,' Hal replied. 'If, however, I was to make an educated guess, I think there is an outside chance that he'll be making his way to Russia. On the other hand, he might try to join a fighting unit of the British Army if they would have him.'

'My guess is the former,' said Dean, 'particularly as Natalia Orlofski is now in Russia, according to information I've just received from John Duff at the *Record* in Liverpool.'

'Yes,' replied Hal. 'He never fully overcame the strange obsession he had about her. If I were you I would alert our embassy in Petrograd to keep an eye out for Michael. Our ambassador is George Marye who I remember from way back. Would you like me to contact him?'

'Thanks, Hal,' said Dean thoughtfully. 'That would be very helpful.'

During the following week Dean had time to appreciate fully the obstacles that they would have to surmount if O'Donnell's was to survive. In the past, when things had gone wrong, they had always seemed to lead a charmed life, but this time it looked as though fate had dealt them a dangerous hand. One afternoon, as Sam sat by him, he gazed down from his office window into windswept Franklin Square.

'Nothing seems to have gone right since Tamara's death,' he said, pacing up and down. 'I've had a call from Stewart at the bank this morning, and he tells me that he can't give us any more time. They insist that the land in Brazoria County be put on the market now that the geological reports are completed.'

'I hear they're very good,' said Sam, 'and that there are already one or two big fish interested.'

'That's not the point,' snapped Dean. 'I was hoping that we might have got away with it by selling the Texas hill country land at Wimberley, but so far we've only had one buyer come forward, and he's offering about half of what it's worth. Much as I dislike him, I wish Michael was here. That land was bought by his stepfather and it's his inheritance.'

'Come on, Dean,' said Sam. 'Are you really telling me that Michael cares a fig about some wild land in Texas? He's never seen the place and I refuse to believe he's got any sentimental attachment to it.'

'You misunderstand me, Sam,' said Dean impatiently. 'I'm just trying to do things as Tamara would have wished. She would have been really cut up if she'd been here seeing us with no option but to sell,' he continued.

'The land adjoining ours, west of the Brazos River at Damon Mound, came into production last year, and news

228

has travelled fast about the result of our geological surveys,' said Sam, making his point convincingly. 'The Humble Oil Company has already got wind of our difficulties. The nationwide reporting of the Davis and Eisner fraud case has put us under the spotlight. They will probably be ready with their bid the moment we put the land on the market.'

'Well, it goes against the grain,' said Dean, 'but as you have so ably pointed out, we have no options left.'

'Well, since we're forced by circumstance to agree, let's get it over with by telephoning Stewart,' suggested Sam. 'Tell him we'll come over tomorrow to sign the necessary papers to secure our overdraft formally until the land is sold.'

'There's little else we can do. The only consolation is that we're not selling off parts of our core business,' said Dean dejectedly. 'It's just possible I still might have an ace up my sleeve', he continued, brightening, 'as I'm almost at the point where I intend to seek a meeting with Bernstorff at the German Embassy. It will be interesting to see just how much pressure I can put on him. There's mounting evidence directly linking the embassy with allegations of espionage and sabotage against this country that would make the Dumba scandal seem very small beer.'

'You realise that revelations of that sort could precipitate the entry of the United States into the war with all its consequences?' said Sam gravely.

'I would, naturally, reveal my hand to the State Department before taking any action that might be against the national interest,' replied Dean. 'If you remember, Sam, it is this paper's declared policy to crusade for us to join the Allies. If we can achieve that it will shorten the war and save so many lives. We may even have our money returned legally through government channels when the German assets in this country are frozen.'

'You're playing with fire, Dean, at a difficult time in O'Donnell's fortunes,' came the stern warning. 'It's a very dangerous game and the Germans know the stakes are high.'

'Don't worry, Sam, I'll let you know when I'm ready to

show my hand,' said Dean, gathering up the papers on his desk and placing them in a neat pile. 'I sure appreciate your help, Sam,' he said. 'I don't know how all this will end, but you've certainly proved your loyalty to the company.'

Sam smiled, 'Just pleased to be of service.'

Sam waited as Dean called Josh to his office. He knew that, as chief financial officer, he was having a tough time dealing with O'Donnell's suppliers. He had had little option but to delay payment to many of them, a situation which they bore stoically at first, although panic soon spread as rumours abounded of O'Donnell's insolvency. Josh faced an added difficulty as the major newsprint suppliers were now asking for cash on delivery instead of the usual, generous credit terms that had applied before.

'We've got to do something to restore confidence in our finances if we're going to brazen this mess out,' he said looking wearily at Dean. 'There are now major suppliers who aren't giving us any credit at all, let alone our usual thirty days. We can't last out for more than another three weeks at this rate unless Frinksteins are prepared to raise our borrowing limit substantially.'

'I'm hoping to have some good news within the next day or so,' said Dean. 'Sam and I are doing all we can to hurry through the deal with Humble Oil but they know the longer they keep us waiting the more vulnerable we become. If only we could make contact with Michael. I'm sure he would agree to allow his stepfather's trust fund to be put at the company's disposal. It would see us over this short-term problem until the oil deal is concluded.'

'That would give us the break we need,' said Josh, 'but the chances of finding him seem pretty remote.'

'I've got the embassy doing all they can,' said Dean, 'and Sloan at the Midland Bank in Liverpool is being very helpful but it's a forlorn hope. He just seems to have disappeared into thin air. As a last-ditch stand we've even contacted our embassy in Petrograd to see if he's followed Natalia Orlofski.'

'I've stopped believing in miracles this week,' said Josh wearily. He leaned forward and pushed a sheet of figures across Dean's desk. 'You and Sam did a great job in increasing advertising revenues but I'm afraid they've slumped below normal levels again and we're simply not generating enough cash to keep up with our short-term repayments.'

Dean grunted his acknowledgement impatiently, 'I know it's a pretty dire situation. However, while you're both here I'll telephone our agent in Texas to see if he's got any news,' he said, picking up the receiver and asking the operator to put him through to Joe Dunlop of Brink and Co. 'What's the latest position, Joe?' he asked as the line crackled ominously.

'I'm afraid I've got some bad news, sir.'

'Come on then, tell me the worst.'

'Humble says that they're not satisfied with the geologicals we've had done', he began, 'and they want their own people to undertake an independent survey.'

'How long will that take?' said Dean, looking across at Josh, his face saying it all.

'Anything up to six weeks, depending on how soon they can start. From what I gather, the adjoining areas have been producing well, but they want to be absolutely certain of the potential of the land they're buying.'

'They've never raised this before,' said Dean. 'It's obviously a delaying tactic to see if we'll drop the price. Tell them we're not playing that game, Joe. Either they buy at the agreed price or we sell elsewhere.'

With that he put down the telephone and explained the gist of what he had been told to Sam and Josh.

'In the circumstances I'll go along with you,' said Sam carefully. 'There are bound to be other buyers and, if you and Josh agree, I'll go to Houston at once and start negotiating. It's a hell of a risk but I know we can rely on Stewart and the board of Frinksteins to help us. They'll see the sense in what we are doing. After all, it's in everybody's interest that the land makes its full price in a rising market. How long can we hang on before they set the wolves on us?'

'Three weeks, Sam, at the very most a month,' said Dean. 'Josh is doing his utmost to keep things on an even keel here and I'm hoping to get Frinksteins to do what they can to increase confidence in the City by making encouraging noises about our future prospects.'

'I've already heard that Randolph Hearst is waiting in the wings to pick up the pieces,' said Sam, 'so we've got to pull a few rabbits out of the hat. I'll tell you the situation when I get to Texas and find out how the land lies.'

31

'May the Great God of All the Russias bless you, Princess,' said Yuri as he greeted Natalia at the railway halt. 'We have never forgotten you,' he said, tears welling up in his eyes as he knelt before her.

'Dear Yuri, it's so good to see you, but please get up,' she said. 'I am no longer coming to Ivanhov as an Orlofski and all that that used to mean, but as a nurse.'

'It's terrible at the castle now, Princess, I just hope you won't be too upset,' Yuri said looking downcast, 'but we still have Sasha,' he continued, pointing proudly to one of the three grey horses harnessed to the sleigh. 'He's nineteen but can still trot with the young ones.'

As she sat behind Yuri's bear-like figure for the twenty-mile journey to Ivanhov, Natalia was inwardly dreading seeing the castle again. She knew it would be stripped of its furniture and paintings but she consoled herself with the knowledge that, thankfully, the family silver had been taken into the care of Count Freedericksz in Petrograd. She felt many mixed emotions as they sped past the great gates and down the familiar drive to the massive front door.

An old, stooping man came forward to greet her as she

alighted from the sleigh and, in spite of the years that had passed, she clearly recognised him as Dr Kuropatkin.

'Good afternoon, Princess,' he said gravely. 'I'm sorry that I have to welcome you back to Ivanhov in such circumstances.'

She smiled and embraced him as she blinked back the tears. 'I heard from the Empress that you're in charge,' she said, regaining her composure. 'It's like old times seeing you again.'

'We're so desperately short-staffed here, Princess,' he said, 'and, to make it worse, last week they took my senior nursing staff to the field hospital at the Front. I'm afraid that we are working under the greatest pressure.'

'I will do what I can,' she replied, fixing her brown eyes on him, 'but please realise that I have very limited experience of nursing.'

'But you have the Orlofski name, Princess, and the village girls, who do such wonderful work here, will respect you.'

As they walked across the huge entrance hall with its blazing fire, Natalia put aside memories of her childhood. The doctor led her up the familiar wide stone staircase to a small room in the west tower.

'I deeply regret that you cannot have your own room, Princess, but we have ten wounded men in there and it would be impossible to move them.'

'I understand,' she said. 'Give me a moment and I will join you downstairs and you can show me what my duties are.'

'Very well, Princess,' he said, shutting the great oak door behind him.

In the space of a week Natalia had well nigh accomplished the impossible. Owing to the dire circumstances that existed at the hospital, Dr Kuropatkin had little option but to give her the role of administrator. It was a masterstroke and lifted the spirits of both staff and patients who all loved having an Orlofski back at the castle and in authority.

'It's wonderful to see her with the wounded,' wrote the

doctor in his report to the Empress. 'They seem to gain so much courage just from her presence. Many cry out for her to come close to them and she holds their outstretched hands with such tenderness. It's often the final blessing they receive from this side of the grave, and it helps them to face the final hurdle more peacefully.'

It therefore came as no great surprise to the doctor when, during the following month, he received a letter from Count Freedericksz. 'The Empress has commanded me to advise you that she graciously intends to visit her hospital at Ivanhov. Father Gregory Rasputin will accompany Her Royal Highness and she will be attended by Anna Vyrubova.'

Natalia accepted the news with no outward sign of emotion. Count Freedericksz had already written to tell her that such a visitation was in the wind, advising her that he would do all he could to prevent the Empress from bringing Rasputin. However, he held out little hope of this as Rasputin could do no wrong in the Empress's eyes at the moment as she maintained that he had saved the life of the Tsarevitch. From the start, James had advised Natalia to keep her distance from Anna Vyrubova and Natalia knew this to be sensible as the last thing she wanted was for Rasputin to give his blessing to the staff and patients.

The following morning she received a letter in the Empress's rounded hand, advising her that: 'I will be bringing Our Friend together with Anna to see the dedicated work of your staff.'

Natalia felt a chill of apprehension as she put the letter down. She was near to panic but tried to keep calm as she braced herself for what she knew would be the greatest ordeal she had had to face since returning to Russia.

On the day before the imperial visit, Natalia telephoned the British Embassy and waited impatiently until the operator put through her call to James's office. 'I just had to speak to you,' she said in a hoarse whisper. 'As you know, the Empress, with Anna Vyrubova and Rasputin, is visiting the hospital tomorrow and I'm not sure if I can go through with it.'

James sensed the apprehension in her voice. 'Just calm down,' he said. 'You must use this opportunity to prove to yourself that you've overcome the ghosts that have dogged you since childhood. You mustn't let Rasputin see even the smallest trace of fear or anger in your eyes.'

'That's all very well, James,' she replied, 'but I don't quite know how I would cope if I was left alone with him.'

'Just make sure that one of your nurses remains near you at all times. You've simply got to go through with it. You would betray everything your family has stood for over the years if you ducked out now.'

At three o'clock precisely, the Empress, accompanied by Anna Vyrubova and Rasputin, passed through the gates leading to the hospital. After a final check with Dr Kuropatkin that everything was in order, Natalia had assembled the nursing staff by the entrance to the echoing great hall of Ivanhov. When the Empress's entourage came into sight, she drew her cloak round her and ventured out with the doctor into the freezing cold afternoon. The Empress and Anna travelled in the first car while Rasputin travelled with court officials in the second.

Natalia now stepped forward and made a deep curtesy to the Empress before introducing Dr Kuropatkin. Rasputin, meanwhile, had jumped out of the second car. He looked unkempt, his long hair hanging over his shoulders as he helped his crippled friend into the wheelchair that had been provided for her. Once Anna was in the chair he pushed her over to where they were standing.

Natalia wondered what it would be like to come face to face with those famous blue-grey eyes and she could feel herself tremble as she lifted her gaze and faced Rasputin.

Anna Vyrubova was the first to speak, 'I don't think you have met Princess Orlofski who is doing such a wonderful job here?'

Rasputin stepped forward.

'My God, he's going to kiss my hand,' Natalia thought in horror.

Seeming to sense her apprehension, Rasputin stopped in mid-action and, instead, released her hand and made the sign of the cross, thus disguising his intended action. 'Such acute awareness,' she thought, admiring his quick reflexes. She knew now that she was going to be able to handle the situation and, her courage bolstered, she acknowledged him with dignity.

'Good afternoon, Father,' she said.

'Blessings be upon you, my child,' he replied simply, his eyes fixed on hers.

Quickly returning to the Empress's side, Natalia said quietly, 'It's cold here, Your Majesty, let me take you inside.'

'Thank you, Natalia. I've heard so much about your good work from Dr Kuropatkin that I'm anxious to see with my own eyes what you are doing.'

'It's an uphill struggle,' Natalia replied. 'First of all you must meet the nurses. They're all from the village and I've known them since we were children.'

While this conversation was taking place, Natalia could feel Anna's eyes watching her every movement from the wheelchair. The presentation completed, they started their formal tour of inspection of the wards where the party was received with a reverent silence by the patients. Natalia could see that they viewed Rasputin with a mixture of fear and suspicion as he walked past the rows of beds, intoning prayers in a low voice. A few held out their hands and he went to them, bending low to deliver words of divine inspiration. Anna's eyes followed him everywhere and she could not disguise her admiration of the man she had brought to such prominence through her influence with the Imperial Family.

Natalia remained impassive but polite. She could now see signs that Rasputin's initial relaxed cordiality was turning to boredom. As they made their slow progress from ward to ward, it became increasingly clear that the party had seen enough and they should return to the great hall. Rasputin now recovered his good spirits. Looking directly at Natalia, he began a long dissertation on divine healing. 'Your doctors should not always cling to conventional medicine,' he argued. 'I have recently advised the Tsar to consult the great Tibetan herbalist, Batmaef, and he has already done so much for His Imperial Majesty with herbal treatments.'

'It's not so much herbs they need here, Father, but basic things like amputations and more drugs to combat infections.'

'True, my child,' he said, 'but never turn your back on the power of the Holy Spirit.'

'God is never far from us here, Father,' Natalia said defensively.

She could see that Anna was taking a great interest in the conversation. She had been unusually silent for the last few minutes, before interrupting. 'I must congratulate you, Princess, on the smooth running of the hospital. I personally recommended that the Empress should come as soon as her duties permitted and see your good work for herself.'

'Dr Kuropatkin and I are deeply honoured,' Natalia replied.

Rasputin now stepped forward and took her hand again. She felt the touch of the delicate smoothness of his white flesh with revulsion. 'You must always feel free to come and see me if anything troubles you, my child.'

'Thank you, Father,' she answered, quickly collecting herself, 'but my heart and mind are at peace with God.'

'It must please you to see your former home used as a state hospital for the wounded.'

Natalia knew the first carefully worded challenge had been laid down. 'It pleases me that I can serve my countrymen here,' she said, 'but you, of all people, know the injustices and deceits of the past.'

'Humility is the path to godliness, my child,' he said, smiling. 'That is the great lesson I preach to all who listen.'

'I prefer to believe that taking pride in the family and the noble traditions of service is the way, Father,' she said returning his gaze, anger now welling up inside her.

'We shall see very soon who is right, Natalia. Now we must not keep the Empress waiting.'

Natalia was strangely composed after they had left. 'Now let's get back to work,' she said smiling at the awestruck staff who were still excited and keyed up by the events of the day. She thanked Dr Kuropatkin and returned to her office where she put through a call to James at the British Embassy.

'How did you cope?' he asked anxiously.

'Better than I thought I would.'

'Was there any trouble with Rasputin?'

'No more than I expected,' she replied. 'He tried to lecture me on Ivanhov but I wasn't going to let him get away with it.'

'Good for you,' said James. 'By all accounts he can be pretty persuasive when he wants to be.'

'It's his eyes, James. They seem to light up like fire when he looks at you. He's hard to make out – a strange mixture of profanity and piety.'

'You may be interested to hear that the gossip now going around the city is that he is a German agent who is pulling the strings in concert with a German-born Empress.'

'The Empress would never allow such a thing,' said Natalia defensively.

'Perhaps not, but you can't stop people talking. I also meant to tell you that George Marye, the American Ambassador, was asking us if we had any ideas on where Michael Korsakov has got to.'

'What did you tell him?'

'Nothing,' was the firm reply.

32

'There's an important message for you, Mr Goldman,' said the clerk as Sam signed the register on his arrival at the Rice Hotel in Houston.

Taking the envelope, Sam opened it expectantly. Although tired after his long journey, he could feel the adrenalin pumping as he read the request from the Stevens Oil Company to enter into negotiations over the tract of land near Damon Mound.

Once Sam had showered in his room on the seventh floor, he came down to the lobby and put through a call to Lee Stevens.

'That you, Mr Stevens?' he began.

'Yessir, sure is,' came the jaunty reply.

'This is Sam Goldman from New York.'

'You got my note at the hotel, I hope?' Stevens said.

'Yes, that's why I'm calling you. Can we meet tomorrow?'

'Yep, sure can.'

'What time?' asked Sam.

'How about ten o'clock at my offices at the intersection of Main and McKinney?'

'That'll do fine.'

Sam knew that Stevens and Humble were in fierce competition to exploit the oil-rich lands in Brazoria County, but he also knew that Stevens was small in comparison with his rival. That evening in his room Sam studied the brief on the oil companies operating around Houston that Frinksteins had prepared for him, and he was pleased to see that Stevens was highly rated as a medium-sized independent operator.

The following morning it took him fifteen minutes to get to Stevens's office by cab and he heard the nearby clock strike ten as he entered the building. Stevens was a bluff, amicable giant dressed like a cowboy with a stetson hat and alligator-skin boots. His office reflected his down-to-earth approach with its massive oak furniture. The place fascinated Sam after the elegant grandeur of his own city office suite.

'Hear you've got some land for sale near the Humble field in Brazoria County,' Stevens started. 'We'd sure like to do business with you if we can work out a deal. What prices are you asking?'

'We're looking for offers in the region of eight hundred and fifty thousand dollars,' said Sam. 'The geologicals are excellent and the field should be very productive if exploited correctly.'

'Heard that Humble Oil are giving you a hard time,' Stevens said looking at Sam. 'Now I hear that you need the money real bad so I've a proposition that may help both of us.'

'Let's hear what you have in mind, Mr Stevens,' said Sam sitting back in his chair and clasping his fingers together.

'Just call me Lee,' boomed the giant. 'Now I reckoned on offering you a deal that would give you five hundred thousand dollars now and a thirty per cent royalty on every barrel of oil produced from this field. We're a relatively small company and it will be difficult to persuade our bankers to lend us the money to purchase the field outright. The way I'm proposing you get your cake and also get to eat some of it,' he added, smiling. 'We're told in Texas that Frinksteins are flexible and know the oil business. They should be happy to have the security of the future income from a field based on the geologicals they've seen.' Sam nodded as he continued, 'Don't forget it was Eastern investors who helped Captain Lucas bring in that oil gusher at Spindletop Springs south of Beaumont City in nineteen hundred and one. You probably know that's how Frinksteins accumulated their expertise in the oil business.'

'It's an interesting proposition,' said Sam, 'but my instructions are that we must have six hundred thousand dollars immediately to reduce our borrowings. If you can raise that we might consider being flexible on our future royalties. How soon, anyway, do you see the field producing?'

'We should be in business in nine months to a year, depending on the luck of the draw,' said Lee.

'I'll have to contact New York,' said Sam carefully. With that, Lee poured out two huge glasses of bourbon. 'I know it's a bit premature,' he said, 'but let's drink to a profitable future. You never know, I might even find time to come up east and see you fancy Yankees one day.'

Sam downed the bourbon with difficulty. It wasn't his drink. Over the years he had developed a taste for Scotch whisky and it seemed harsh in comparison. 'I'm hopeful we may be able to do business, Lee,' he said carefully, 'but it all depends on my colleagues in New York. For my part I shall recommend that we thrash out an agreement that is fair to both parties.'

'That will suit me, Sam, just as long as you don't ask me to find too much extra cash. I've been straight with you, mind, so if we're going to have to get along as partners, we might as well get off on the right foot.'

'We're just as anxious to get things settled,' said Sam, 'so let me see what comments my colleagues have to make.'

With that Lee grasped Sam by the hand nearly breaking it in his vice-like grip. 'Stevens may not be the biggest,' he said with pride, 'but by hell we're going to be the best oil company in Texas. Now, let's go down and look at this land. We can talk in my car.'

That evening, tired and dusty, Sam arrived back at the Rice Hotel at six-thirty feeling strangely elated by his encounter with Stevens. He picked up the telephone and was soon speaking to Dean.

'How did it go, Sam?' was the urgent enquiry.

'It was a useful meeting. With Frinksteins' approval I think we might have a deal that could resolve our short-term financial difficulties and give us a good income from the fields in future.' Sam went on to explain Lee's proposal and Dean listened with interest. 'It's my feeling', he continued, 'that we can push them to six hundred thousand dollars and thirty cents a barrel. I would recommend we go for it, but I realise that Stewart needs to agree to it first.'

'I can't see it being a problem, Sam. Get back to Stevens tomorrow morning and work on the deal. I'll try and make sure Frinksteins don't raise any objections.'

'Now you're certain you don't want to take further advice before making a decision?' asked Sam.

'First impressions are important, I've always said,' replied Dean, 'and I trust your judgement. I'm glad you think Stevens would make a good partner. Looks like Humble Oil have missed the boat.'

'It may be one deal they regret passing over,' said Sam.

'You did a great job for us in Houston,' said Dean shaking Sam by the hand as he walked jauntily into his office at O'Donnell's two days later.

'In retrospect, I really enjoyed the challenge,' Sam replied grinning. 'Lee Stevens is quite a character and at one stage I almost despaired of prising over half a million dollars out of him let alone thirty cents a barrel as well. It sure helped having Stewart's assistance and Frinksteins' knowhow behind us, as I've no real experience of these complicated oil deals.'

'I don't think any of us can claim to know much about the oil business,' replied Dean, 'but Stewart tells me that Frinksteins are now thinking of opening a branch in

Houston to help others wishing to exploit the new fields. It's good news for us. They can keep an eye on Stevens and make certain we're getting all the royalties to which we are entitled.'

'First things first,' said Sam. 'I just need your signature on this contract to make it all legal. Stevens now has a week to complete the deal.'

Dean sat down at his desk and signed the document with a flourish. 'We can now get on doing what we know best without always having to look over our shoulders,' he said. 'As we're solvent again I'll ask Josh to call a meeting of our major suppliers and get Stewart over here to tell them the financial facts of life. There's no harm in giving them a bullish view of the income we shall receive if the Texas fields are as productive as we've got reason to believe. It will be a smack in the eye for our competitors who thought we were dead and, in particular, our German friends who will not be overjoyed.'

Dean allowed himself a rare moment of satisfaction before turning to Sam again, 'The only thing that makes me uneasy is Michael's continuing absence. The longer we go without hearing from him, the more concerned for his safety I become. I've decided to ask Hal to go to Liverpool – ostensibly to strengthen our team in England – but his brief will be to leave no stone unturned until he gets a lead on where Michael may be.'

'It's a dangerous assignment as things are at the moment,' said Sam.

'I know, replied Dean, 'but Hal knows the risk of an Atlantic crossing and he's really quite excited about the whole thing. He says that he's lived long enough in an academic backwater and now's the time to break out, especially as he has no family ties.'

'Good for him,' said Sam. 'As far as I can see this country is drifting nearer and nearer to declaring war on Germany and joining the Allies so, just as long as he knows the dangers . . .'

The announcement of O'Donnell's deal with Stevens Oil made a big impact on the financial pages of the specialist press. Most of the *Chronicle's* rivals played it down and, when they did make passing mention, gave all the credit to Frinksteins. Dean was pleased to see, however, that *Business and Commercial World*, the respected organ of Wall Street, featured Stevens Oil and the colourful Lee Stevens over the following weeks. The articles attracted much favourable attention, particularly when Frinksteins made an unexpected announcement of their expansion into Houston. Stevens was portrayed as a flamboyant Texan, brash and unsophisticated but with a nose for a good deal and a flair for exploiting the fields he owned with clinical efficiency. One headline in another independent even went as far as shouting, 'Stevens Humbles The Opposition' and went on to praise the O'Donnell management and their advisors for their shrewd thinking under pressure. It was just the boost that O'Donnell's needed to bolster their flagging fortunes. Confidence now seemed to surge back after the bad times.

Stewart and the bank had been impressed with the rapid turnabout in O'Donnell's fortunes. At the same time they had been mildly embarrassed by the publicity that they had received over the Stevens deal and Dean was at pains to point out that, while the bank had lent its expertise, it was Sam Goldman who really deserved the credit for the way the deal was put together. The board of Frinksteins had taken the hitherto unheard-of step of sending a confidential letter of support to the *Chronicle*.

In this frenzied atmosphere, Hal departed by steamer for Liverpool. He had spent the previous afternoon with Dean discussing how best he might use his time in England now that an arrangement had been confirmed between the *Record* and the *Chronicle* for the syndication of reports from both sides of the Atlantic. It was agreed that Hal, from his base in Liverpool, would follow up every lead in a concentrated effort to find Michael, and that he should seek the help of the Liverpool police if they could be persuaded to take the case seriously. Dean knew that Hal would be a good ambassador for O'Donnell's in Britain and he was confident that, with his measured approach and old-world charm, he would be able to repair much of the damage that Michael had done. He just hoped that the continuing speculation caused by Michael's disappearance would not undermine the new-found confidence that had permeated all levels of O'Donnell's management. It was, he mused, the first really positive news the company had received since the setback of Tamara's untimely death, and he now desperately wanted to ride his luck through the stormy days that lay ahead. However, Hal's last words as he left the office kept ringing in his ears.

'Believe me, Dean,' he had said sombrely, 'Michael's obsession with Natalia could well be the death of him.'

33

'Natalia really must have a break from that place,' said James. 'She may not admit it but it's beginning to tell on her.'

'I agree,' said Sir George Buchanan, looking at him searchingly across his mahogany desk at the embassy. 'She's been there for over four months working seven days a week without a break.'

'Wouldn't it be an idea to get Count Freedericksz to ask her to come to Petrograd next weekend?'

'Good idea, James,' he answered smiling. 'I know Prince and Princess Yussoupov would want both of you to dine with them if they don't have a previous engagement. Why don't you let me contact them for you?'

'I would be very grateful,' said James. 'I know it would liven things up for Natalia. After all, she has known Felix and Irina Yussoupov since she was a child.'

'The Empress tells me that she is devoted to her work,' said Sir George, 'but I know she worries that Natalia sometimes drives herself to the limit.'

'She's always been the same,' James replied. 'Give her a cause and she throws herself into it heart and soul.'

James knew Natalia would need some persuading to leave

Ivanhov, even for the weekend, but he also knew that the elderly courtier would be at his most persuasive with her. A veiled reference to the Empress wishing her to report in person would be sufficient. There was, he speculated, much for them to talk about and he knew from their fleeting discussions that Natalia felt that Count Freedericksz held the key to many Orlofski secrets that would help her to understand the past so much better.

James left the office keyed up at the prospect of seeing Natalia again. Half an hour later, he telephoned the Count who readily agreed to his proposal.

'Delighted to be of help, Mr Ponsonby,' he responded. 'I had a letter from the Milners only yesterday, asking how things were with Natalia, so I'll be able to let them know at first hand. They tell me her letters are full of enthusiasm for what she's doing but she doesn't say much about how she's coping in other ways.'

James looked out of the window on to the cold street below. He studied the motley band of cabbies sitting on their horse-drawn *droshkys*, protected from the cold by their long collarless overcoats. He knew that his next encounter with Natalia would be critical if he was to bring about a subtle change in their relationship. One false move could ruin things. 'Be patient, James,' he said under his breath as his mind wandered back to those now distant days in Vaduz with Peter when they had all first met.

James was delighted when, later that afternoon, Count Freedericksz telephoned with the good news. 'Natalia will be coming on Friday evening by train from Ivanhov. I will arrange for someone from my household to meet her.'

'That's really very kind, Count,' James said. 'However, if the embassy can be of any assistance, then please let me know.'

'Thank you, but it won't be necessary. Natalia can stay with me. We have much to discuss.' For a moment James's heart missed a beat. 'However,' the Count continued 'I know that she's looking forward to seeing you on Saturday

248

evening. Sir George tells me you're both invited to the Yussoupovs.'

'It will be a great pleasure, Count,' James replied stiffly, feeling that his emotions were too close to the surface to hide adequately.

'I was really pleased to receive Count Freedericksz's invitation,' Natalia said as she sat in the back of the embassy car with James on the way to the Moika Palace.

'I thought you might not come,' he said, smiling.

'I very nearly refused, but he's so persuasive. Anyhow, it's time I saw old friends again. I also had a suspicion that you might have had a hand in things.'

James hesitated before replying, 'I can't deny that we were all very worried about you,' he said evasively.

'Well, you can see I'm none the worse for my experience,' Natalia replied brightly.

'Did Count Freedericksz tell you that the American Ambassador, George Marye, and his wife would also be dining with the Yussoupovs this evening?' he said, changing the subject.

'Yes,' said Natalia carefully. 'I just hope that we don't have to hear about his efforts to find Michael Korsakov.' Then, turning to James, she said earnestly, 'Has there been any news? Have they found him?'

'No,' he replied, 'and for reasons that I won't go into, they're very unlikely to.'

'I understand,' said Natalia. 'I just hope he rots in hell!'

Felix and Irina Yussoupov greeted Natalia and James warmly as they entered the magnificent drawing room at the Moika Palace.

'I was hoping it could have been just the four of us for dinner this evening,' Felix said to James when they were out of earshot of the others. 'That American chap really is so boring. All he wants to talk about is work. He may be the American Ambassador but he's not in the same league as Sir George.'

249

James smiled tactfully, 'Yes, he can be a little hard going.'

'Anyway, thank God we've got Natalia back to civilisation, even if it is only for a few days,' smiled Felix.

True to form and predictable to the last, George Marye attempted to dominate the conversation before dinner. 'What do you know about this fellow Korsakov?' he asked James as they sipped champagne. 'It seems he's disappeared and his people in New York are worried about him.'

'I've absolutely no idea, Your Excellency. We've all heard the rumours, but he could be anywhere.'

James shot a glance at Natalia who was attempting to listen to the conversation while still continuing her own animated discussion with Felix. 'All I know', he continued, 'is that his mother was a friend of the young Rasputin when he first came to Petrograd. I think that says it all – like mother, like son.'

Marye nodded and, realising that his line of questioning was not bringing him any social accolades, was suddenly saved when Irina took his arm and led the guests into dinner.

After the starchy atmosphere of the embassy, James was determined to enjoy himself. The Yussoupovs loved informality and Felix, dressed in a red velvet smoking jacket, told his guests racy stories. Natalia and James entered into the spirit of things while Marye struggled for conversation.

'I don't know why we ever let Natalia leave Russia,' said Felix once the men were alone after dinner. 'She's the most beautiful creature I've ever seen, Irina excepted, of course,' he laughed. 'That mad devil Rasputin had a hand in her family's downfall you know,' he continued, turning to James, his face suddenly pale and serious. 'He's the devil incarnate and he's destroying this country. The Empress seems powerless to resist his influence. God knows where it will end.'

'These are dangerous times,' interrupted Marye, 'and it certainly looks to me as if a very serious situation is developing. With the Empress at the heart of affairs, now that the Tsar is at the Front, it appears that she will only assign the highest offices of state to those of whom Rasputin approves.'

'That's not all,' replied Felix, his eyes alight. 'He's setting us on course for military disaster with his predictions on the course of the campaign, which Alexandra believes implicity. Something has got to be done', he confided, 'and the sooner the better. Has Natalia ever said anything to you about Rasputin, James?'

'No, we keep off the subject but, deep down, she's never forgiven him and the Korsakovs for destroying her brother. She's got spirit and it's only human nature to try to redress the balance. If one waits long enough an opportunity always presents itself.'

'Hm,' Felix said thoughtfully. 'We might be able to kill two birds with one stone. I'm told Rasputin is now living with his daughter Maria in a very ordinary third-floor apartment in Gorokhovaya Street.' After a moment's pause, he continued, 'I find it hard to believe that a man of such ambition should choose such a dreary part of town.'

'With him nothing is as it appears,' said James. 'I'm told he's got no real interest in money. He's got people queueing up all day asking for favours of all descriptions. It appears he takes money from the rich and then distributes it to the poor.'

'Don't tell me he doesn't keep plenty to pay his bills at some of the most notorious places in Petrograd,' said Felix, his eyes narrowing. 'We all know he's pretty good at making women of all classes pay for his help in another currency. It's scandalous to think that, on a whim, he will write to the Empress, knowing that whatever he suggests, no matter how outrageous, will always be granted.'

'It certainly seems a very strange way to run a country,' replied James thoughtfully. He couldn't help but smile at Felix's outrage as he remembered the endless stories that abounded in the city of his own indiscretions.

'If you were in my shoes, how would you plan Rasputin's

251

downfall?' Felix enquired suddenly, directing his gaze at the startled diplomat.

'I really don't know,' replied Marye, stiffening. 'I suppose you might start by cultivating his friendship. He would be flattered by someone of your rank showing interest in him because, as you know, he's been shunned by a large section of the nobility.'

'That's exactly what I think, Ambassador,' Felix said, frowning.

The party broke up after one o'clock, with Natalia asking to be excused as she had the long journey back to Ivanhov the following day. James was only too pleased to leave with her. As the chauffeur-driven limousine sped down the city streets, he began, 'You've heard that Rasputin is with the Tsarevitch again?'

'Yes, Count Freedericksz told me about it this afternoon.'

'Everyone is gossiping about him being a German agent who is pulling strings in concert with a German-born Empress.'

'That's a terrible thing to say,' said Natalia, genuinely shocked.

'But it's what the people really do think,' James replied. 'Felix has asked me to go and see him next week,' he confided. 'He says he's got something of the greatest importance to tell me.'

'Just be careful, James. Believe me, Felix is a good friend but he's also impetuous and often doesn't realise the likely consequences of his actions.'

'I shall take the greatest care, I promise you,' James replied.

'I'd bet you anything, he's planning to get rid of Rasputin. As you know we both loathe the man after what he's done to my family and Russia.'

'I'm only just beginning to realise the full significance of the danger he poses,' said James thoughtfully.

'You're an Englishman and you will never fully understand,' said Natalia. 'The whole sorry mess is magnified by the myths and superstitions that hold sway in this country, particularly as the Empress has fallen prey to many of the attitudes left over from the Middle Ages concerning the occult.'

'Has Felix got the guts to get rid of him?' asked James, eyeing Natalia intently.

'Don't underestimate him. He may seem to lack backbone but I'd put my money on him in a crisis any day. His ancestors didn't build up and consolidate one of the largest fortunes in Russia without having something special about them.'

'Well, I promise you I shall watch with interest from the comfort of my diplomatic corner while battle is joined,' James said solemnly. Suddenly, he placed his arm around Natalia. It was more by way of a spontaneous reflex action than premeditation. For a moment, James despaired as he felt her stiffen, then she slowly began to unbend as she turned to face him. She inclined her head slowly towards him and kissed him softly.

'Don't rely on me to fulfil your dreams, James,' she said tenderly. 'I'm ashamed to say that I'm not certain if I know what love is anymore.'

James caught his breath as the words he wanted to say seemed to stick in his throat. He longed to hold her tighter and release all the feelings that had tormented him over the past months. He just wished that all the world could be filled with the love that he felt for Natalia and he wondered how anyone could be so vulnerable on the one hand, and yet so forceful and determined on the other.

'You must give me time to come to terms with myself,' she began again, looking at him over her furs. 'There are so many things you don't understand.'

34

'I'm very glad I asked you to be my best man,' said Randle, grinning at Paul Wigram over breakfast at Weathersfield. 'One needs a sensible chap like you along at times like these.'

'Well, thank you for the compliment,' replied Paul. 'At least I was able to stop you from getting blotto on that claret last night.'

'Be kind enough to bring me some more coffee, Crabtree,' said Randle turning to the old manservant who was hovering nearby, 'and then get one of the men to fly the family flag from the pole on the roof. If I wasn't so damned out of puff I'd do it myself. Now, are you certain you've got the ring?' he enquired earnestly, looking at Paul.

'For Heaven's sake, Randle, trust me. I promise not to lose or drop it during the service.'

'Sorry to be a bit edgy,' said Randle, 'but it's a bit of an ordeal having John Duff at the service. I'm afraid that every time he claps eyes on me he'll think, "That's the man who killed my wife and now he's marrying my daughter".'

'I thought all that had been straightened out,' said Paul anxiously.

'On the surface it has, but who knows what he's really thinking.'

'Now listen to me, Randle. If you aren't man enough to put all this behind you, it will dog you for the rest of your life and ruin your marriage.'

'I know,' he replied. 'That's just what worries me.'

As Randle had forecast, the daffodils in early April were a riot of yellow on the grassy banks at Weathersfield as the family and guests began to assemble in the small fifteenth-century stone church on the estate. Randle's side of the family, however, was not much in evidence. The Baguleys appeared not to be the marrying kind and, when finally bound by the ties of matrimony, they seemed to have had a poor breeding record. All Randle could muster were his two elderly maiden aunts and a distant cousin with whom he had always kept in touch. On Emma's side there was Lucinda's family, the Camerons, who saved the day by swelling the congregation with a good representation.

Emma stayed the night with Randle's close friends, Richard and Caroline Malpas, at their rambling home, Blackthorne Lodge, some two miles distant. It was to Caroline that Emma had confided that, for the first time, she felt a fleeting cloud of doubt scudding across an otherwise blue sky. She found herself saying, 'I just hope he's not marrying me to try and make amends for what happened so long ago,' only to be swiftly admonished. Try as she might, Emma was unable to control the wave of homesickness that flooded over her and, if she had dared admit it to herself, she was close to panic.

It was only the following day, when John Duff arrived with Grainger in the Rolls-Royce to take her to the church, that she fully regained her composure. She always felt safe with her father. He was big and reassuring and she held his hand as they drove the last mile to the church.

At the lych gate John squeezed her hand as Grainger opened the car door to allow them to alight on to the mossy path. For a moment she paused. 'Do you really think Mother is watching now, Papa?' she asked looking directly at him. He could see the tears in her eyes.

'Yes, I'm sure she is,' was his definite reply. 'You must get on with your life, and live it to the full with Randle. Now, chin up and smile,' he continued reassuringly as she took his arm.

A large crowd of villagers had gathered outside the church. To them Randle and Emma's wedding contained all the best romantic ingredients. They could see beauty, rank, wealth, youth, courage and tragedy all bonded together in an elaborate mosaic. They jostled discreetly for the best view and gasped as Emma, on John's arm, entered the church by the west door.

The organ music swelled as they walked up the broad aisle and they could feel every eye riveted on them. Emma carried a prayer book together with a small, fragrant posy. She had chosen a simple ivory silk dress and her tulle veil was held in place by a coronet of fresh orange blossom from the greenhouses at Weathersfield. It complemented the way she had swept up her dark hair in a neat style which suited her oval face. She knew that these were difficult times for the country and the village and she realised it was not the time to make a splash.

She made her vows quietly but with serene confidence, while Randle spoke his with ringing clarity.

While the bridal party was in the vestry signing the register, two small bridesmaids in ivory silk dresses distributed blossom to the guests from wickerwork baskets.

As Randle and Emma emerged from the church a large cheer went up. 'Don't forget, you're all invited to the village hall this evening to celebrate with my wife and myself,' said Randle as he received the good wishes of the estate workers and tenants who gathered round them smiling and nodding.

Just then, to their surprise, they saw before them a carriage that had belonged to Randle's Uncle Edwin and which had lain discarded for some years in the coach house at Weathersfield. Instead of a fine pair of Cleveland Bays, however, the estate workers had attached two ropes and were intending to haul them the short way back to the hall. They laughed as they entered the carriage before it set off to the accompaniment of cheers from the onlookers.

'They're a wonderful bunch of people you've got working here,' said Emma turning to Randle as the family guests sat down in Weathersfield's magnificent Georgian dining room.

'They're the salt of the earth and my best friends,' said Randle proudly. 'Even the new landgirls they have sent are absolutely first class. My only sadness is that so many of my old friends from the estate will never come home. Many of the families have been working here for generations and this year alone we've lost three fine young men in action at the Front.' Taking Emma by the hand, he continued, 'I just hope you will be as happy here as I've been.'

Before she could answer, Jimmy's wet black nose came pushing in between them, and Randle patted his head and fondled his ears. 'Did you see him sitting at the back of the church during the service with Gregson the gamekeeper?'

'Yes, of course,' replied Emma. 'I knew you would want him there, and he was perfectly well behaved.'

The speeches were short and informal. It was, therefore, a surprise when Paul rose to his feet again and announced, 'I've got one more important telegram to read out which has just arrived. Looking at Randle and Emma he began, 'It's from Natalia in Russia and reads: "WITH ALL MY LOVE TO YOU BOTH FOR ALL THE YEARS AHEAD".'

There was a buzz of approval around the room as Emma carefully averted her gaze from where Lucinda was sitting. 'If only I hadn't been so short-sighted, she'd be here now,' she thought.

Once the formalities of the reception were over, Randle and Emma went upstairs to change. It was 8.30 that evening before they arrived at the village hall where celebrations were in full swing, with rabbit pie and all manner of country delicacies served to the estate tenants and workers who sat at long trestle tables.

Randle and Emma took their places at the centre of the top

table. After a few minutes one of the old tenant farmers, Ernest Poole, unable to contain his enthusiasm any longer, rose, banging the table, and asked for silence.

'Begging your pardon if it's the wrong time, Squire,' he started hesitantly, 'but on behalf of us all I'd like to present you and Miss Emma with a token of our respect and affection.' When he had made his way to the top table where Randle was now standing, he thrust a silver-plated horse-shoe, mounted on a board, into his hands. Beneath the shoe was a simple inscription, 'Columbia 1900–1914'.

'We saved one of her shoes when she was put down. Good luck and good health to you and Miss Emma in the future – begging your pardon, Mrs Baguley,' he said looking sheep-ishly at Emma.

'Thank you, Ernest,' replied Randle. 'You couldn't have given us anything more precious. My wife and I will treasure it as we will treasure the memory of this happy day. I had hoped', he continued, 'that nineteen sixteen would have brought an end to this dreadful conflict but, in spite of our prayers, it rages on. I thank God that this ancient estate continues to feed us, thanks to you all, and it only grieves me to remember those whom we have lost. Let us hope that soon we shall all have cause to rejoice and that those who are far away will return safely.' With that he sat down, fighting for breath, and Herbert, his farm manager, poured him a glass of water. 'I'm all right, Herbert,' he protested. 'Just give me a moment.'

Emma knew not to take these attacks too seriously. Randle was always at his worst when under strain, and she put her arm round him reassuringly. Five minutes later, when he had recovered his breath, he took Emma by the hand. 'I'm sorry if that presentation was a bit tactless,' he said, 'but they meant well.'

'I know,' she said softly. 'It didn't worry me one little bit. I'm just pleased that they've got so much affection for you.'

'Yes, I'm very lucky,' he said. 'I'm just proud to think that our children will one day inherit this estate and continue to farm here. I still think it's a miracle that your father has accepted me into the family. It takes an exceptional man to forgive what happened to your mother.'

'That's all in the past now, darling, don't let's dwell on what happened so long ago.'

'It's all very well you saying that,' replied Randle, 'but it's burned into my memory and a day never passes without me reliving those fateful seconds.'

35

'I think at last we're getting the message across,' said Dean, looking pointedly at Marvin Jeffries as they sat in his office after the monthly board meeting.

'Yes, I agree,' he said. 'I think our editorial policy supporting the Allies is very much in tune with the public's mood.'

'There's no question that circulation and advertising have soared in the last month, so we must be doing something right.'

'We've got to help force America into the war on the side of the Allies,' said Marvin, 'so let's not be afraid to be seen as giving a rallying call to all true patriots and supporters of a free society.'

'That's exactly where we're trying to position ourselves, Marvin,' said Dean, 'and only today, as you know, we've asked the question, "What would happen if Britain, with her command of the seas, was defeated?" Why, if Germany usurped her supremacy it would spell disaster for our trade with Europe and South America. Just think of the hardship that would ensue if we were denied access to such important markets.'

Marvin nodded as he puffed blue smoke from his pipe into the air.

'We've got to make certain that public opinion pressurises the President to take firm steps against Germany,' continued Dean.

'It's surely obvious to everyone by now that their propaganda machine is blatantly trying to influence German-Americans.'

'Yes, I agree,' said Dean. He got up, went over to his desk and put a copy of *New Yorker Staats-Zeitung* in front of Marvin with a flourish. 'Just look at what Herman Ridder is trying to do to promote Germany's interests.'

'Personally I'm more worried by *The Fatherland*,' Marvin said, tossing the paper aside. 'As you know, Dr Heinrich Albert, the Kaiser's man over here, is behind it and he gives them almost unlimited financial backing to promote the German point of view.'

'Yes, but they're swimming against the tide, Marvin. Our next crusade must be aimed at making the American public aware of what would eventually happen to Mexico, Central America and even Texas if the Germans inflicted a heavy defeat on the Allies. Why, after a period of consolidation, they might even move to annexe these territories before we had time to mobilise ourselves. We could kiss goodbye to all those oil revenues that will be so important to us in the future.'

The *Chronicle's* warnings did not go unheaded and Dean waited to choose their moment to mount a full-scale campaign urging the President to make a declaration of war on Germany. Phrases like, 'bringing the nation face-to-face with its destiny' were regularly coined by the *Chronicle's* feature writers while Dean bided his time. It was the softening up of public opinion that was important before a full assault began to occupy the moral high ground.

Large corporations now flooded the *Chronicle* with advertisements laced with heavy overtones of patriotism and the newsboys groaned under the *Chronicle's* weight as they delivered the papers. It was as though the boom times had returned almost overnight and Josh Wilson walked around the O'Donnell building with a spring in his step that would have been unimaginable a few months earlier. He was, however, cautious in making predictions about future revenues to Dean.

'Lee Stevens is pretty pleased with the prospects for the Texas field,' was as far as he would speculate. 'It would be silly to give you an estimation of net revenue for nineteen seventeen. It's all so hypothetical, I could be way out.'

'Come on, Josh, just give me an educated guess,' said Dean. 'You must have some idea.'

'Sorry, Dean,' he replied. 'All I will say is that I'm cautiously optimistic that, within two years, the revenue from the oil may change the face of the O'Donnell balance sheet and open up all manner of options for us in the future.'

'That's great, Josh,' Dean said, smiling.

'Yes, but don't forget that you've also got to pursue the monies fraudulently stolen from O'Donnell's.'

'I promise you I haven't forgotten,' said Dean. 'If, during the course of the year, war is declared on Germany then all German assets in this country will be frozen. It would then be easy for us to put up a good case for the return of the funds embezzled from O'Donnell's, together with the interest.'

'But what about the short-term position,' asked Josh. 'Isn't there anything that can be done?'

'It's a question of timing,' said Dean carefully. 'Rock the boat unnecessarily now and we might damage our case.'

'I see that, Dean,' he replied, 'but don't forget it was you who was so certain that the Germans would be forced to make restitution.'

'That's true, but let's not forget that one of our main objectives now must be to find Michael. If we are able to believe the rumours that are circulating, the Germans are also trying to find him as he could be crucial in confirming their contention that the *Lusitania* was carrying American arms to the Allies.'

262

'Yes, I fully understand what you're saying,' said Josh pushing back his mane of greying hair, 'but I've always felt that the Russians had a hand in his disappearance. Hal was coming more and more to that conclusion before he left for England. He thought it might be to do with the feud Michael's family had with the Orlofskis, going back a long way.'

'Hal may be right. So why on earth didn't he emphasise this to the board when we asked him if he knew anything that would help us to find him?'

'Well, as you know, he never deals in speculation,' replied Josh. 'His precise academic training makes him cautious about coming to any definite conclusion until he has all the facts.'

'I understand,' said Dean testily, 'but he owes a duty to us to be frank and open. Good God, we're all working on the same side.'

'What's he sent over the wire from England since he arrived?' asked Josh, determined to pin Dean down.

'He's drawn a blank as far as Michael is concerned. It seems he's just vanished into thin air.'

'Has Hal been to see John Duff?'

'Yes, but he's not been able to help much. He's put Hal in contact with the private detective he hired to follow Michael but he can't add anything to what he's already told the police.'

'What about the manager of the bank Michael left instructions with?'

'Sloan at the Midland Bank, you mean?' asked Dean.

'Yes, he must know something.'

'Hal's tried him. He went to see him yesterday as it happens. Seems he's as baffled as all of us and Hal tells me he's beginning to take a very serious view of the whole business.'

'How do you mean?'

'Well, in his limited experience of cases like this, the missing person rarely turns up, especially if they have given

263

such detailed instructions before disappearing as Michael did.'

'Yes, I can see that. I just think Hal should pursue the Orlofski lead.'

'A bit difficult,' replied Dean impatiently. 'Natalia Orlofski is in Russia working in a hospital. She's gone back to her old family home near Petrograd which is being used by the state for the war wounded. On the brighter side, however, Hal has sent some useful despatches from England. Used properly they're dynamite and could help shorten the war drastically.'

'All right,' replied Josh. 'Just as long as Hal remembers that his number-one priority is to find Michael at all costs. We still might need access to the trust Joe left him to give us a cushion in case anything goes wrong with the Texas operation.'

'You worry too much,' said Dean, smiling for the first time.

'I just don't have the ability to put my head in the sand sometimes,' Josh replied frowning. 'I can only hope that Michael is still alive but he's got too many enemies for me to give him more than a fifty-fifty chance.'

'Now, just listen to me, Josh,' said Dean. 'You worry about the balance sheet and I'll worry about Michael.'

'Fine, Dean,' Josh replied, 'but it's not a bad idea to remember that the two things are very closely linked.'

'We've always managed without Michael and I think we can manage for a little longer,' Dean said, smiling thinly at Josh. 'Anyway, it would be just like him to deny us access to his trust even if we could find him.'

Dean was annoyed by what he thought of as Josh's all too cautious and unhelpful attitude. To his credit, however, he had always found him resourceful and reliable and he knew that he had the best interests of O'Donnell's at heart. 'Perhaps I'm becoming too sensitive,' he thought as his anger became focused on Michael. He and Michael had been long-standing adversaries and he remembered exactly how

Michael had treated Tamara. 'She deserved better,' he said under his breath. 'Thank God I've got Sam and Stewart to rely on.'

It amused him suddenly as he remembered something Sam had said to Michael one day when fiercely provoked. He searched for a moment for the exact words Sam had used before they came back to him. 'One day, Michael, you'll be famous,' he recalled Sam shouting at Michael. 'You'll probably have a disease named after you.'

He could even remember the slight curl of Michael's lip as he glared at Sam before walking defiantly out of his office.

'It's the scandal more than anything that will damage us', he thought, 'if he really has met with a nasty end.' Tamara, he remembered, was always worried that Michael would end up the victim of his own aggressive nature. She put his ruthlessness down in some part to the genes he had inherited from the Korsakovs who had been involved in a thousand scrapes in Russia only to be saved by their name and rank. 'Bad blood,' he repeated over and over again.

36

'It's good of you to come,' said Felix Yussoupov as he welcomed James to his private study at the Moika Palace. Motioning his visitor to sit on one of the gilt empire chairs, he walked to the large double doors and checked that they had been tightly closed by the liveried servant who had announced James.

'Sorry if I seem unduly cautious,' he began. 'You must be curious to know what I wanted to talk to you about,' he added, scanning James's face.

'Yes, I must admit you've had my imagination working overtime. If I was a betting man, however, I'd lay money that it's something to do with Natalia and Rasputin.'

'Very perceptive,' replied Felix, 'but before I tell you more, what news from the embassy?'

'Not a lot,' said James carefully. 'As you know, Felix, these are difficult days for the Allies. George Buchanan is gravely worried by Russia's predicament and you know he's been talking to Maurice Paleologue at the French Embassy to try to counter the threat Rasputin is posing.'

Felix paused and fiddled anxiously with a silk handkerchief stuffed up the sleeve of his jacket. 'What I have to tell you, James, is of the greatest importance to Russia and, dare I say it, the world at large. I therefore need your word that what I tell you will never be disclosed.'

'Well, Felix, that's a bit difficult,' said James, smiling. 'I think you'll just have to rely on my sense of loyalty to you and Natalia.'

'That's not good enough,' was the reply.

'I can only repeat that you must trust me, especially as Natalia's welfare is at stake,' James replied, firmly holding Felix's gaze.

'Very well then,' said Felix. 'It shall be so.'

'Now, please let me know what you have on your mind. Sir George is expecting me back at the embassy in just over an hour.'

'Very well,' said Felix drawing himself up to his full height and rocking forward on the balls of his elegantly booted feet. 'I'm going to get rid of Rasputin once and for all. It's my supreme gesture for Russia.'

After a short hesitation James enquired, 'What exactly do you have in mind, Felix?'

'Murder, assassination, call it what you will,' was the reply.

'After what you hinted at the other evening, I guessed as much. Just don't involve me, Felix. Do what you have to do but for God's sake leave me out of it.'

'You have my word on that,' he replied. 'Do you think Natalia will agree to help me?' he said, lowering his voice. 'I may just need her to act as bait for the trap, together with Irina.'

'You know how she feels about all that happened in the past. If you genuinely want her help then I'm sure you'll get it,' replied James. 'She's got the strength of character and determination not to let you down when it comes to the moment of truth, but Rasputin must never be underestimated.'

Pausing for a moment, they sat staring at one another as if overcome by the enormity of their discussion, before Felix began again: 'You can be of great assistance by telling me if, in the future, you hear a whisper on the diplomatic grapevine about my plan. If one word gets out then our cause is lost.'

'I'll certainly do that for you,' said James, 'but as a British citizen I can do no more. If we were discovered just think what a hell of a diplomatic stink it would cause. Why, it might even end in a rift between our two countries. I would be able to hide behind my diplomatic immunity but it would still be madness for me to be implicated.'

'I agree entirely,' said Felix. 'Now for Natalia's and Irina's role. Rasputin is, as you know, notoriously fond of beautiful aristocratic ladies. I intend to use them both as bait for the trap. Irina knows nothing of this, I might add, but I am going to tell Rasputin that she will be at the palace and is eager to meet him. She will, in fact, be on holiday in the Caucasus. In addition, I will tell him that Natalia will be present as I know he would welcome another chance to meet her. He said as much after the visit to Ivanhov with the Empress and Anna Vyrubova.'

'What would you expect her to do?' asked James, looking at Felix in alarm.

'Just to be there in case we need help. With Irina being away we've got to have another attraction for him in case he should get to know of her absence and decide to call it off. He certainly would not do that if he knew Natalia was to be at the palace.'

'As long as that's all you want I'm certain you'll be able to count on her,' said James returning Felix's steady gaze.

'That's what I thought,' said Felix jumping up from his chair and pacing around, his hands clasped behind him.

'Just keep it simple,' said James, 'and remember, one word out of place could spell ruin and dishonour for you and your family. If you are able to get rid of Rasputin then Russia will owe you a great debt. Why, she might even have the chance to save herself,' he said with a wry smile.

'What do you think would be the reaction of the British

and French Governments to Rasputin's removal?' asked Felix eyeing James.

'I'm sure that, privately, they would be quite delighted but, of course, they would refrain from commenting publicly. It would be quite improper to make official any views held privately but the Americans might let it be known by an "official" leak that they approve whole-heartedly,' he laughed. 'George Marye, as you can see, is so out of touch with reality that I don't think it will be long before he is replaced as ambassador. President Wilson will eventually see that he just hasn't got the necessary qualifications for a job that is going to be vitally important. There could be great changes ahead.'

'So many of my friends are now saying that the empire is doomed,' said Felix. 'There's a silly superstition that the Tsar's reign was tainted from the start when the chain he was wearing at his coronation, symbolising the Russian Empire, fell to the ground. Even he, it was said, regarded it as an omen. It had a profound effect on him.'

'I thought it was only the Empress that went in for that sort of thing,' said James.

'There's so much you still don't understand about my people,' said Felix.

'I must admit sometimes I do find them very hard to understand,' said James sadly. 'Here we are talking of murder as a last resort to save Russia and, only a short distance away at the Maryinsky Theatre, Karsavina is dancing before an audience who seem oblivious to the fact that a war is being fought. Nobody seems to bother about those shirkers who are at this moment taking extended leave from the Front and swilling champagne down as though there is no tomorrow.'

'Perhaps there will be no tomorrow', said Felix frowning at his friend, 'if we do nothing and let the empire collapse like a pack of playing cards. When Russia's history is told you will know you were here in her time of need and on the side of the angels.'

'That's a bit strong,' said James. 'I just hope I can live up to the image.'

Felix saw the funny side of that and burst out laughing. 'One request, please,' he said anxiously. 'Irina must know nothing of what we have discussed.'

Without saying a word James nodded and shook Felix by the hand. 'I shall pray that you may be given strength for what you have to do.'

That evening, in his room at the embassy, James brooded over what Felix had told him. 'I just wish he hadn't tried to involve me,' he thought. He was also anxious about Natalia's potential role in this plot. Knowing her headstrong ways, he was certain she would risk anything to help Felix and he just hoped that time and circumstances might resolve the problem that Rasputin posed before she became too deeply involved. He knew she had buried herself in her work at Ivanhov and he was already concerned about the long hours she worked.

They corresponded regularly and James had written suggesting another visit to Petrograd which Natalia had tactfully declined.

'There are never enough hours in the day,' she wrote. 'The Empress's visit did so much for morale, but conditions are truly appalling in spite of all we're doing. We gain strength from knowing that we are united in a common cause to support the brave men of Holy Russia who are bleeding and dying in millions.' She went on to give him an account of the horrifying conditions in their primitive operating theatre, the lack of proper medicine and drugs, and the utter dedication of Dr Kuropatkin. James could tell that, in some strange way, she was working out her anger and frustration over the dramas of her childhood that had centred around Ivanhov. It had been the focus of her childish world and now, stark and stripped of all its finery, it was allowing her a chance to put her life into perspective. Seeing the suffering of others and by being involved in their pain was helping to blunt the memories of her own traumatic early years. James noted with increasing interest that Count Freedericksz's name appeared regularly in her letters and he knew, from past experience, the influence the Count had with the Orlofskis. It would be most useful, he thought, to delve deeper into the background of the elderly courtier so trusted by everyone and so obviously ruthless in protecting those he cared for.

He took his bunch of keys and descended the mahogany staircase to the file room. His position allowed him unobstructed access to this restricted area and he soon found the shelf he required. His eyes flicked across the Fs until he pulled out one marked 'Freedericksz (Count)'. He skimmed the contents:

Freedericksz – Count Vladimir Borisovitvch, began his career as an officer in the Horse Guards. Appointed by Alexander III as First Master of the Horse. Later assistant to Count Vorontzov, Minister of Court. Appointed Minister after Vorontzov resigned. Received title of Count from Nicholas II.

Descended from Swedish officer taken prisoner by Russian troops and interned at Archangel. Ancestor won distinction as banker to Catherine II and ennobled with the title of baron. Father ended his career as General ADC to Alexander II. Private residence in the Potchtamtskaya opposite the Horse Guards' barracks.

Smokes large cigars and enjoys the best Bordeaux. Subject to effusions of blood on the brain and suffers loss of memory.

James replaced the file on its shelf and noted that the coding indicated that further highly confidential information was held in the embassy's high security area.

'Just as I thought,' he muttered as he left the room, locking the door behind him.

Over the next two months, James weighed up his case for asking Sir George to give him access to Count Freedericksz's top secret file, only to decide against it for the moment. He believed that he might set a hare running unnecessarily. Anyway, he didn't want his private thoughts to spoil what was becoming one of the most fascinating periods of his life.

Spring had now given way to early summer and the face of the city had changed from a slushy nightmare to blossom and greenery. He had known from his earliest days in the Diplomatic Service that Petrograd was a city seething with intrigue, but it was a different thing altogether now to be a part of it. Rumour, counter-rumour, gossip and fact all seemed to merge into a mist of speculation from which it was often very difficult to distil the truth.

He knew the secret police, or Ochrana, had always had considerable power and a shiver went through him when he pondered how Michael Korsakov might be faring. 'The ruthless old devil,' he said under his breath when he thought of Sir Edward Milner and speculated how, with one telephone call to Sir George at the Embassy, Michael's fate had been sealed by orders from Count Freedericksz. 'He's probably better off dead than at their mercy,' he thought. At the same time he wondered how Natalia lived with the knowledge of what had happened to Michael. 'She's certainly got a pretty ruthless streak,' he murmured. He had often despised men who had fallen under the spell of beautiful but calculating women, but he now understood the attraction. He could see that it only heightened their allure, and he was almost proud to put Natalia in that special category.

From what he had gleaned from Natalia, he knew that Count Freedericksz was holding what remained of the Orlofski treasures. He had often wondered what vestiges of the past had been saved when Natalia had left in those dark days after her mother's death. There was silver, he knew, but surely, he thought, there must be family archives and family heirlooms.

Natalia was so unlike the English girls he knew. Everything about her had an air of fascination for him. From her high cheekbones and chiselled beauty to her often high-minded and imperious behaviour, she personified everything he had ever desired in a woman. The trouble was that he still didn't understand what made her tick, and what she had said to him in the car on their way back from the Moika Palace still weighed heavily upon him. 'What on earth did she mean?' he pondered.

He was jerked suddenly out of his contemplation by the telephone ringing.

'That you, Ponsonby?'

'Yes, Ambassador,' he replied.

'Have you heard anything about a rich German banker called Manus?'

'I'm afraid not.'

'Well, find out all you can about him. Maurice Paleologue has just been in contact to tell me that Rasputin was seen at his house yesterday.'

'I don't follow the significance, sir,' James said.

'Well, all I can tell you is that he's supposed to be Germany's chief agent in Moscow.'

37

'It just seems to be one thing after another,' said Randle gloomily as he toyed with his breakfast.

'What's happened now?' asked Emma deftly slicing the top off her boiled egg.

'Herbert Parker tells me that Frank Kennedy, the new man we've taken on at Home Farm, has made one of the landgirls pregnant. It's the last straw,' he snapped.

'He's also probably told you we're expecting a record harvest.'

'I just hope he's right,' replied Randle and he smiled and reached over the table to squeeze her hand. He looked at her wistfully for a moment. 'You know, the trouble is that I feel uncomfortable stuck here while the regiment is in the thick of it.'

'For Heaven's sake, Randle, how many times do we have to go over that?'

'I know,' he replied. 'Anyway, at least it's some small comfort to me to see the gun teams being trained on the estate. Why, I almost forgot to tell you what Herbert told me yesterday. One of the teams, some large Argentinian mules, ran away in the village. They went for two miles or so before they could be stopped.'

'They're nasty, vicious creatures,' said Emma. 'It's the poor horses I feel sorry for when they leave here and go to the Front.'

'I know. I've seen what happens to them at first hand. It's not pleasant.'

'Now, let's get a move on,' interrupted Emma, getting up from the table. 'You've promised to drive me into Liverpool this morning. I hope you haven't forgotten that I'm supposed to be meeting George at his office.'

As they arrived in the city traffic, Randle crunched the gears as the car moved slowly forward following a horse-drawn brewery dray.

'I'm going to the club after I've dropped you at the *Record*, then on to see my comrades at the hospital. I'll pick you up at four-thirty.'

'Don't be late,' Emma replied, 'and for Heaven's sake do cheer up.'

After Randle had left her at the *Record's* office in Dale Street, he went directly to his club. Two hours with his friends was usually quite enough and from there he went to the hospital to see the disabled from his regiment who were still undergoing treatment and rehabilitation. He found it singularly depressing to see the pitiful state of so many fine men whom he had fought beside. As usual, it put him in a reflective, almost morose, state of mind as he left for the *Record's* offices to collect Emma.

'Miss Emma has left a message for you, Mr Baguley,' said the commissionaire. 'She may be fifteen minutes late.'

Entering the building, Randle now looked for some diversion. He was anxious to renew his acquaintanceship with Hal Morrow who had recently arrived from New York so he asked the receptionist to see if Hal was available. He had enjoyed meeting Hal the previous week at dinner with Emma and the Duffs at Charnley Lodge.

'Dr Morrow will be pleased to see you, Mr Baguley. You know where his office is, on the third floor?' asked the woman behind the desk.

'Yes, thank you,' said Randle getting up.

Since Hal had arrived in Liverpool he had quickly gained a reputation for his charm and polished manners. At first John Duff had been wary of him, knowing of his close connection with Michael Korsakov, but curiosity had got the better of him when George Gerrard had invited Hal to the *Record's* offices. It was then that John, seeing him as a potential future ally, had suggested that he might care to use one of the smaller offices in the *Record's* building. The offer was gratefully received and already Hal had become quite a celebrity with the staff who consulted him on all manner of topics.

Hal greeted Randle cheerily as he entered the office he was using while he searched for Michael and where he prepared his dispatches for the *Chronicle* which were syndicated in America.

'How do you like this?' he asked, passing some papers to Randle. It was copy for a new column on current affairs entitled 'American View' which George had recently commissioned for the *Record*. 'I'm also researching an article on the Russian Royal Family which is proving fascinating,' he continued. 'You may be interested to know that I've been speaking to Sir Edward Milner. I was hoping for some good background material.'

'I would think he was a mine of information,' said Randle.

'On the contrary, he was very guarded, which I suppose is understandable. He terminated the conversation very promptly when he remembered I was connected with the *Chronicle* in New York.'

'It's the old story of that stupid feud between the Orlofskis and the Korsakovs,' said Randle, 'Did you know he's Natalia's guardian?'

'Yes,' replied Hal thoughtfully. 'I should have remembered that Sir Edward lives near Henley. As you possibly know, Michael was there rowing in the Harvard crew, and he even went as far as visiting Larkhill to see Natalia.'

'I bet he got a chilly reception,' chuckled Randle.

'Yes, it wasn't a success for either of them,' commented Hal ruefully. 'Michael could never see further than the end of his nose where women are concerned.'

'Wasn't it a bit more than that?' asked Randle.

'Yes, but it's a long story,' replied Hal wearily.

'Is there any news of him?'

'No, not a word.'

'Have you tried the Salvation Army?'

'Yes, they've been very good. I've followed every lead imaginable, but he seems to have vanished.'

'What about the police?' Randle continued.

'They're not overly interested in one missing foreigner when so many local people are missing without trace.'

'I see your point,' said Randle. 'Has there been any news from America?'

'Not a thing, except that we have received confirmation from our embassy in Petrograd that Michael has not officially entered Russia.'

'Why don't you see Sloan at the Midland Bank? He's only just a stone's throw away in Castle Street.'

'I was there last week,' said Hal. 'He's inclined to think Michael either lost his memory or has been kidnapped.'

'What do you think?' asked Randle, anxious to see what line he was taking.

'I discount the former, and regard the latter as improbable as no ransom demand has been received. My own instinct tells me that he's been involved in some lowlife fracas which has ended with him being killed.'

'I suppose it's quite possible that Michael has fallen foul of the same people who knifed him when he first arrived here.'

'Quite so,' said Hal matter of factly. 'He's always had a terrible temper and, try as I might, I was never able to get him to curb it.'

They looked at each other in silence for a moment.

'I'm his only remaining lifeline if he's still alive, Randle,' said Hal solemnly, 'and in spite of what he may have done, I won't let him down.'

'Has George shown you the file he holds on the Korsakovs?' Randle enquired.

'Yes, it's been a big help. It confirmed what I had suspected all along. Tamara always tried to hide the circumstances of Michael's conception. It explains a lot.'

Randle now excused himself, explaining that he had to meet Emma, and made his way to John Duff's office to see if she had arrived. The late afternoon sun was still streaming into the building and a light breeze off the Mersey wafted the curtains at the half-open windows. Randle was anxious to get back to Weathersfield and he hoped that John wouldn't keep them too long.

'Has Mrs Baguley arrived?' he asked the secretary.

'Yes sir, she's with her father in his office. I'm sure it will be all right if you go straight in.'

Emma was sitting chatting to John as Randle entered. They both beamed at him.

'Do come in, Randle,' John said as Emma jumped up and put her arms around him.

'Now, I want you both to sit down and listen to what I've got to tell you,' Emma said, her eyes dancing from one to the other. 'I wasn't going to say anything until I knew for certain, but I've been to the doctor today and he confirms I'm going to have a baby. Isn't it wonderful news?'

Randle sat transfixed in his seat for a moment before jumping up and hugging Emma with delight and surprise.

'I just couldn't wait to tell you both,' she said beaming with pleasure.

'This calls for a celebration,' said John going over to Emma and kissing her before shaking Randle warmly by the hand. He then took the key to his cabinet and produced a bottle of champagne. 'Lucinda will be so pleased when I tell her the news,' he continued excitedly. 'It's important when you get to my age to know there's going to be continuity in the family. You need an heir, Randle,' he said shooting a glance at his son-in-law, 'and I need to know there's a new generation to take over Albany after Emma and Natalia.'

After a moment's pause he looked at Emma. 'When's the little one expected?'

'Doctor Martin thinks it will be mid-January.'

'Ah! A Capricorn,' said John. 'Now just remember to take things easily.'

'You'd better not ride that new horse of yours,' said Randle anxiously, only to be cut off by Emma.

'Now wait a minute,' she said firmly. 'You're not going to wrap me up in cotton wool.'

On their way home Randle talked excitedly about the plans he had for their child. He was convinced it was going to be a boy and he was anxious that he should eventually inherit the Weathersfield Estate in good heart and carry on the Baguley tradition. Emma listened with pleasure as Randle poured out his delight, but it worried her that he seemed set on her producing a boy.

'I'd better put his name down for my house at Shrewsbury,' he said thinking aloud, 'and we'd better make sure the old nursery at home is given a good spring clean.'

'Just hang on a minute, Randle, you're going too fast,' laughed Emma. 'Let's just enjoy the moment and then tomorrow we can get down to planning the future.'

When Crabtree met them at the front door of Weathersfield Randle could see he was slightly peeved that they were back late. 'Cook's worried about the meal,' the elderly servant croaked wearily. Seeming not to hear his lament, Randle told him the good news.

'Mrs Baguley is expecting a child, Crabtree,' he said proudly. 'You have my permission to tell the staff.'

'My congratulations, sir,' Crabtree said with genuine delight. 'It will be good news for everyone when you have an heir.'

Randle looked for a piece of wood to touch, muttering, 'Thank you.' He was very superstitious and had learned to be even more so in the trenches. Some soldiers at the Front said that the habit of touching wood came from the early Christians who touched part of the cross of Christ. The origins of the story didn't really matter, but Randle was conscious of how many of the Baguley women had had miscarriages, and he was very aware of how few relatives he had.

38

For some time Dean had been worried about the small mountain of mail that had accumulated for Michael. In the first months of his absence, it had lain in piles waiting to be forwarded, but then Dean had instructed his secretary, Kate Jones, to wade through it to see if there was anything that might throw some light on his disappearance. Kate had known Michael since he was a boy and Dean had always joked mischievously to Tamara that she must have had her sense of humour removed with her tonsils when she was a child. In spite of this, they got on well enough as Kate was fiercely loyal, possessing all the protective instincts of an ageing spinster looking after an adopted family. Tamara had taken to her when she was first hired. On principle she didn't like overly attractive women working at O'Donnell's and Kate, with her close-cropped ginger hair, pointed face and piano legs, filled the bill.

Dean instinctively knew that Kate could be trusted with such an assignment as she was shocked by nothing. Her instructions were that any bills were to be sent to Stewart for immediate settlement from the funds Michael had left on deposit with Frinksteins, while his private correspondence was to be answered with a brief letter explaining that he was in England and could not be contacted at the moment. There was nothing that shed any light on his disappearance, leaving Dean even more mystified.

The following morning's post, however, brought a letter addressed to Michael in a delicate hand that Kate was sure was female. The envelope was obviously expensive and, on the top left-hand corner, it was marked 'PRIVATE AND CONFIDENTIAL'.

Without hesitation, Kate opened it and began to read. She scanned the writing slowly at first, only speeding up as the power of the sentiments expressed caught her attention. When she finally finished reading the fragrant paper, she went immediately to Dean's office. She found him at his desk studying a sheaf of papers.

'I'm sorry to interrupt you, Dean,' she said quietly, 'but I think you ought to see this right away.'

'What is it, Kate?' he asked testily. 'Can't it wait? I'm extremely busy.'

'It's a letter to Michael from Olivia Simmons. She's the widow of Senator Harry Simmons who killed himself in such tragic circumstances a few weeks ago.'

'Yes, I remember it was big news,' said Dean putting down his papers and looking up at Kate quizzically. 'Let me see.'

Handing him the letter, she waited while he read it, watching his face impassively. 'My God!' he exclaimed. 'Is there no end to the damage that boy can do? Hal told me some time ago that Michael was seeing this woman, but even he had no idea that she was expecting his child.' He paused for a moment, looking at Kate. 'What a terrible thing that this poor man should have been driven to kill himself while so disturbed.'

'Who do you think wrote the poison pen letter that told him of his wife's infidelity?' asked Kate.

'It could have been any of Michael's old enemies, including the Russian secret police,' Dean replied. 'He used to boast quite openly about his conquests of society ladies.

He found it humorous to imagine their horror if they had only known whom he slept with the night before.'

'But this lady is obviously very distressed,' said Kate. 'Do you think that Sam Goldman, as Michael's attorney, should go and see her if I make an appointment?'

'Yes, get hold of him right away, and make certain you take the letter round to him personally. Whatever you do, don't leave it with anyone in this office. The only good thing is that Harry Simmons's inquest didn't reveal any of this. His suicide was simply put down to pressure of work while the balance of his mind was disturbed, if I remember correctly.'

'Do you think there's more to this letter than meets the eye?' said Kate, always alert for the undertones that she knew were present in the ebb and flow of Michael's life.

'It would be difficult to prove, Kate, but, after all, Michael's a rich man,' he said. 'It's not beyond the bounds of possibility that she wants a pay off.'

In spite of his outward calm, Dean was worried. Olivia Simmons's letter concerned him and he set about reviewing the facts of the situation, drawn from careful study of the file the *Chronicle* held on her husband.

Harry Simmons had been born into the patrician world of money-based Republican society. The family lived in a fashionable New York apartment, spending their summer vacations at their farm in the blue grass country of Kentucky. Harry's father, it was rumoured, had bought votes for his son at the start of his political career but otherwise very little mud had stuck in a blameless, if ineffectual, life. Harry had married the former Olivia Warzycha, the glamorous daughter of a first-generation Polish-American family, who was twenty years his junior. The marriage was ill-starred from the beginning, with Olivia quickly becoming disenchanted with the long periods her husband was away. While she had not overtly sought outside diversions, Michael had swept her off her feet at their first meeting. He was everything that Harry Simmons was not, and she had evidently enjoyed the danger of the illicit nature of their relationship, which Michael pursued with fiery passion. Harry Simmons, meanwhile, had been completely unaware of Olivia's unfaithfulness, believing her to be the perfect loving wife.

Dean was still contemplating the contents of the brown file when Kate knocked on his office door. She had brought him a cup of coffee – black with no sugar.

'Interesting?' she asked, raising her eyebrow in an unattractive gesture which mildly contorted her mouth.

'Yes,' he replied thoughtfully. 'It was obviously a terrible shock when the Senator learned the truth about his wife and Michael. It appears the anonymous letter was sent just a week after his wife returned from hospital with the baby.'

'Do you think there's any truth in the allegation?' asked Kate.

'Oh yes, I'm pretty certain that the story holds water. It's just the sort of thing that would amuse Michael and he will probably still be able to tell you what colour underwear the poor woman was wearing.'

'Had it finished before Michael left for England?' asked Kate, unperturbed.

'Yes,' replied Dean. 'Michael gets bored easily.'

Sam, meanwhile, had promised to contact Hal in England to see if he could remember anything about the lady and her affair with Michael. Over the years he had become adept at brushing off calculating women who had tried to pin paternity suits on Michael, often after the briefest of encounters. This case, however, seemed altogether different and would need careful and sympathetic handling, especially as it involved the possibility of a potential heir to the O'Donnell empire.

Dean agreed to let Sam handle things but the more he thought about it, the more he realised that they must, at all costs, keep any news of Michael's possible involvement from leaking out. He was already the subject of so much speculation that if they let the cat out of the bag the

Chronicle's competitors would have a field day at its expense and undo all they had achieved in the past six months. He poured himself a brandy and drained the glass with one gulp, at the same time cursing Michael for all the misery he had caused. Old Joe O'Donnell had predicted this would happen and now it was all coming true.

Sam arranged to meet Olivia Simmons at her apartment overlooking Central Park. She was a small, delicate woman with a flawless complexion and soft blue eyes and Sam immediately warmed to her vulnerability.

'It's good of you to come, Mr Goldman,' she said gently. 'As you can imagine, the events of the past few months have been very distressing. However, I must face the future and do the best for my son.'

'I'm very sorry for the way things have turned out,' said Sam, feeling his way carefully, 'but may I ask you how you know that Michael Korsakov is the father of your child?'

'Harry and I had difficulty in having children and we both went for tests. About the same time I had an affair with Michael and, by the time the doctor told us the results of the tests, I was pregnant. He told Harry that he had a low sperm count and it was highly unlikely that he could ever have children. When I announced I was pregnant Harry just thought we had got lucky.'

'But that might have been the case,' said Sam cautiously.

'Almost impossible, Mr Goldman. I checked with the doctor afterwards and he told me they never like to tell a man he's infertile, as Harry was, as it often leads to psychological complications. The plain fact of the matter is that Harry could not have children and I have no doubt that Jack is Michael's son. I want to tell him who his true father is rather than hide behind a lie all my life.'

'Have you thought about this carefully, Mrs Simmons?' asked Sam. 'The implications of what you tell me need considering thoroughly; a lot of people could get hurt. Things are also made more difficult as we have no idea where Michael is at this moment or even if he is alive or dead.'

'Mr Goldman,' she said, stretching out her hand and placing it on his arm, 'you are a wise man with a lot of experience. You must know that in life there are some things better swept under the carpet while other matters are best faced fair and square. I desperately want Jack to have a father and to that end I am prepared to face any amount of gossip and innuendo. If Michael can be found, I'm certain he would want to know that the boy is his son. It would then be up to him to make some important decisions. He could either ignore us and life would continue as at present, or he could take a real interest in Jack and he might change his name to Korsakov by deed poll.'

Sam sat back in his chair and gave a long, low whistle. 'I've got to give it to you, Mrs Simmons, you're a courageous and far-seeing lady. I'll do all I can to help you but you do understand I can promise nothing?'

'Harry left us very comfortably off so I may assure you that the motive of this approach was not financial.'

'I don't think you needed to tell me that,' said Sam grinning. 'I'll be in touch.'

On his way back to his office, Sam couldn't put Olivia Simmons out of his mind. She seemed so different from any of the other flashy women who had attracted Michael, and Sam just hoped that if Michael ever reappeared she and the boy might be a stabilising factor that would enable him to settle down. 'It's all such a damn mess and most inconsiderate of him,' Sam thought, 'but let's hope this is the lucky break we've been looking for. Find Michael and who knows what the future might hold.'

While Sam was wrestling with Michael's problems in New York, Lee Stevens was wasting no time in his endeavours to get the Damon Mound field into production. His test wells had all proved above expectations and the smile on his face grew wider by the day.

'You cotton pickin' Yankees sure had a slice of good luck when you bought this old tract of land for a few thousand dollars,' he reported cheekily in his last communication to O'Donnell's. Lee had now overcome his initial wariness of Sam and Dean and was beginning to treat them as partners. He was shrewd enough to see that they could bring their own special talents into play on his behalf and, after all, he was enjoying the publicity of being involved with such establishment names from the East.

He had been brought up to be distrustful of what his father called 'effete Easterners'. He was still not certain what the word meant but he had a good idea of what the old man had been driving at. He had watched with great interest when Frinksteins had opened their branch office in Houston. They now had a long list of investors who wished to cash in on the oil bonanza they could see was coming. Sam had long since decided to put a lot of faith in Lee for he trusted his down-to-earth approach and obvious knowledge of the oil business in all its forms. He was just the man to help them to exploit the area on a large scale and, with the money the bank could put at their disposal, Dean was confident of substantial rewards for Frinksteins and their investors.

'You just wait and see,' Lee would say to anyone who would listen. 'Soon this place will grow till this ranch land, as far as you can see, will be covered with highways and developments. Houston's going to make more millionaires than any other city in the whole country,' was his proud prediction. 'I just hope most of it stays right here rather than giving some city boy in New York or Philadelphia an income fit for an Indian prince,' he would add.

He chewed heavily on a plug of tobacco when he was in a reflective mood, spitting it out as he downed his bourbon. Lee was a fighter and he was determined to extract every last drop of oil from his newly acquired lands. His eyes sparkled as he thought of the rewards but the thought of O'Donnell's taking thirty cents per barrel tempered his rejoicing. 'God damn it, O'Donnell's did get their cake and got to eat it,' he said under his breath.

Like so many others, he heard the rumours that were

circulating about Michael's disappearance. He had even asked Sam about him, only to have the question brushed aside.

'But he's a major shareholder of O'Donnell's, Sam, so you'd better level with me,' Lee had persisted.

'Some time, when we've got all day to spend, I'll tell you about him, Lee,' Sam had said. 'All you need to know is that he could well have been born a Texan.'

'Why do you reckon that?' asked Lee.

'Well, he's big and brash and his ego's almost as large as yours!'

39

With the Tsar away commanding the army at Supreme Headquarters at Mogilev on the Upper Dneiper River, Rasputin was able to use the long summer of 1916 to strengthen his position as the Empress's trusted friend and advisor. Day by day his influence seemed to grow and James Ponsonby had almost ceased to keep count of the number of ministers and high-ranking officials dismissed from their posts at Rasputin's whim. More worrying to him and the British Government was the fact that reason and logic played no part in the selection of those who now ran the country. There was no coherent policy in the Councils of State which seemed to be governed by those versed in the occult and acting only in the interests of themselves and their friends.

Dissent, alarm and confusion were the order of the day as James sat with Sir George Buchanan in his office to give his weekly report.

'The changes just seem endless with good men ruined on the turn of the tarot cards, Ambassador,' he said. 'I've checked on this chap Manus as you instructed, and as well as being indecently rich, our people confirm that he's working for the Germans.'

'I'm still not certain that there's substance to these stories of an increasingly pro-German stance being adopted by the Empress. It's simply that she's being manipulated unmercifully.'

James nodded. 'She's unable to see the danger that her association with Rasputin is precipitating. All he really wants, in my view, is to be left alone to continue to enjoy his uniquely outrageous lifestyle. I can't believe his ultimate desire is to rule in Russia.'

'I agree with you, James. It's transparently clear that, above everything, he wants to perpetuate and increase the Empress's belief in autocracy. In that way he can see a way of survival for himself against those legions of powerful men that he has crossed. He's very shrewd. He understands the peasant point of view of the monarchy as divine and he plays along accordingly.'

'But you must agree, Ambassador, that things are very volatile,' replied James. 'It doesn't help that Saranov, the Foreign Secretary, has just been summarily dismissed for proposing a separate kingdom of Poland.'

'I know,' replied Sir George. 'The Empress had a blue fit. She said it was tantamount to endangering the throne.'

James knew that this brief exchange was simply a prelude before Sir George brought a subject that was more important to the table. It was the way he always worked and James's imagination was racing, wondering what could be the focus of such urgency. He was soon to understand as Sir George began, 'Now, James, what news of Natalia? Sir Edward has asked me to keep him informed, and I know you saw her last weekend.'

James had been waiting for this enquiry and was guarded as he framed his reply. He knew Sir George was fishing for information and was perceptive in reading the slightest expression or gesture that indicated evasion. 'On the whole, she's bearing up very well,' he began. 'However, I tried to persuade her that she can't stay at Ivanhov indefinitely.'

'What was her reaction?'

'Guarded, in a word,' replied James seriously. 'She's very stubborn, as you know, Ambassador. All I can say is that it's a good job she decided to stay with Count Freedericksz rather than the Yussoupovs when she came to Petrograd.'

'I agree. I don't altogether trust Felix. He's wild and irresponsible.'

'I know what you mean,' said James. 'The attraction of staying with the Yussoupovs is that they've so much in common from the past but, as you know, she regards the Count as a second father.'

'Yes, I do know,' said Sir George, leaning back in his chair. 'I just hope that she takes his advice. You have some influence with her, James. Just make certain that Felix doesn't involve her in any of his hair-brained schemes.'

'I'll do what I can,' he replied, 'but Felix can be very persuasive.'

'The rumour is that when he was born his mother, Princess Zenaide, wanted a girl. Felix was actually kept with long hair and wore dresses until he was five which wasn't very healthy, if you follow my drift.'

'Yes, it must have had a profound effect on him,' replied James. 'Funnily enough, at our first meeting Natalia reminded him of how he used to walk around the city in his mother's clothes. I didn't think she was serious at first. Irina just laughs at him and doesn't take him seriously.'

'Well let me tell you it all nearly got out of hand before he married when he was in Paris,' said Sir George gravely. 'At the Theatre des Capucines he was handed a note from a man who had been eyeing him. It was King Edward VII who thought he was a woman before he realised his terrible mistake.'

'It's easy to imagine,' replied James. 'He's at his most eccentric when he's been reading Oscar Wilde whom he greatly admires.'

'Well, just keep Natalia away from him. I know initially I encouraged you both to see Felix and Irina, but it was a mistake.'

'Very well, Ambassador,' said James, hoping that his interrogation was over. He knew Sir George was perfectly well aware that he had more than a passing interest in Natalia, and that the old man's concern for her was well intentioned. He would now be able to write to Sir Edward with a clear conscience, reassuring him that Natalia was safe and well.

After a moment, Sir George got up from his chair and walked to the window clasping his hands behind his back before turning round to face James again. 'There's something further of importance I feel you should know,' he began. 'You may already have put two and two together.'

'I'm not sure I follow,' said James genuinely puzzled.

'It's about Michael Korsakov. I think you understand that we know precisely what happened to him and where he is now.'

'Yes,' replied James. 'Natalia told me that Sir Edward had contacted Count Freedericksz through the embassy and he had instructed the Ochrana to wreak their own particular justice on him.'

'They're pretty vicious people and are trained, as you know, to be extraordinarily unpleasant,' said Sir George.

'Mutilation, such as Michael suffered, being one speciality of theirs,' interrupted James.

'I'm afraid so,' he said deliberately before continuing.

'Sir Edward asked Count Freedericksz to deal with things as he saw fit, and we simply reported the result to him. Natalia showed herself to be as cold as ice when she heard what had happened to him. She must have had a burning desire for revenge.'

'I know,' said James thoughtfully before continuing, 'Where is he now?'

'In a lunatic asylum in Liverpool under the name of Michael Brady. The Ochrana in England have been very thorough. We don't mind going along with it, as Korsakov could well be an embarrassment to us over the munitions the *Lusitania* was carrying.'

292

'Yes, it is quite convenient,' said James matter of factly.

'Now you realise, James, that Natalia knows everything and that Count Freedericksz will have kept her fully informed.'

'Yes I understand, Ambassador.'

'Just be careful what you say,' he said solemnly. After a moment's pause he began again, 'The final piece in the jigsaw has been a carefully guarded secret which I doubt if Natalia has ever told you about.'

James inwardly tensed himself as he wondered what the next revelation was to be.

'Count Freedericksz and only a few others, including Sir Edward, know what I'm going to tell you. It may help you to understand the deep-seated animosity and rivalry between Michael and Natalia.'

James feigned calm concentration as Sir George coughed as he came to the moment of his revelation.

'Michael's mother, Tamara,' he began, 'was the lovechild of Natalia's grandfather Boris Orlofski. Natalia, however, was only told the facts a short time before her mother's death. She resents it deeply and has blown it up out of all proportion. Michael, no doubt, has the same feelings. Sir Edward thinks one of his motives for chasing about after her is to have an illicit and, some would say, incestuous relationship. It's just the sort of thing that would appeal to his perverted mind.'

'Good grief,' gasped James.

After a moment's pause the ambassador continued, 'Now you probably know that Igor Korsakov's will provided for Tamara who was then his established mistress. She was left a very considerable fortune which, on her death, passed to Michael. Ivanhov, however, was left by Igor to an elderly uncle who lived in Paris. He fell on hard times and the estate was sold in quick succession before being purchased by the state.'

'So neither Natalia nor Michael has any stake in the property that had been owned by their common ancestor and his forebears for so many generations.'

'Yes, strange isn't it?' replied Sir George with a thin smile.

James sat looking thoughtfully at the portrait of the King which occupied pride of place on the wall behind the Ambassador's desk. The whole affair was laced with intrigue and a spider's web of hurt going back generations. He was suddenly overtaken with an urge to probe further with a question to which he already knew half the answer.

'Ambassador, what do you think was the most bitter pill that Natalia had to swallow in the whole unhappy episode?'

'Well, it's funny you should ask that, James,' he replied. 'Do you know I really think it was seeing her mother having to sell the famous Orlofski emeralds to Fabergé to pay some of her debts. She regarded them, above everything, as a symbol of her family's rank and position over the generations and it had a catastrophic effect on her.'

'That's just what I think,' replied James.

'Count Freedericksz, I'm certain, would have bought them from Catherine,' continued Sir George, 'but her pride wouldn't allow it. As it was, he was keeping a roof over their heads and she felt she couldn't impose on his generosity further.'

'I can only add, Ambassador, that when Peter Duff and I first met Natalia in Vaduz she was a virtual refugee. She asked my mother if she knew who had purchased her family's emeralds. If I remember correctly it turned out to be Eugenie Shepilov, and now it all fits into place. Mother told me that she lived in Paris and that her husband had inherited a large estate in Russia.'

'Ivanhov?'

'Yes, the very same. Mother told Natalia that they had bought the necklace from Fabergé's shop in Petrograd just before her husband lost all his money on the Bourse. I have known for a long time that the necklace was very precious to Natalia and that she would do anything to have it back. I feel that being back at Ivanhov is all part of the same need to relive her childhood. She's seeking a different ending to a difficult time in her life.'

'I know exactly what you mean, James,' he replied. 'You've been very perceptive. It's like the effect it has on some people if they are unable to cry after the death of a loved one.'

James flushed for a moment. What Natalia said in the back of the embassy car now all made sense. The phrase: 'I'm not certain I know what love is any more', had haunted him but now he understood every word perfectly.

'Thank you, Ambassador,' he said. 'You've helped me enormously by telling me the facts. You may rest assured of my discretion.'

In the days that followed, James's thoughts became more and more focused on Michael. Although he had never met him, he felt he knew him intimately because so much unhappiness had centred upon him or followed in his wake. Instinctively, he knew that, with his background and steely make-up, Michael would have learned how to cope with his enforced removal from society. He would, no doubt, have passed through a long period of withdrawal and despondency but, although the future would still look bleak, he would at least have come to terms with his situation as far as was possible. James reasoned that Michael would be sustained by the thought that if he waited long enough the opportunity would surely come when he could exact terrible revenge on those who had put him away. It wasn't difficult for James to imagine the deep anger that would burn inside him, allowing him to endure any mental or physical torment as long as he kept his goal in sight. He could even imagine Michael subduing his natural aggression and becoming a model of good behaviour, patiently enduring the taunts and humiliations that were handed out on a daily basis, knowing that one day his captors would lower their guard and he would have the element of surprise on his side when he needed it most.

40

James Sloan was still waiting for the elusive Michael Korsakov to walk into his office at the bank and claim what was rightfully his. In case his wayward customer had suffered from a bout of temporary amnesia, he had alerted his staff to advise him immediately if anyone answering Michael's description came to the counter. He hated loose ends and, in a final effort to resolve the mystery, went as far as placing small photographs of Michael by the tellers' windows to help them to recognise him if he showed his face.

It seemed extraordinary to Hal that Michael would behave in this way. It felt quite wrong and out of character.

'I can give you no rational explanation, Mr Sloan,' he began as they sat in the ground-floor office overlooking Castle Street. 'I'll give you that Michael is unpredictable and eccentric but he cares about money and possessions and wouldn't let them go without a struggle,' he continued, rubbing his chin. 'At long last the police are taking his disappearance seriously but it's like looking for a needle in a haystack.'

'For the last ten months he hasn't withdrawn a penny,

which leads me to conclude that the chances of Count Korsakov being found alive are slim indeed,' replied Sloan gravely. 'In all my banking career I've never experienced anything quite like this before.'

'What would you advise me to do?' asked Hal in exasperation.

'I can add very little to what I've already said,' replied Sloan gravely. 'There are only six weeks to go before a year will have passed since Count Korsakov's disappearance. I am then bound to open the envelope he left at the bank, with all that that may mean.'

'What are you driving at?' asked Hal, his gaze riveted on Sloan. As if seeing him for the first time, Hal suddenly noticed the immaculately groomed moustache grown to conceal a mouth so full of teeth that they seemed jarringly at odds with Sloan's otherwise precise image.

'You may recall, Dr Morrow, that Count Korsakov expressed his wishes to me quite precisely. If we do not find him by the thirtieth of November, he will be officially listed as a missing person, presumed dead, with all the implications such an announcement will make.'

'I understand,' replied Hal. 'It could be very damaging to O'Donnell's image in America. I shall have to write to the board advising them to prepare a statement well in advance so that they're not caught on the hop.'

'Very prudent,' murmured Sloan. He paused for a moment, sucking his teeth in a way that only increased his resemblance to a walrus. 'What do John Duff and his colleagues at the *Record* think of the situation?' he asked tentatively. 'I know you're using an office in their building.'

'I don't think he can help us,' replied Hal bluntly. 'Anyway, he and George Gerrard have got their hands full.'

'Quite so,' said Sloan.

'Emma Baguley, however, has been very helpful,' Hal confided. 'Naturally, at first she was very defensive, but now we get along famously. In fact, I'm off with her tomorrow to interview the superintendent at the City Asylum about shell shock.'

'It should be fascinating,' replied Sloan with a slight shudder. 'Just make certain they don't keep you there by mistake,' he continued in a monotone as he smiled grimly.

Emma had been watching Hal out of the corner of her eye as they left Albany House and threaded their way through the dense city traffic. There was something about his face, she thought, that inspired confidence and respect. His eyes always looked directly at one, but never probed too deeply, and his mouth was full and generous without a hint of coarseness. He had the look of a patrician with the gentle manner of a poet, which set him apart from his fellow men. 'You're a good man,' she thought to herself, averting her gaze. She and Randle had often remarked that Hal would have made a fine politician or priest, and few who knew him could understand how he had managed to reach the age of fifty without marrying. There was much she still didn't understand about him but, given time, he might be more forthcoming and talk more freely about his past.

Soon they turned off the main road and passed through a large ugly gateway with an ivy-covered lodge to one side.

'This place always gives me the creeps,' said Emma as Hal stopped the car on the gravel drive outside the forbidding brick façade of the asylum. 'It would horrify me if I had to spend just one night in there.'

'It's surprising what you can get used to,' said Hal, smiling.

They walked up to the massive entrance and reported to the superintendent's office, situated to the right of the echoing hall. A small, unkempt woman greeted them with a questioning glance.

'We're here on behalf of the *Record* to research a feature on the extreme effects of shell shock,' began Hal. 'This is Mrs Baguley, and my name is Morrow – Dr Hal Morrow.'

'You're expected,' came the curt answer. 'Please sign your names in the visitors' book. Dr Simpson, the superintendent, will be with you presently.' With that they were shown to a wooden bench where they waited in silence until a white-coated figure appeared. Dr Simpson was a man in his early fifties, with curly grey hair receding at the temples. His manner was brusque and it was obvious that he regarded them with considerable suspicion.

'Just as long as I can exercise my right to see any copy and approve it before publication,' he stated. 'It's the board's policy, you know,' he added blinking behind a pair of thick spectacles.

'We're only interested in helping to bring the plight of these unfortunate people to the public's attention, Dr Simpson,' said Emma defensively. 'I'm certain you and your board need support, financial and otherwise, and we can help to provide a platform for you to put your case for extra funds.'

Hal could see that Emma's last statement made Dr Simpson shift his position almost imperceptibly. Gradually, he became more talkative as they started their tour of the massive building. The first wards they visited confined those who were only mildly deranged and were not considered a threat to the staff or themselves. They stopped at the miserably furnished dayroom where some ten or twelve inmates were either sitting hunched up in chairs or leaning against the sickly green walls. It was a pathetic little group who communicated sparsely and spent most of their time looking at a fixed point on the ceiling with blank eyes or rocking backwards and forwards. Dr Simpson pointed to a large man sitting slumped at the table.

'This chap', he whispered to them, 'showed outstanding courage at the Front. After two years of suffering high explosive bombardment day and night, and seeing almost all his men killed, something snapped. He's now terrified of his own shadow.'

'Can we put some questions to him without upsetting him?' asked Emma tentatively.

'Better not, Mrs Baguley. You could undo all we are trying to achieve by asking him about his past. The strange thing is that patients with his problem often can't remember all that much about the fighting; a shutter seems to come down in their minds and blank it out.'

Leaving the room Hal could see that Emma was visibly upset. He put his arm around her as they walked down a seemingly endless bleak corridor before entering the high-security wing.

'This is where the most dangerous and disturbed men are kept,' started Dr Simpson, at the same time calling for a male nurse to accompany them. 'Most of these patients are kept in restraints or are on a specially formulated drug programme to keep them from being violent. We have psychopathic killers in this part of the hospital, and men from the Front who have been so brutalised they only know how to do one thing – kill.'

'As you know, we're only interested in those who have been at the Front,' said Hal. 'Our brief is to report on the aftercare and rehabilitation of those who were shell shocked or mentally damaged by war.'

'I understand perfectly, Dr Morrow,' said the superintendent indicating to the nurse to unlock the door in front of them. 'In here is a corporal from the Dockers Battalion who has to be kept sedated. The other fellow is a strange kettle of fish who was admitted for trying to mutilate himself. He was also supposed to have received injuries on an Irish boat in a storm, but we were never really told the full story. We've got him stabilised now, but keep a safe distance from these men, Mrs Baguley. You're in no immediate danger, but it's always better to be safe than sorry.'

As they moved across the stale-smelling room they could see two men lying on their beds. Hal sat on a plain wooden chair by the soldier.

'Would you mind if I asked you a few questions?' he said softly. 'My name's Hal; what can you remember about things before you were brought here?'

The man blinked through bushy eyebrows and tried to speak, his lips trembling as he raised his head from the

300

pillow, only to fall back, his face contorted.

Emma, meanwhile, had averted her eyes and was looking towards the other end of the room to where a young man was curled up in a ball on his bed. She could see that he was thin to the point of emaciation, and his dark hair was cropped short. His bright blue eyes watched them intently. Suddenly he jumped up and Hal swung round from where he was sitting, anxious for Emma's safety.

The young man cringed as he saw the superintendent and nurse move ominously towards him.

'Wait!' shouted Hal. 'Don't touch him!'

Emma was looking directly towards the pathetic figure who was now standing in front of them, tears running down his cheeks.

'My God!' Hal exclaimed. 'Michael!'

The figure shrank back to his bed, sobbing as though drained by the effort. Hal ran across the room and cradled Michael's head in his arms while Emma and Dr Simpson looked on in disbelief.

'You know this man, Dr Morrow?' he asked anxiously.

'Of course I do,' Hal replied angrily. 'It's Michael Korsakov. His presence here is going to need some explaining.'

Turning to Emma, Michael looked at her with pleading in his eyes, 'Emma, for God's sake tell them you know me.'

'I warn you he's a dangerous and cunning character,' said Dr Simpson, ordering the nurse to restrain Michael. 'I'm sorry you have been worried by this man.'

'Leave him alone!' shouted Emma. 'There must be some terrible mistake.'

It took a while for Hal to comprehend fully what he had witnessed. There was absolutely no doubt that the trembling young man was Michael and he felt sick and outraged. He knew, however, that this was not the time to confront the superintendent with retribution. All he wanted to do was to let Michael know that within days he would be free and to ensure that he was not victimised while he remained in the asylum. Although he, more than anyone, knew Michael's faults, he was deeply saddened to see him in such distress.

'How long have you been here, Michael?' asked Hal once he had regained his composure.

'I don't know exactly, Hal,' Michael replied, 'but I think it's almost a year. Please, for Heaven's sake, get me out of this goddam place.'

'This man is Michael Brady. His family visited him only last week,' said Dr Simpson angrily. 'Now let's have an end to this farce. You've obviously arranged this little stunt purely and simply to provide a good story for the *Record*. I know your sort,' he raged. 'Now get out of this hospital or I shall have to report you to the authorities.'

'Keep your spirits up, Michael, and we'll soon have you out of here,' Hal shouted as he and Emma were escorted out of the room.

'You lay a finger on Count Korsakov, Dr Simpson, and I shall see to it that you face criminal charges,' said Hal as they left. 'Mrs Baguley is a witness and you will be hearing from our solicitors within the day.'

As Hal struggled to start the car engine, they stared at each other in disbelief.

'We've got to get Michael out of there without a moment's delay,' said Hal. 'We'd better go straight back to the *Record* and wire Sam Goldman in New York. What time is it by Eastern standard time?'

'It should be eight-thirty in the morning,' replied Emma, 'so by the time we get back to the office Sam should be at his desk. Come on, Hal, do let's get moving.'

A moment later the engine sprang into life and they careered down the drive and out into the city traffic. When they reached the *Record's* offices in Dale Street, Hal jumped out of the car and bounded up the stairs to his office, leaving Emma to take the lift.

'Send a wire to Sam Goldman's office in New York,' he barked, picking up the telephone.

'Very good, sir,' came the prim reply. 'What's the message?'

Hal waited for a moment to collect his thoughts, the palm of his hand flat on the desk. 'Michael Korsakov found alive in City Asylum stop please advise course of action stop,' he dictated.

After a few moments Emma appeared. 'On the way up here I called in at my father's office and told him what has happened,' she said. 'He's as amazed as we are. He's going to waste no time in contacting our solicitor, David Mulley of Jason, Lock and May. He's asked him to contact you as soon as possible. He's also going to contact Sloan at the Midland Bank and let him know the position.'

'Thanks, Emma, that's a great help,' said Hal.

The telephone rang and Hal seized the receiver.

'Mr David Mulley is on the line, sir,' the telephonist announced.

'Hello, Mulley,' said Hal, cutting across the operator. 'Good of you to respond so quickly.'

'What's the full story?' Mulley asked anxiously. 'I've just heard the news about Michael Korsakov from John Duff.'

'It's quite true,' replied Hal. 'He's been placed in the City Asylum under the name of Michael Brady. It appears he's been there almost a year. I suspect he's been the victim of a conspiracy. He even had a visit a few days ago from some individuals claiming to be his family.'

'Have you seen him with your own eyes?' asked Mulley calmly. 'Mistakes do happen sometimes in these cases.'

'Yes, there's no doubt about it,' replied Hal. 'We're waiting for instructions from Sam Goldman in New York.'

'I've advised John Duff that he is right to contact Sloan at the bank as soon as possible,' said Mulley. 'It's also important that we have two independent medical reports to place before the court. Remember, Dr Morrow, you're the most important ally Michael has at the moment and there's a lot riding on you.'

'I shan't let him down,' said Hal defensively.

It was six that evening before a reply was received from New York.

'What does it say?' asked Emma impatiently.

'It's simple and to the point,' said Hal. 'In plain language Sam instructs us to use every device known to man to get Michael released in the quickest way possible, regardless of cost.'

41

'Another poisoned chalice, no doubt,' sighed Dean as he pondered the implications of Michael being found in the asylum. He had been deep in thought, finalising his plan to recover the money syphoned off from O'Donnell's by Eisner and Davis and their German masters, before leaving the following day for Texas. The urgency in Kate's voice now diverted his thoughts.

'Mr Goldman's here to see you, Dean. He says it's important.'

'Very well, show him in,' he said wearily, realising that Michael's shadow once again lay crookedly across the future of the company.

Sam didn't waste any words. 'I've contacted David Mulley in Liverpool and we've agreed on the path he must take with the courts to secure Michael's release.'

'But I thought you said earlier that it wasn't going to be easy?' queried Dean, a little surprised.

'Well, Mulley's a good man,' Sam replied. 'He just has to overcome the problem of proving that it really is Michael.'

'If I remember correctly, he was certified by two doctors when he was admitted. It won't go in his favour that he was so violent at first.'

'Mulley's pinned his hopes on the police and the doctors who saved his life being able positively to identify Michael.'

'There's got to be more to this than just a case of mistaken identity, Sam,' said Dean anxiously. 'It seems very suspicious that Michael had a visit from certain individuals claiming to be his family within the last couple of days.'

'That's a very strong lead for the police to follow, but if they're true professionals they will have covered their tracks pretty well I should imagine,' replied Sam thoughtfully.

'There's obviously something more important at the root of this,' said Dean. 'Only Michael will be able to give us the full story. Knowing him, I should think it's all a bit murky, and I don't really think it's going to enhance either his reputation or that of O'Donnell's if it gets out.'

'My advice would be to concentrate on getting him out and then to decide on what line to take once we know all the facts,' said Sam. 'It's a good job that Emma Baguley was there to corroborate the story. Hal might have been on shaky ground if he had been alone. I just worry that some nut will get a crazy idea into his head that Michael's worth kidnapping a second time.'

'Lightning only strikes in the same place once,' replied Dean, smiling. 'You know I never really thought we'd see that son of a bitch again.'

'Well, it was a million to one chance. Michael has Hal and Emma Baguley to thank,' Sam replied. 'Why, he could have rotted away in there but for them.'

'I know. It's a terrible thought. Well, I suppose when the dust settles it will become clear who masterminded the whole sorry story.'

Realising that there was little more they could do to help Michael, the two men now turned their attention to Stevens Oil. Dean had decided that it was time he travelled to Texas to monitor progress. Stewart Armstrong, he knew, was also anxious to visit Frinksteins' outpost in Houston and had agreed to meet Dean in a few days' time. Sam was well pleased with this turn of events as it saved him the long and tiring journey.

Lee was waiting at Great Central Station, Houston, holding a notice bearing the legend 'STEVENS OIL' when Dean's train arrived. Dean, however, couldn't have missed the giant of a man, standing six feet seven inches, waiting at the barrier wearing a large white stetson and grinning amiably.

'Howdy, Dean,' he said shaking his hand with a vice-like grip. 'I'm real delighted that you've been able to find the time to come and see your interests in Texas.'

'I've been looking forward to this for some time,' Dean replied, 'Sam tells me that you run a good operation.'

'We don't all run dude ranches down here,' said Lee, smiling. 'I've booked you in at the Brazos Hotel in Washington Avenue – it's just over the street.'

As they entered the vast lobby, Dean was struck by the rows of wooden rocking chairs. Seeing his interest Lee said, 'We oil men get to behaving like the nodding donkeys at the field!' They both laughed. 'Now you wait till I take you to the Majestic Theatre tonight,' continued Lee. 'They've got the best vaudeville show in Texas.'

The following morning they made an early start and were at Damon Mound by nine o'clock. Lee had made considerable progress with the field and a forest of wooden derricks and their engine sheds littered the landscape. Around each derrick a gang of men worked on the metal oil-storage tanks. The occasional mule train of materials would arrive but, in the main, Lee prided himself on his modern fleet of lorries.

'We struck oil at one thousand feet,' he said waving his hand airily. 'As you probably know, Dean,' he drawled, 'the process of sinking a well is pretty goddam simple. The drilling costs have not been excessive here, especially as the natural yield could reach two thousand barrels a day from each well. When the critters cease to flow we torpedo 'em by exploding six or eight quarts of dynamite at the bottom of each shaft. The black gold becomes free and squirts up again,' he said rubbing his hands in pleasure.

307

'Presumably the oil is then collected in those vast tanks?' asked Dean.

'Yep, then it all goes by pipeline to the oil siding by the railroad. The tanker trains you saw this morning hold about twenty-five thousand gallons each and take it to the refinery.'

'How do you know what quantity has been shipped and what royalties you should pay us?'

'Simple,' replied Lee. 'When the well tank is full one of our men comes and opens the locked stopcock on the pipe and releases the oil. Three certificates are made out. One is for the well manager, one for central office and one for your agent at Frinksteins who will have the option of being present when the pipe is opened. Credit is given by the refining company, less three per cent which is deducted for evaporation and sediment.' During the explanation Lee had been enthusiastically chewing a plug of tobacco which he now spat out into the dust.

'It all seems very workable,' said Dean, 'but before you go into production, we need to standardise our procedures with Frinksteins' office in Houston and let Josh Wilson in New York know what has been decided.'

'That's fine by me,' replied Lee. 'Now, how about meeting some of the men?'

'I'd like that,' said Dean suddenly conscious that his city clothes were entirely inappropriate.

'Most of the guys are local,' said Lee, 'but some families moved here for work from Galveston after the great hurricane of nineteen hundred when five or six thousand people died on the island. It's a case of the sand crabs of Galveston moving in on the mud turtles of Houston!'

That evening Dean and Lee met Stewart Armstrong at the Rice Hotel where he was staying.

'Heard about your boy Michael being found,' said Lee looking at Dean before pushing an unbelievably large quantity of bread into his mouth with one huge hand and chewing vigorously.

'Not my boy, Lee,' Dean said good naturedly as Stewart smiled.

'Quite a story by all accounts,' he continued. 'He's just the sort we could do with down here. We need men with a real spirit of adventure. You can forgive them a lot if they've got drive,' he announced beaming at his fellow diners. 'Now, just one word of warning. I know you folks from the East think you know it all, but just be careful not to upset things here by making any statements about Germans.'

'What are you driving at, Lee?' asked Dean, puzzled.

'Well, I get that newspaper of yours, and it's all for getting us into the war. Just remember there are a lot of German workers employed here. I'd also keep it quiet that you're hoping to get the German Government to pay damages to O'Donnell's.'

'I know what you mean, Lee,' interrupted Stewart. 'Our office has given us the same advice and we all know the dangers of adverse publicity.'

'Good,' replied Lee, smiling. 'Then I won't have to mention it again.' He went on to advise his guests that he was now almost ready to put the new field into production. There had been, however, a series of minor set backs which had worried him. At first it was nothing he could pinpoint but all the time there were delays in obtaining equipment and spare parts which Stevens Oil had never encountered before. Added to this was a host of breakages and minor failures of plant and machinery. Much of the trouble had started after the announcement of the deal with O'Donnell's and it had crossed Lee's mind that it might not all be simple coincidence. After all, he had received a massive amount of publicity in Houston and he knew that the *Chronicle's* hawkish stance over joining the war on the side of the Allies was not to everyone's taste. There were large communities of Germans living in the southern part of Texas, and Stevens Oil employed a fair percentage of them.

'Just take a very low profile, Lee,' said Dean. 'This whole thing will blow over.'

'Too right it will, but in the meantime we lose valuable time and money. Seems to me it's all to do with the vendetta you boys have with the Germans.'

'Now wait a minute,' said Dean. 'I acknowledge there probably are saboteurs working to make our lives difficult but I don't think we're a prime target.'

'Well, that's not what I hear,' Lee retorted. 'Word has it that you've really upset the German Embassy in Washington.'

After Lee had departed, Stewart and Dean sat together in the empty lobby of the hotel.

'I wasn't going to say anything in front of Lee,' Dean began, 'but I just had a wire from Sam.'

'Oh yes. What does it say?' asked Stewart, cocking an eyebrow suspiciously.

'Well, the gist of it is that it looks likely that Michael will be released tomorrow.'

'That's about what we thought, isn't it?'

'Yes, but there's more. It appears that the new theory the police are following up is that Michael was the subject of an orchestrated plot by the Ochrana.'

'You mean the Russian Secret Police?' asked Dean, screwing up his face in an incredulous smile.

'Yes. It's not too fanciful to anyone who knows their methods. Apparently, the Russians were anxious that he should not follow Natalia to Petrograd. Sam says that it now appears Michael had some of his Harvard friends working with the Soviet revolutionaries to overthrow the Tsar. I'm sure you can see that someone with his background and influence might have been potentially very dangerous.'

'Go on,' said Stewart, listening intently.

'The British, on the other hand, probably connived to keep him out of circulation in view of his knowledge of the cargo of the *Lusitania*. This, coupled with his newspaper background, made him a particular danger to the government and the British propaganda machine. Sam says that he's in a pretty bad state. Time alone will tell how he's going to be in the future.'

'This experience could send him over the top or we might even see a reformed character,' said Stewart gravely.

'I'm just hoping that the publicity we receive on both sides of the Atlantic will be sympathetic and responsible.'

'Well, if you take it in its true perspective, even Michael isn't as much news as a major European war,' said Sam.

Dean was silent for a moment. 'I wonder what his reaction will be when Hal tells him about Olivia Simmons and the child?' he began.

'I doubt if he'll mention it for the moment. It would be better to wait until he's back in New York. With luck he'll be travelling back with Hal as soon as he's released if they can find a ship.'

'I just hope that Hal keeps him from getting himself into any further trouble,' said Stewart.

'I agree,' said Dean. 'I know Sam's worried that he may do something silly when he gets out. Without question he'll put two and two together. He's probably already decided to wreak revenge on those who put him away and realised that Sir Edward Milner was the only person who was in a position to ask the Secret Service for a personal favour.'

'Yes, I suppose it's possible,' agreed Stewart.

'Michael's always subscribed to the biblical doctrine of an eye for an eye,' said Dean.

'The other thing I couldn't fathom out was about this family who visited him while he was put away,' Stewart said.

'It must have been the Ochrana cell working in Liverpool checking to see he was still safely incarcerated. No doubt it's the same people who were involved in the first attack.'

'It makes a strange story but the ends do seem to tie up,' replied Stewart. 'I doubt, however, if we'll ever know the whole unvarnished truth.'

42

James was becoming increasingly alarmed as the conspirators gathered round Felix, united in their desire to rid Russia of Rasputin. They were an unlikely but effective alliance. Felix Yussoupov and the twenty-six-year-old Grand Duke Dimitry Pavlovich were blue-blood aristocrats and had known each other since boyhood. Pavlovich was a leading right-wing member of the Duma, while Sukhotin and Lazovert were serving officers in the army.

Fearful for his safety, the Empress appointed an imperial detective to watch over Rasputin who was becoming evermore concerned by the hostility that all levels of society showed to him. As the months passed he took little comfort from the fact that his influence remained constant with the Empress. He became increasingly preoccupied and obsessed with his own mortality. In such a dark state of mind he had a clear premonition of his own death after which he dictated a letter to his friend Simonavich. It was entitled 'The Spirit of Gregory Efimovich Rasputin-Novykh of the Village of Pokrovskoe' and read:

I write and leave behind me this letter of St. Petersburg. I feel that I shall leave life before January 1st. I wish to make known to the Russian people, to Papa, to the Russian Mother and to the Children, to the land of Russia, what they must understand. If I am killed by common assassins, and especially by my brothers the Russian peasants, you, Tsar of Russia, have nothing to fear, remain on your throne and govern, and you, Russian Tsar, will have nothing to fear for your children, they will reign for hundreds of years in Russia. But if I am murdered by boyars, nobles, and if they shed my blood, their hands will remain soiled with my blood, for twenty-five years they will not wash their hands from my blood. They will leave Russia. Brothers will kill brothers, and they will kill each other and hate each other, and for twenty-five years there will be no nobles in the country. Tsar of the land of Russia, if you hear the sound of the bell which will tell you that Gregory has been killed, you must know this: if it was your relations who have wrought my death then no one of your family, that is to say, none of your children or relations will remain alive for more than two years. They will be killed by the Russian people ... I shall be killed. I am no longer among the living. Pray, pray, be strong, think of your blessed family.

Gregory.

James constantly warned Felix that rumour and counter-rumour abounded about a plot to assassinate Rasputin, all of which sprang from the excited chatter of one of Felix's friends, Poroskewitz, who was unable to keep silent.

'The man's lost his nerve and will be the downfall of all you've planned,' he said urgently.

'We've gone far too far to go back,' replied Felix with as much conviction as he could muster. 'The Empress and Anna Vyrubova are fearful for Rasputin's life and are warning him to take the greatest care. You've got to see, James, that I must take the opportunity now or it may never present itself again.'

313

'Just as long as you know that your name is frequently mentioned and that speculation is rife,' James replied anxiously.

'The die is cast. We've set the date for the twenty-ninth of December. Rasputin has accepted my invitation to a party and Lazovert, disguised as a chauffeur, is going to drive me to collect him from his home at Gorokhovaya Street.'

'My only advice is never to underestimate that man,' said James, feeling a chill of apprehension.

'When are you collecting Natalia from the station?' asked Felix.

'This afternoon at three,' replied James.

'Just remember, don't, on any account, allow her to try to join us this evening. It'll be quite enough for Rasputin to know she's in Petrograd. News travels fast.'

'It would be a fatal mistake and too much of a coincidence for her to have just arrived from the country. Everyone knows of your friendship and when news of Rasputin's assassination gets out, there'll be questions asked.'

'I know,' said Felix. 'She's far better spending the evening with Count Freedericksz. She then has the perfect alibi. She won't like it but she's already involved by association and the consequences for her are quite serious enough. Just give her this note,' he said thrusting an envelope into James's hand. 'It explains everything to her, and she'll know that, if she disregards my instructions, she'll put all our lives at risk.'

'You may rest assured that I shall do as you say,' said James.

'Just make sure she burns it when she's read it.'

James nodded. He felt a wave of relief sweep over him now that Natalia was to be kept away from the fateful events of the coming night when so much could go dangerously wrong.

'Where will you spend the evening, James?' Felix asked.

'I shall stay at the embassy. I've a card school organised.'

At eight o'clock that evening, Rasputin, smelling of cheap soap, was brought by car to the Moika Palace. He strode into the newly painted basement room with Felix as the conspirators waited in an apartment on the first floor that was connected by a winding staircase. They were playing 'Yankee Doodle' on the gramophone in an effort to convince him that Princess Irina's supposed party was in full swing. The room was plainly furnished except for an ebony cabinet standing in one corner upon which was placed a sixteenth-century Italian crystal crucifix. In the middle of the floor, which was covered with a Persian carpet and white bearskin rug, was a low table on which rested a samovar surrounded by a plate of cakes containing the poison potassiun cyanide. On the sideboard stood a variety of bottles flanking a bottle of lethal Madeira. The time was approaching midnight. Rasputin seemed relaxed and asked Felix to play a gypsy song to him on his guitar as he lay back having gulped down two glasses of the poisoned Madeira and some of the cakes. He seemed perfectly normal and in good spirits as he listened to song after song. Those waiting upstairs now became more and more apprehensive that something had gone seriously wrong. Lazovert's nerves were nearly at breaking point when, at 2.30 a.m., Felix, perspiring freely, joined them, his hands trembling.

'What should I do, the poison does not seem to be working?' he asked.

'For God's sake,' interrupted Dimitry, 'I've had enough, let's call it off,' only to be overruled by Poroskewitz who thrust Dimitry's Browning revolver into Felix's hand saying, 'Go and finish him off!'

When Felix returned to the basement Rasputin was slumped at the table breathing heavily. 'Let's go and visit the gypsies, with God in thought but mankind in the flesh,' he said in a low whisper.

Felix helped him up and leading him to the ebony cabinet said, 'You'd better look at the crucifix and say a prayer.'

He knew that further delay was impossible and as

Rasputin crossed himself he took aim and shot him at point blank range in the back. With a terrible cry the monk fell heavily on to the bearskin rug where he lay motionless.

A few seconds later Lazovert burst into the room and rushed over to examine the body.

'The bullet has entered the heart and pierced his liver,' he pronounced. 'He's dead.' Shocked by the dramatic and terrible events of the night he made the sign of the cross and dropped to his knees beside Felix where they prayed together that Russia might at last be saved.

Five minutes later as the conspirators met in the upstairs room to decide their next move, Felix became increasingly anxious and suddenly announced, 'I'm just going downstairs to make sure there's been no mistake and that he really is dead.'

Bending over the prone body, he checked for a pulse and found nothing. Then suddenly, without warning, Rasputin leapt up and clutched at his throat, before ripping the epaulette off his uniform. Felix was now convinced that he was dealing with the devil incarnate. Breaking free, he ran upstairs in panic to where Poroskewitz was waiting, the others having gone to fetch the car in which they were going to dispose of the body.

'My God! he's still alive!' he shouted. 'He tried to kill me!'

'Take a hold of yourself, Felix, you're out of your mind.'

'Go and see for yourself if you don't believe me.'

With that the two men went on to the landing. To their horror they saw Rasputin clawing his way up the staircase on all fours. They shrank back while he staggered to his feet and crossed the hall before opening the courtyard door and lungeing into the darkness. Poroskewitz then picked up the pistol and fired four shots at Rasputin who was shouting, 'Felix, Felix, I will tell everything to the Empress.' The first two shots missed, while the third hit him in the shoulder, and the fourth in the chest. Rasputin fell in a pool of blood on to the snow and, running over to him, Felix hit him repeatedly over the head with a rubber truncheon.

The commotion had alerted the police who started to make enquiries about the shots that had been heard. Felix was temporarily able to satisfy the investigating officer.

'Don't worry, it's only the Grand Duke Dimitry who had been dining with me. We killed a dog by mistake in the courtyard in high spirits.'

The explanation, plausible as it was, did little to convince the night officer at the police station, who asked his colleague to return to the palace where he found Poroskewitz, obviously drunk, blurting out 'We've just killed Grishka Rasputin, the enemy of Russia and the Tsar.'

'He's gone out of his mind,' interrupted Felix. 'All that happened was that the Grand Duke Dimitry shot the dog and my friend said, 'What a shame it wasn't Rasputin.'

Intimidated by Felix's rank, the officer retired for a second time.

Rasputin's body was now rolled up in a blue curtain and put in Dimitry's car which carried a flag on the bonnet exempting it from being stopped by the police. Poroskewitz and Lazovert were entrusted with disposing of Rasputin and on arrival at the Neva they hastily pushed the body through a hole in the ice, carelessly leaving one of his boots where it could be seen.

The following day rumours of Rasputin's assassination were rife in Petrograd. Protopopov felt it his duty to advise the Empress about the circumstances surrounding the night's happenings at the Moika Palace. His message only reinforced the conversation she had just had with Anna Vyrubova who told her that Rasputin's daughter, Maria, had telephoned in some distress to say that her father had gone out last night in Felix Yussoupov's car and had not been seen since.

Turning to Anna the Empress began, 'I knew from the moment you told me that our friend was going to the Moika Palace to see Irina and Felix that there must be some mistake. Irina's in the Crimea.'

'I took the icon to our friend as you asked yesterday

afternoon and he was in good spirits,' replied Anna, 'but it worries me that Poroskewitz, although drunk, has claimed he murdered him.'

'I think it might be an idea if you were to telephone Prince Obolensky and see if he was with Felix last night,' said the Empress. 'After all, someone must know what is going on and where he is.'

Before Anna was able to bring her any news, the Empress contacted Protopopov's office and asked that Felix and Dimitry be put under house arrest. This caused an instant shock wave as only the Tsar had the power to confine a grand duke of Russia.

Felix was anxious to disassociate himself from the killing. He telephoned the Empress only to be told that she was unavailable and that if he wished to communicate it must be by letter. He dashed off a hurried note claiming to have no knowledge of the events of the previous night.

Meanwhile, James had been waiting anxiously for news of the assassination attempt. He dared not communicate with Natalia but he knew that Rasputin was missing and that Felix, Dimitry and Poroskewitz were considered to be the major names under suspicion. He had been asked that morning by Sir George to comment on the rumours in the light of his friendship with Felix, and he knew there was no point in trying to deceive the Ambassador.

'Felix often talked about ridding Russia of Rasputin, Ambassador,' he began. 'There's every reason to believe that he may well have been murdered.'

'Did you have any part in this?'

'No, I was at the embassy all evening, playing cards with Baskerville and Johnson. I lost a packet, I'm afraid.'

'What connection, if any, might Natalia Orlofski have had in the plot if our assumption proves correct? Think carefully, she is now a British national, and if she was implicated it could be embarrassing.'

James sat back and took a deep breath. For a moment he was undecided as to how he should handle this question. He knew any attempt to cover up the truth would be transparent to Sir George who was an old and wily campaigner.

'She knew what Felix was planning and supported him,' he replied carefully. 'I can only assume that if it was Felix who murdered Rasputin, then she would be implicated by association.'

'That's exactly the conclusion I have come to,' replied Sir George. 'In the light of all this I'd better wait till things become clearer before I tell Sir Edward Milner. It's almost certain the Empress will insist that the conspirators are brought to justice, and it's going to be a very ticklish situation. London is waiting for definite news before we are advised on the official Foreign Office line.'

Three days later, on 12 January 1917, the tell-tale boot was found on the icy Neva, After a short search of the river, divers brought Rasputin's body to the surface. It showed signs that he had still been alive when put in the water as he had freed one arm which was held upright as if in a grotesque benediction.

The news spread quickly through the city and crowds of people ran through the streets rejoicing. Yussoupov, Dimitry, and Poroskewitz were acclaimed as saviours of Russia. The Tsar, when informed, confessed to being 'horrified and shaken' and went on to express the grief he felt over the incident when he returned to Petrograd. The Empress, however, bore the news with amazing resilience and waited silently for the results of the post mortem which was being carried out at the Veterans' Hospital near Tsarkoe Selo. When the results were given to the Tsar they showed that Rasputin's lungs were filled with water, certain proof that he must have been alive when thrown into the river.

Two days later he was buried in a corner of the Imperial Park in the presence of the Imperial Family, Anna Vyrubova and another friend of the Empress named Lilli Dehn. Before the coffin lid was closed the Empress placed an icon, signed by all her family, inside it, together with a letter. It read simply, 'My dear Martyr, Give me thy blessing that it may follow me always on the sad and dreary path I have yet to tread here on earth. And remember us from on high in your Holy prayers. Alexandra.'

The question now remained as to what to do with the conspirators.

In the days that followed, the Tsar's health became precarious and Sir George and Paleologue were shocked by his ghost-like appearance. Rumours again circulated that Batmaef's herbal potions, as recommended by Rasputin, were slowly weakening him in body and soul. The Empress was preoccupied by thoughts of death and disaster. Uppermost in her mind was the prediction, made with such certainty by Rasputin, that if he were to die, the crown would be lost within six months.

Natalia made no attempt to contact the Empress but sent a letter of condolence through Count Freedericksz. She knew, however, that her days in Russia were numbered and it came as no surprise when James telephoned to say he was sending a car for her and she must prepare to leave the country. 'I'm afraid that the embassy has received a direction from Protopopov's office that you must return immediately to England on the Tsar's orders. You would be wise to comply and I am making all the necessary arrangements.'

'But what about my patients and the staff at the hospital?'

'You must leave them to others now,' replied James gravely. 'You have done your duty.'

'What news of Felix and Dimitry?' she asked hesitantly.

'They are safe for the time being,' replied James, 'but who knows what the future may bring to this turmoil.'

'Has the Ambassador told the Milners about all this?'

'Yes, they know all about it and send you their love. They're looking forward to seeing you at Larkhill. Now you really must start your packing, there's very little time. Delay and all may be lost.'

43

Lavinia Milner sat in silence in the dining room at Larkhill. At the other end of the table Sir Edward was finishing his breakfast as Lovatt brought in a copy of *The Times,* which he had just ironed, and placed it before him. This was a ritual important to both of them as it gave the household a feeling of order and stability. Sir Edward opened the paper and scanned the pages eagerly.

'There's a full account of Rasputin's funeral,' he announced loudly. 'The Tsar's come back specially to Petrograd from headquarters to be near the Tsarina, and there's even mention of Natalia being in Petrograd on the night of the murder.'

'I really can't understand what they're trying to achieve by involving her,' said Lavinia. 'It's just so unfortunate that she had to leave in such haste.'

'Felix bungled things, I'm told,' he replied. 'He'll be lucky to escape the Tsar's wrath.'

'It's not him I'm worried about. Natalia really doesn't need all this unwelcome attention. I'm certain that she would have had the good sense to keep her distance.'

'Don't be too sure, Lavinia. You know she always swore

that one day she would take revenge on Rasputin and the Korsakovs for her brother's death.'

'I know what you're saying has a grain of truth, dear,' she replied, looking over her glasses at Sir Edward, 'but I also know that Freedericksz wouldn't let Natalia get directly involved in such a plot.'

'To rid Russia of Rasputin has always been a sacred cause to her,' he replied. 'She saw him as a demon and was only too happy to support Felix and Dimitry in what she thought was right for her country, as well as settling an old score.'

'Don't you think we ought to contact the Duffs?' Lavinia asked suddenly, changing tack. 'After all, they must be wondering what's going on.'

'I spoke to John last night,' replied Sir Edward airily. 'He's been kept up to date by the Foreign Office. I was going to tell you if you'd given me time.'

Lavinia saw there was little point in arguing.

'I told him the facts as I know them', he continued, 'and advised him that Natalia was going to be staying with us for a while.'

'How did he take it?'

'Didn't have much to say on the matter,' said Sir Edward brusquely. 'He already knew about Felix being banished to his estates in Central Asia, and that Dimitry had been ordered to join the army in Persia.'

'What about the other three men?'

'They've wisely left for the Front.'

'What saved them from standing trial?' asked Lavinia, intent on wringing out the last bit of information.

'Public opinion is a strong master. The Tsar could never have dared to allow them to be put on trial and punished. They are heroes in Petrograd.'

'Well, I can't help but admire Natalia if all you say is true,' said Lavinia, her eyes sparkling. 'Good for her, I say.'

'I agree, my dear,' replied Sir Edward cagily. 'There's no doubt she's got spirit and, if she has been involved, she has helped to shorten the war. With that dreadful man out of the way, it will save hundreds of thousands of lives.'

'I do hope so,' she sighed. 'I just hope it doesn't give way to a greater evil. I always remember you saying that infringements of the law by privileged people, for whatever reasons, often lead to severe consequences and the breakdown of law and order on a much wider scale.'

'You've got a good memory,' said Sir Edward.

Two weeks later Grainger was dispatched to London in the Daimler to meet Natalia's train. Victoria Station was crammed with troops either going or returning from overseas, and he had to hunt to find her in the milling throng. She greeted him warmly and waited while he struggled to secure her copious array of suitcases and portmanteaux in the car.

Once they had cleared the outskirts of the city, Natalia could see the remains of a snowfall that still clung to the hedges and fields. As they gingerly descended Henley Hill and crossed the bridge into the town, a wave of memories washed over her before they turned and headed up the Fairmile to Larkhill. The lodge keeper was waiting to open the impressive wrought-iron gates almost before Grainger had honked his horn. Passing between the great stone gate piers they drove up the long, straight avenue leading to the house.

As Lovatt opened the front door, Natalia rushed in and flung her arms around Sir Edward and Lavinia in turn while Lovatt went to attend to her luggage.

'We've been so worried about you,' began Sir Edward as he took Natalia by the arm. They walked to the library. The room looked just as she remembered it with its pine bookcases and elegant furnishings. They sat down before the blazing log fire.

'You'd better get warm before you tell us your adventures,' he said.

'I never fully appreciated that England in mid-January can feel almost as cold as Russia,' said Natalia, rubbing her hands.

323

'It's simply that we have a damper cold here which penetrates the bones,' complained Lavinia. 'Now, I want to hear about James first and then we can hear the other news.'

At that moment there was a knock on the door and Lovatt entered with a tea tray which he left on the low table in front of the fire.

'James is fine,' Natalia started. 'He's been a wonderful friend to me and a strong shoulder to lean on.' Natalia could sense that Sir Edward was anxious to hear of the important matter and he sat clapping his hands in excitement as the story of Rasputin's murder unfolded.

When she came to describe what Count Freedericksz had told her of the fateful night, he let out a bellow. 'God bless Felix and Dimitry! Never thought they had it in them. How did James say the news of the assassination was received in diplomatic circles?'

'With mixed feelings,' replied Natalia. 'While almost everyone at court was delighted, there were disturbing reports that the peasants in the provinces felt it was yet another blow struck at one of their kind.'

'They'll soon forget him,' said Sir Edward, 'and a bit of common sense will return to Russia.'

'It's important that you both know that I didn't become involved in the plot just to revenge my family for the part Rasputin played in their downfall,' said Natalia seriously. 'It was my decision, taken in the cold light of day. It was vital to save the monarchy and, at the same time, free Russia from the Empress's misguided rule. From the comfort and safety of Larkhill it almost seems as if it never happened.'

'But how did Freedericksz say the other members of the Imperial Family reacted?' asked Sir Edward intently.

'I'm afraid that, instead of uniting them, it only widened the breach within the family. Why, before I left James even told me of a plot among the Grand Dukes to remove the Empress from power, by force if necessary. He had heard from the French Embassy that Prince Gabriel Constantinovich had given a wild party for his mistress just before I left at which the topic on everyone's lips was the plot against the Empress.'

'It's a sad state of affairs,' said Sir Edward thoughtfully. 'I don't envy the job Sir George has to do but I know from personal experience that we couldn't have a better man at the embassy.' After a pause he continued, 'It's that bloody man Protopopov who's not giving the country firm or decisive leadership. I'm going to chance my arm and write to Buchanan suggesting he should seek an audience with the Tsar and tell him bluntly that time is running out for Russia and the Romanovs unless something drastic is done to save the situation.'

'You can try,' replied Natalia softly, 'but it's my opinion that things have already gone too far to be put right. I fear very much for Russia.'

'I can only hope you're wrong,' he replied. 'If she's weakened by internal unrest then the Germans will make capital out of the situation and we will have to rely on America coming in on our side.'

'I've got a feeling that the Tsar may have done us a greater favour than he knows by expelling you, Natalia,' Lavinia said with a wry smile. 'At least you've come home to safe ground. Now why don't you go and have a nap before dinner and then you might like to telephone the Duffs and tell them you've arrived safely.'

In the weeks that followed Natalia's departure, James was overcome with a deep sense of unease. He knew he was coming to a pivotal point in his life and, deep down, he felt lonely and unfulfilled. If his time in Petrograd had taught him one thing, it was a sense of crisis, and that each moment seemed more urgent than any in the preceding years. The Diplomatic Service had fallen short of fulfilling his wider ambitions and, although he had made steady progress, he could only see himself ending up as ambassador to some princeling state or principality like his father. Time was running out and if he was to take the major step of leaving the service he knew it must be now. He had hoped to talk to Natalia about his more secret thoughts but her sudden departure had upset his plans. With iron determination he controlled a strong impulse to go and see Sir George immediately and tell him he had thrown in his hand. He realised that it would only be a matter of time before he cut loose. He knew, with ever-increasing intensity, that it was his feelings for Natalia that were at the root of his problems.

The following day James walked into Pierre's barber shop in the Bolshaya Moroskaya to have his hair cut. As he entered the fashionable establishment he met Count Freedericksz who went there to be shaved as part of his rigid daily routine.

'James,' he said in his avuncular manner, 'I'm glad to see you. You have been very much on my mind. Could you spare the time to come and visit me at five o'clock this afternoon?' Without waiting for an answer, he continued, 'Come to my private apartments at the Potchtamtsaya which is directly opposite the Horse Guards' barracks.'

'I shall be honoured, Count,' was all James had time to say before the elderly soldier was submerged in a lather of white soap as Pierre started the daily ritual.

At five o'clock precisely, James was ushered into Count Freedericksz's study by a liveried footman. The old man was sitting in a big easy chair and he signalled James to sit opposite him. The room was comfortably furnished, and it was obvious that its focal point was a desk strewn with papers and a cluster of pictures of the Imperial Family. On the wall hung a large picture of the Count's regiment deployed in formation on the parade ground.

'It's good of you to come at such short notice,' he began. 'To tell you the truth, I've been in poor health and out of action since Natalia left. In view of the circumstances, it would not be politic of me to write to her formally so I am asking you to convey to her my very warmest regards and sentiments.' He fumbled in his pockets and brought out a small, beautifully wrapped parcel, saying, 'Please be kind enough to give her this memento when you see her on your next leave.'

'I shall be only too pleased to ensure that both your message and this gift are delivered safely,' replied James.

'Never forget, my boy, that she comes from a very remarkable family and it's a tragedy for Russia that they are not here now, putting some backbone into the affairs of this country.'

'I know what you mean, Count,' replied James. 'It's at times like these one becomes frustrated by diplomatic language and conventions. It's such a temptation to try to get to the truth and speak plainly. If only the ambassadors of the Allies would speak their minds to the Tsar.' He stopped abruptly, feeling he had gone too far before he saw a twinkle in the old man's eyes.

'I think it will not be long before Sir George will be asking me to arrange an audience with His Imperial Majesty. Now, if you will accept some advice from an old man, don't leave it too long before you contact Natalia. It may interest you to know that, when we talked privately, you were the one she always spoke of. She holds you in very high regard and, after all, you're one of her oldest and most valued friends. You mustn't let her escape, James,' he said eyeing him.

'I don't think she would ever consider marrying me, if that's what you had in mind, Count,' said James, flushing.

'That's exactly what I meant,' he replied, tapping his cane on the parquet floor. 'Now pour yourself a drink. I can't join you, unfortunately, as those damn doctors have stopped me.'

James did as he was instructed and mixed a powerful pink gin before quickly resuming his seat.

'My mentor and predecessor in this exalted position', Freedericksz continued, 'was Count Vorontzov. He was eventually appointed viceroy to the Caucasus. One of the most important things he taught me was always to go to the heart of the matter. At the same time it's vital to choose the moment to deliver your message with the greatest care. It must be like a rapier thrust – quick and purposeful.'

James nodded, which was all he could think of by way of a reply to this totally unexpected piece of advice.

'I am glad that Natalia has gone,' Freedericksz continued. 'There's no place for her here now as the forces of another god are poised to take over Russia. A spiritual gangster, as our American friends call Rasputin, has been removed but he leaves a potential vacuum to be filled by revolution and terror.'

'I know what you mean only too well, Count,' replied James. 'Britain, with all its faults, seems a haven of stability compared with Russia at the present time. There can be little doubt we're headed for dangerous times.'

'Just so,' he replied gravely. 'Now, take my advice and don't let your own dreams collapse by worrying about the overthrow of an old system here. To some extent we all have blood on our hands but at least we don't use the water Pontius Pilate washed in.'

James was still wondering precisely what Freedericksz had been driving at as he left carrying Natalia's parcel. 'It's always riddles and intrigue in this place,' he murmured. He just hoped that he had understood the message the old man had been anxious to put over to him. To have understood correctly, he knew, might change the whole course and direction of his life.

Almost exactly one week later, Sir Edward came into the library at Larkhill bearing the morning's mail. 'George Buchanan has written to me,' he said turning to Natalia. 'James intends leaving the Diplomatic Service at the end of February. He has suggested that he might be able to spend a few weeks here until he's able to find more permanent accommodation. As you know, both his parents died last year and, after all, we're not exactly short of accommodation. What do you think?' he asked eyeing her intently.

'I know he was concerned about his future,' she replied, 'but it's a shock to know he's actually resigned. We've known each other for a long time and we get along very well. You must, however, be careful you don't turn Larkhill into a refugee camp for displaced persons.'

'George tells me James is looking for a house in Cheshire where his parents lived for a brief time in their retirement. It's a shame he let their place go, but it's always easy to be wise after the event.'

'Randle and Emma might have a cottage to let on the Weathersfield Estate,' said Natalia. 'I'll write to them today and see if there's anything available that might be suitable.'

Although she would not admit it, Natalia was hurt and annoyed that she had to learn of James's resignation from the Diplomatic Corps second-hand from Sir Edward. 'The very least he could have done was to write and let me know,' she thought angrily. When, however, a letter from the embassy duly arrived, she forgot her annoyance and read it eagerly. James had always written entertainingly and she smiled as he recounted his meeting with Count Freedericksz and the details of how he had asked that his kindest sentiments be expressed to her. He went on to tell her that the old man had entrusted him with a gift which he would bring to Larkhill. As she expected, he didn't dwell on his decision to change the course of his career, simply explaining it away as, 'Something I had to do before I was too old and set in my ways'.

It was, however, his proposal of marriage that took her completely by surprise and left her unsure of her own emotions. It had taken her a long time to get over Peter's death and she had been very defensive where men were concerned. She knew James understood her feelings and she appreciated the way he had never pressed his attentions on her. He finished the letter by saying that the answer would wait until he came back to Britain but he would '… appreciate a pointer as to which way the wind blew'.

'I'll bet it's that wily old fox Freedericksz up to his tricks again,' she thought.

She slipped the letter into her pocket and went upstairs. The following morning she sat down at the writing desk in the library and started to write in her firm, bold hand.

Dearest James, Many thanks for your belated letter. In answer to your question; the wind was blowing from the east but it has suddenly changed to a much more favourable direction. Come back soon and you will have your answer. Love, Natalia.

Natalia now found a new contentment at Larkhill. She had loved the house from the moment she first saw it and it was the nearest thing to home she had known since her childhood. Everything about the place had a particular magic for her. It was England personified with its classical proportions, elegant yet discreet furnishings and rolling parkland. The whole place had an air of serenity and peace and it was only now, in these Arcadian surroundings, that she began to realise how much strain she had been under in the preceding year and how much she needed a stable and loving relationship.

44

Several weeks passed before all the formalities of Michael's release were completed to the satisfaction of the court, the police and the medical authorities. He had been examined by two independent doctors who had certified him to be of sound mind. Many questions remained to be answered but at least he had his freedom and he wept openly with joy as Hal collected him from the asylum and drove him to the Adelphi, where he was booked into his usual suite. He was thin and unkempt and for several days he stayed in his rooms unable to face the world. Hal was careful not to ask too many questions at first but, as the days passed, he gradually built up a picture of what had happened. The police were also anxious to reconstruct Michael's movements before and after his capture but in spite of repeated requests, he was unable to help them identify the house in which he was held captive. The fashionable residential areas of the city had endless houses that answered the description he had given and, anyway, he reasoned, even if they did succeed in finding it, his captors would be long gone.

'Dean and Sam are anxious that we return home as soon as

possible,' said Hal. 'There are difficult days ahead and if America goes to war it's going to be almost impossible to go back with any degree of safety.'

'I'm not going back just yet, Hal,' said Michael firmly. 'I need at least a month to recover and, anyhow, I've still not finished what I came here to do.'

'What on earth are you talking about?' asked Hal. 'If you're talking about your plan to take over the Albany Group then you can forget it. I've been working close to the family for almost a year. By now I know almost as much about them as anyone. There's no chance of the Duffs selling, especially as Emma has married Randle Baguley and there's a child on the way.'

'We'll see. Now tell me what's happened to Natalia Orlofski,' asked Michael, looking aggressively at Hal.

'It's a long story. She became involved on the fringes of the plot to murder Rasputin and was expelled by the Tsar. She's now come home to live with the Milners at Larkhill.'

It took Michael some time to take in the news. He walked over to the sideboard and poured himself a whisky. 'Drink?' he asked curtly.

'It's too early for me, Michael. Now don't start that nonsense about the Orlofskis again. There's been enough trouble in the past. I can only advise you to keep well away from her.'

'How do you know what happened?' asked Michael, erupting in anger. 'It's nothing to do with you!'

'Maybe not but I've researched the *Record's* files and found a mass of material on the Orlofskis. It's helped to fill a lot of gaps,' he said, returning Michael's icy stare. 'If only your mother had told me more I might have been able to stop you making some silly mistakes.'

The two sat looking at each other as Michael lit a cigarette, lazily inhaling the blue smoke.

'I wasn't going to tell you this until we got home,' started Hal after a moment's pause, 'but I've some news which I think you will want to hear about. It may, however, come as a bit of a surprise.'

Michael looked questioningly at Hal, without emotion.

'I'm sorry to have to tell you that Senator Harry Simmons killed himself over six months ago.'

'So what?' countered Michael irritably.

'Well, it's simply that his wife, Olivia, has claimed that their son is actually your child. She's anxious to speak to you and wants you to see the boy.'

'The stupid bitch,' replied Michael angrily. 'I don't want anything to do with her. I'd be grateful if you, Sam and Dean would keep out of my affairs. Just stop meddling in things which don't concern you.'

'Now calm down,' said Hal anxiously.

'What with this crazy story and all the pain and suffering that dreadful man Milner made me endure at the hands of his friends, it's lucky I'm not really mad,' he spluttered. 'He's helped Natalia to gain her revenge on me but I'll get even no matter what it costs.'

'For God's sake, Michael, calm down,' said Hal alarmed by this outburst which only served to confirm what he knew was in Michael's mind. He now saw, with great clarity, that a visit to Larkhill in the near future was important if another disaster was to be averted.

As the train hissed its way into Henley Station, Hal got up from his seat and put on his overcoat. He waited for the engine to grind to a halt and gathered up a battered leather case before stepping on to the platform. He quickly found a taxi on the station forecourt and asked the driver to take him directly to Larkhill Park. As they drove up the long avenue to the house, he could feel the sweat on his palms and, for the first time, he wondered if he would be able to get away with visiting Sir Edward under an assumed identity. When making the appointment by letter he had said that he was a visiting American writer undertaking research into the role of the Social Democratic Party in Russia, and had used the name Jack Duncan. He knew from his first conversation with Sir Edward that he had strong views on the subject and that he would welcome the chance to get his opinions better known in America. If only, by some twist of fate, Natalia could be there he might just be able to draw her into the discussion. Discretion, however, was the key and he knew he must not reveal his true identity.

Upon arrival at Larkhill, Hal was shown into the study where he was greeted warmly by Sir Edward who poured him a glass of Madeira.

'I just hope that I can be of some help, Mr Duncan,' he said looking at Hal. 'At least I see we share a mutual, if somewhat eccentric interest in the new forces that are active in Russia. It looks like those who follow the gospel of Marx and industrial socialism are going to have an increasing voice in the months and years to come.'

'I agree entirely,' said Hal. 'That is why it is so important to have the views of someone of eminence such as yourself who has held high office and knows the country and her people intimately.'

'I'm a bit out of touch now,' replied Sir Edward, 'but I still keep in contact with some of my old colleagues. They help to fill me in on the latest news.' Much to Hal's dismay, Sir Edward started a long dissertation on Russia and her problems, which lasted almost unbroken until Lovatt knocked on the study door and announced that lunch was served. In the dining room Sir Edward introduced Hal to Lavinia. He was disappointed that there was no sign of Natalia, and throughout the course of the lunch he tried carefully to steer the conversation in her direction by mentioning the shock waves that Rasputin's murder had caused. Lavinia was anxious to hear Hal's views on whether America would join the war and she nodded approval as he came down firmly on the side of their joining forces with the Allies as soon as possible. As she got up to leave the table she shot a glance at Sir Edward saying firmly, 'Now don't forget that Grainger is taking us into Henley at three-thirty this afternoon. We've an appointment in the Red Cross Committee Rooms with Natalia.'

'Glad you reminded me,' he replied. Then turning to Hal he enquired, 'What time is your train, Mr Duncan?'

'Four-fifteen, Sir Edward,' replied Hal.

'Capital. We can drop you off at the station on our way.'

By now Hal had come to the stark realisation that he was not going to learn anything from the Milners that was not directly connected to the stated purpose of his visit. After lunch, Sir Edward gave him a short tour of the house and it was a merciful relief to him when Grainger announced that the Daimler was at the front entrance. Sir Edward and Lavinia got into the back of the immaculate green limousine while Hal climbed into the front passenger-seat. A glass division separated the front seats from those behind and he felt strangely isolated sitting beside Grainger as they passed through the park gates on to the Henley road.

'Turning out a bad day, sir,' said Grainger without taking his eyes off the road.

Hal nodded, merely relieved that he had successfully survived the day without detection.

Michael was furious when he opened the note Hal had left for him. 'It's just not good enough, going off for the day and leaving me here alone while he interviews some idiot for his feature,' he muttered. 'Why, he's not even left me a telephone number to contact him.'

Resigned to his fate, he sat down and decided to read the copious memorandum that Dean had carefully prepared for him. It was clear from what he read that the German Government had now discarded any pretence and a policy of unrestricted submarine warfare against the Allies had been defiantly announced.

Zimmerman and the German Foreign Office had proclaimed that this would shorten the war dramatically. The *Chronicle* had faithfully printed the draft of Zimmerman's remarks to the United States Ambassador in Berlin, James Gerard, in their edition of 1 February 1917. Readers had been left in no doubt as to where the paper's sympathies lay. 'The announcement by the German Government of a hostile zone around Great Britain, France and Italy and in the Eastern Mediterranean in which all navigation including that of neutral countries is at risk has caused the gravest alarm,' it stated. It went on with the bald statement: 'All ships within the zone will be sunk.'

Michael noted that the following morning's edition of the *Chronicle* concentrated on: 'The insulting concession made by Germany in stating that only one American passenger ship each week might sail for England on the express condition that it was painted in wide stripes and adhered to a predetermined course laid down by Germany.'

'END THIS FARCE!' bellowed the headline and, on cue, President Wilson, swept along by a wave of public indignation, severed diplomatic relations with Germany on 3 February and dismissed Count Von Bernstorff.

Dean went on to explain how he was now concentrating on continuing to whip up anti-German fever with a series of blistering attacks on the Fatherland and its expansionist policies. Sales of the paper, he announced, were now running at record levels, and they had even brought out a supplement detailing the so-called outrages that 'the enemy' had perpetrated against the United States. He published cartoons lampooning the arrogant posing of the embassy personnel in their heyday and now openly printed the names of heavy industrial plants where sabotage had taken place.

The *Chronicle's* readers, meanwhile, had been promised new and shocking revelations about Germany's intentions for the dismembering of the United States. Dean confided that he was anxious to emphasise to the readers that Texas, New Mexico and Arizona could be taken under the control of Germany acting in alliance with Mexico. 'Don't like the son of a bitch but he's got his priorities right,' muttered Michael under his breath. 'Always knew those Texas lands would be worth something if we waited long enough and it will be over my dead body if anyone gets control of those oil revenues. Now, where the hell is Hal?'

45

John Duff was sitting at his desk reviewing the *Globe's* circulation figures with Paul Wigram when Emma came in. In spite of the fact that she was well advanced in her pregnancy she still looked immaculate in tweeds and pearls.

'Sorry to disturb you but I'm looking for Hal. I wondered if either of you know where he might be found? His secretary doesn't know when he will be back and we've got to send his syndicated column to New York urgently.'

'It's not like him,' said Paul. 'He's always unfailingly punctual with his copy. Have you checked his hotel?'

'Yes, they said they haven't seen him since yesterday morning,'

'I shouldn't worry if I were you,' replied John, 'Hal won't let us down and I don't want you worrying about trivia.'

'It's not trivia, Papa,' replied Emma irritably. 'We've never been late with copy for New York and I don't intend to start now even if I have to write it myself.'

'George will probably have everything to hand, Emma,' replied Paul. 'Why don't you ask him? Come to think of it, he had lunch with Hal on Monday and I believe they discussed Hal's forthcoming feature on Russia. I think there was mention of asking Sir Edward Milner to clear up some details that had eluded him.'

'Thanks, Paul' said Emma. 'Let's just hope it doesn't take too long. He's probably at the library scribbling. It's his favourite place for peace and quiet when he gets behind.'

'By the way, Emma, Hugo Ballard was asking after you,' said John. 'It might not be a bad idea if you were to go and see him some time soon and review your affairs. I don't want to meddle but you and Randle ought to consider letting him talk to David Mulley before he draws up new wills for both of you. It's particularly important now there's a baby on the way.'

'All in good time, Papa. Randle has already talked to him on the telephone. We both know his views.'

'Don't leave it too long,' said John picking up a sheaf of papers off his desk.

'As a matter of interest,' Emma said, turning to Paul, 'have you heard any more about Michael Korsakov lately? Hal's been very secretive.'

'Not a lot. It appears he's survived his ordeal pretty well, but I don't think the police have made much progress in solving the mystery of who attacked him and put him in the asylum. It's widely thought that one of the doctors who signed the certificate was implicated in some way. I believe he's soon to come up before a disciplinary panel on a number of serious charges. He'll almost certainly be struck off.'

'That young man seems to attract misfortune like a magnet,' said John, puffing at his cigar. 'It's a good job Lucinda was so perceptive in seeing through him.'

'I'll see you before I leave this evening, Papa,' said Emma, hastily gathering her things. 'I've got to rush now. I have an appointment with the gynaecologist in Rodney Street and I've promised to meet Randle at three.'

'Just do me a favour, Paul,' said John after Emma had left. 'I didn't want to say anything at the time but it's not like Hal to have neglected his copy and there's no one answering his telephone at the hotel. I'd be grateful if you'd go round to the Adelphi and check that things are all right. If you can't raise him then speak to Korsakov if you have to.'

'Are you sure that's a good idea?' asked Paul anxiously.

'Just do as I ask please.'

Enquiries at the front desk of the hotel drew a blank so Paul asked to be put through to Michael's suite.

'My name's Wigram,' Paul began.

'What the hell do you want?' was the surly reply.

'I've been asked to come and check on Dr Morrow by John Duff. We need his copy for New York.'

'I've no idea where he is,' came the terse answer. 'He just left a note that he was going to be away for a short time to research an article.' With that the telephone went dead.

Paul hurried back to the office. Deciding not to report to John Duff until he had all the facts, he asked to be put through to George Gerrard's office. 'Is that you, George?' he began. 'What do you know about Hal having to rush off to research a feature?'

'What's all this about?' asked George defensively. 'All I know is that he's doing some work on the rise of the Social Democratic Party in Russia and I've given him a contact who might be able to help.'

'Sir Edward Milner?'

'Yes, as a matter of fact, it was.'

'Isn't Natalia staying at Larkhill?'

'Yes.'

'Well, don't you see the connection, George?' Paul asked anxiously.

'You mean with Michael Korsakov out of the asylum, Hal's gone to see Milner to ward off further trouble.'

'More than likely.'

'What do you think has happened?'

'Could be anything, but it must be serious as Hal always telephones if he's unable to fulfil what he's promised.'

'You'd better tell John. He knows Sir Edward and he'll be able to find out what's going on.'

John Duff hated disorder. It was in his nature to cling carefully to the prepared way. He didn't like to bother Edward Milner but things were now becoming urgent and he needed to know where Hal was. After all, he thought, if Edward was not in he would be able to speak to Natalia and it would give him the opportunity to catch up on her news. Lucinda and he had been careful not to invade her privacy after she telephoned them when she first arrived at Larkhill but two weeks had now elapsed without further contact. He picked up the telephone and asked for the number, Henley 222. It rang for what seemed an age before Daisy the housemaid answered.

'I'm afraid, Mr Duff, there's no one here at the moment.'

'It's important I contact Sir Edward as soon as possible. Can you tell me when he will be back?'

'Grainger took Sir Edward, her Ladyship and a guest to Henley about half an hour ago. I think they were going to drop the gentleman at the station.'

'Do you know who he was?'

'No, sir. He's not been here before. However, I think her Ladyship said his name was Duncan. From the way he spoke I assumed he was American.'

'Where is Mrs Duff?'

'The Princess went to Henley this morning to the Red Cross Committee Rooms. Sir Edward and her Ladyship, I think, will be going on there as well.'

'Thank you,' said John replacing the receiver with a click.

'Find me the number of the Red Cross Committee Rooms at Henley,' he said to the telephonist as he sat drumming his fingers on his desk.

'Please may I speak to Sir Edward or Lady Milner,' he began, 'or failing that, to Mrs Duff.'

'One moment, please,' was the measured response. After a minute or so Natalia came to the telephone.

'Thank God it's you,' she began. 'Something terrible's happened. The police have just told me that Sir Edward and Lavinia have been killed in an accident.'

'What on earth happened?' asked John, shocked.

'It just seems they had a puncture and their car skidded and overturned before catching fire.'

'My God,' said John catching his breath, 'Was there anyone with them?'

'Yes, Grainger the chauffeur and another man. They're all dead. We don't know who he is yet.'

'Well, I think I can tell you,' he replied solemnly. 'It's Dr Hal Morrow, Michael Korsakov's old tutor.'

'I don't believe it,' said Natalia. 'Are you sure?'

'As certain as I can be, I'm afraid. Now give me a few hours and I'll be with you on the next train. I'll help you all I can. Just go back to Larkhill and wait for me.'

John now telephoned the Henley police, advising them that he was travelling down immediately to identify the body. The last thing he wished was to have Michael travelling to Henley with all that might entail, especially as Natalia would be so vulnerable. He knew that the news would be difficult for Michael to take and he asked George Gerrard to wire Dean in New York, telling him that Hal's briefcase and passport had been found in the charred remains of the Daimler. Paul, meanwhile, was given the unenviable job of breaking the news to Michael.

It was ten o'clock when John arrived at Larkhill. Natalia kissed him as he held her close in a rare moment of intimacy. He could feel her pulse racing and he wondered how many more disasters she would have to endure. 'Surely', he thought, 'she's been through enough.'

Once seated before the large fire with a glass of whisky, he was able to study her face. There were a few more character lines but it was the same old Natalia, with her high cheekbones and those dark eyes still able to weave their spell in spite of the shadow of grief that hung over her.

'Don't worry about tomorrow,' he said reassuringly. 'I'll be with you every step of the way. We'll do everything together.'

After breakfast Natalia braced herself for the visit to the

town mortuary. Once inside the clinically tiled building they were shown into a small room where three bodies were laid out under white sheets. John went first to identify Hal.

'Yes, that's him,' he said. 'His name's Dr Hal Morrow.' He then moved quickly to where Natalia was standing. 'Be brave,' he said pressing her hand as the white sheets were turned back by the attendants, revealing the badly burned features of the Milners. She shrank back in horror and, finding herself unable to speak, merely nodded her head before John walked with her from the bare room. A terrible feeling of nausea engulfed her and she sat down pale and shocked on a hard pine bench.

It was with the utmost relief that they eventually stepped into the police car which had been provided to take them back to Larkhill. They sat in stunned silence for most of the journey with Natalia looking straight ahead, her slender fingers pressed together in her lap. For once John was lost for words and only when they saw the house in the distance did he attempt to speak.

'Just let me know when you feel able to talk about things,' he said. 'I know exactly how you feel.'

The following day Natalia received a visit from Richard Granville, the solicitor in charge of Sir Edward's estate, who had travelled from London.

Natalia had by now composed herself and she greeted the tall, hawkish man warmly as he entered the room.

'Sir Edward always talked about you with great affection, Mr Granville,' she said graciously. 'I should like you to meet Mr Duff. He's the father of my late husband. He has been a great strength to me.'

Granville shook John firmly by the hand and, once they were seated, he stared uneasily into the fire before speaking.

'I must, first and foremost, express my most sincere sympathy, Princess, for the great loss you have suffered. It was Sir Edward's express wish that if anything was to happen to him or Lady Milner I was to come and see you at the earliest possible moment.'

John then broke in to suggest that he left the room in case his presence might be an embarrassment to them both.

'Please stay,' said Natalia. 'You're family and I need your support more than ever now.'

'It was Sir Edward's wish', resumed the solicitor, 'that you be told immediately on his death that you are the sole beneficiary of his will after several charitable donations have been made. Naturally, I shall be reading the will formally after the funeral on Monday, when the exact terms will be revealed.'

After a long silence Natalia lifted her head and looked at him. 'I really don't know what to say, Mr Granville. This is such an unexpected turn of events. It's all been a terrible shock.'

'I fully understand, Princess,' said Granville. 'When you feel up to it, I'm afraid I'm going to have to burden you with making certain arrangements.'

'I think it might be a good idea if we waited until after lunch,' said John, looking anxiously at Natalia.

'I'm perfectly all right,' she protested. 'Things of this nature are better faced up to. Sir Edward always told me that in the event of anything happening to him or Lady Milner they wanted a simple funeral conducted in the family chapel.'

'His wishes are clearly set down,' said Granville. 'You are perfectly right, Princess, in saying that the funeral is to be kept simple but in view of his links with the Diplomatic Service there should, of course, be a memorial service held in London at a later date.'

'That goes without saying, Mr Granville. It's strange, you know, what you remember of past conversations,' she said, looking at John. 'They both always said that the best way to go to the grave was on a farm cart behind a fine pair of plough horses. Sir Edward said the thought of travelling in one of those dreadful macabre hearses gave him the shivers.'

'I think we can see that his wish is fulfilled without too much difficulty,' said Granville sombrely. 'The details I hold for the funeral arrangements are comprehensive. Sir Edward had obviously given them much thought. My instructions are that after the service in the family chapel the coffins are to be taken by horse and cart across the estate land to the boathouse at the river. The family steam launch will take them the short journey up the Thames to Henley Bridge together with the mourners. On arrival at Riverside, the estate workers will carry them to the family vault at the parish church for burial.'

'I shall leave the details for you to sort out, Mr Granville, but I must ask you to make immediate financial provision for Mrs Grainger,' said Natalia. 'I have been to see her. She is, naturally, very distressed.'

Granville acknowledged this request before turning to John. 'Who is in charge of the removal of Dr Morrow's body, Mr Duff? I believe he worked in association with your newspaper and is an accredited foreign correspondent working for the *Chronicle* in New York?'

John could feel Natalia's eyes suddenly focus on him.

'I thought he was your man, not the *Chronicle's*,' she said icily, turning her head away. It was not the time for lengthy explanations.

46

Lee Stevens was sitting in BJ's bar drinking beer and relaxing as he surveyed the rough and ready company.

'Hear you've had some trouble with folks tampering with your equipment, Lee?' said BJ.

'Yep, it's been a real problem.' replied Lee, looking at him questioningly. 'What do you know about it?'

'Not a lot, but I hear things.'

'What things?'

'Nothing real particular but enough to make me curious.'

'Go on BJ,' said Lee, leaning forward on to the bar.

'Just thought you ought to know those Germans don't like your running mates in the East. There's a lot of unrest hereabouts, and the Mexicans that come in brag about Germany joining forces with them and taking over Texas.'

'Makes me so damn cross,' said Lee downing the last of his beer. 'There seems to be no law and order around here anymore and that there Sheriff Parker is as much use as an alligator with rubber teeth. Looks as though I'll have to take the law into my own hands if we're ever to go into production.'

'Now don't do anything silly, Lee,' said BJ waving his finger reprovingly. 'Y'all got to remember that this is a law abidin' community.'

Lee gathered up his coat and walked across the crowded bar and out into the chill February evening. He crossed the forecourt, stumbling on the potholed surface and talking to himself all the time under his breath. As he was about to get into his car he saw two men coming out of the darkness towards him.

'You Mr Stevens?' said one.

'What's it to you?' replied Lee who was swaying unsteadily as he fumbled for his keys.

'We've been sent to find you by the security guard at the field. Seems like he's found some explosives attached to the derricks, sir.'

Lee tried hard to put his thoughts in order. 'Drive me to the field,' he said as he pushed the keys of the car into one of the men's hands.

The cool air of the evening helped to bring him back to his senses as they rushed along the country road at breakneck speed, the car bounding on the ruts made by an endless stream of heavy lorries and carts. He hoped against hope that Luder Carn, his foreman, would be there when they arrived as he had more experience of explosives than anyone else. Soon the forest of timber derricks came into view, silhouetted against the full moon. The area looked unreal in the silvery light as they sped to the centre of the field.

'They've placed the explosives where they will do the maximum damage,' said the guard as Lee jumped out of the car.

'Let's just get a feel of things,' he said cautiously. 'Where's Luder?'

'Not here, boss,' said one of the men.

'Anyone else about?' asked Lee

'Nope.'

Seeing he wasn't going to get much information from the frightened guard, Lee made a quick inspection. Although his head still throbbed, he was now thinking clearly. He could already see the explosives strapped to the derrick and further careful examination showed him that the engine shed would be blown to pieces if there was an explosion. Even more worrying was the fact that the surrounding well tanks had been wired up to explode simultaneously in one huge fireball that would cause enormous damage and put back the opening of the field by months. Lee knew well that if he lost those months it would put a great strain on his already precarious financial position and might even lead to insolvency. As all this raced through his mind, he sought desperately to find the timing device that was set to trigger the explosion. In spite of the cold of the night the sweat ran down his face as, oblivious to danger, he hunted for the detonator box.

Lee now started to work methodically. He traced the wires back from the engine shed. At last his patience was rewarded and careful examination revealed that the detonator box lay beneath an old green tarpaulin. Placing his face close to it he could hear the device ticking. A quick look at his watch showed him it was nearly midnight. His mouth was now dry and he tried to wet his lips with his tongue. He swallowed nervously as he debated what should be done. If only Luder could be found, he would know how to render it safe, he reasoned.

A few seconds later the night sky was illuminated by an enormous flash and the explosion that followed sent timber and fragments of hot metal flying in every direction.

In New York, Dean was still stunned by the news from Britain. Hal had always been his friend and he knew how much he had done behind the scenes to support Tamara when Michael was growing up without a father. He was sitting with Sam in his office and they had a critical decision to make.

'The only feasible solution as far as I'm concerned is that Michael must come back with Hal's body,' began Dean.

'I agree,' said Sam readily. 'I'll bet you any money that Hal was with the Milners with the sole intention of trying to prevent Michael from doing something unspeakable. Leave him alone in England and God knows what could happen.'

'We must rely on John Duff for help. He and George Gerrard have become friends in spite of Michael and perhaps they can help to persuade him to return.' At that moment the telephone rang. 'Excuse me a moment,' said Dean picking up the instrument. The conversation was short and to the point.

'You'd better listen carefully, Sam,' Dean said, putting down the receiver. 'It seems we've got major trouble on our hands in Texas. News has just come in from Frinksteins' Houston office of massive sabotage at the field. First reports say that Lee's been seriously injured and is in hospital fighting for his life. I'm told that a major part of the field has been blown up which will put our schedule back by months, not to mention losing a key man at a vital time. It seems for some strange reason that all our troubles come at once. No sooner do we get one crisis resolved than another bombshell hits us.'

'Couldn't agree more,' said Sam. 'Stewart tells me that Lee had trouble enough before this happened. The sabotage put him behind and cost him a lot of money. Seems he had serious cash flow problems.'

'You know, it occurs to me', said Dean thoughtfully, 'that Michael might just be the man to sort out this mess. We've always known Lee's weakness was that he operated a one-man company. Someone is obviously going to have to replace him in the immediate future to safeguard our interest so why don't we send Michael to Texas? You never know, it might be the challenge he needs. Furthermore, I know that Olivia Simmons has gone to live in San Antonio with her mother and I'm sure Michael will want to see this supposed child of his.'

'It might work,' said Sam cautiously. 'If he is to come back then he'd better book passage within the week as the international situation is worsening. If he isn't careful he might find it impossible to get back at all.'

'In the short term', said Dean, 'I think it's vital you get down to Houston and assess the situation at first hand. Stewart, I know, will give you all the help you need from Frinksteins' office.'

'I'll try to leave tomorrow when I've cleared up a few things,' replied Sam. 'I need to study the fine print of the contract with Stevens Oil. I'm certain that we put in a clause giving O'Donnell's the right to negotiate a takeover of the company if they become insolvent or lost key personnel.'

'I knew you'd leave nothing to chance,' smiled Dean. 'Incidentally, I heard only a few days ago from Senator Whinney that our case for compensation by the Germans has had a favourable hearing in the appropriate sub-committee. It appears that if America declares war on Germany, we may get our money in full from German assets that will be frozen over here.'

'Let's cross one bridge at a time,' said Sam cautiously. 'You deal with Michael and his problems and I'll see to things in Texas.'

Dean knew that news of the troubles in Texas would travel fast and that, unless he took positive action, the predators would gather. He was still convinced that Michael might be the saviour of the situation. In spite of all his faults, he had flair, courage and charisma, and it would be good to be seen to have an O'Donnell on the spot. Reports from Britain had suggested that he was near to a nervous breakdown after Hal's death but Dean knew that revenge and anger were great motivations in Michael's life. Give him a grievance and it would really get his blood up. This time, he hoped, he might temporarily forget about his feud with Natalia and concentrate his venom on the German saboteurs in Texas. He knew that, deep down, Michael was very loyal to Hal and had already indicated that he would bring his remains back to New York. Even as he was speaking to Sam a cable had been received indicating that he was to sail the following day.

'Let's hope he doesn't change his mind,' said Sam.

'No, he'll do as he promised.'

'I wish you'd tell me what you're really thinking, Dean,' Sam said, looking at his friend whose face was creased with a strange expression.

'It's something better not said.'

'Try me.'

'Well, I just wish it had been Michael who had been killed, not Hal.'

'Life's a bitch,' replied Sam. 'It's full of surprises and perversities.'

'Let's hope I'm right and that when he gets back here he'll have matured a bit. We're going to need all the help we can get in the next few months.'

'The choice is his. He can either become involved in the business on a day-to-day basis or get out. If he does decide to stay then he'll have to get his personal life in order.'

'You mean Olivia Simmons?'

'Yes, I've no doubt he'll make a beeline for her. She's got what he wants more than anything – a son and heir.'

By the time Michael arrived back in New York, the revolution in Russia had started to catch fire. The Ochrana headquarters had been ransacked and it seemed like a strange omen to him when he read reports in the *Chronicle* of soldiers and workers flooding into the great hall of the Tauride Palace which had been the gift of Catherine the Great to his ancestor. Dean, meanwhile, had made arrangements for Hal's body to be interred at Greenwood Cemetery. O'Donnell's stopped all their operations for a one-minute silence at noon as a mark of respect for their dead colleague, while he was laid to rest among the handsome monuments as the chill rain lashed down.

Michael had been very reserved since he returned and Dean and Sam were worried by the fact that he seemed almost to hide himself away in his apartment. When Dean managed to persuade him to come to the office for lunch, he listened without expression as he was told of O'Donnell's fortunes since he left on the *Lusitania*. It was only when Sam joined them after the meal that he showed any spark of interest.

'We had hoped, Michael,' he began, 'that you might feel up to helping us put the Texas operation back on its feet. Lee Stevens will be out of action for at least six months and then he'll be confined to a wheelchair. He's had both legs amputated. We're talking to Frinksteins about taking over Stevens Oil. They're going to need a considerable injection of cash if the field is to be exploited properly. Sam's talked to Lee in hospital and he's persuaded him to consider the offer.'

'What about Humble Oil taking them over?' asked Michael.

'Our contract specifically forbids Stevens from seeking other purchasers or investors. We have a sixty-day option which expires at the end of next month so we mustn't delay.'

'But I've no expertise in the oil business, Dean,' Michael protested.

'That's true, but Lee's got a good man in Luder Carn to help you and, don't forget, you've now got Frinksteins' office in Houston.'

'I must say it appeals to me to run my own show,' Michael replied. 'Who would I have to report to?'

'You'd be ultimately responsible to the board of O'Donnell's,' replied Dean, 'but as you and I technically own the company you'd just have me to kick your ass if things were mishandled.' He sat back, smiling.

'I appreciate the confidence you've placed in me Dean,' said Michael with an air of surprise. 'I can't seem to settle in New York so I'll consider the proposal very carefully. I'll give you my answer when I've taken time to think about it.'

'I shall wait with interest for your decision,' said Dean.

The following morning Michael arrived at Dean's office. He was now much more like his old self and had already insulted Kate by telling her that she should do something about her bad breath. 'For God's sake, go and get your teeth

351

fixed,' he had snarled. Pushing past her, he sat down, eyeing Dean with the gaze of a predator. 'Those bastards in Texas need a lesson,' he began. 'What they've done has got me mad as hell. I'm considering going down there as you suggested. I'll enjoy the challenge.'

'Good,' said Dean. 'But you must remember that if you do, you'll have to keep your temper under control.'

'For God's sake!' Michael replied angrily, 'Don't lecture me. A year in a mad house teaches you a hell of a lot about human nature.'

'I can imagine.'

'Anyway, I also want to see my boy in San Antonio. I'll let you and Sam know my decision by the end of next week.'

47

In the days after the funeral Natalia had found it difficult to accept her new position as mistress of Larkhill. She was acutely conscious that she had inherited a large house furnished with accumulated treasures brought together over the centuries by generations of Milners. The responsibility weighed heavily on her, particularly as she was all too well aware of her lack of experience in running a large estate.

She had called together all the staff, telling them it was her intention to carry on the estate in the best traditions of Sir Edward's family, and that they might rest assured that their jobs would be safe. She knew that Martin Kershaw, the newly appointed agent at Larkhill, was as solid as a rock, and she promised him full authority to run things without interference. In the past Sir Edward had often tried to intervene in estate matters, often with disastrous results, and she was determined not to make the same mistake. Martin was a man of around fifty with a direct but pleasing manner, who had recently been widowed, leaving him to bring up two teenage daughters. Natalia found him comforting, without feeling threatened by him, and she felt protected by his air of competence and authority. Everything about him suited Larkhill, from his restrained tweed suit to his brown brogue shoes. It was just his hands that were at odds with the rest of him. Where his face was sensitive and alert, his hands were like the roots of a tree, strong, sinuous and earthy.

At breakfast Natalia read the paper that Lovatt had delivered to her in the time-honoured way. She noticed that he had placed it on the table to reveal the first news of the events of 18th March and the Russian Revolution.

'What a blessing Mr Ponsonby has already left, Princess,' Lovatt ventured.

She nodded gravely. 'This really is the end of Russia,' she thought. 'If only the Tsar had stayed in Petrograd there still might have been a chance.'

The problem of James's accommodation was exercising Natalia's mind. He obviously could not stay at Larkhill and all the houses on the estate were occupied. The Red Lion at Henley might be a temporary refuge but it didn't provide a long-term solution. She wondered if she could ask Martin to allow him to stay at Manor Farm until things became clearer.

Natalia got up from the table and made straight for the estate office.

'You're up and about early, Princess,' Martin smiled.

'Not really. I'm always up at the crack of dawn. I just wanted to ask you a favour.'

'Fire away,' he said, looking at her directly, intrigued as to what the request might be.

'I wonder if it would be a grave imposition if James Ponsonby was to come and stay with you for a short time? Just until he gets somewhere else arranged, you understand.'

'But of course,' he beamed. 'I was going to suggest it myself, but I thought he might find the girls a bit too noisy in the school holidays.'

'I think he'll enjoy their company,' smiled Natalia.

'Well that's settled then,' said Martin decisively. 'The girls need stimulating conversation to broaden their minds and I shall greatly enjoy James's company.' He saw a smile flicker over Natalia's lips. 'If I may enquire, Princess, what does James consider turning his hand to now he's left the Diplomatic Service?'

'I don't think that he knows himself,' replied Natalia vaguely.

'Have you ever thought that with his administrative skills he could be an enormous help in running and developing the ancillary business enterprises on the estate? As you know I've always maintained that the forestry here could be made very profitable. Our properties in Henley have great potential. James could give you a balanced report.'

'I'd never thought of that,' said Natalia pensively. 'It's not at all a bad idea. Perhaps you could mention it to him when he arrives?'

'I'd be glad to,' said Martin, picking up his papers from the desk and jamming them into a battered old leather case. 'As you know, I've got great plans for the estate,' he continued as he looked for his cap. 'By the way, thank you for your vote of confidence. I think you know that I love the place almost as much as you do. Now, if you'll excuse me, I've got to be down at the dairy in five minutes.'

When he arrived at Larkhill two days later, James was grateful to Martin Kershaw for his offer of accommodation. He was painfully aware that circumstances had dramatically changed since Natalia and he had exchanged their last letters, and he knew he must tread carefully. He needn't, however, have worried as Natalia greeted him with a fondness that almost took his breath away.

'I've been so worried about you,' she said as he sat in the library facing a large silver tray containing an array of thinly cut sandwiches and a pot of his favourite Lapsang Souchong tea.

'If only I could have been here to help you when you needed it most,' he began.

'Funnily enough, it's probably a good thing you weren't,' replied Natalia. 'The main thing is that you're here now. It would have been terrible if you had been caught up in the revolution.'

'I'm sorry in a way I didn't stay,' he replied. 'Real revolutions don't happen every year. I'd like to have seen just one so that I could tell my grandchildren about it.'

'Don't joke,' said Natalia. 'It's all a bit too close to home for comfort. Fate has been kind with Sir Edward leaving me this wonderful estate; but there's not a day when I don't wish he and Lavinia were still here.'

James now listened carefully for some clues as to the direction of her thoughts and feelings towards him.

'You must be wondering where you stand with me?' she said, looking at him with her big, dark eyes.

'It did occur to me, more than once, that things are a bit different now,' he admitted hesitatingly. She took his hand and, seeing the look of apprehension, squeezed it gently.

'So much seems to have happened in a few short years, James. I'm not yet thirty and I seem to have lived through a lifetime. I'll be happy to spend the rest of my life here at Larkhill. Hopefully I'll have a bit of peace and quiet for a change.'

'Not you,' said James. 'You're not made to take a back seat.'

'Maybe not, but we'll have to wait and see. Everyone thinks that we Russians have a dark, brooding side to our natures but it's not really true.'

'I'm glad to hear that you're going to disprove my theory,' replied James smiling.

'Just wait a year or so for the war to be over and we'll make this place the most brilliant house in the country.'

'We?' murmured James raising his eyebrows.

'Oh! Did I forget to tell you that I've accepted your proposal?' she said airily.

'You most certainly did,' said James. He could feel the soft contours of her body as he pulled her close and kissed her before she gently pushed him away.

'It would be terrible if Lovatt came in and found me in your arms,' she said, smiling. 'The scandal it would cause in the village! I know we're still in mourning but I'm certain the

Milners would be glad that we're going to be happy in their home. Is it wrong to enjoy the gift of life while still respecting the memory of the dead?'

In the days that followed, Natalia asked James all manner of questions about the repercussions of the Rasputin affair. He explained to her that, before he left, the embassy was getting daily reports of the activities of the President of the Duma, a man called Guchkov. 'He's a rich man, powerful as well, but I know he fell from favour with the Tsar by supporting Felix and Dimitry.'

James went on to explain the latest rumour centred around the powerful anti-monarchical Union of Nobles joining forces with Guchkov. 'They seemed hell-bent on a palace revolution.'

'It doesn't surprise me,' replied Natalia. 'The Ochrana and all manner of secret movements have been conspiring for months.'

James now explained his theory that the recent visit to Petrograd by a British minister, in concert with the French and Italian delegations, might have stiffened Russian resolve and got all classes to pull together.

'It should have given the people hope,' he sighed, 'but instead they seem to feel a growing despair.'

'It's probably all down to the Tsar's attitude,' replied Natalia. '*The Times* commented that he had withdrawn into his own world at Tsarkoe Selo with the Empress and contemplated going back to military headquarters at Mogilev.'

'Gross folly. His place was in Petrograd. It wasn't only the wild men who preached revolution, you know, it was also senior members of the Duma. Why, only two weeks ago the Duma sent the Tsar a letter stating that they feared revolution was at hand and he completely ignored it.'

'So Felix's brave act did nothing for Russia?'

'I'm afraid not,' James replied. 'The situation was so tense and brittle after Rasputin's assassination that it almost seemed to have an adverse effect. There were rumours and

357

counter-rumours about plots against the Imperial Family every day but it was the bread rationing that really did it.'

'I can imagine,' said Natalia reflectively. 'Now you still haven't told me about the people at Ivanhov – how are they all. Is there any news of Kuropatkin?'

'I checked before I left but, as I said before, there's very little I can tell you. Yuri used to get messages back to us when he visited the railway halt, but nothing was coming through in the final days.'

'I only hope and pray they're all right. If anything was to happen …' Natalia's voice trailed off and she sat looking into the huge log fire.

'One question,' said James after a moment, 'What was in that parcel from Count Freedericksz? I've been dying to know.'

'Well as it happens, I've no idea. When I came to open it there was one of his little notes attached sending affectionate greetings but also a stern warning not to open the package until either he was dead or on the night before I marry.'

'How odd.'

'Yes. I must say it's all a bit puzzling but then he has a great sense of the dramatic.'

'Have you written and told him of our news?'

'Yes. I sent him a letter yesterday – I just hope it gets through.'

'It'll be safe if you did as I told you. All mail must now go in the diplomatic bag. My replacement, Ian McIntosh, will look after all letters and see they're delivered safely.'

'What sort of a man is he?'

'He's a fine fellow with a good record. Eton and Oxford and a first class degree. Now he can take all that lecturing from Sir George about "… the revolution born of the cold wind from the Front and fermented in the cities" as he puts it. You know, he's certain the Germans have a master plan to dominate the world,' he said, mimicking Sir George's precise tones. 'I can just hear him saying "being here is like standing transfixed on the doorstep of history".'

Natalia laughed.

48

Emma and Randle were overjoyed by the news of Natalia's engagement but it had come as a bit of a shock to John Duff. He still considered that she was married to Peter but, inwardly, he knew he must accept that she should have the chance to rebuild her life. It was a major hurdle for him to clear, and Lucinda listened patiently as he tried to set his thoughts in order. Subconsciously, she knew that he resented the fact that Natalia was on an equal footing with Emma as a shareholder in Albany.

'There's nothing wrong with James,' he reasoned. 'It's just that Natalia was married to Peter and it seems wrong that she should marry his best friend.'

'I don't see it that way,' said Lucinda soothingly. 'There's something rather reassuring in the fact that she should find happiness with a friend of Peter's. At least we know that he will look after her properly and that he's a young man of principle and integrity.'

'Just as long as she doesn't think that she's going to get him a seat on the board at Albany,' he replied.

'I really don't think that will be an issue,' she said. 'From what I hear Natalia is an extremely rich woman now, and the dividend she gets from Albany will be neither here nor there.'

'She was glad enough to have it in the past,' said John angrily.

'But times have changed,' insisted Lucinda. 'I shall be cross with you if you go on talking like that. You've got to accept things as they are, hard as it may be, and not harbour any ill will.'

'I bear her no ill will,' said John sighing. 'It's just that she'll always be Peter's wife to me.'

'I'm afraid that there is a phrase in the marriage service that says "till death do us part",' she prompted.

'I know, I know,' he said.

'I hear that Emma is thinking of asking Natalia to be godmother to the baby when it arrives,' said Lucinda.

'Yes, thanks to you, my dear, those two seem to get on now that business over Korsakov is in the past.'

'I'm just delighted that Emma saw the light before it was too late. It would have been a case of "marry in haste and repent at leisure", if ever there was one.'

'I wonder what poor girl's life he's ruining now?' sighed John.

Emma's baby arrived at three o'clock on the afternoon of 2nd April. It was a girl, weighing six pounds, and Randle was summoned from the gun room to be told that mother and daughter were doing fine. Secretly, Emma had been desperately hoping for a boy as she knew Randle wanted a son and heir for Weathersfield.

Now, however, all she cared about was that her child was healthy and normal. She had almost forgotten the long and excruciating labour pains and the final supreme effort of birth. She cradled the small, wizened child in her arms as Randle came into the bedroom. He gently kissed Emma on the forehead before looking in wonder at his daughter.

'She's the most beautiful thing I've ever seen,' he said smiling. 'You know I always wanted a girl as the Baguleys have had a strictly boys-only tradition in the past. You've given me a wonderful present today,' he said as he touched Emma's cheek.

She was so pleased and surprised by what Randle had said that she burst into tears. Handing the child back to the midwife, she dried her eyes and kissed him.

'She's going to be quite as beautiful as you,' he said beaming.

Jane Elizabeth Duff Baguley was christened at Weathersfield Church by Rector Howard on the last Saturday in April. Her godparents were Natalia, Sir Hugo Ballard and Caroline Malpas. Preparations for the service, however, had not gone entirely without a hitch. The family christening robe had split asunder and had had to be hurriedly stitched by Nanny Brown. Randle had refused to allow the rector to use the supposed Jordan water that had been brought home by Sir Hugo from a visit to the Holy Land as he pointed out that the Jordan River was now an open sewer and contained all manner of dreadful diseases. On reflection, Sir Hugo agreed with this logic and the offending water was ceremoniously poured away.

When the service was over the small party made their way back to the Hall where a buffet had been laid out in the dining room. Crabtree presided over the proceedings with increasing difficulty and Cook and the staff were invited to come in to see the christening cake cut by Emma. Sir Hugo made a speech on behalf of the godparents and finished by wishing the child: 'Roses, roses all the way'.

John and Lucinda had given Jane a beautiful little diamond cross on a gold chain which had been the property of Lucinda's mother, but it was Natalia who amazed Randle and Emma with the generosity of her gift. She had placed her Albany share certificates in a large manilla envelope and appended a simple note in her own hand. 'To dear little Jane, I give you these shares as I know Peter would have wanted you to have them – remember him always – all my love, Aunt Natalia.'

361

The following Monday John Duff and Paul Wigram presented themselves at Sir Hugo Ballard's office at the Cheshire Bank in Liverpool. They proudly showed him the month's figures for the *Globe* which had achieved a circulation of over a million copies for the first time, and John carefully placed a cheque on Sir Hugo's desk which effectively cleared the loan Albany had taken out to secure their place as a major force in the newspaper world.

'This is quite an achievement, gentlemen,' said Sir Hugo, beaming. 'I'm glad that things have worked out so well and that the bank has been able to play a small part in your success.'

'Thanks, Hugo,' said John. 'You were with us when we started all those years ago and you've always been a good friend through thick and thin. My only regret is that Peter can't share in all this success, but it is a great comfort to me to know that little Jane has shares in Albany.'

'It was a fine and generous gesture by Natalia,' replied Sir Hugo looking at John. 'Peter would have been proud of her.'

The following day Randle went to Liverpool, leaving Emma at Weathersfield. He made a point of calling at Dale Street to see John and was pleasantly surprised when he encountered Lucinda on her way up to his office.

'How's Emma, Randle?' she asked as they walked together up the stairs.

'She's just fine,' he replied. 'She's never looked better but I can't stop her still eating for two!'

'Just make sure she goes on a diet,' said Lucinda smiling.

'Don't worry,' he replied, 'I've spoken to her very severely.' They both laughed as they were shown into John's office suite.

'I'll tell Mr Duff you're here,' the secretary said softly. 'It's a good time to catch him. He doesn't have an appointment for lunch.'

After a moment John walked in, kissing Lucinda before he shook Randle warmly by the hand and patted him on the shoulder.

'Why don't I order lunch and we can crack open a bottle of champagne. I've got something important to tell you.'

'Don't keep us in suspense,' said Lucinda. 'You never were much good at keeping a secret.'

'Well,' he said, lighting a large Corona, 'it's to do with Michael Korsakov.'

'Now don't start all that nonsense again,' said Lucinda angrily, 'or I shall not stay in this office a moment longer.'

'Just hold on,' said John. 'I said it was good news.'

'Tell us what's happened.'

'He's moved to Texas and seems settled there according to Dean.'

'Thank God for that,' said Randle. 'The damage that young man has done is irreparable. It may sound callous but, like so many others, I wish that it had been him who was killed in Hal's place.'

'Life so often is unfair,' replied John. 'But at least we shall have the satisfaction of knowing he's thousands of miles away and we can let someone else deal with him.'

'I've never trusted that bounder,' said Randle. 'I'm only surprised he decided to go back so quickly after Hal's death.'

'George tells me that it was a dreadful blow to him,' interrupted John. 'Apparently he blames himself for it but at the same time he still feels that Natalia must be held equally responsible.'

'For what reason?' asked Lucinda astounded.

'I've no idea,' said John. 'George just puts it all down to that blood feud that's been going on since childhood. Let's just be glad that he showed one spark of human decency by wanting to do the right thing by Hal and returning with his body.'

'Hang it all,' said Randle, 'Hal was almost a father to him. It's the least he could have done.'

'Don't make the mistake of judging Michael by your own standards,' replied John. 'He lives by a different code. Now, more importantly, how are you keeping, Randle?'

'Not so bad,' he said. 'I still get caught very short of breath occasionally.'

'Can anything be done?'

'Not a lot. I'll be better now that winter is behind us.'

Lucinda could see that Randle did not wish to pursue the subject and shot John a warning glance. From what Emma had told her she knew there was no chance of his condition improving. All they could do was to hope it stabilised. She would never have dreamed of confiding her thoughts to John, but she knew after talking to Emma at the christening that the outlook was bleak for Randle. Emma had told her exactly how far his lungs had been affected by the gas and the look in her eyes said the rest.

For some reason that neither of them could explain, Hal's death remained a point of contention between Randle and Emma. Fate had played strange games and Hal's relationship with Emma, which had begun so ill-starred, had developed into one of trust and mutual admiration. Randle had not been keen on Emma's suggestion that Hal should be asked to become a godparent to their unborn child. He had regarded him as far too close to Michael Korsakov and thought that the idea was asking for trouble. He could see that finding Michael in the asylum, with all its psychological overtones, had created a bond between them, but it was a link he had wanted to sever.

Hal's untimely death had not only left a gap in Emma's personal life, it had also left her with another problem at the office. There was no one with Hal's ability and knowledge to write his syndicated column, and it had been with deepest regret that she had suggested to George that it might be discontinued. Dean had thought he might be able to find a replacement for Hal, but Randle, on hearing the news, had made certain that any future links with the *Chronicle* were now kept to a minimum.

'It just spells trouble,' he said. 'Let's forget the column and let it die a natural death.'

'But it was so readable and dynamic,' argued Emma.

'I'm just being practical.'

'Bigoted and short-sighted, you mean.'

'Perhaps, but I've learned to keep clear of minefields. There's been too much unhappiness and I want a clean break. Jane's future is the most important thing we have to think of. It would be a disaster if history repeated itself.'

'The same argument could just as well apply to Natalia,' she replied crossly.

'Yes, it could, but she just happens to be family and she's proved her loyalty by her love and generosity to Jane.'

'That's true, but you know how she hates Michael. I know in my bones that their saga will be played out to the last act. Revenge is a terrible master and they're both in chains.'

49

'I never thought Michael would take to the oil business so well,' said Dean as he sat in Stewart Armstrong's office at the bank. 'I am glad to tell you that he's really got things moving.'

'Let's hope it's not a flash in the pan.'

'We'll just have to wait and see, but I'm confident he'll do a good job. More importantly, things are moving pretty quickly in Washington,' continued Dean. 'The President is addressing Congress at this very minute and word has it that he is going to pillory Germany as a "natural foe of liberty" and recommend a declaration of war. If that happens then I have Senator Whinney's assurance that O'Donnell's will be paid a million dollars in compensation out of German funds frozen over here.'

'I think there's little doubt about the course of action Congress will take,' replied Stewart. 'Why, after all, we've already broken off diplomatic relations with Germany after Secretary Lansing made public the dispatches sent by Zimmerman to the German Minister in Mexico.'

'They must have been crazy to propose an alliance against us with Mexico and Japan and think they would get away with it.'

'Desperate times require desperate measures,' replied Stewart seriously, 'and Texas, New Mexico and Arizona were big prizes to be won. Now, if I foresee your question accurately, you are going to ask me to lend you part of the million dollars you need to buy Stevens Oil, with only Whinney's word to rely on?'

'Precisely,' replied Dean. 'You've got it in one.'

'I've got to say at the outset that I'm not too happy about it. It's a big gamble and the only real argument you have in your favour is that, with war imminent, this nation is going to need all the oil it can get its hands on.'

'Right again,' said Dean.

'Obviously, I can't give you an answer one way or the other at the moment. It will have to be a main board decision based on the report we get from our office in Houston. By the time we receive the relevant information I think that Congress will have made up their mind and the nation will know where it stands.'

'That's good enough for me,' replied Dean. 'I just hope that you and your colleagues will take into account the remarkable turnaround in the company's fortunes in the last six months and see that we have a really strong management team now.'

'You include Michael in this team?'

'Yes.'

'I'm just curious to know why.'

'Things have changed a lot for us,' replied Dean carefully. 'Sam and I have been very pleased with the attitude he's shown since his return. We're going to put our faith in him. After all, even if he makes a mess of things, we can always bring him home.'

'That may not be as easy as you think,' said Stewart cautiously. 'Don't forget that he can match your shareholding in O'Donnell's. He could give you a very rough ride if you're not careful.'

'I know all that, Stewart, but I'm still going to give him the chance.'

'That's fine, but don't expect the bank to take the same line.'

'I can see your point but I'm sure the bank will give favourable consideration to lending money to expand industries that are vital to your new markets in the southern states and to the war effort. Also, just think what effect it would have on your credibility in Texas if you pull out of this one.'

'You always were a good talker, Dean,' said Stewart. 'I'll do the best I can for you but I really can't promise anything at this stage.'

Sam had travelled to Houston at Michael's request and they had arranged to meet at Frinksteins' office.

'I wonder if you'd mind if Mr Goldman and I were to have a few minutes in private?' Michael asked tentatively. 'We've got a bit of catching up to do.'

'The boardroom's free all afternoon.'

Once they were alone, it didn't take Michael long to broach the subject of Olivia Simmons and the child. 'I've had a lot of time to think things over recently, Sam,' he began, 'and, because of the injuries I suffered in England, I can no longer father children. I would be most interested to see this boy.'

'It can be arranged,' said Sam carefully. 'I must advise you, however, that in deference to Mrs Simmons the whole thing must be played tactfully.'

'Do you think she's making the whole damn thing up for some purpose?' asked Michael defensively.

'I've never thought that,' replied Sam. 'She's too straightforward a person to play silly games. I knew you would ask for proof that he was your son so I arranged to take a statement from her husband's doctor confirming his infertility.'

'Well?' asked Michael, leaning forward in his chair.

'It proves conclusively that he is your child with all that implies,' said Sam gravely. 'I need not tell you that we are all

368

relying on you to use this information with care. It would be a disaster if you were to burst into this little boy's life and cause him and his mother hurt. When you have considered your position carefully, we can talk again.'

'No need, Sam. The events of the last two years have slowed me down a bit. I've only got one old score to settle, and that's with Natalia Orlofski. Sir Edward Milner got his just reward for what he did to me, but I shall always feel that Hal's death could have been prevented and that I was partly responsible. Looking back on it, he was trying to protect me from myself.'

'It's no good blaming yourself,' said Sam, 'and you'll soon realise we can't put the clock back. I must, however, caution you about pursuing this old feud with the Orlofskis. It will only lead to more grief.'

'Deep down I know in my heart of hearts you're right, Sam, but there's some devil just drives me on.'

The following day, 6 April 1917, the war that had been started so casually by Austria-Hungary and Germany on the banks of the Danube entered a new phase with the United States of America joining forces with the Allies. It had now become a truly global conflict.

For the first time in his life, however, Michael was almost contented. For some reason, Texas seemed strangely remote from the hostilities and he found it difficult to grasp the full significance of the momentous days as the nation mobilised. The root of his happiness was the meeting that Sam had arranged with Olivia Simmons in San Antonio. Since their conversation in Frinksteins' office, Michael had given the matter considerable thought and he was now convinced, in spite of his earlier scepticism, that the child was his. Olivia was, by his own admission, a cut above the other women he had known and he felt flattered that she wanted to see him again, even if it was only for the boy's sake.

Sam had arranged for them to meet for lunch in the fashionable River Room restaurant in San Antonio. For once in his life, Michael felt nervous as he sat in the back seat of

369

the cab taking him into town from the station. The meeting had somehow assumed huge significance for him, and he hoped against hope that he wouldn't say anything out of place that would offend Olivia. As he sat fingering the brim of his hat with agitation, he determined that nothing must prevent him from seeing the child.

Olivia was sitting at a corner table with a middle-aged, balding man. As Michael approached, the man got up and hurried away.

'Hello, Olivia,' he said gently before taking his place opposite her. 'Who's that?'

'Don't worry,' she smiled. 'I know the place very well and I arranged with the owner that his brother would sit with me as chaperone until you arrived.'

Michael laughed as he saw the twinkle in her eye. 'I nearly got the wrong impression,' he replied.

Now that the ice was broken, he began to relax. He hadn't remembered just how attractive Olivia was with her long auburn hair and well-proportioned features but, above all, she had charm and poise.

'I hear from Sam Goldman that you've had some bad times recently,' she began.

'It's not been a vintage year I have to admit. You too?'

'Yes, it's been a bit difficult, but that's in the past now. There's nothing to be gained by looking over your shoulder.'

'I agree with you,' he said, taking a sip of iced water. 'I was really pleased that you wrote about Jack.'

'I was in two minds at the time as to whether I should tell you, but I knew that you would want to know. He's one and a half now and pretty lively.'

'I would never have forgiven you if you hadn't written,' replied Michael, looking down at the table cloth. 'I'm just sorry you had to face all your problems alone.'

'Mother has been a great help,' she said. 'Jack and I have been down here for two months, and I just hope we haven't outstayed our welcome.'

'Mothers are the most forgiving people on earth,' replied

Michael, 'as I know from personal experience.'

Olivia gave him a knowing smile. She had, from the outset of this encounter, kept the initiative, anxious for him to know that while she wanted him to see their son, she was going to give no quarter. She was quite determined that Jack should get a father on the terms she dictated, rather than have one thrust on him. As the meal progressed, Michael became increasingly impatient.

'I do hope that we can get off to see Jack before too long,' he began. 'I can't remember when I've been so nervous about anything. It's a strange feeling to be about to meet your own flesh and blood for the first time.'

'Then let's not keep you waiting a moment longer than we have to,' smiled Olivia. Michael summoned the waiter and paid the bill without even checking it.

The drive out of town to the sprawling, Spanish-inspired house took them the best part of twenty minutes. When they arrived, Michael helped Olivia out of the car and they walked together to the front door which was opened by a smiling Mexican manservant with gleaming white teeth and a fine head of shining black hair.

'Where's Master Jack, Pedro?' asked Olivia.

'In the sitting room with the nurse, ma'am,' he replied, smiling.

Olivia led Michael along a tiled corridor before opening a large wooden door. In the centre of the elegantly furnished room was a small child, playing with a young woman.

'You may go now, Ellen,' said Olivia picking up the boy and kissing him. Michael waited impatiently as she held Jack close to her as if to establish ownership. Only then did she turn to face him. The boy had a strangely piercing gaze for one so young. He had large brown eyes which dominated a slightly compressed face, giving him the look of a pugilist. He held Michael's gaze then pointed to him crying, 'Man, man'. After a moment or so Olivia signalled Michael to come close to her before handing Jack over to him. She could see at once that he was totally unaccustomed to holding small children in his arms. The boy immediately sensed his apprehension and let out a deafening wail which continued for what seemed an age to Michael before he looked at Olivia helplessly and offered the child back.

'I hope I didn't do anything to upset him?' he enquired earnestly.

Olivia smiled before replying, 'He's just anxious to make an impression so that you'll know who he is in future.'

'As sure as hell, I shan't forget him in a hurry,' replied Michael. 'He's got the makings of a filibustering senator, and he might even make a good oarsman the way he held my hand ...'

'Just wait a moment,' said Olivia. 'There's a lot to discuss before we start thinking of all that.'

By now Michael was enchanted with Olivia and amazed at his good fortune in seeing the son he thought he would never have. He was anxious to impress on her that he would like to take up her offer to allow him to change Jack's name of Simmons to Korsakov.

'Sam can fix things up in no time,' he said, 'but I've a better idea.'

'What's that?' asked Olivia guardedly.

Michael waited a moment. 'Why don't we legitimise him by getting married?'

'Now just hold on a minute,' she said, smiling. 'Don't you think you're going a bit too fast?'

'I've learned by past mistakes that if you want something badly enough you should act decisively.'

'I like the style,' she replied, 'but I'm not certain of the motive.'

'What do you mean?'

'Is it just Jack you want?'

'Sure I want him, but I want you just as much,' he replied looking at her directly with those piercing eyes she remembered so well. She almost believed him, but something made her hold back. The first time they had met she had fallen under his spell but she reminded herself that she was older and wiser now.

372

'Your offer is very flattering, Michael, but I can't possibly give you an answer right away. I will promise you, however, that I'll think it over very carefully and let you know my decision at our next meeting.'

'What about Jack, then?' asked Michael anxiously.

'There's no problem as far as he's concerned. You can see him when you want, within reason, and I should be happy to let you change his name to yours.'

'That's very generous of you,' he replied. 'In fact it's more than I deserve.'

'It's not a question of what either of us deserves,' she said. 'It's Jack's best interests that I want to protect. You, of all people, must know how important it is to have a father to turn to when you're growing up.'

Michael looked straight ahead. 'There was a certain person who was father to me in all but name, and he died trying to save me from myself,' he said bitterly. 'It's something I deeply regret and one day I shall have revenge on those who I feel were responsible for his death.'

'I'm sorry to hear you speak like that,' said Olivia. 'Bury the past and live for the future. It's what I've had to do.'

When Michael arrived back at the Damon Mound field, Luder Carn was waiting for him.

'Got some real good news, boss,' he grinned. 'Dean just 'phoned and left a message for you.'

'Well?' asked Michael impatiently.

'He said to tell you that Senator Whinney has been as good as his word and a cheque for one million dollars has been lodged with Frinksteins' head office.'

'Thanks, Luder, that's the best news I've had in months,' said Michael. 'I'd better go and see Lee in hospital. Now we can sign the papers that will make me the owner of Stevens Oil and he'll be a rich man.'

'Just go carefully,' warned Luder. 'Knowing him as I do, he'd rather be comfortably off and able to walk than very rich and in a wheelchair.'

'I know what you mean,' replied Michael. 'I'll break it to him gently. I realise that Stevens Oil was his whole life until the accident. I'm hoping that when he's fit enough he's going to come back and work with us again.'

'We sure need him,' said Luder. 'It would be just dandy if he could be back for the inauguration of the field. Now war has been declared and all that sabotage has stopped, we should be on-stream for the end of July.'

'Thanks for all you've done to help me get to grips with things here, Luder,' said Michael. 'I couldn't have managed to cope in the short term without you.'

'Been a real pleasure, Boss,' Luder replied grinning.

Michael had taken an instant liking to this unruly half-breed. Although their backgrounds were miles apart, they worked well as a team, each supporting the other with their particular talents.

'How did things go with that pretty lady in San Antone, Boss?' Luder asked, smiling.

'You're too damn nosy,' replied Michael good humouredly. 'I just about got to first base if you must know,' he said, striding off towards his car.

50

In the short time since James had returned from Russia much had happened in that unfortunate country. The Tsar had abdicated leaving the Liberal and Labour elements of British politics applauding; even the United States appeared to rejoice. Natalia was delighted when Winston Churchill spoke out in the Tsar's defence but there were few who supported him. In the following months King George V had been greatly concerned for his cousin's safety and Sir George Buchanan had reinforced his fears by sending a telegram to the War Office asking if something might be done for the Imperial Family whose safety was now in danger. Lloyd George was steadfastly against any plan to let this course of action succeed but he was forced, reluctantly, to agree that they might seek asylum in Britain if the provisional Russian Government would be responsible for all the costs involved. When they first got wind of the plan, the Petrograd Soviet denounced it as dangerous as they were staunchly against the Romanovs ever returning to what they called 'the historical arena'.

James and Natalia discussed the crisis for hours on end.

'It's all very well you offering to put Larkhill at the

disposal of the Tsar and his family,' he said anxiously, 'but it's a plan with no hope of success.'

'And why not?' she asked.

'Our Royal Family would find them more suitable accommodation at either Sandringham or Windsor,' he replied. 'Your offer is ill-advised and foolish. Just think what it would cost. They have little or no funds and, rich as you may be, it would nearly bankrupt you.'

'I know you're right, James, but the idea of doing nothing to help them appals me.'

'You did what you could for Russia,' he said quietly. 'Now live for me and the future.'

When she awoke next morning, Natalia was strangely depressed. At times like these she sought refuge out of doors where she could breathe. She had hardly noticed the spring had quietly passed into summer at Larkhill and the gardens were a riot of colour. Gabriel Gleeve, the head gardener, was a perfectionist of the old school, and was pleased and flattered by the interest Natalia took in all he did.

'Lady Milner was interested but all Sir Edward wanted was a garden that was neat and tidy,' he said as they walked between the immaculately tended rose beds. 'It'll take some time to get things back as they should be but I'm certain it can be done. After the war, when we get some experienced men back, it'll be a different story, just you wait and see.'

'It will be quite splendid, Gabriel,' replied Natalia excitedly. They walked on, deep in conversation, across the lawn that spread like a carpet down to the lake. Here they stopped to look at the arum lilies that were now well established along the bank. Natalia took the white petals in her fingers, almost caressing them as she admired their beauty.

'We propagated some this spring, Princess,' said Gabriel proudly. 'They do say round 'ere that a bride should always carry 'em.'

The whole estate seemed infused with an optimistic spirit in spite of the terrible happenings both at home and abroad.

James shelved any plans he had for a survey of the estate for the time being. Instead he suggested to the War Office that his skills as a translator and interpreter might be useful to them on a part-time basis. His offer was accepted and he was soon kept busy working on an infinite variety of material from the highly classified to the mundane.

The last Saturday in August saw close friends and family gather at Larkhill to see James and Natalia married. It was a simple but dignified service and, after the guests had departed, Natalia and James were watching the last rays of the dying sun flood the gardens and meadows around Larkhill with a soft golden light.

'The chapel looked wonderful with all those flowers that Gabriel brought in for the service,' said Natalia, holding James's hand. 'Fate plays a strange game,' she continued. 'Who would have thought a year ago when we were both in Russia that we'd be sitting here at Larkhill, married?'

'I certainly wouldn't have put any money on it,' said James. 'The whole world seems in turmoil, but we've got the most perfect peace here.'

'I can see why the Milners always wanted to come back,' she replied. 'It's just so sad that they couldn't be here.'

They sat in silence, wrapped in their thoughts, until James spoke.

'It was good of John Duff to give you away. It must have taken quite an effort after what happened to Peter.'

'Yes, it can't have been easy, but it might have helped him to come to terms with Peter's death. He's never really accepted it you know. I was a bit worried about him at one stage when he had to sit down after the service,' replied Natalia. 'I hope there's nothing wrong with him.'

'It's possible that he got a bit emotional, or he might have been feeling off colour,' said James. 'Lucinda or Emma would have let us know if there was anything wrong.'

'I suppose so,' she replied. 'It would be unthinkable if anything was to happen to him.'

'I agree,' said James thoughtfully before turning to Natalia and taking her hand in his. 'I can see there's something else troubling you,' he said anxiously. 'Please let me share it.'

'It's nothing really,' she replied, 'but I suppose ever since the Romanovs were taken to Tobolsk in Siberia I've had the most dreadful fears for their safety. I know they were blind and stupid in so many things but they don't deserve the fate I know is coming.'

'You mustn't start that all over again. Even if they had come to Larkhill as you wanted, there would have been intolerable pressure from the Socialists over here. There might even have been attempts to assassinate them.'

'That's true, James, but at least we would have been doing something positive. Just imagine what those poor children must be going through.'

'They're not children any more, except for the Tsarevich,' replied James, 'and at least the little boy has Sidney Gibbs, his tutor, with him for moral support. It's funny how someone like that can bolster one's spirits in difficult times.'

'It just seems so unreal, me being with you in this beautiful place when Russia is on its knees. Promise me you'll never leave me, James?' she asked fixing her gaze on him.

'I promise on one condition.'

'What's that?' said Natalia, looking at him anxiously.

'That you get a move on or we'll be late for the party Martin Kershaw has laid on for us with the estate staff at the tithe barn. No more sad thoughts, please,' said James. 'Let's not spoil the day.'

'There's just one thing I must do,' said Natalia. 'When you brought the letter and present from Count Freedericksz in Petrograd I think you knew that I had already made up my mind to marry you. I wrote back to him saying that I was going to open the parcel on our wedding day and I'm dying to know what he sent me.' She went over to the Regency sofa table and, finding the key, unlocked one of the drawers before taking out the package. She slowly and carefully removed the wrapping paper, finally revealing a case with the distinctive logo of Fabergé's Moroskaya Street shop. James heard her give a small, startled cry as she looked inside. He craned forward to see an exquisite golden egg set in protective wrapping. As she gently eased it from the elegant container she noticed a miniature portrait set in a cluster of rose diamonds on the egg.

'Oh James,' she gasped, 'it's Mother.' She sat down on the sofa, half alarmed by the significance of this discovery but anxious to know what secret was to be revealed.

'Well, go on, open it,' said James as she carefully felt for the catch which released the two halves of the egg. As it swung open on the delicate hinges she found, to her amazement, a tiny folding screen of three miniatures. The centre panel depicted her mother while the other panels clearly showed her brother Alexander as a boy and the unmistakable features of the Grand Duke Constantine. Natalia now turned her attention to the letter Count Freedericksz had placed beside the egg.

'What does it say?' asked James.

She began to read the untidy hand of the ageing nobleman.

My dear Natalia,

Please accept this golden egg. It contains the secret that I have kept for so many years to protect your mother. As we now seem to be in danger from all quarters, it is my duty to pass it to you before I die. You may well ask why your mother and brother are depicted with the Grand Duke Constantine. The explanation is quite simple – your brother Alexander was really Constantine's son, and I was the only one to share the secret with them. I knew all the secrets of the Imperial Family. Unfortunately, after that fateful card game in the mess, when Alexander lost Ivanhov, Igor Korsakov found out about the indiscretion between your mother and Constantine. He threatened to make it public so Alexander had two good reasons for

killing him. Your mother returned the Fabergé egg to me
for safe keeping before she died and asked me to give it to
you when I judged the moment to be right. You may be
assured that this information was never divulged to other
members of the Imperial Family.

Your loving friend, Freedericksz.

51

By late August Dean had been pleased to confirm Michael as President of O'Donnell-Stevens Oil. He congratulated himself on his masterstroke as it allowed him to get on with running O'Donnell's in New York without interference and, at the same time, put Michael to work on something for which he showed a natural flair. Even Stewart Armstrong had to admire the way he seemed to have changed and buckled down to running Stevens's existing enterprises as well as looking after the Damon Mound field. Dean knew that Michael had been seeing a lot of Olivia Simmons and that she had put back returning to the East with the boy so that she could be near him in Texas. He was, therefore, not surprised to receive a letter from Michael informing him officially of their engagement.

Olivia had decided to accept Michael with all his faults. Her decision was partly influenced by the fact that Jack would now be legitimised in her eyes, even though, to all outward appearance, he was still Harry Simmons's child. She was pleased that Michael had moderated his excesses since he had returned from Europe. She knew that outward appearances are often deceptive but she was prepared to take the chance for Jack's sake. They had decided to buy a house in Houston and set about looking for suitable property near the golf club at the end of San Felipe Road. Both shunned the elegant Main Street mansions which were well within their joint financial compass and settled for a large colonial-style residence set well back from the road in secluded gardens. It was from here that Olivia would, in due course, be launched into the Thalian Club which some thought marked acceptance into fashionable Houston society. The war, however, seemed to have put a damper on such frivolities.

Another great milestone was reached when Michael presided over the formal inauguration of Luder's Mound field. With Lee and Dean by his side, he welcomed the large contingent that had come from New York and which included Sam Goldman, Stewart Armstrong and John Wilson, plus a large slice of the local oil community including such famous names as Ross Sterling and Robert Lee Blaffer. Howard Hughes came in for considerable praise in Michael's speech for the part his 'roller bit' had played in exploiting the find, and Olivia felt a glow of pride as she watched him mingle easily among the guests. Even Sam, who had been mildly sceptical about the wisdom of such a gathering, heaped praise on Michael.

'You sure managed to put on a great show,' he beamed as he looked across the forest of derricks and oil storage tanks.

'Thanks, Sam,' Michael replied. 'I owe you a great deal for getting Olivia, Jack and me together.'

'Just pleased it worked out. Olivia looks as pretty as a picture and I needn't tell you you're a lucky man.'

'Sure am,' he replied, 'especially as Jack is part of the package. If you hadn't acted promptly I'd have had no son to inherit all this. Some day we must talk about the possibility of splitting O'Donnell's from O'Donnell-Stevens. Dean can have one hundred per cent control of the operation in New York if he'll let me have the oil company.'

'Sounds as if it might be the basis of a deal,' said Sam warily. 'Have you talked to him about it?'

'No, not yet.'

'Then why don't you and Olivia join us at the Rice Hotel this evening for dinner? You can put your proposal to Dean before we eat.'

'That's a fine idea,' said Michael. 'Now you must let me go and see if Lee is coping all right.'

Finding Olivia, they walked over to where Lee sat in his wheelchair surrounded by Luder and the men.

'This is a great day for both of us, Michael,' he said, looking up. 'Thanks for seeing the work through to completion.'

'We've hardly started yet,' Michael replied. 'Just wait till we're an international corporation known to millions.'

'Now simmer down, boy. Don't let the sun get to you,' Lee laughed.

As Luder and the men drifted away to the beer tent, Michael sat down beside Lee.

'I've a big favour to ask,' he said earnestly.

'Fire away.'

'Olivia and I have been talking and we'd very much like you to be best man at our wedding.'

'What, a legless old fool like me?' he replied. 'You're not serious are you?'

'Absolutely.'

'Well, I'll be damned!' he said. 'That's just about the best compliment you could pay a man. I'll be there, you can bet your life on it.'

'Thanks, Lee,' said Olivia. 'It means a lot to both of us.'

'Now Olivia, don't start getting any ideas about me wearing fancy clothes,' Lee began nervously. 'I don't know how we're going to manage in church with this damn contraption,' he continued, pointing to his battered wheelchair.

'There's not going to be a church, Lee,' said Michael. 'It'll be just ten minutes at a civil ceremony. It's the second time

383

around for Olivia and, what with me being a Catholic, it's all a bit difficult.'

'Just tell me the date and the place and I'll be there,' Lee grinned.

'That was quite a day,' said Michael as he drove down San Felipe Road with one arm round Olivia.

'It was quite like something out of the Keystone Cops,' she replied, smiling. 'Did you see Lee and Luder arriving at the courtroom in Houston in that old Ford with Lee's wheelchair strapped to the roof?'

'It looked decidedly dangerous to me,' said Michael, 'and I thought Luder was going to split his pants getting it off the car.'

'Anyway, we couldn't have had a better day if we'd spent a million dollars,' replied Michael. 'Sorry I can't take more time off for a honeymoon but the government are pressing us for all the production we can manage. I need to be with the men almost all the time if we're going to meet the targets we've set ourselves.'

'I understand,' she replied reassuringly. 'I'm just glad that Dean agreed to your suggestion about splitting the two companies.'

'I never thought that I would end up in Texas in the oil business,' replied Michael reflectively, 'but these last few months have been the happiest days of my life. Looking back, I wasn't cut out to be a newspaper baron.'

'If I had been older and wiser I should have known that I shouldn't have become a senator's wife,' Olivia said seriously.

'Let's just hope that you and I can be happy now with Jack.'

'One thing, Michael,' she began warily. 'Why didn't you use your title when we were before the registrar? I was rather looking forward to calling myself "Countess".'

'All that's better forgotten now,' he replied, looking at her earnestly. 'The aristocratic half of my ancestry has never brought me any peace of mind. It's brought feuding, sorrow and despair on so many occasions and it's time now to forget all that. Like Luder, I'm a bit of a half-breed,' he laughed.

'There's so much I don't know about you, Michael,' said Olivia looking at him tenderly. 'One day we're going to have to sit down while you open the closet door and let out all the skeletons. So many people in New York used to talk in hushed whispers about a certain Natalia Orlofski and her connection with your family. Mother knows the story but has never told me for some reason.'

'Don't let's go into all that now,' he said, dismissing the subject. 'It would be a pity to spoil the day. All I want now is a secure future for Jack and for him to have a better childhood than I had. When I was small the kids gave me a hard time and I just hope he has a happier life. Now, let's see if we can banish all those ghosts from the past. I have my bad memories to live with like you.'

While he had been speaking, Michael's thoughts were in turmoil. Fragmented, random pictures of the *Lusitania*, Natalia, Hal, Emma and the asylum flashed through his mind in a jumbled kaleidoscope. For some reason he remembered that a doctor had once told him that the events of each day of life were accurately stored in the brain's filing system. Perhaps, he thought, the brain might also have a memory-destruction button, if he knew where it was.

By some twist of fate the month of August had seen both Michael and Natalia marry their respective spouses. Michael, the Ivy League college boy, had found himself in a rundown register office in a small town in Texas — a far cry from St Patrick's Cathedral, with a fashionable reception at the Pierre to follow.

On the other hand, Natalia, until recently an impecunious Russian refugee, found herself marrying in her own private chapel amid her thousands of green English acres. Both had been battered by the winds of fortune, but each was now determined to take the chance of the happiness that presented itself in such differing surroundings.

For once, the old feud that had cost the lives of those dear to them and had almost ruined their youth seemed unimportant.

BOOK TWO

1

The space of twenty years had not diminished Natalia's beauty. She was still superbly slim and elegant and maturity had only emphasised the fine bone structure of her face. Her skin had kept the lustrous, almost peach-like softness which had always set her apart from other women. Marriage and security had allowed her to blossom, and she repaid James with the coin of faithfulness. Over the years she had laughed with him when she told him of the maladroit approaches of over-ardent admirers. She kept her relationships on a strictly formal basis, but men friends were permitted a kiss on greeting or departure, mixed with carefully chosen words of affection. Older men simply wanted to admire from afar for they knew that any serious attempt to possess would result in a rapid distancing of friendship.

James, too, had preserved his distinguished good looks. His hair was now greying at the temples and he had put on a few pounds but he still retained his engaging charm and innate good manners. He had always been solid and reliable. Even in his Oxford days he had never played the field and had mildly disapproved of those who had. He could now watch with detached amusement the antics of some of his friends who ran around with their tongues hanging out, seeking to rediscover their youth. With a wife like Natalia, to him that game was not worth the candle. He was in every way the epitome of the benevolent country gentleman and few of the younger generation realised that it was Natalia, not he, who owned Larkhill.

Their daughter Ludmila had been born in 1920. She was now eighteen and was both beautiful and intelligent. She had the high cheekbones of her mother and it was obvious from an early age that she had inherited the Orlofski dark good looks.

For several years after her birth, they had hoped for another child but Natalia had had a series of miscarriages and was finally advised by her doctor that it would be dangerous and foolhardy for her to become pregnant again. This left Ludmila sole heiress to a fortune which had remained intact and had even grown despite the Depression, a fact which had not been lost on her many suitors.

Since Sir Edward's days, Larkhill had undergone a sympathetic transformation at Natalia's hand. She had lovingly restored the house and gardens to their former splendour and, following the death of Count Freedericksz, had brought what was left of the Orlofski treasures from Russia. The ground-floor rooms had been redecorated and regilded and the ornate painted ceilings were much admired. Upstairs great care had been taken to restore the delicate Chinese wallpapers, depicting birds and flowers in a domestic setting, and the whole house shone with a new-found brilliance.

In sharp contrast to the affluence of Larkhill, Randle and Emma were fighting for survival. During the last two years Randle's health had seriously deteriorated and he was now in the final stages of emphysema which left him struggling for each breath. The estate that he treasured so much was rapidly becoming rundown through neglect and lack of investment. The terrible state of the nation's economy in previous years had seriously eroded Randle's investments and he was now forced into selling off cottages and small parcels of farm land to help to bolster his depleted income.

Since John Duff had died suddenly of a heart attack in the worst days of the Depression, Emma had taken increasing responsibility at the Albany Group, together with Paul Wigram who was managing director. Her father had left her an empire that was slowly bleeding to death as a result of its alarmingly high borrowings, and she knew that the spring that had always watered her life was finally running dry. The world she had known as young woman had become a very different place. Gone were many of the old values, to be replaced by a society worshipping a different god. The old establishment figures, like Sir Hugo Ballard of the Cheshire Bank, had either retired or died, and the hitherto secure world seemed much less friendly. The *Record* continued to make profits but even its success was unable to prop up the *Globe* and various other titles which were losing circulation and revenue at an alarming rate. Every day seemed to bring a new anxiety and Emma was devastated to find evidence of another major problem when looking through her father's papers. According to documents kept under lock and key in the safe at the Cheshire Bank, it appeared that he had formed a liaison with the notorious, and latterly discredited, honours broker Maundy Gregory.

On investigating the position carefully with Paul Wigram, Emma soon established that John had paid Gregory the sum of fifty thousand pounds in bonds redeemable in 1930 on the understanding that he would procure a peerage for him. The position was further complicated by the fact that, under the 1924 Prevention of Abuses Act, it had been deemed an offence to pay or promise money for titles or honours. Emma could only assume that the chill wind of official disapproval had removed Gregory's power and that John had been left without the title he had paid for. She could only imagine her father's distress at being unable to press for the return of the money for fear of charges being preferred.

It was clear that Lucinda knew nothing of the Gregory

affair and Emma had not discussed it with her, feeling it kinder to spare her the distress that she would undoubtedly have felt if she had known the facts. After John's death, Lucinda had continued to live at Charnely Lodge in spite of the size of the house and the cost of running such a large establishment. She had never remarried but led an active social life, cushioned by the generous provision John had made for her. In addition to this, she had invested her own money wisely after inheriting a sizeable sum from her parents. Her life was now devoted to good causes and Emma often joked with Randle that Lucinda was more concerned with the Liverpool Dogs Home than what was happening within the family.

To compound their troubles, Emma and Randle worried about their daughter Jane who, at twenty, was rebellious and sulky. From a child she had known that she could never take the place of the son her father had so badly wanted to keep alive the Baguley name at Weathersfield. She had her mother's oval face and fair colouring and, on the occasions when she allowed herself to smile, she could almost be called pretty. Her parents' dearest wish was that she should work for the Albany Group but it was a prospect that Jane viewed with a mixture of amusement and horror, preferring to spend all her time with the horses that consumed her life with a passion, and which Randle could now ill afford.

Matters now reached breaking point. With Randle so ill and the estate's finances creaking badly, Emma knew that it was imperative that she act decisively if Weathersfield was to be saved. That evening, after dinner, she sat in the study watching Jane over the top of her bi-focal spectacles. What she had to say couldn't wait and she was glad that Randle was upstairs.

'I do wish you would give the *Record* a try,' she began. 'After all I worked there with Grandpa when I was your age.'

'That's different. It's not for me, Mother,' came the stony reply.

'It would be good experience for you and you do own a

sizeable amount of shares in the company.'

'No, I'm sorry. Absolutely no.'

'But why are you so against it?'

'It just wouldn't work. Ever since Aunt Natalia gave me my shares when I was small, I've always felt that you and father resented me having them and that you wished that she had given them to you.'

'That's most unfair and quite untrue, Jane,' Emma retorted angrily.

'Is it? With all the problems here and Father being so ill, it would probably be better for both of us to sell our shares to Aunt Natalia.'

'It would be humiliating to have to ask Natalia to buy the shares she gave you. Have you no pride?'

'Of course I have, Mother,' Jane replied, 'but just think it over. If we both sold our shares then Aunt Natalia would get control of Albany. It might just appeal to her and Uncle James. It would certainly be the answer to our prayers if we got a fair price.'

It was only a matter of weeks before pressure from the bank and a basketful of unpaid bills left Emma no option but to write to Natalia proposing that she purchase her own and Jane's shareholding in Albany. It was a good letter, but if she was to try to help, Natalia needed to be convinced that the acquisition would bring benefits to both sides. Charity, she knew, was never a good basis on which to build family unity, but her first instinct was that Albany had the strength to rebound.

Over lunch at Larkhill, Natalia told James the bones of Emma's proposal. 'I'll show you the letter later. It's on my desk.'

'What did she say?' he asked quizzically.

'Just that Randle was very ill and that it would be sensible for her and Jane to sell their joint interest in the company. I get the feeling things are a bit desperate.'

'Yes, me too. It must be difficult for her,' said James sympathetically, 'especially as you gave Jane the shares you inherited from Peter as a christening gift.'

'That's not the real issue. I would really like to help,' replied Natalia, 'particularly as Randle is so ill. Emma must understand, however, that it's got to be a viable proposition.'

'What's the asking price?'

'Two hundred and fifty thousand pounds or thereabouts, for both blocks of shares.'

'They'll never get that,' James commented drily, putting down his paper. 'However, I think you ought to consider making an offer. It would be quite a feather in your cap if you were to join the ranks of the press barons.'

'Are you serious, James? I must say you never cease to amaze me,' replied Natalia, smiling.

'Offer them two hundred thousand pounds and let Emma keep her seat on the board, and I think they'll be quite delighted,' he said looking at her intently. 'You'd be dealing with Paul Wigram, whom I trust implicitly. He'll drive a hard bargain for Emma and Jane but you'd need his expertise if you were to buy Albany. It's about time you lived dangerously again and, after all, you would be keeping the company in the family. I had a great regard for John Duff and I'm very sorry things have come to this sorry state.'

A month later Natalia became the majority shareholder in the Albany Group. The arrangement was a source of mutual satisfaction to all parties and, most important, Baguley pride and family unity had been preserved and even strengthened. Control of the business empire she had been so close to when Peter was alive was just the challenge Natalia was looking for, and she set about the task of rescuing Albany with her customary vigour and determination.

Michael Korsakov bent his head as he led his flock in prayer. It was now ten years since he had completed his studies at Austin Theological Seminary where he graduated *summa cum laude*. As Pastor of the First Evangelical Church of Texas, he was a revered and respected man. His conversion, like that of Saint Paul, had come on the road, the only difference being that he was driving an expensive car at the time. 'It came like a blue flash from God,' he said to the congregation who hung on his every word. 'I was a sinner. My, how I sinned. Yet God had a purpose for me and He called me to serve Him in His Holy ministry. Praise the Lord for He showed me the way and saved my soul!'

Both Michael's ministry and the church prospered as a result of the enormous income he received from O'Donnell-Stevens, enabling him to crusade on a national scale. In an unusually magnanimous gesture, he had recently given Jack all his shares in O'Donnell Publishing which was now a closed chapter in his life.

Lee Stevens ran the O'Donnell-Stevens Corporation from offices in Houston with his customary efficiency, but Luder Carn had disappointed Michael. He wanted no part of the big time and had married an easy-going Mexican woman, who had given him eight legitimate children, as well as fathering at least two other offspring from liaisons with local girls he had met at BJ's bar. Michael had tried to show him the light when he came to church but Luder was sheepishly unrepentant, comfortable in the life that fortune had bestowed on him, and he had no intention of changing his ways.

Olivia had put up with Michael's eccentricities for nine long years. The final straw came when he told her he was going to dedicate his life to God in his own special way. She couldn't even begin to understand how he had got mixed up with 'a load of religious crackpots' as she called them. In desperation, she gave him an ultimatum, spelling out that he would have to abandon any thought of being ordained to serve in such a sect if she was to stay. The Church, as most had predicted, won by a mile. Sadly disillusioned, she left the house on San Felipe Road and bought a fine residence in River Oaks. Much to Michael's annoyance, she started a relationship with David Delaney, an eminent Texas lawyer, who had been married but was childless. For the moment Michael was quite prepared to accept a formal separation but divorce was another matter and he would not consider it.

Jack had seemed remarkably relaxed about his parents splitting up as, after all, he had seen little of his father over the years. Physically he was like the Korsakovs, strong and athletic with a mop of dark hair which needed to be controlled night and morning. He had inherited Olivia's charm and undoubted intellect, and a broad smile which exposed perfectly regular, pearly white teeth. His face was noticeably softer than Michael's, but the forward set of his jaw gave a strong indication of his forceful character.

Compared to his father's turbulent youth, Jack's progress to manhood had been smooth and relatively trouble free. Olivia and David had provided the loving and stable home environment that Michael had never known, and it had borne fruit. Jack had turned out to be a thoroughly decent and level-headed young man who found it difficult to grasp how someone like his father, brought up a Catholic in New York, could espouse such radical and eccentric religious views. His own faith was strong and robust, owing much to the Baptist Church which had been a rock in his mother's life through her troubles. Since boyhood Jack had known the circumstances of his birth and, in spite of her own private thoughts, Olivia had encouraged him to take pride in his father's name, stoically enduring the gossip and innuendo.

Olivia worried when Jack was offered a place to read law at Harvard. She knew that Michael would still be remembered, his exploits even now causing a frisson of excitement among those who had known him. Most, she reasoned were too discreet to say much, but a few would undoubtedly bring out the well-worn stories of his prowess with women and liking for booze and every vice imaginable and unimaginable. She begged Jack to turn down the place but his mind was made up and no amount of persuasion would change it.

As his mother predicted, Jack's first year at Harvard was beset with difficulties. Michael's reputation hung about him like an all-enveloping dark cloud, attracting those at the university who sought cheap sensation and a free handout. On both counts they soon found they had backed the wrong horse and, slowly but surely, they drifted away. Jack was glad at last to be free of his father's unfulfilled dreams and ambitions as set out in the lifeplan he had shown to Hal before leaving for Harvard himself some forty years previously. Now, to his relief, the worst he had to endure was an infrequent letter reminding him earnestly how the good servant had handled his investments in the parable of the talents.

Michael did, however, take more than a passing interest when, the following year, Jack was chosen to row for Harvard at Henley. Leaving nothing to the imagination, he wrote a long and rambling letter, describing in detail his involvement with Natalia and her family. His spidery handwriting was punctuated by fierce underlining and exclamation marks littered the untidy pages as the sad story was told. He described fully the bitter legacy of hate and jealousy that would be Jack's should he decide to pursue the past. 'My advice', he wrote sternly 'is to keep your distance, especially as Natalia Ponsonby lives only a few miles from Henley. Keep away from them,' he repeated. 'Disobey me, Jack, and I shall never forgive you.'

2

Emma had found a new lease of life now that her financial worries were eased by the sale of her Albany shares to Natalia who had also allowed her to keep her seat on the main board, with the generous salary that went with it. She and Randle were delighted that Jane's money from the sale of her shares had been invested wisely by Paul Wigram to ensure that she received a substantial regular income. With matters now on a better footing, Emma had agreed to guarantee the estate's overdraft at the Midland Bank, Liverpool to the tune of forty thousand pounds so that the most urgent problems that beset Weathersfield could be tackled without delay. Her first decision was to take Turville Farm and its two hundred acres off the market.

'There's going to be no more talk of selling land or property,' she said smiling at Randle as he sat ashen-faced and breathless in his wheelchair. 'We can now afford to start work on the new milking parlour and then get to grips with Crown Meadow and the surrounding land and see that it's drained properly.'

'I really don't know what we would have done without you coming to the rescue,' he said after a moment's silence, noticing the premature grey in her hair and the worry lines round her eyes.

'It would have broken my heart as well as yours to see Weathersfield go to rack and ruin,' she replied. 'Now let's get on with repairing the fences. You know how you hate disorder.'

He smiled, reaching for her hand which he squeezed gently. It had grieved Randle that the last five years had been so hard for Emma, and it was his greatest regret that on account of his failing health he had not been able to support her more actively, both at Weathersfield and in her battles at the *Record*. Subconsciously he still felt that he was being punished for the events of that dreadful day in a rainswept Cheshire field when Emma's mother had died beneath his horse's hooves.

'Everything seemed so predictable when we married,' he thought. 'The estate always made a handsome profit and my investments seemed so secure.'

In spite of his disability, Randle had led a nearly normal life up until a few years ago when his condition worsened, leaving him in a wheelchair. He now knew that he would not see another summer so it was with great delight that he gave his consent to Jane's marriage to the fresh-faced Toby Lytchwyke, heir to the Earldom of Ranmore. Impoverished Toby might be, but he had the qualities of integrity and common sense that would qualify him, one day, to live at Weathersfield and take on the guardianship of his precious acres along with Jane. Randle was delighted to see that Jane was now taking a welcome and unexpected interest in the estate and that Toby, a newly qualified land agent, encouraged her.

'Father lost the lot in the Depression I'm afraid,' he said as he sat opposite Randle on the terrace. 'It was a bit of a disaster.'

'Same thing nearly happened here, Toby,' Randle replied. 'It was a damn close-run thing, and we're still not out of the wood.'

'I'll do all I can to help,' Toby ventured. 'It's quite one of the most beautiful places I've seen.'

'It's nothing to my sister-in-law's place at Henley,' Randle wheezed before lapsing into a fit of uncontrollable coughing.

As the weeks passed, Randle's condition steadily worsened and he now rarely came out of his bedroom in the east wing which had come to resemble the hospital ward in Liverpool where he and Emma had first met. As fluid built up in his damaged lungs, he was forced to fight for every breath until, at 8.30 in the evening on 2 December 1937, he died, his family at his bedside.

To the end he had remained dignified and patient in his suffering and although his last days had been a trial to him, it seemed to those who knew and loved him as though a strange inner light was already becoming visible. Death, when it came, must have seemed a welcome deliverance and Emma thanked God that the end had come swiftly.

His funeral was a simple affair. The estate staff carried his casket from the house and placed it on a horse-drawn brake drawn by two elderly Cleveland Bays on the short journey to the church. As they passed the old yew tree beside the drive, Emma's eye was caught for a fleeting moment by Jimmy's plain, flat gravestone and she remembered clearly the legend it bore: 'Jimmy – 1904–1918. Born a dog. Died a gentleman'. She smiled as the memories of their youth came flooding back.

Michael's warning about the Ponsonbys had only served to fuel Jack's imagination. Unwittingly, he had rekindled a fire, the flames of which had almost destroyed two noble lines in former generations. From boyhood Jack had become used to hearing his father's stories about Natalia and her family. In those days he had had no particular feelings one way or the other on the subject and would even often silently take the side of Natalia, the perceived underdog, when her name was mentioned in anger by Michael. Until now he had never seriously thought about the reality of Natalia having children so it made him sit up and take notice when his father had alluded to Ludmila. He reasoned that she must be about his own age and in his mind's eye he increasingly saw her as the beautiful offspring of a famous mother, possessing all the elegance and breeding inherent in the Orlofski genes. It was something that absorbed him and overwhelmed him with curiosity. Olivia became seriously concerned and begged him to abandon what she called 'your childish infatuation' but Jack, for once in his life, took little notice of his mother.

It was in this obsessive frame of mind that Jack now set sail for Britain with the Harvard crew, as his father had done so many years before. The only difference was that he lacked any trace of the Korsakov malice that had shown itself so strongly in the young Michael.

At Larkhill, Natalia and James had carried on the tradition started by the Milners of inviting the overseas crews and other distinguished guests of the regatta to a reception at the house. The arrangements were undertaken in a grand manner, and invitations were highly prized. It was only when Natalia read through the guest list after dinner that she came across the name of Jack Korsakov.

'What on earth possessed you to invite a Korsakov here?' she said, looking angrily at James. 'You really seem to have lost your reason this time.'

'I can only assume that you are referring to the invitation sent to the Harvard crew along with all the other competitors from overseas.'

'Yes, precisely.'

'We can't leave one out – it would be an unforgivable snub.'

'You do understand the implications?'

'Yes.'

'And that doesn't worry you?'

'Not unduly.'

'Well you must be mad.'

'I hear he's a very civil young man, quite unlike his father.'

'You mean you've checked?'

'Yes, I've made extensive enquiries – he won't cause any trouble, mark my words.'

'Well, the least you could have done was to discuss it with me.'

'I was going to tell you tonight but I wanted to be quite certain of my facts, and I've only just received word on him from the American Embassy in London.'

'What the hell do they know about him?'

'Quite a lot it appears, and all highly praiseworthy.'

'Just don't try my patience any more,' said Natalia looking at him with her intense brown eyes. 'I'm holding you responsible for the consequences, James.'

Jack was intrigued and excited when the Harvard coach told the crew that they had an invitation to dine at Larkhill. Casting aside his father's advice, he joined in the general enthusiasm for a break from training in the week before racing started in earnest.

'I just hope that some of these famous English roses that we've all heard so much about will show up,' began Jack. 'I've only seen the thornier variety so far.'

'I heard that the Ponsonbys have a beautiful daughter who's stinking rich,' said Ed Ford, the diminutive sandy-haired cox. 'She could just be your type, Jack – she's part-Russian,' he said, grinning.

'How do you know my preference, Ed?' Jack asked. 'Anyway, she may consider herself far too good for the likes of us.'

'But I thought your old man was a dook or count before he came to New York?'

'Yes, he was, and for that matter still is, but it means very little now.'

As they approached Larkhill Jack was deep in thought, oblivious to the good-natured banter that was going on around him. It was hot and the sun beat down on the airless charabanc as it slowly climbed the hill. He was acutely aware of the drops of perspiration running down his face and he reached for his handkerchief to mop his brow. As they passed the lodge gates to the estate, his heart was racing. 'Is this all a huge mistake?' he asked himself over and over again. When they finally reached the end of the long avenue of trees, he could see the majestic front elevation of the house and for a moment he was almost in awe of the grandeur of his surroundings.

He walked slowly across the crunching gravel towards the front door and it was with a certain sense of unease that he stepped on to the marble floor of the entrance hall. He had little time to look at the high ceiling and the impressive collection of pictures before being ushered into the library and eventually out through the french windows on to the velvet lawn. A string quartet was playing softly under an elegant awning and the guests, many in striped blazers and white flannels, were standing in groups talking and laughing. It was exactly how he had imagined life in an English country house to be and he stood for a moment drinking in the scene. The view was spectacular, with a panorama over the gardens stretching as far as the eye could see. In the middle distance a Palladian bridge spanned a corner of the lake. Like the house it had been restored to its former magnificence and its reflection seemed to shimmer in the clear water. Stone and lead figures of satyrs and pagan gods complemented long colonnades before the vista almost imperceptibly merged into the densely wooded background.

When the guests were assembled, James and Natalia, accompanied by Ludmila, stepped out on to the terrace from the house. As they did so, a momentary hush seemed to blanket the onlookers. It was unexpected theatre, with all eyes fixed on them. Natalia was used to being the centre of attention but Ludmila flushed when she sensed she was being discreetly admired by so many eager young men.

'That must be Ludmila,' said Ed, elbowing Jack in the ribs and making him spill his champagne.

'Yes, I know,' he replied, trying to sound casual as he wiped his blazer.

'Oh, come on Jack, show some enthusiasm. She's beautiful

and so is her goddam mother for Heaven's sake.'

Jack smiled as he pushed his hair back from his face in a nervous gesture. He had been careful not to show his real feelings or to seem over-anxious to meet Ludmila but at the same time he was determined to ensure that he didn't leave without being introduced. He was still acutely conscious of the grim consequences of his father's ill-starred visit some twenty-five years previously but the difference was that he was not here today as an interloper, but as a recipient of a formal, if reluctant, invitation.

In the end, help came from a most unexpected quarter. Jack had hardly noticed that Ed had slipped away from the knot of Harvard supporters and crew who were standing around sipping champagne. He was, therefore, taken aback when, some ten minutes later, Ed walked up to him chatting animatedly to Ludmila.

'I should like you to meet Jack Korsakov – he's half Russian,' he began.

Jack flushed. 'It's entirely my pleasure, Miss Ponsonby,' he managed at last.

'Jack Korsakov?' she repeated.

'Yes. My father is Michael Korsakov,' he began warily. 'You've probably heard of him?'

'Oh yes, I know exactly who you are,' Ludmila replied with disarming directness.

'I only hope you don't consider my presence here an embarrassment.'

'Quite the contrary – it's about time all that silly nonsense was forgotten.'

Jack took a deep breath and smiled.

'Why don't you join me for some strawberries,' she continued. 'They're quite delicious. We have a lot of time to make up, Mr Korsakov.'

After their guests had departed, Natalia and James retired early. Natalia lay propped up against large, billowing pillows in their lavishly gilded four-poster bed, while James attempted to read.

'How could Ludmila be so stupid as to encourage that Korsakov boy?' she began angrily. 'Why, she even sat next to him when she knows the harm his family has caused.'

'The young look at things differently to the way we do,' James replied softly. 'The war taught them that forgiveness is important and they seem to accept each other at face value.'

'I can't possibly agree with you especially as no one knows better than you what's happened in the past. It's unthinkable. She must never see him again.'

'I agree that she must be on her guard,' replied James. 'But if we make a great song and dance about her seeing him it will make her doubly determined. The odds are stacked against him but, on the face of it, he seemed a decent enough young man.'

'How can you say that?' replied Natalia in exasperation. 'His father is both violent and mad. Why, I've even heard a rumour that he's joined some eccentric wing of the church and has become an evangelist in America.'

'That sort of thing can only happen over there,' said James dismissively. 'Anyway, at least the boy can't be after her money. I didn't tell you but the financial papers are full of him inheriting a slice of the O'Donnell millions before he was twenty-one. His father must also be worth a mint of money. You probably heard he has an oil company in Texas.'

'I don't know anything about that and I don't know what he wants,' said Natalia, 'but it makes me desperately worried. I just wish to God that you hadn't invited him.'

'I understand your concern, my dear,' said James, 'but don't forget I know the full story.'

'What do you mean?' asked Natalia, turning angrily to face him.

'Well, if you remember you did tell me about your grandfather's indiscretion with Tamara's mother.'

'How could you bring that up? It's disloyal and unworthy of you.'

'Now hold on. All I'm saying is that it's been one of the major sources of trouble between your families over the years.'

405

'Stuff and nonsense. It goes back much further than that and you know it.'

'Yes,' he persisted, 'but there's a drop of shared blood in both of you and I know that rankles.'

3

O'Donnell's turned in record profits for 1937 and the first quarter's results for the new financial year made encouraging reading. The group had carefully expanded its operations over the years since Michael had handed over control and, at long last, Dean felt he had achieved his goal of making it the second largest independently owned newspaper group in the United States. The old firm of Stewart Armstrong and Sam Goldman still helped him to run the show but Mike Kransky was now president of the group and had proved to be an able and shrewd operator in what was still a highly competitive business. He was a bluff, uncomplicated, career journalist who had risen the hard way and was widely acknowledged to be heir apparent to the O'Donnell crown. Both he and Dean were acutely aware that new blood was needed in the board room and Sam's son, Harold, an abrasive and highly qualified lawyer, had recently been asked to join the board. It was a time of consolidation and of looking to the future.

Dean died suddenly and peacefully in his sleep. He was seventy-six but had seemed as fit and active as a man of sixty. He had hardly missed a day through illness in his long working life and everyone at O'Donnell's had considered him immortal. It seemed impossible to think that he would never again stride into the building, his familiar Derby at a rakish angle.

He had never married and had recently moved into a small suite at the Waldorf Hotel where he kept about him a few precious possessions. A photograph of Tamara held pride of place on the Steinway grand piano that he had treasured and which dominated the room. He had invested his money shrewdly and his collection of fine English sporting pictures was considered of international importance.

He was buried quietly, by his own request, with just his old friends present.

Much speculation centred on the future of O'Donnell's and it was a relief to everyone when Sam Goldman made an announcement to the staff reassuring them that their jobs were safe. He confirmed formally that Dean had left Jack Korsakov his entire shareholding in O'Donnell Publishing. Just as, so many years ago, Tamara had made him the custodian of her inheritance, he, in turn, saw it as a matter of honour to return control of the company to the Korsakov family upon his death.

'The board, as presently constituted, will continue to run O'Donnell's and Mike Kransky will now become chief executive,' Sam said in a low monotone. 'You will also be pleased to hear that the new owner of the company is Mr Jack Korsakov, a relative of our founder, Joe O'Donnell.'

A rustle of surprise went round the meeting and, when quiet had been restored, Sam continued, 'Mr Korsakov is at present studying at Harvard University and will be joining the company when he has completed his studies. We are lucky that control of the business will remain in sympathetic hands and I can assure you all that Jack is an outstanding young man.'

Sam knew that many of the older generation of O'Donnell employees still remembered Michael with considerable distrust and that stories of his excesses had passed into company folklore.

'Let's just hope they give him a fair chance and don't tar him with the same brush as his father,' he said under his breath to Stewart who was sitting next to him.

'The boy will stand or fall by his own efforts,' was the distant reply. 'All I know is that he'll have a hard act to follow.'

Mike Kransky wasted no time in calling a series of high-level planning meetings to examine the best ways for O'Donnell's to continue their careful expansion into the next decade. Sam and Stewart were impressed by his clinical approach and meticulous attention to detail. He was wise enough to leave room for Jack to take up a senior position in due course, but he was also of the opinion that Jack must get practical experience before he could exercise his rights of proprietorship with any authority. Jack's reaction was predictably modest. He knew that in such a competitive industry it was vital to know all facets of the business. He was quite prepared to take a back seat until such time as he felt confident enough to be involved in the decision- and policy-making process. In any event, he still had another year at Harvard before he graduated. As usual, Sam Goldman waited until the pendulum of discussion had swung to and fro and his view was the last expressed. Mike always took an interest in his carefully judged opinions.

'Michael had his faults,' said Sam, 'but he was right in attempting to expand into Britain all those years ago. As you all know, he targeted the Albany Group but we understand a considerable shareholding has recently been sold to Natalia Ponsonby who seems to have invested a large amount in attempting to revive the family fortunes. The shares were never offered on the open market so we weren't in a position to submit a bid.'

'It's a pity that we didn't send someone to replace Hal Morrow when he was killed,' said Mike. 'The syndication deal was great, and in those days it meant that we were able to keep close to John Duff and George Gerrard. I'd like to think that by nineteen forty', he continued, 'we will have purchased a substantial number of titles in Britain.'

'Why not start from scratch?' interrupted Harold. 'It's an orderly way to expand.'

'Too expensive,' snapped Mike. 'We've got to watch our costs as it could run away with our money.'

'I agree,' said Stewart. 'Let's bide our time until something enticing comes up for sale. In the meantime there's no harm in keeping an eye on Albany and watching how things work out. After all, there's no guarantee that Natalia Ponsonby and her lieutenants have got the flair to make the group viable.'

'Dangerous ground,' sighed Sam under his breath.

September 1938 saw the first signs of Europe edging nearer to the brink of another war while America looked on, a nervous spectator. In New York, Mike Kransky was making a significant impact at O'Donnell's and profits were at an all-time record. He had already established a reputation for strong leadership and he was determined that nothing would be allowed to blow the company off course. Michael Korsakov had visited him briefly when he was evangelising in New York, to ask if he would consider launching a new publication which he hoped would become a vehicle for the further teachings of the First Texas Evangelical Church.

'The idea of launching a new religious title is totally impractical, Michael,' was the firm reply. 'I suggest that you go to a specialist publisher in the Bible Belt. As you know, we're operating big battleships, and the kind of magazine you suggest would never attract the sort of mass readership we would need to make it viable. Don't you remember Dean always said, "Never mess with religion if you're a class publisher. Leave it to those who know better"?'

Michael scowled.

Since their first meeting at Larkhill Jack and Ludmila had become inseparable. On the day before he returned to the United States with the crew, Jack had proposed to Ludmila and she accepted. Much to the disquiet of both their families, they formally announced their engagement. Michael was left speechless by the news which came as a bombshell. He was further dismayed when Jack told him that he had presented the Orlofski emerald necklace to Ludmila as an engagement present, even though, years ago, Michael had bought it in New York with the sole purpose of eventually seeing Natalia wearing it. Michael grudgingly remembered the frisson of pleasure he had received at the thought of putting the necklace round Natalia's neck and seeing the stones highlighted against her flawless skin. These, however, had been the reckless dreams of his youth and he now retired with the elders of his church and prayed that Jack might see the light and be purified. The whole business gnawed at his soul and a cancer of resentment began to grow inside him. The thought of a Korsakov marrying an Orlofski was seen by him as symbolic of a great angelic conflict against the forces of evil. He could understand that Jack might be physically attracted to the girl as he, in his turn, had found Natalia desirable. It was, however, the idea that, in the eyes of the church, Jack and Ludmila would be locked in some indissoluble union that he found too dreadful to contemplate.

He thought of the thousand absolutions he had given to sinners in his own ministry, hopeful that he might eventually find it in his heart to forgive Jack. The shining miracle of reconciliation, which so many of his friends had prayed for, never had a chance in reality and he set his face grimly against the marriage.

'I pray for you,' was all he would say to Jack when he telephoned.

By contrast, Olivia and David were delighted. They supported Jack in every way possible and knew the match was for love even if it was fraught with complications. Against her better judgement, Olivia wrote to Natalia asking her to think carefully of the implications before opposing the

411

marriage. Her letter produced no response.

'Have you thought where you might live when you marry Ludmila?' asked David, looking at Jack over the top of his horn-rimmed glasses.

'I've still got to finish my degree, but if by some miracle Princess Natalia comes round', he replied, 'I'd like to work for the Albany Group. It would mean living in England, but it would help me gain some important practical experience before returning to New York. The problem, as you know, is that we're up against a lifetime of animosity between our two families. It's going to be difficult to change her opinion.'

'Your father had a stupid idea that Natalia was a she-devil. And to think he's now a priest!' exclaimed Olivia angrily. She looked at David for reassurance before beginning again after a moment's pause. 'I put it all down to the drugs he took when I first knew him,' she blurted out. 'I've never told anyone before but he once told me that he started taking heroin before he went to Harvard – Hal apparently knew what was going on and was able to stop him by getting Tamara to cut off his allowance. He started by buying the stuff on street corners and he used it regularly until he overdosed snorting the stuff and went blind for almost three days. It really scared him.'

'You never mentioned this,' said David.

'No, and that's not all. When I met him he had started again and he was worried about the state of his nose because sniffing was beginning to destroy the septum. He then started "skin popping" as he called it, or injecting himself. I worried about all the needle-related infections he might have contracted, such as syphilis and hepatitus. It was like playing bacterial roulette and that's why I stopped seeing him before you were born, Jack, in case I became infected. I only know that Luder tells me he's recently started again.'

'It just gets crazier by the day,' said David, looking at Jack. 'He'll do something really stupid soon, mark my words.'

The distress and resentment caused to Michael by the

412

announcement of Jack and Ludmila's engagement was mirrored by Natalia's feelings. She made her disapproval abundantly clear to Ludmila and the usually happy and relaxed atmosphere at Larkhill had become strained and difficult.

James attempted to calm Natalia by pointing out that Jack, in contrast to his father, seemed a gentle young man with perfect manners. He also advised Natalia not to be too hasty in her judgement as Jack was blessed with a huge fortune. He even dared to make the point that a strategic liaison between the Ponsonbys and the Korsakovs would create a massive alliance which would ensure the future prosperity of the Albany Group. Natalia would have none of it. A lifetime of animosity between the two families had created too large a barrier for her to cross easily.

As the weeks passed the gulf between Natalia and Ludmila grew steadily wider. It was as if a wedge had been driven firmly between them, and it appeared that there was nothing James could say or do to help heal the rift. He could only hope that the relationship between Jack and Ludmila was of a transitory nature, but in his heart he knew he was deluding himself.

He hated to see such unhappiness and to clear his head he took his dark green Bentley on its final spin before putting it away for the winter. As he left Henley and started back up the Fairmile, he engaged the supercharger and the lazy burble of the exhaust turned to an urgent wail. The 'blown' four and a half litre was his pride and joy and by the end of the straight the speedometer was registering one hundred and ten miles an hour. He felt he needed the fresh autumnal air to clear his head before he saw Ludmila and talked to her about the future and, more important, her involvement with Jack. He braked hard for a corner before changing down to third gear and felt the Bentley surge forward again. It would take only a few minutes to get to the house by the estate roads and he pressed on recklessly.

His mind was focused on what he had to do. Whatever his

views were about Jack, he knew that Natalia would do everything in her power to stop the marriage and it was up to him to talk frankly to Ludmila and point out the stark reality of the situation. He was also a good listener and he knew that she would open her heart to him. The matter would have been so much easier, he thought, if Jack had been like his father. He could then have taken Natalia's side but, as things were, there were no grounds for him to take anything but a positive view of Jack. After all, everyone spoke well of him and he had found him charming when they had met briefly at Larkhill. He felt trapped by his loyalty to Natalia on the one hand, and by compassion for Ludmila on the other. He smiled wryly as he remembered the number of lost causes he had championed over the years and the pleasure he had always felt whenever a victory for common sense and justice had been won against the odds.

It was then that he remembered what John Duff had said all those years ago at Shewsbury when he had been invited out to lunch on speech day with Peter. The words surfaced from the deep recesses of his memory and they worried him. He clearly remembered John talking to Peter about the dream Elizabeth Duff had had of owning two great publishing empires on each side of the Atlantic. It had seemed idle talk to him then but now he couldn't help wondering if he might live to see it a reality.

Arriving at the house James dismissed the thought from his mind. He had opened the front door and was hurrying across the hall towards the library when Lovatt attracted his attention with a discreet cough.

'Excuse me, sir, but there's an urgent message from Mr Wigram in Liverpool for you to telephone him.'

'Did he say what it's about?' asked James anxiously.

'No, only that it's most important.'

'Very well. When you've got the call on the line, put it through to my study.'

He waited, drumming his fingers on the desk, until the telephone rang.

'Good morning, Paul,' he started. 'What's the problem?'

'Bad news, James, I'm afraid,' Paul answered. 'I'm sorry to have to tell you that the news desk had an unconfirmed report from Reuters that there's been a shooting in Houston.'

'How does that affect us?' James asked, puzzled. 'There must be a lot of crime over there.'

'This one's a bit different,' Paul confided. 'It concerns the Korsakovs.'

4

The First Texas Evangelical Church in Houston was the product of both Michael's imagination and his deep pocket. It was situated on Fannin, facing Courthouse Square near the Opera House. When it was built, critics lambasted its austere architecture which made it look more like a cinema than a place of worship. The only difference, to the eye of a casual observer, was the onion dome surmounted by a cross, which Michael had deemed a necessary statement for his church but which, in reality, looked like a cumbersome after-thought. Everything about it was on a grand scale, with seating for over a thousand of the faithful. A much remarked upon feature was the magnificent Würlitzer organ which rose on a lift from below the floor, with the organist playing at full volume, when Michael stepped forward to greet his adoring but respectful flock, wearing the gown of a Harvard graduate and with a large gold cross hung about his neck.

The choir were spectacularly robed in deep blue cassocks and sang from a gallery with a melodic precision that would have graced a Hollywood musical. Everything was staged for effect, and in this charged atmosphere Michael was able to hold the congregation in the palm of his hand.

The only concession he made to formality was the altar with its brass crucifix flanked by simple candlesticks and dressed with a plain white frontal with a dove embroidered in gold thread. Not for him formal mahogany pews with elaborate carved ends and the stereotypical stained glass depicting the crucifixion or the pascal lamb. 'We need to speak a new language,' he would say. 'Leave the garbage and baggage of the past behind and look for the true light.'

'Hallelujah' was the only practical response from a thousand voices.

Jack had made a special effort to see his father that evening and had driven from River Oaks to the church in his new Chevrolet. The first of the worshippers were drifting into the parking lot as he arrived and he found Michael in the robing room where he was shocked to see him sitting on a wooden chair rocking back and forth, his head in his hands. Looking closer, Jack was alarmed by the unmistakable evidence that betrays any drug addict, littered on a nearby table. It was clear to him that Michael was mainlining heroin by intravenous injection, and he knew he must act fast.

From experience gained working at a drug rehabilitation unit in his vacations, Jack reckoned that his father had used adulterated heroin from one of the junkman dealers in the city. Before he knew what was happening, Michael suddenly sat bolt upright, vainly trying to clear his head of the psychedelic veil that had come down on reality, distorting his thoughts and images. The devil incarnate was now uppermost in his mind and was the basis of the sermon Michael was about to deliver. In this pitiful deluded state he could clearly see the horns on Jack's head and his forked tail.

Michael slowly put his hand inside his gown and unsteadily drew a revolver from its shoulder holster. He was now an avenging angel, the four horsemen of the apocalypse and Saint George slaying the dragon all rolled into one, as he aimed the gun at Jack. For one agonising second Michael seemed to hesitate as Jack stared at him in horror and disbelief. Then, with God as his solitary witness, Michael fired two shots in quick succession and Jack fell heavily backwards knocking over a bottle of communion wine which shattered leaving jagged shards of glass on the ornate mosaic floor.

It was a bright, late-summer evening, made comfortable after the heat of the day by a breeze that cooled the house and rustled the foliage of the lush garden shrubbery. Olivia and David were seated on the veranda, deep in conversation.

'I just hope that Michael isn't too hard on Jack,' said Olivia. 'He's always had a vicious temper if he feels he's being crossed.'

'Well, talk of marriage to Ludmila Ponsonby isn't exactly going to put him in the best of moods. Let's just hope that he's mellowed since he joined the Church.'

'I really can't see it,' she said, 'but I know Jack is desperate to talk things over with his father. He's never been able to confide in him and that's half the problem.'

'Yes, it must have been a body blow for Michael that Jack should want to marry an Orlofski. It must have made him doubly mad when Jack gave Ludmila those emeralds.'

'Those wretched stones have always brought bad luck,' sighed Olivia, only to be interrupted by the telephone ringing. 'Why don't we leave it?'

'No, it may be important,' he said, getting up and walking briskly across the wooden veranda and into the house. After a moment he reappeared. 'Luder Carn's on the 'phone. He seems upset – hurry!'

Hearing the urgency in David's voice, Olivia ran to the table in the hallway and picked up the telephone.

'Luder?'

'Thank God I've got you,' Luder began. 'It's Jack.'

'What?'

Luder was breathing hard and Olivia knew something terrible had happened as he struggled to tell her.

'For God's sake, Luder, what happened?' Her question

seemed to break the log-jam of words that shock had held locked up.

'It's terrible,' Luder began again. 'I only went to the church to deliver some junk to Michael. He went to get changed and then Jack arrived. The next thing I heard two shots. We rushed in and there was Jack in a pool of blood. He's bad, Olivia, real bad.'

'Where is he now? Where have they taken him, Luder?'

'To the Hermann Hospital, I think.'

'Oh my God!'

'There's more,' he continued hysterically. 'Then Michael turned the gun on himself and blew his brains out.'

'Why, oh why, Luder?' she sobbed.

'Michael said something about the Lord having the final say,' Luder replied. 'Didn't really follow him too well.'

Olivia and David left the house without even shutting the front door. David reversed the car out of the driveway, bumping into the road and raising a shower of sparks from the fender. He drove fast and in silence as Olivia repeated in a low monotone: 'Don't let him die, please God don't let him die.'

When they arrived at the hospital to their amazement there was already a small knot of photographers and press. They pushed their way through, Olivia running awkwardly to the reception desk in her high heels.

'I'm his mother,' she breathed hoarsely. 'I'm Jack Korsakov's mother. I must see him.'

'I'm afraid that's not possible, ma'am,' was the reply. 'He's already in theatre – they're doing everything possible for him.'

News of the tragedy spread quickly and was soon on the front page of every newspaper in the country. The presses were made to work overtime as the embers of the Orlofski-Korsakov feud were fanned into flames by news rooms working at fever pitch.

The *Chronicle* took a defensive and conservative line, reporting the minimum amount it felt was consistent with its duty to its readers. While other papers went in for sensation and lurid descriptions of the death scene, Mike Kransky and his team relegated the story to the inside pages. It was a time when a cool nerve and a brave face were required if there was not to be a crisis of confidence in the *Chronicle's* boardroom.

'Jack's engagement to that Ponsonby girl must have caused Michael more anguish than we thought,' said Mike Kransky, looking at Sam Goldman over a mound of paperwork on his desk. 'It really is the final irony that he should want to marry her of all people.'

'I agree, Mike, but it's shameful that Michael should have wasted his life and brought infamy on all of us by association.'

'Yep, it's a real mess. Trust him to make a grand gesture.'

'I suppose he would have called it atonement for the sins of past generations, and to stop what he saw as the insanity of the proposed union,' said Sam wearily. 'You probably already know that he's left his O'Donnell-Stevens shares to the Church, but it may amuse you to hear that he's left instructions that he is to be embalmed and to "lie in state" as he called it, in an open coffin in the church. Then he wants his remains sent back to Russia to be buried beside his father.'

'The new regime over there are going to love that,' chuckled Mike. 'And what about Olivia?'

'She gets very little – just some personal items.'

The two men sat facing each other; Sam waiting for the question he knew would inevitably come.

'What happens if Jack dies?'

Sam looked hard at Mike. He saw the shiny dome of his bald head, the ears that stuck out just a bit too much, and the perspiration that was showing on his sallow face. 'Sorry, but you're not going to like this, Mike,' he said. 'Jack came to see me after he returned from England. We talked at length about his wishes and he was quite definite in his instructions.'

'Go on,' said Mike impatiently.

'You might as well know that, in spite of my words of caution, he's left the bulk of his estate to Ludmila Ponsonby, including the shares Dean left him in this company, so you'd better pray that he pulls through.'

'You mean that if Jack dies that Limey bitch gets control of O'Donnell Publishing?' Mike asked, unable to conceal his anger. 'I'll contest it!' he shouted, jumping up and walking round his desk to the window where he stood clenching his fists.

Sam could see the large vein on his neck throbbing as the anger welled up inside him. 'I'd advise you not to do that, Mike,' he said calmly. 'It would be a waste of time and money. I drew up the will.'

Ludmila was stunned when James and Natalia broke the news of the shooting to her. By coincidence, she had received a letter in the post that morning from Jack, and she now held it pressed against her like some talisman. Even Natalia was shocked by the violence of the previous day's chain of events and she held Ludmila close as she sobbed uncontrollably.

Natalia was secretly pleased that Michael was dead and, as if to set her seal on his departure, she said a short prayer for the repose of his soul. With Michael gone she was free to look on Jack in a new and slightly more favourable light now that his father's earthly shadow no longer fell across him. It was almost as though death had brought hope of reconciliation.

Meanwhile, in Houston Jack lay between life and death with control of O'Donnell Publishing depending on the skill of his surgeon. If the pendulum swung towards life, then he would marry Ludmila and follow his destiny. A swing in the opposite direction would mean that Ludmila and Natalia, with their undisputed control of both O'Donnell's and the Albany Group, would be a new force in publishing on a hitherto unimagined scale. Fate would now decide if

Elizabeth Duff's vision of a publishing empire spanning two continents would become a reality. It seemed a special irony that Natalia Orlofski, once a high-born refugee with little or no money, should now be waiting to see how the wind blew the final seeds of fortune for the last of the Korsakovs.

Bibliography

At the Court of the Last Tsar, A.A. Mossolov, Methuen & Co. Ltd, 1935

Carl Fabergé, Goldsmith to the Imperial Court of Russia, A. Kenneth Snowman, Debrett's Peerage Ltd, 1979

My Russia, Peter Ustinov, Macmillan, 1983

Native Houstonian – A Collective Portrait, Ann Quin Wilson, Houston Baptist University Press, 1982

Nicholas and Alexandra, Robert K. Massie, McCelland and Stewart Ltd, Canada, and Atheneum, New York, 1967

Russia – Painted by F. de Haenan, text by G. Dobson, H.M. Grove and H. Stewart, A. & C. Black, 1913

Russia Under the Csars, Henry Moscow, American Heritage Publishing Co. Inc. 1962

St. Petersburg – A Travellers' Companion, Laurence Kelly, Constable 1981

The Duel, Robert Baldick, Chapman and Hall, 1965

The Duchess of Devonshire's Ball, Sophia Murphy, Sidgwick & Jackson Ltd, 1984

The History of the War, The Times, 1915

The Last Tsar and Tsarina, Virginia Cowles, George Weidenfeld and Nicholson Ltd, 1977

The Lusitania, Colin Simpson, Little, Brown & Company, 1972

The Reason Why, Cecil Woodham-Smith, Constable, 1953

The Vanished Pomps of Yesterday, Lord Frederic Hamilton, tenth edition, Hodder and Stoughton

Years of the Golden Cockerel – The Last Romanov Tsars 1814–1917, Sidney Harcave, Robert Hale & Company, 1968